DAY FOR NIGHT

DAY FOR NIGHT

STACEY E. BRYAN

Strange Fictions Press

DAY FOR NIGHT

© 2016 by Stacey E. Bryan

ISBN: 978-0-6927-2611-2

Strange Fictions Press
An imprint of Vagabondage Press LLC
PO Box 3563
Apollo Beach, Florida 33572
http://www.vagabondagepress.com

First edition printed in the United States of America and the United Kingdom, June 2016

10 9 8 7 6 5 4 3 2 1

Cover designed by Maggie Ward and Fawn Neun.

DAY FOR NIGHT

DEDICATED TO MY HUSBAND AND TO MY FATHER.

IN MEMORY OF MY MOTHER AND MY BROTHER.

PART I

There's a beer in my hand that feels like an aspirin
There's a beer in my hand that feels like a weapon
There's a beer in my hand that feels like an aspirin

— Jim Mason, *Love Poem*

CHAPTER 1

The world came to an end on a balmy Tuesday evening while I was doing laundry in my Glendale apartment building. Not on a Monday so I could start off the week fresh with the apocalypse, knowing just where I stood. Or a Friday so I could say, "Thank God, it's the weekend. I need to de-stress from the End of Days." It was a Tuesday. Four weeks to the day that I had been voted off one of the most popular reality shows running: *Muscle Beach Midlife: Sand in your Face*. I guess it didn't matter that *Muscle Midlife* had no voting. Details, schmetails. They did it anyway, and it made for good TV. If ratings were sharks, I was the bloody, mashed-up chum.

I was multitasking. For me, this involved doing laundry while I mused about regret. What better time to muse on the nature of regret than when the world was about to end? Of course, I had no idea such was the case as I made my way deeper into *Single White Female* territory—my building's dank basement—gripping my basket tight and my rage tighter. I shouldn't even be here. Forced out of escrow on my dream condo in Hermosa Beach, bad timing left me scrambling, and I'd ended up here, surrounded by elderly Armenian gentlemen who seemed to disapprove of women wearing pants. Parents? They lived out of state. Sister Margarite? Not an option in this life or the next. You found out fast who your real friends were when you got kicked off a TV show. When anything went wrong in this town, Los Angeles, especially if even remotely connected to The Biz, you'd blink twice and find yourself in the middle of a boiling, empty desert with nothing but the cacti and a lizard doing pushups on a rock. Two handfuls of "friends" condensed overnight down to just Hama and Rex.

So, back to regret, back to the end of the world. An overall discontent, kick-started by *Sand in your Face*, had bogarted its way past the borders, routed the castle walls. The castle being the state of denial I lived in, discontent being reality. It was funny that I was thinking of reality as I neared the laundry room, basket on my hip, because I was expecting a certain series of circumstances ahead of me. I was expecting the machines to all be occupied, except for one, which wouldn't be enough to accommodate my load. I was expecting the light bulb to be stuttering in its usual migraine-inducing pattern. Even before I arrived, I could hear them all busily humming. All the machines, all being used. The one poster on the wall would be there, Truffaut's *Day for Night*, dusty, the plastic cover cracked in one corner. I even expected my right shoulder to jackknife with pain when I hitched the basket up on my hip. It was injured almost a year ago after a failed Pap smear attempt.

What I wasn't expecting was to turn the corner and find my thirty-something neighbor Annie, eyes open, silent, encased by a cone of light and suspended in midair just inside the doorway. Nope. Wasn't expecting that at all. Floating beside her was the small, big-headed creature I'd seen a million times on TV and in the movies, so hilariously clichéd that I laughed out loud. There were some young filmmakers in the building. It must be an experiment, a joke. But then the creature turned, and it just wasn't funny anymore.

I stopped breathing. Because I forgot how to. If I had been older, I probably would have collapsed, dead before I hit the floor. The creature's eyes moved, found me, and froze. It was a monster, but I had startled it. The laundry basket tumbled from my hands. Bras and socks and panties and jeans spilled out onto the floor, bleached of color under the buzzing lights. The being glanced at the laundry (was that disgust I saw, or was I projecting?), and then something happened. My laundry basket was sailing through the air, aimed directly at the creature. Without thinking, I had retrieved it and launched it, Olympian-style. Mistake. Shoulder. Agony.

The basket bounced off the thing's torso while a yellow bra pin-wheeled through the air and fell onto its head. The being/creature/monster visibly jerked, and triumph spiked behind my terror. It was a familiar feeling from my surfing days. From being battered and strangled by the surf, then caressed and buoyed high moments after. The sea was like an abusive lover, harboring beauty and terror within, including sharp teeth that came up out of nowhere to claim parts of your body as if it was a free buffet.

A deep-seated scream corkscrewed upward from the center of my intestines. It poured out, brittle and clawing. "GAAAAAAAAAAAAHHHHHH!" It was like a thousand times louder than a rape whistle. And it must have worked, because the next thing I knew, the light was gone, the creature and my yellow bra were gone, and Annie was flopping down on top of me as I pitched backward to the floor. For such a tiny thing, she was really heavy. Or maybe it was just the impact from falling. I thought, "I wonder if Annie's the one hogging all these machines." And then I blacked out. Just a little.

Okay, not the end of the world in the traditional sense, but the end in every other sense. The end of my world. As I knew it. The end of my reality. Of everyone's reality, I might add. I wasn't alone in this. When I came to seconds later, I was thinking of the show again. Suddenly, getting kicked off *Sand in your Face* wasn't the worst thing that had ever happened to me, as it had been moments ago. Correction—voted off. Illegally voted off. No, having Annie blink her already-open eyes, roll off me, then sit up, and ask blankly, "What happened?" was worse than getting voted off the TV show I'd been counting on to help me buy my condo, my future, my dreams.

"Holy shit, did I pass out again?" She was a petite brunette, and it was always weird to hear her swearing. It was like listening to a filthy-mouthed ten-year-old. The name didn't help either, as it conjured up images of Little Orphan Annie unloading a raunchy diatribe at Daddy Warbucks, who stood, speechless, while his left arm slowly went numb.

I helped her to her feet. The stubs of my missing fingers ached horribly. I hadn't been in this building that long, as I mentioned before. I only knew Annie's name because her boyfriend was always bellowing it from somewhere in the building. Or, unfortunately, from the apartment next door to me where they lived.

"You don't remember what happened?" I asked.

"What happened?" she said, now with some suspicion. She glanced around the room quickly, then back, as if Hannibal Lecter might step out from behind me.

"You…fainted," I suggested. It wasn't exactly a lie.

Annie sighed. "God." She sounded genuinely weary and sagged a little. "I quit drinking four months ago. WTF?"

Note to self: do laundry somewhere else.

I decided to take myself up on that and put it into immediate effect. I packed my 280Z with my laundry accoutrements and then sped off down the street, trying to put as much distance between me and my new Glendale apartment building as fast as possible. Evidently, before you decide to move in somewhere, you have to inquire about the regular stuff…*and then some.* Is there on-site laundry? Is there covered parking? Is alien abduction once or twice a month? I have to know because once is doable, but twice will take some scheduling.

It was beautiful and sunny outside, belying the day's ludicrous events. I was thinking about cigarettes for the first time in ten years while shock and denial held hands and started making out. As I accelerated toward Central, I glanced over to see a police cruiser pulling up alongside me. Jesus Christ, what now? I had terrible cop karma. They were drawn to me for some reason, but I never got a ticket. It was almost like I was the secret daughter of Osiris or something, floundering down here on earth but encased in his invisible protection. I'd always loved the stories about Osiris in school because he'd been the god-king who'd evidently been responsible for giving civilization to Egypt. Serious props. Much more than I'd done with my life. I could see him up there, my secret father Osiris, reclining on a golden chair in midair, waving his hand dismissively.

Osiris: (preoccupied and about to tuck into a platter of raw, sun-dried fish) She must learn her lessons. Let the authority manage her. But do not let them fine her mercilessly.

Resigned, I cranked down my window. My pumpkin-colored 280Z was a classic and had no power anything. I was proud of the fact that it was such a hands-on car, very difficult to roll down windows and manipulate the steering wheel. I had purchased it ten years ago in Ventura from a mysterious Belizean man who, although he'd been wearing a metal body brace from the waist down, could not stop staring at my missing fingers.

There were two officers in the car and a guy sitting in the backseat. Possibly a perp. They were all slightly blurry to me. My eyesight had started to go astray several years ago, and in my usual fashion, I still had done nothing about it. The officer in the passenger seat with ruddy good looks lowered his window with a power button and gave me a lopsided grin. If he knew what had just happened a half-hour ago, he wouldn't be smiling like that—a creepy Ted Bundy smirk.

"Something wrong, officer?"

This was how I always started my conversations with the men and women in blue.

"Hey, how do you keep the gasoline smell from permeating the rest of the car?"

No traffic infraction today. It was to be classic car chitchat. Mentally, I rolled my eyes. The 280Zs from 1978 had a design flaw where the odor of gas permeated the interior. There was very little one could do about it. This, of course, was beside the fact that I had just witnessed an almost-alien abduction in the laundry room of my building. I had to manually lift up the entire memory, put it aside, and then switch gears to deal with the cops. *Focus focus focus.* I drifted forward and talked to the cop at the same time, amazed that he was encouraging such unsafe driving.

"Oh, well, I've gotten that checked out over and over. The car's safe, though. There's nothing I can do about it."

"Oh, yeah, I'm not accusing you of anything. I just got one myself, and I can't get rid of the gas smell. There's nothing you can do?"

"No, I'm afraid not, officer. " I offered the shaky smile of a coke addict and glanced forward to make sure my tires weren't about to roll over a baby's head. The cop didn't seem to give a crap if I was about to kill anybody. He just kept staring at my car, aglow with pleasure in that way that only men could get with machines that they admired. The guy in the backseat, a smallish-looking Soviet Bloc type, stared moodily out the window at me. Suddenly, he said something. His window was up, so I couldn't hear him.

"Hey. Hey, hey, hey!" said the ruddy cop, turning his head slightly around. "Shut the fuck up. SHUT THE FUCK UP."

The man in the backseat said something else.

"SHUT THE FUCK UP. I WILL KILL YOU. I WILL FUCKING KILL YOU. DO YOU HEAR ME, MATILDA? DO YOU FUCKING HEAR ME?"

Silence. Matilda bored holes into the back of the ruddy cop's neck for five seconds. Then he shrugged. Then he looked back at me and suggestively licked his lips.

"Okay," said the ruddy cop to me. "Thanks." I started to roll up my window. "Oh, hey," he called. I sighed and rolled my window back down. The police officer seemed conspiratorial suddenly. I fully expected him to say, "We have two dead women in the back of our car. Would you like to join them?" That's how freaked out I was. "We're gonna kill this guy," he'd say, "and put him in back. You ever been in a trunk with a dead body? We can take a long road trip, drive over to Barstow with you rolling around in back with this guy for hours and hours. Would you like that?"

Instead he said, "Hey...hang in there. You got a raw deal from that Ricardo guy." He looked pointedly at my left hand for a minute, resting on the steering wheel, with its three remaining fingers. Then he aimed his hand and pantomimed shooting me. The guy in back said something. Officer Ruddy craned his head around one quarter and screamed, "SHUT THE FUCK UP, YOU DUMB FUCKING FUCK." Then he turned back to me and smiled and said, "Go get 'em." He rolled up the window and the car accelerated away at top speed and disappeared down the road in about 3.5 seconds. It was like watching the *Millennium Falcon* transitioning into hyper speed.

As far as my encounters with cops, this one had been fairly benign. Who knew they watched reality TV too? Probably his wife did, and she went on and on about it. Women were heavy into *Sand in your*

Face because of sexy Jamaican Dante with his dreadlocks and then the added sympathy factor of his being completely deaf. Cayman, the professional cowboy with his sun-leathered skin and rough ways, also drew his fair share of female admirers.

We tried to be different on our show but, really, we were like every other reality show. We eschewed the bleached blond Sustainable Youth route of The Real Housewives by avoiding plastic surgery and plumped-up mammary glands, but we were still composed of the same shallow, self-involved DNA that animated those others. I was pretty sure I hadn't been that way before I got on the show, but being on the show tended to foster that behavior. I appreciated the support from the cops. I appreciated thinking about the show and not thinking about people floating in mid-air and receiving the evil eye from big-headed creatures I had heretofore thought of as an urban myth.

Since it was the middle of a weekday, the laundromat was semi-empty. At least that's how it looked from my car as I sat parked outside at the curb, unable to make myself go in. A few skinny palm trees waved gently in the breeze. The Verdugo Mountains stood in the distance, gently cupping the East Valley. I stared out the windshield, watching my mental hands begin to pick the abduction memory up and bring it around to center stage. The stagehand was waiting, reaching for the spotlight switch. I dropped the memory and tackled the stagehand, wrenching his hand away from the switch. *NOT YET!* I screamed right in his face. The stagehand jerked, wounded. I could tell he was going to quit.

My cell phone shrilled. I jumped in my seat, heart pounding. *Get a grip, get a grip, get a grip.* I panted and leaned back on the headrest. When I'd recovered enough to look at the display, I saw that it was Cola, my agent. A nickname, as you can imagine, needing no explanation. He was a quiet, unflappable man of indeterminate age (anywhere from forty to seventy). Cola wasted no time, as usual.

"Rae, there's a red carpet event involving PETA. Andrygen is hosting. I told them you'd be there."

My name was actually Raine, but everyone called me Rae. It was like the universe was gently trying to help me, to get my mind off the recent horrific events by bombarding me instead with all things annoying concerning the show. Of course, Andrygen was hosting for PETA. She was a pet psychiatrist, after all. She was the one who San Fernando Valley denizens paid oodles of cashola to come over, grip their Pomeranian's paw, and discover why it wouldn't go number two on the evening walks or preferred chirping crickets over the rushing surf on the sound machine. She had four children who were named after the moons of Jupiter.

"Is Ricardo going to be there?"

Pause. "Yes."

He knew what was coming.

"Okay, then no. I'd rather have hot coals shoved in my eyes." I might have gone if Dante was going to be there. The beloved sweetheart of Muscle Beach had tried to warn me, in sign language, that trouble was brewing, but he signed way too fast, and I'd thought he was talking about hotdogs. Only Moeyner, Krumping Champion of 1999, named from a combination of Moesha and Jackie Joyner, had taken the time to actually learn American Sign Language well enough to communicate with Dante. So, as usual, I had blown him off. I guess you could say I'd had a hand in my own demise.

"You can't despise him that much. He deserves your pity, not your anger."

"He deserves my what? Not my what? You know, you're the one who convinced me to get on this show and play my real age when I'd been playing a lot younger forever and doing fine. Now I've been outed from the younger demographic, and I can't go back. I mean, people might have *guessed* that I was older, but they didn't know for sure. Now they know for sure." I never said my real age out loud. I had stopped at a certain birthday several years ago, and it would pretty much take a team of time-traveling Schutzstaffel agents to pry it out of me.

"You've turned down the last four things I've offered you. How do you expect to make a living?"

"I don't know, Dad."

I could feel Cola stiffen on the other side of our electronic connection. What had I said? Jeez!

"Go back to teaching gymnastics." Ha. Unlikely. Not with *this* shoulder.

"Your AFTRA is going to run out. Can you afford Cobra?"

I couldn't think about AFTRA or Cobra right now. What did bureaucratic paperwork have to do with abduction and anal probing? *What did it have to do with the scene from a sci-fi horror movie taking a crap in the middle of my life?*

"Look, Cola, something weird just happened, so I'm not..." I trailed off.

Pause. "What happened?"

"I can't tell you. You'll think I'm crazy. You'll drop me as a client. You'll see me in The Grove one day and walk past me holding your newspaper up to your face."

"I would never do that."

"You would do that if you were smart. I would do that if I was you and you were me."

There was something about Cola that had started to bother me for the past several years. I wasn't one of his more prestigious clients, and I hadn't even had much success as an actress. Okay, I wasn't prestigious *at all*. Yet Cola not only kept me on as a client, he seemed to often make me a priority. Who did that? It was strange. I guess this was where you weren't supposed to look a gift horse in the mouth.

"You know," Cola said, "whatever happened to you...maybe it's good to have the nature of reality questioned now and again, don't you think?"

My hackles rose. "What do you mean?" I looked around at the street in paranoia, much like Annie had just done in the dank basement. "What do you mean, the nature of reality?"

"You said something weird happened," he answered. "I was deducing."

Unflappable.

"Oh." I reached sideways to hoist my purse up off the passenger seat, and my shoulder zinged with shimmering pain. I really had to do something about that. "I guess you're right." I felt crazy. I felt like I was going to look up and see one of those things coming toward me, its big head eclipsing the entire sky. And right behind him would be a vampire. Why not? Five minutes ago, I hadn't believed in aliens. Who knew if there were vampires or not? Or werewolves. Or Fairies. Who knew? I searched mindlessly through the purse, having forgotten what I'd wanted. *I needed a beer.*

"Talk to you later."

I needed pain killers.

We disconnected.

CHAPTER 2

A year ago. I was at the doctor's, engaged in everyone's favorite activity involving stirrups and knees spread wider than was considered acceptable anywhere else in polite society. I went to a GP to get this done because I figured she could do everything at once while I was there: check the blood pressure, the glands, take some blood, invade my innermost being. The only problem was I had these gigantic fibroids growing in my abdomen, and the doc couldn't get past the monstrous benign growths in order to acquire the smear. Fibroids were still a mystery to the medical community, the Planet X of the uterus. I felt a little sorry for my doctor. It must have been akin to being on the set of *Land of the Giants*, difficult to maneuver your way around because everything was so oddly dimensioned.

She was down there below the sheet draped across my knees, twisting this way and that, muttering to herself. Finally, she sat up, sweating lightly. She disengaged the speculum with an audible pop. My thighs relaxed. "Nope. Can't get in there," she announced cheerfully, as if returning from a failed Everest expedition. Or, more accurately, a journey to the center of the earth. She hadn't taken enough rope with her, and her compass had malfunctioned. "You'll have to make an appointment with a gynecologist. I'm sure they'll have better luck. In the meantime, when was the last time you had a tetanus shot?"

Seemed like an innocent question. Seemed like an innocuous thing to do, get a tetanus shot. After all, I hadn't had one since I was about nine. And I was pretty clumsy, always tripping, falling, bumping into things, stepping on things. What was the harm, right? Two days after the shot, I couldn't lift my arm; it burned with fever and turned black and blue. I all but developed a third head on it. A concerned call to the doctor's office left me assured this was "normal." It was so great when people said things like that. What did that mean?

"Blood is pouring from my eyes, and I can barely breathe."

"Oh, that's normal. If your heart implodes, and you can't breathe at all, call us back."

A week later the pain was gone, but my shoulder was stiff and worsening. But then I got the show, started buying the condo in Hermosa Beach, and just learned to live with it.

Back in my apartment, I made the dreaded call to physical therapy. Might as well. I had time to do it now and no more excuses. The therapy people were very accommodating. They suggested that I come in two days from now. My heart sank. Two days? I sighed and agreed, and we both hung up. The ease with which I'd gotten the appointment was troubling. The therapy place was going to stink. I could just tell. But there weren't that many covered under my present insurance, so what was a girl to do? I caught myself and had to smile. I was bitching about physical therapy and health insurance as if Annie hadn't almost been abducted and defiled two hours ago. And not by someone in a Liam Neeson movie. If only! At least human against human violence was normal, understandable. But alien violence against humans? Unacceptable.

Despite the recent inexplicable events, the duties of everyday life still made their obnoxious demands. For now, laundry was a no-go. I switched my attention to the living room instead. It was still stacked with unpacked boxes. *Keep busy, keep busy* I heard my mind telling me. I viewed my mind as something separate from myself, like a visitor renting a room in my head. My *Green Splendor* posters I and II were leaning against the wall, still sheathed in plastic. After I'd quit surfing, those were the only two movies I'd made. I decided to get the mail first then come back and clear at least a foot of floor space. I yanked open the front door and almost walked into my neighbor, Mr. Dadalian, standing stoically in the hallway, his hand raised to knock. His apartment was right across from mine. I remembered his name because he had tutored me once, my third day here, in its pronunciation. He wouldn't let me leave until I had said it right, on my own, ten times in a row. I threw the door open wider. "Mr. Dadalian. How are you?"

He appeared pleased that his training seminar had succeeded. He held his hand up. Pinched between two fingers was a rose-pink bra. "Dis is yours, no?"

I looked at it. "How do you know it's mine? Maybe it's your wife's."

Mr. D. pushed the bra at me. "I seen it enough times on you," he said, ignoring my comment about his wife's underwear, "coming out from your clothing."

"Really? No one else in this building has pink underwear?" I plucked it from his grasp with my good hand. Mr. Dadalian wasn't very adept at hiding his disapproval. I suppose pink bras by themselves were an affront, much less ones visible outside of clothing. "Thank you, Mr. Dadalian." He nodded sternly and turned away as I closed the door. I understood that women were supposed to present themselves in a certain way, in his mind, but this wasn't Armenia, after all. We were in L.A., for God's sake. Was he aware that he was in L.A.? Nobody had any sense of what was correct here, me most of all. The sooner Mr. Dadalian accepted this, the sooner he'd be much happier.

I simply ignored the fact that Mr. D. obviously had discovered the bra in the laundry room downstairs where it had fallen during the "event." I just didn't have the fuel supply to revisit that planet right now. Especially since my yellow bra was still missing, and it had been one of my favorites, sewn as it was with tiny little silk flowerets along the front. It wasn't a good time to think of it hanging, lopsided, on the fat head of the creature and where it could possibly have gone when that creature had disappeared. In fact, it felt like a really good time to get the mail later, have a beer now. Maybe a few Ibuprofen to boot. Hmm. Déjà vu.

CHAPTER 3

So, I have to admit: the world had almost ended for me already once before when the Tiger shark chewed off two of my fingers. I guess this world-ending thing; it was a pattern for me. I'd been surfing with my buddy Rex, just hanging out on our boards in Huntington Beach. Back when we were kids. Belly down, butt to the sun. There was no warning, no sense of danger, just a tug on my left hand, a very wrong feeling. Later, I imagined how my hands must have looked to the shark as it cruised the dark depths beneath me: like fat worms, like baby squids, like little wriggling fish. Something yanked. My brain tilted. The sun blossomed. I thought I'd screamed but had made no sound at all. I was tugged off my board into the sea. Rex only saw what was happening because he turned my way to ask something. He threw himself forward on his board, pounding his hands into the water like shovels, hoarsely screaming, "Shark, Shark!" I'm sure the sight of his sun-bleached head closing in on my bobbing sun-bleached head from above was a charming one for the seagulls circling obliviously beneath the clouds. Or maybe they were thinking, "Better her than me."

I'd never really gotten back on the horse, and I missed the waves. I've always remained near the beach, however. Except now, here in Glendale. Surfing was one of the few places where I'd felt included, surrounded by like-minded folk. When you were born and raised in Sherman Oaks, California, and the product of a mixed marriage, being an outsider was nothing new. The Sherman Oaks of my childhood had been a tucked-away suburb in the hills just below Mulholland Drive, laid-back but exclusive at its core. I grew up without wanting for much, with my older sister Margarite. She tried to drown me once when we were children but denies it to this day. Margarite had been living a wonderful life for several years, absorbing the endless love of our parents as an only child. Several years was like a hundred years in child time. It must have been a shock when, one day, I'd burst in on the scene. I guess technically, that was the first time the world almost ended for me, floating in the blue chlorinated water of our swimming pool. For a while after the attempted murder, water became my life.

Think *The Brady Bunch*. The episode where they hung out with the ethnic friend. Remember that? No? That's because there was no such episode. We grew up to the polite smiles and invitations of neighbors and friendliness of neighborhood kids, well aware of the invisible wall that stood between them and us, my weird mulatto sister and I. Mom was black, Dad was white. The funny thing is, at first glance, we looked like a couple of white kids with a nice summer tan (that never went away), but everyone around us knew we weren't. Why did that matter? I don't know. You'd have to ask them. Think *Body Snatchers* with the gaping mouths and the pointing fingers and the horrible screeching. When we got older, we had to remove our earrings more than we liked to prepare for the street brawl, the catalyst usually a racial epithet. That's why, as soon as she moved away, Margarite started to pass. Today she has a psychotherapy practice out of her home where she caters to anorexic and bulimic girls with whom she had acquired a degree of success. They had affectionately dubbed her "The Eating Monster."

It might be hard to believe, but my childhood and the Tiger shark and the alien abduction were all inextricably intertwined. Because my childhood alienated me. Because the Tiger shark increased the alienation. And in the next couple of days when the whole tableau would play out again, the familiarity of being outcast, of being alone, was the very thing that kept me from going completely bat-shit crazy.

Before that happened, though, life seemed to return to normal. A few days went by, and the incident began to fade. The event was already slipping away, breaking up. It looked the way people did on *Star Trek* as they were beaming on or off the ship—swirling bits of energy and light rapidly disappearing, accompanied by a high-pitched humming. In case you've never experienced it, this was called denial. I knew. I was an expert at it. I could open a Denial School tomorrow and do very well for myself.

"Okay, Lauren, what are you doing?"

"Making notes."

I would grab her notes and tear them up. She would be writing them down because she was too afraid to learn how to use a computer. Therefore, she was pretty much unemployable everywhere in the world.

"No. No notes. Go the other way. "

"What other way?" an older gentleman would ask, confused.

"This is denial, people. The only As I'll be giving out here are the people that deny they're in Denial School. Kara. Kara!" I would snap my fingers, startling her. "Pop quiz! When should you make a decision about the baby?"

Kara's eyes would roll slowly toward the ceiling as she searched her memory. She would be 17 years old and in the class because she was three months pregnant.

"At the last possible minute…or until I'm forced to?" she would answer hesitantly.

"You got it! Up high!" We would high five each other while awe and understanding slowly filled the faces of the rest of the class.

I was clearing away the foot of floor space I'd promised myself when my friend Hama called.

"Hey," she said, "feel like substitute teaching some gymnastics for a few hours?"

I looked at my watch. It was 5:00.

"Um…I guess as long as I don't have to lift my arm straight up or sideways. Or make any abrupt movements. Or move it at all, actually. Yeah, sure. "

"You haven't taken care of that shoulder yet?"

I read not a small amount of derision in her voice.

"Actually, I'm going to physical therapy tomorrow."

She snorted. "Yeah, good luck with that. Let me pound you in a workout. You'll be fixed by the end of the week." Then she added. "Well, just come over and keep me company."

Hama was a professional body builder, one of the requisite careers of a good culture-abiding Angelino. I guessed at this point, though, she was a fitness model, which meant she had shed half her muscle mass and got so shredded for competitions she looked like she hadn't eaten in five years while the muscle she had cultivated stood out glorious mounds and stark ravines of flesh.

We had met as kids, flipping under the watchful eye of Patric, our Austrian coach, at Adventures in Gymnastics. Hama had been chewing gum one afternoon, and Patric made her spit it out in his hand. Our eyes met, and we couldn't stop giggling. I didn't remember why Hama was giggling. I was giggling because Patric had let Hama spit on his hand, essentially.

Since we were disrupting practice, Patric made everyone in the gym assume an exaggerated push-up position with their butts pointing straight up, creating a tunnel through which Hama and I were forced to crawl, like soldiers through the fox holes, trying to reach the commander so we could get advice on how to stay alive. Only there was no commander at the end that we could talk to. If there had been a commander, he might have told us, "Maybe you girls should stop effing around and pay attention before you break your necks. Do you think Patric wants your parents to sue the shit out of his Austrian ass because you're not following instructions? Hmm? Do you? Now, pull yourself together. All that sniveling's gonna rain Charlie down on us like a shit storm."

As we pulled ourselves beneath the seemingly endless tunnel of bodies, I surreptitiously started crying. Amid the humiliation and remorse during and after our punishment, a friendship was forged. Hama was too tough to cry. The first time I asked if I could come over, she told me no, because she had been raised by jackals.

CHAPTER 4

I tooled the Z over to Van Nuys where Hama worked at Gymnastics Abounds! We'd quit the gym game after high school because my surfing hobby had turned more serious by then, and Hama had succumbed to the call of iron. I'd reluctantly returned to Adventures to coach for Patric after everything fell apart years later. Meaning there was not going to be a *Green Splendor III*, and even my modeling jobs had begun to dry up.

Hama was in the middle of catching a girl in midair when I walked into the gym. The girl was in the fetal position on her back in the air with only Hama's hands holding her aloft. This was the position one was supposed to assume when one was doing backflips correctly.

"You got it. You got it. Okay, good." Hama set the girl down gently with her bulging arms. She was between competitions, so she wasn't as cut as usual and was actually covered with a tiny layer of fat, like a slathering of butter over a bagel. She saw me and waved her hand. A girl thought this was her signal and took off running toward Hama like a locomotive. "I meant Rae, not you…" she said half-heartedly, then sighed and waited until a string of flip-flops had been completed before the tiny girl catapulted herself into the air backwards like a whirling dervish. She landed and stuck it.

"Bitchin'!" Hama yelled and patted the girl on the back. She cupped her hands around her mouth and screamed down the mats toward a waiting line of gymnasts, "Did you see Juana? Did you see Juana? That's what I'm talking about!"

I walked over and stood beside Hama. She had obtained handsome

Middle Eastern looks from her mother and a generous donation of exotic stoicism from her Japanese father. Her father, of all people, was immensely proud of her accomplishments in the world of weight lifting. Her mother had been tepid, wanting Hama to be a model. "Why can't you be more like Raine?" her mother used to harangue her. Hama went through a period where she hated my guts, often screaming at her mother, "Well, why don't you just fucking adopt Raine and replace me? You love her so much!" At some point, after she started packing on the muscle, all she had to do was pop a bicep if her mother started up. Muscle was an instant silencer for many situations. Hama had learned to use it well.

Hama grabbed my arm and cranked my shoulder into a position that ground my bones together. I emitted a strangled shriek, and my right knee buckled. It was like the shark attack all over again. A girl went flipping by while Hama studied my shoulder joint.

"Good!" she called, preoccupied. "When are you going to physical therapy?"

"Tomorrow."

She let go of me and clapped her hands together. "Okay, girls, come on, back whips now. Back whips!"

I used to love doing back whips. Essentially, they were straight-legged back-flips where you whipped your legs over your head at the speed of sound. I loved thinking about back whips and not thinking about the weird event that had happened in the laundry room earlier this week. For a moment, I considered telling Hama about it, but I didn't have the energy for the questions that would follow. I could never be the White House Press Secretary. I would be fired after my first press conference. Before I had dropped out of UCLA, I had been a journalism major, intent on being a sports announcer. Sitting and watching other athletes performing while I narrated in a stream of consciousness about what was going on, compared it to my own experiences, predicted what I thought might happen—that was my idea of a dream job.

Another girl went flying by, and Hama reached up and plucked her from the air like she was removing a can of soup from a kitchen cabinet.

"Do you know how far your butt is sticking out?" She held the girl up in front of her like a Raggedy Ann doll, face-to-face.

"No."

"You're arching your back. Curve it, baby, curve it."

"Okay."

Hama set her down, and the girl looked at me. "Are you on that TV show with the cowboy and the lady that talks to dogs?"

I was pleased that she didn't soil the air of the gym with Ricardo's name or description.

"Yes, honey."

"Can I get your autograph?"

"After class! After class," yelled Hama, clapping her hands together. "Get back in line! Okay, come on. Let's see some full twists. For those of you who can't do those yet, do halves. At least *try*." Hama turned to me, raising her arms straight out, inhaling deeply. "Come on… don't you miss it?" She looked around suggestively.

"I do miss it. Sometimes." I didn't really miss it. Gymnastics was painful. "I miss surfing." I realized I didn't really even miss surfing that much anymore. But I still loved the ocean.

"Up, up, up!" Hama screamed. I wonder if I used to sound like that when I was coaching. No. Not even Patric had sounded like that. Hama was terrifying. It seemed like the girls loved her, though.

"Yeah, but you're not surfing." She started listing things on her hands, and her biceps bulged as she did so. She was wearing a racer back leotard and a tiny pair of short shorts. "You're not on the show. You're not modeling. You're not doing a movie. You haven't done a movie for a *long time*," she added pointedly. She looked at me. "How the hell are you planning to make a living? UP HIGHER OUT OF THE—YES!" She screamed in my ear.

"What, are you and Cola conspiring together or something? He said the exact same thing."

The last girl who had gone high enough and earned Hama's roar of approval trotted past and smiled at me.

"Cola!" Hama did an exaggerated wink. "How is your *agent*?" Hama had a boyfriend, but she also had a healthy lust for life. She had a crush on Cola, whom she had met once at a fundraiser she had attended with me several years ago. He reminded her of the lead singer for Bush, Gavin Rossdale. He had also played Balthazar in the movie *Constantine*, one of Hama's favorite rentals of all-time.

"All right, all right!" Hama strode forward, clapping her hands. "Get some water and meet me over at the parallel bars—STAT." She turned to me. "And you," she continued, "Good luck tomorrow. Give me a call when it doesn't work out. You'll come back. They always come crawling back."

The funny thing about Hama was she was right a lot of the time. I had such a good time talking to her and signing autographs for some of the girls' "mothers," that when I noticed a strange man staring at me from across the street as I left for the evening, I wrote it off as coincidence, as usual, and forgot about it five seconds later.

CHAPTER 5

The therapy center was in Glendale and looked like it had been there since the disco days. The building was long and low, rectangle-shaped, and painted a faded light green. If I were to wake up somewhere chained to a bed, this was the color I imagined the room would be. Inside was no better. My suspicions had been correct. Think the YMCA, the years of wear and tear, the worn-down wooden floor, the dingy athletic hopes and dreams of the masses.

When I walked into the front office, a 14-year-old Filipino boy was engaged in a passionate conversation with the front desk girl, screaming in Tagalog. I thought his mother had forgotten to pick him up, and he was having a tantrum. He stopped screaming when I came in and broke into an angelic smile. I was too startled to smile back.

"Rae Miller?" he said and held out his hand.

"Hi." We shook.

"I'm Chrislann. I'm going to be working with you!"

I glanced around the room, looking for his mother. I looked back at Chrislann.

"Christian?" I said.

"Chrislann."

"Christlian?"

"Chris-lan. Chris-lan. You can call me Chris."

I couldn't even imagine the millions of times he must have had to say to people, "You can call me Chris."

He gestured at the girl behind the desk. "Sorry about that," he said happily. "I was telling Maria what happened on the 405 this morning. Crazy fucking drivers. I can't believe I'm still fucking alive!"

He was smiling. "Somebody fucking loves me," he yelled, throwing his arms up toward the sky and, I guessed, God. "Thank you!" he shrieked.

"Chrislann!" Maria gasped.

Chrislann slapped a hand over his mouth. "Oh, shit, I'm sorry." He glanced to the right toward a big, open room where a number of elderly people were tottering around, performing a variety of slow-motion exercises, then back at me.

"It's okay. I love to swear," I told him.

Chrislann and Maria guffawed as if I was Richard Pryor. Chrislann bent over and slapped his thighs.

A few moments later after he'd recovered, he said, "Okay, Rae, let's get started."

"Do you have some ID?" I said. "How old are you?"

"I love your show!" Maria intoned from behind the desk. "Before you leave today, please pay $25."

Chrislann started to pull out his wallet. I held up my hand.

"I'm just kidding. You just look like you're a teenager."

"Well, thanks!"

"So do you," offered Maria, kindly. I shot her a wry smile.

"Well, let's not go that far," Chrislann said cheerfully, and then before I could gouge his eyes out he said, "but what are you doing on that show? Isn't it about middle-aged people?"

I smiled.

"I don't know," I shrugged. "Different surveys have different numbers. Some say middle age starts around thirty-five. Like anywhere between thirty-five and fifty."

Maria shook her head slowly.

"I heard it was like forty-five to sixty," she said.

We both looked at Chrislann, who shrugged, oblivious. "I have no idea!" he said. "I think it depends on the person."

How could he know? He was only eleven, himself.

"But generally," Maria persisted. "Yeah," she nodded to herself. She had decided. "About forty-five."

"Well, I'm not forty-five," I said, as if I was being accused of something. As if it was a sin to be forty-five. Which it was. In this town. In America.

"It doesn't matter. You look great!" said Maria again. I was beginning to loathe her.

"Okay," I said to Chrislann. "Let's go."

He smiled and placed his hand gently behind my shoulder blade, pushing me forward.

Half an hour later after a lot of questions and Chrislann marking a form and taking movement measurements, he had me on my stomach on an examination table identical to the one that had gotten me into all this trouble to begin with, sans the stirrups. He held my arm gently and asked me to push up. My whole arm shook and didn't move an inch. I was flabbergasted at how weak I was. When I got home, I was going to tear my ex-doctor a new one on Angie's List.

"It's okay, it's okay. The muscles are gone. They're just *gone*, Rae. How long has it been since the tetanus shot?" I had relayed my tale to him about the tetanus shot, without the Pap smear, and he was amazed. He knew you could have an inflammatory response, but he'd never seen anything this bad. Of course, I had waited a long time to take care of it…

"About a year."

"Yeah, a year. You haven't been using the arm because of the shoulder. You're not aware of it, but your left arm started taking over. It turned into a fascist. It started doing everything, and your body just obeyed. Your right arm said, 'Sounds good to me!' and took a fucking vacation. Now the muscles are just *gone* in your right arm." He patted me on the back while he massaged my shoulder. "We'll get you well. Come on, let's go into the big room."

We went into the big room. There were fewer elderly people in it by now. Chrislann had spent a long time on the examination table telling me that his wife (he was married!) and everyone he knew thought Ricardo had given me a raw deal. Part of the reason Ricardo had convinced the others to vote me off the show was because of my missing fingers. His reasoning had something to do with my energy being bad, otherwise why would the shark have stolen part of my body? Nature was responding to my lack of balance. My chakras were out of order. Chrislann almost went ballistic talking about it.

"That man is supposed to be a 'yoga master'? What *is* that anyway? And if it was true, wouldn't a fucking yoga master have more compassion? And how can a chakra be out of order? My wife is a holistic masseuse. A fucking chakra isn't out of order! You're not a soda machine!"

Chrislann managed to calm down a little as he set me up with a giant red rubber band and showed me how to do several types of exercises. Then he pressed the button on a timer and said, "Three sets of ten each. I'll be right back."

I started doing the exercises carefully. My shoulder was sore now, and a small part of me despised Chrislann and the pain he had ushered into my life. Across from me, an ancient-looking man was trying to do sideways steps without losing his balance. A young woman held his arm and kept saying, "Good, good, good," even though he was doing a terrible job. I was at the point between in this room. I was between all the young therapists and all the old codgers. One part was done for me and the other lay ahead. It was the wrong thing to think, because immediately, my energy waned, and I had the urge to sit down. But I could see that the old man across from me was thinking that too, probably in triplicate. Probably for the last thirty years, all he wanted to do was sit down. Billy Crystal had been right in *City Slickers*. Except it wasn't just your twenties that were a blur. It was *all* a blur. Time itself was a blur. All of time was like my eyesight, except for a five- or six- foot radius directly surrounding me. One small circle of clarity. The rest was scenery rushing past your car window.

Out of nowhere, Chrislann's complete physical opposite entered the big room from some back way and strode purposefully across toward the front office. He looked to be slightly older than me, with thick black hair spiked at the temples with gray. The forearms coming out of his rolled-up sleeves were thick and dark, and the left displayed a nasty scar running from above the elbow to the wrist. Motorcycle accident? Knife fight? Of course, this was all seen by me as if through a camera lens smeared with Vaseline, due to the limited scope of my eyesight.

As he neared the doorway leading to the front desk, he suddenly stopped walking and looked across the room directly at me. It was as if he heard something or sensed something. Electric eye contact sizzled and sparked between us. I was surprised the room didn't explode. Blowing me up, with the red rubber band and the old man teetering on his oversized sneakers, into the sky, spinning end over end. We would even out at some point, and just before we started to plummet back to earth, the old man would look at me and say, "Seriously?"

I yanked on my rubber band and grinned crookedly at Salt and Pepper. After several seconds of intense staring, like he was trying to place me from America's Most Wanted, his face softened, and he smiled back before disappearing into the front office.

CHAPTER 6

There was a lake in Toluca Lake, but I had never actually seen it, and nobody I knew had ever seen it. It was only a rumor at this point, more mysterious and enigmatic than fibroids. It defied reality that I had actually seen an alien abduction before I had seen Toluca Lake. As I drove down Riverside a few days later, I told myself for the billionth time to turn down one of these side streets and try to find that goddamn lake. Then I could take pictures and email them to my mom. When Mom would drive with Margarite and me out here for whatever reason—to visit Travel Town in Griffith Park, drop us off at a school friend's house—the invisible lake, without fail, would come up in conversation.

Trolling for the lake was soothing and occupied my mind. I liked the hum of the Z's motor, the sunlight filtering down through the trees. These were normal things, earthly things. I needed to stay away from the sky, where *they* were, and bend down and kiss the dirt of the world. So in this capacity, as I drove aimlessly around, falling into a kind of fugue state while I craned my head to and fro, I happened to spot a young boy standing on a corner. He was holding the leash to a large German Shepherd that was wearing one of those Elizabethan collars. I recognized Ganymede, Andrygen's ten-year-old son, at once. I had met him several times at various charity events catering to children's causes. Whenever anything had to do with children, Andrygen hauled her four moons, Ganymede, Io, Callista, and Europa with her. Ganymede was the only boy. He was also black and adopted. He had confided that his mother had tried to treat Ralph, his dog, for excessive barking, and had caused a psychotic break instead. I assumed this must be the wayward Ralph.

I pulled over to the curb where Ganymede and Ralph eyed me suspiciously. Ganymede was wearing a T-shirt that said "Honey Badger Don't Care." There was a picture of a honey badger lying on his back, greedily consuming the remains of what looked like a field mouse. Ganymede's face lit up, and he leapt forward toward the car. The Shepherd remained wary, eyeing me moodily from within the cone of his collar.

"Hi, Rae!" Ganymede bent over and looked through the window.

"What the hell are you doing here? Are you here with your mother?" I looked over my shoulder and up and down the street.

Ganymede grinned from ear to ear. "No. I got a ride from a friend."

"A ride? From where?"

"Topanga Canyon."

His hair was growing into an impressively wild afro.

"Is your ride coming back?"

He shrugged and straightened up. "We didn't plan that far ahead," he said. "I don't know where he is."

"Okay, get in."

Ganymede opened the door and ushered Ralph into the rear hatch area. 280Zs don't have backseats. There ensued much grappling and some slapstick while all three of us tried to maneuver the Elizabethan collar through. Finally, they were both situated.

"Okay." I slapped the wheel. "A friend drove you here. You don't know where he is. Does your mother know where you are?"

Ganymede became coy. "Literally?" he asked, "or symbolically?"

Oh, God. I'd forgotten. He was one of *those* kids. I closed my eyes for a minute then looked at him.

He was gazing at me adoringly. He wasn't even looking at my stumps the way most kids did, with their mouths hanging open.

"Hey, wait a minute. Aren't you supposed to be in school?"

"It's summer vacation," Ganymede informed me, preoccupied. He was rubbing his hand up and down along the cherry vinyl of my car seat. I thought for a minute. *Oh, yeah. It was June, wasn't it?* Behind me, Ralph sneezed. "I take it this is the famous Ralph you told me about."

"Yeah." He glanced at Ralph. "He's doing a little better." He looked back at me as I pulled away from the curb. "My mom misses you on the show. She talks about you all the time."

"What?" I found that hard to believe. It was difficult to respect anyone called Andrygen who had named her kids after the moons of Jupiter. Wasn't one crazy name in the family enough? Did she have to spread the craziness out evenly over the toast, or couldn't she have missed a spot here and there, for the sake of the children?

Ralph uttered a muffled woof from the backseat. "Ralphie, hush," Ganymede said immediately. I could see Ralph in my rearview mirror, constantly licking his lips. It made me nervous just watching him. It made me want to lick *my* lips.

"But anyway, my friend gave me a ride 'cause I was going to the hobby shop on Laurel Canyon. I guess we overshot it. Then he was driving around in circles. Then we got a little lost. Do you know all the streets in Burbank sort of go in weird directions and double back on each other?"

I smiled. "*All* the streets in Burbank?"

Ganymede sighed and pushed his hand into his hair, where it disappeared completely.

"A lot of the streets."

"So, you never made it to the hobby shop, I take it?"

"No. I told him to let me out. I'd find it by myself. I guess we got into a fight."

I was having trouble imagining the "friend" who could drive and who had gotten into an argument with a ten-year-old and then abandoned him on the street.

"Should we call your mother?"

"She's filming. You could call the nanny if you want. She thinks I'm in the library. Shh, Ralphie!" he said distractedly, even though Ralph hadn't said anything. I looked in the rearview and saw Ralph eyeballing Ganymede, confusion mixed with doggy worship.

"Okay, look, I'll take you to the hobby shop, and then I'll drive you home. How does that sound?"

He flashed a smile, and I realized at that moment that I'd been hard on his mother. There was no way a child could exude such radiant, celestial energy and be named anything but Ganymede.

❊ ❊ ❊

We had finished our business at the hobby shop on Laurel Canyon and were headed across town for Topanga. Luckily, it was still early, and I wasn't hitting much traffic on the 101 yet. It was turning out to be a nice day.

"Have you ever gone horseback riding in Griffith Park?" I asked. We were passing by Sherman Oaks, which made me think of my mom, who used to love horseback riding. My parents had up and relocated to Arizona several years ago so Dad could run a smaller podiatry practice with an old friend.

"No."

"Me neither." Pause. "Maybe if I go someday, I'll call you."

Ganymede grinned. "Yeah, I wouldn't mind."

It was so much easier to make dates with ten-year-olds than with adult men.

"Does your mother horseback ride?"

Ganymede took a fairly long time to answer.

"She's not really into bigger animals," he informed me. "I think she likes the smaller brains for some reason. She thinks she can access them easier."

Hmm. I decided to change the subject.

"So what are you doing these days, G?"

"I'm building a robot."

We sailed past the 405 interchange without a hitch. My spirits lifted. Usually the place where the 101 and 405 crossed was a beautiful car museum where every make and model of car in Los Angeles was displayed, frozen in time, for the gods above to look down upon and enjoy.

"Oh, is that what that stuff from the hobby shop was for?" Once we had gotten to Kit Craft, the hobby shop, I remembered it from my childhood. I hadn't been there since I was about 15, when I had been engaged in the delightfully domestic hobby of decorating my own Christmas ornaments. Everyone had been convinced I was going to be the next Martha Stewart. But by the following Christmas, I had already gotten into surfing, and ornament-making disappeared faster than a senator during a brothel raid. I had been floored that the store was still there and, frankly, mystified that it was still open. It must have opened in the '40s, minimum. Who went in there, exactly? Besides Ganymede, I mean. A skinny guy behind the counter had known Ganymede and Ralph by name. They had high-fived each other and started speaking immediately in what sounded like Elvish, but I concluded must be some kind of hobby shop dialect.

"No, this stuff is for something else," Ganymede said, gripping his plastic bag. "My robot's made out of metal and steel, not plastic," he said, affronted.

"Okay. Well, you know, I can't read your mind. How the hell would I know what your robot's made out of?"

"That's true," he answered amicably. "Did you know that the first hand that starts to perform an autopsy is called the prosecutor?"

I changed lanes, attempting to put distance between us and a truck pulling a trailer full of horses.

"You know, I didn't know that. That's pretty interesting."

"Hey, when you drop me off, don't come in. My sisters are crazy."

"Aw. What? That's not nice."

"I'm not kidding. They are. If you go in there, they'll make you crazy, too. I'm already crazy." He tapped his head as Ralph watched with interest. "And I'm stuck there for eight more years, unless I do a Declaration of Independence."

Declaration of Independence? Wow, he'd done his research. *He was serious.*

Andrygen had thought she couldn't conceive, and like many others, she had adopted a child. It had simply been fortuitous that her love affair with Jupiter had eventually borne real fruit, allowing her to bring the rest of the moons down to earth where they belonged. So, the three girls that had popped out one after the other had become Io, Callista, and Europa. I think the father taught at Pepperdine. I wondered if Ganymede's father had wanted to name the children out of a different galaxy entirely and was really pissed off that Andrygen had stayed so close to home.

As I wound the Z up into the Canyon, my heart went out to Ganymede, thinking about his situation. He seemed like a great kid, but his childhood was even weirder than mine, apparently. He was adopted, lived in the Colors of Benetton house up in Manson territory, completely isolated from the rest of the world. He had a mentally unstable dog, and he was building a robot. Was that healthy? I was enjoying his company. For the moment, he was making me completely forget about aliens and any other monsters I hadn't met yet.

"Hey, there's this special bolt on a helicopter they call the Jesus Bolt. You know why?"

According to his directions, we were finally nearing his house. I rounded a sharp curve carefully and said, "No."

"Because if that bolt breaks or falls off, the next person you'll see is Jesus."

Ralph barked.

"Shh, Ralphie!"

Ralph whimpered and hunkered down.

"Wow." I thought about that for a minute. "That's a lot of pressure for one little bolt."

Note to self: never get in a helicopter.

Ganymede grinned.

"It's that whitish house behind the trees."

I pulled over. The house looked to be a typical Topanga Canyon ranch style abode left over from the '60s. "Okay, sweetheart. Do you need help inside?"

"No!" He practically leapt out of the car like I had just suggested we go steady. "Come, Ralph."

More antics ensued as Ralph and his collar struggled to exit the car. Finally extricated, Ganymede closed the door carefully (he worshipped my Z almost as much as he worshipped me) and leaned over into the window with the worldliness of a 35-year-old. Now it felt like he was going to ask *me* to go steady.

"Thank you for dropping me off, Rae. I really had fun today."

I could see the top of the honey badger's paws on his shirt, clinging to the field mouse.

"I had fun too, honey. I learned about the prosecutor and why I'm going to die in a helicopter. Good luck with your robot."

"Thanks." He paused with his head down, staring at the dirt. "It's going to be life-size. I could get in it if I wanted. I could leave space to operate it from the inside. And protect people."

The hair on my neck stood up. I had no idea why, but something felt strange. I couldn't see Ralph, but I heard him emit a low growl.

"Ralph, no!"

"Protect people? From what?"

"I don't know." Pause. "Something." He sounded sad now. "Aliens," he said, as I stared. "Vampires." He shrugged, then he looked at me. "Bye, Rae." He turned around and headed for the house. Ralph skulked along beside him, sort of crouching low to the ground, like he was inching his way through a crawl space. Aliens and vampires? What a bizarre coincidence. Just what I'd been thinking lately. But he was ten years old. If we had been talking long enough, he would have mentioned the Wolfman and Frankenstein and zombies next, wouldn't he? It had to be a coincidence. As Ganymede reached the house, the door flew open. Immediately he whirled around and screamed, "RAE! GO! GET OUT OF HERE! GO! GO!"

The panic in his voice made me panic. After making sure hatchet-wielding ax murderers weren't pouring out of the front door, I floored the Z and took off, tires spinning. I looked in my rearview mirror at the little girl who had come out of the house, standing in the front yard in a white dress that blew softly in the breeze, gazing after me. She looked so innocent, so small and harmless, reminding me of that first glimpse of Lecter in the prison scene in *Silence of the Lambs*.

CHAPTER 7

I continued driving up Topanga, headed for the other side of the mountain and the ocean. Once I reached the peak and started going down, I caught glimpses of frothing waves and endless blue expanse as I rounded certain bends in the road. And this, of course, triggered the memories. As was my habit these days, I mused on the nature of regret. I regretted a lot of things. Dropping out of school. Letting fear run me. Never making it clear to Rex how I felt. It had all become sharper and clearer as time went on, like sinking down into a body of water, everything luminous all around you, but being unable to enjoy this lucidity because you couldn't breathe.

The thing everyone in my life knew and understood, to an extent, was that a shark had tried to eat me once. And I had reacted badly. They knew how the shark, a monster coming out of nowhere, the stuff of nightmares, trying to end me, had filled me with a reckless abandon borne of terror. It was almost a kind of survivor's guilt, a crafty side-stepping of death that had me thinking my days were numbered anyway, as death continued to stalk me. Of course, it stalked us all, but I'd imagined it was on my heels, right there, poised to strike. I'd engaged in the whole nine yards—drinking, drugs, waking up in my car or people's homes with no memory of how I'd gotten there. If *Final Destination* had been made back then, I probably would have had a complete nervous breakdown. Okay. *More* of a complete nervous breakdown.

It was pretty bad. It was fairly miraculous that something serious hadn't happened like herpes, AIDS, flipping over in my car seventeen times on Interstate 10 before it sailed off the side and came to a stop on top of a supermarket roof. My head somersaulting through the air, sliced off clean by the Ralph's sign. My family would still demand an open casket at the funeral, so the mortician would simply tie a pretty scarf around the place where they had quickly sewn my head back on to my body. None of that had happened. Thank God. Thank *somebody*. Strangely enough, despite the present topic, I've always felt like I had someone watching out for me somewhere in the ether.

Ahead of me lay the Pacific, an immense slab of blue stretching to the ends of the earth. Though the sea was moody and capricious, like an omnipotent child, I still loved it. Despite its mysterious depths and terrifying, circling denizens. At the base of the mountain, I turned left onto Pacific Coast Highway, driving until I reached a parking lot, where I forked over some bucks to the attendant and pulled in. The waves were choppy today, and I could see a gaggle of surfers bouncing up and down out there. I leaned against the hood of the Z, relaxing in the weak sunlight, listening to the surf. I closed my eyes thinking: *Everything's okay. It's going to be okay.* I was taking charge of my life. Fixing my shoulder. Going back to school. This was taking charge.

Then I opened my eyes, and God and Zeus and Shiva and whoever else up there hated my guts gazed down and saw that I was having a pretty good day and decided to blast it to hell. Because out on the water, a cone of light had shot down. My heart dropped a thousand feet in five seconds. "Not again, not again, not again," I heard my mouth whispering. With a force of will, I made myself stop. I traced the light up to where it disappeared into a comically shaped flying saucer. I say comically because it was almost cartoon-like: a silver disk hovering in the middle of the gaggle of surfers, encasing one of them in its sheath of light. Everyone around him continued with their activities, oblivious, as the rigid surfer was transported, with his board, through the air toward the waiting machine.

I spun in a tight, hysterical circle, looking for fellow witnesses. I ended facing back toward the sea and the ballsy middle-of-the-day, middle-of-a-crowd kidnapping. I ran forward and stumbled halfway down the small sandy slope toward the ocean. And then the ascension was complete, the surfer having disappeared within. The light went out, and the saucer thrummed once or twice like a hog revving its engine, and vanished.

The surfers bobbed on their boards and called out to each other in casual voices. I turned around and scrambled on all fours up the sandy hill, made for my car, yanked my purse out, and unearthed the packet of cigarettes I'd been carrying around since Annie's event. In one fluid movement, I ripped the plastic off, tossed it aside, and worked one of the little cylinders loose. I was about to shove it in my mouth when someone said loudly, "OH…MY…GOD." I startled and whipped around like the door to my meth lab had just been kicked in. A female bicycle cop was standing right behind me, straddling her Fuji Special Police Mountain Bike in a manner that brokered no foolishness. I hadn't even seen her. She crooked a finger at me. "Ma'am. Come here, please."

Goddamn my frigging bullshit cop karma and the universe that had bestowed it upon me.

"Yes?" I was surprised I was still conscious. I walked tentatively forward. I realized I was in shock. My lizard brain was keeping me aloft, operating my body like a marionette from deep within the temporal lobe.

"Jesus," said the cop. "You didn't see me sitting here?" she asked in amazement. Police officers were always flabbergasted when their authority wasn't immediately recognized and dutifully acquiesced to. It was called "contempt of cop," and you were up shit creek if they thought you were expressing it in any way whatsoever. I had no time to play ego games with the officer, though. I had to get out of here. Now. And she did too, if she knew what was good for her. We all had to get out of here. An alien sighting one time was an accident, an anomaly. An alien sighting twice was an invasion. We were being invaded. Americans were being kidnapped and carted away in broad daylight. It was real. It was happening. It *was* the end of the world.

"You littered," she was saying. "Right in front of me. You littered."

If I had disemboweled somebody here in the parking lot, I could understand her amazement. If she had been able to see what was taking place right in front of her out over the ocean, I think her priorities would have shifted slightly. My knees shook. I was pretty sure I was going to spew vomit all over her front wheel. I covered my mouth politely, as if I had to belch. "I know, o-officer," I said. I held the vomit back. My voice broke. "But I didn't see you. I would *never* litter in front of you."

"Yeah? But if I wasn't here, would you litter?"

"U-Usually I don't litter, ma'am. I like to keep our parks and beaches clean, too. So we can all enjoy them. My sister was a slob when we were growing up, and I really try not to be like her at all. But today—today i-is different, ma'am."

I turned and pointed out at the ocean toward the surfers. My hand trembled. Through my peripheral vision I saw the officer perk up, her alarms jumping from "littering event" to "call for backup" in the blink of an eye.

"Whoa, whoa, whoa!" The lady cop leapt off her bike and put the kickstand down all in one movement. In a minute, she would be searching the Z for drugs, handcuffing me. For some reason, the theme from *Hawaii 50* started playing in my head. I couldn't tell her the truth. I'd be arrested for sure. Pilots, political people, generals, renown scientists had, over time, come out of the UFO closet, admitted they'd kept it on the down low, whatever weird experience they'd had, and they'd all been either ignored, ridiculed, or murdered. Murdered! I couldn't tell this cop what had just happened. I might end up as all three.

"What's going on? Why are you shaking like that? You want to step away from the car?"

I fully expected the officer to pull her gun out and shoot me in the head. This wasn't Great Britain or Canada or even Iowa. This was Los Angeles. Mentally I kicked myself in the butt for never having written a living will. I had two important points to make: Do not hook me up to machines. Do not let Margarite have any of my possessions.

"Sir—ma'am," I pointed out at the ocean again. "I thought I saw a shark. I could have sworn I saw a shark." Now the coup de grace. I held up my hand with its missing fingers. "I know. I used to be a surfer." The lady cop saw my stubs, looked back at me, and the tension flowed out of her like air from a balloon. She removed her hand from the baton on her belt and flexed her fingers.

"Hoo, boy." She peered out at the ocean for a moment. "Whoo! So, were you wrong? There wasn't a shark?" She looked fairly relaxed now, like she was just inquiring politely but didn't actually give a shit about any sharks.

"No, thank God," I sagged, acting out my relief, relief I felt in no way whatsoever. "It wasn't a shark. I don't know what it was. Choppy waves."

She laughed a little. "Jesus, give me a coronary, why don't you? Had a guy last week, shaking like a leaf. Went to give assistance. He pulls a Desert Eagle out of his pants, points it, and fires. Killed a seagull. It fell right on a Bentley parked two spaces away."

"Was he aiming at the seagull?"

"No. He was aiming at my head." She pointed at her temple. "My head. *My head.* It just ended up missing me because he was shaking so bad."

"Oh, my God, I'm sorry. Well, I don't have a Desert Eagle in my pants, officer."

She scanned my tight-fitting jeans for a second like a TSA agent at LAX.

"No. No. I don't think you have one in there either." She grinned.

"Who brings a Bentley to the beach anyway?" I asked. "Seagulls and sand and people walking past with surfboards…"

"I know, right?" She threw up her hands. "Bullets and seagull guts everywhere. When I get *my* Bentley, I ain't bringing it here, that's for damn sure."

"God. Me neither."

"Okay, well, next time, please pick up your trash." She had slipped back into Cop Mode again, but it was Cop Mode Lite, now. "I'll just give you a warning. And there's no smoking at the beaches." Her words were dogmatic and final, backed by city officials and the self-righteous fanaticism of Rob Reiner. Thanks a lot, Rob Reiner! He was so anti-smoking, I figured he must have had something to do with it. Then she added, "You don't want to be like your slobby sister, right?" and she half-winked at me.

"No, I can't stand her."

"Oh…" She turned back to her bike and swung a moderately muscled leg over. "Don't say that." She adjusted the strap under her bike helmet. "It's still there, though," she said.

"Excuse me?"

She pointed. I turned to look at the ground.

"The cigarette wrapper." Beat. "You could pick it up right now if you really wanted to."

"Oh." *Jesus Christ.* "Oh. Yeah. I do. I really want to. Good idea." I bent over and was suddenly chasing the clear plastic wrapper across the parking lot because a wayward breeze had decided to kite it along, just out of reach of my good arm. Oh, my God, Chrislann was right. I *was* favoring the good arm! The breeze kicked, and the wrapper fluttered away. It was the gods again, fucking with me. I couldn't reach the wrapper. I sensed the female cop's eyes on me, observing, monitoring. I would get my revenge. I would get revenge on Ricardo, and then I would go after Zeus. Yeah, Zeus. I switched my sights to him. Why Zeus and why not God? Because I didn't have enough ladders to reach God. But I could buy a shitload of ladders from Lowe's and climb to fucking Mount Olympus and unleash my vengeance. Finally, I plucked up the offending trash.

"Thank you!" called the cop. She had to raise her voice because I'd scuttled behind the cigarette wrapper halfway across the United States. "Okay, be safe," she yelled, and rode off into the L.A. smog. I waved gaily and watched her go. I got back in the Z and headed for Glendale, not that that was any comfort since everything had started there in the Vortex of Evil. I drove down Pacific Coast Highway until I reached Sunset, turned left, and took Sunset all the way to Coldwater Canyon. I took the Canyon home with the *Hawaii 50* theme still blasting through my head no matter how loud I played the radio. I smoked all the way back, coughing and stubbing the cigarettes out one after the other in the ashtray.

At home, I practically raped the margarita mix trying to get it open and get some alcohol in my veins. I called a bunch of people, asking if they were okay. I think I called Margarite, and we ended up in a fight, which concluded with me yelling, "At least I'm not pretending to be white!" and slamming down the phone. I think

Annie's boyfriend pounded on the wall because I was being too noisy. I was too drunk to be enraged at that. I butt-dialed someone who I thought was Dante by accident and a deep male voice answered saying, "Yes? Hello?" as I stared uncomprehendingly at the phone. Then all I heard was deep male laughter. Obviously a wrong number. Or a friend, maybe. I was glad to be of such amusement to whomever it was that had answered. Maybe I would go into standup comedy. It would be easier than going back to school. I continued drinking deep into the night. I continued drinking until there was nothing left to drink.

CHAPTER 8

It was only 10:30 in the morning, and it was already almost 90 degrees. I was outside the therapy center, leaning against the wall, musing on the different levels of the nature of regret. This time, the regret wasn't as far-reaching and soul-plundering as un-archiving all of your life decisions and finding them wanting. This time, it simply involved saying to oneself: "If I had stopped drinking there, right at that point, around 8:30 last night, I would only feel half like shit. I wouldn't feel completely like shit." Sometimes alcohol really was more like a weapon than something meant for peaceful relaxation.

I was wearing a hoodie and sunglasses and smoking until it was time to go in. A red Pontiac GTO pulled up in the parking space next to the Z. Salt and Pepper extricated his manly physique from its interior. He shoved his keys into the pocket of his gray slacks, then turned and looked at me. We exchanged electric eye contact again, even though I wearing the sunglasses. It was as if I was not wearing anything over my eyes. His gaze was made of tiny arms and fists that pummeled their way straight through the cheap plastic of my eyewear. I exhaled some smoke and gave him a small, stiff smile.

"Hi. I saw you last time," he said, stating the obvious. He had a deep voice and an unidentifiable accent.

"Hi."

He held out his hand. "I am Giancarlo."

Ah…

"Hi. I'm Rae."

"Rae." It rumbled out of his mouth. "How lovely."

American men never said lovely. It was charming. We shook hands. Our palms pulsated together as our hearts shoved blood through our bodies. Our hands remained touching for one, two, three, four beats longer than was necessary.

"Nice GTO," I commented.

"Thank you. It belonged to my brother."

Call me crazy, but it seemed like his voice hitched slightly when he said the word "brother."

He gave me a discerning look. "Are you okay?" he asked in a normal voice.

Am I okay? I thought. *No, I am not okay.* I didn't feel I knew Giancarlo well enough, though, to bitch about the alien encounters.

"I'm hung over. I had a bad day yesterday." Why beat around the bush?

"Ah. What happened?"

"Um…"

He nodded. "Yes, I see," he said, as if I had just spilled my guts. Then, "How is the therapy going?"

I sucked in some smoke like it was air and I needed it to live. I exhaled slowly. Feeling a little better now. Regardless of the fact that I'd ruined a nice ten-year stretch of non-smoking. And not because some deluded celebrity decided I should quit. Because *I'd* decided I should quit. But the stretch was over. I had fallen off the wagon, and I was scrambling through the sagebrush on all fours, hiding from the nonsmoking pioneers who were searching for me with a lantern. I didn't want them to find me. I wanted to stay here on all fours. In the sagebrush. With my ciggies. Luckily for me, their lanterns had an unsteady, flickering light, and they couldn't see me. I knew about electricity and batteries, but apparently, they didn't. Morons. Their idiocy was my silver lining.

"You know…I'm playing it by ear. It's only my second session. I feel like it's not enough, though. Like Chrislann's very gentle. I know he has to be. But I feel like they should be making me chop wood, you know, forcing that shoulder to move."

Giancarlo laughed. "That is one way to look at it." He glanced at me appraisingly in that way that men do when you know they're ripping your clothes off in their minds but somehow they're still making polite eye contact with you. Giancarlo's smile disappeared as something caught his attention behind me. I turned around to look. There was a man standing across the street leaning against a light pole, seemingly staring in our direction.

"Do you know him?" Giancarlo asked, eyes locked on the figure.

"No." I paused. "But I've noticed some strangers staring at me lately. I figured it was because of the show." I shrugged. "Weird that it's always guys, though. Women tend to like the show more than men." What the hell was going on with everyone? *Now* strange guys were noticing me, after I'd been banished from TV land?

"Mmm…" he rumbled in a sexy way deep inside his throat. He seemed to tear his eyes away from the guy across the street with a force of will. "Well, Rae, it is so nice meeting you. I guess I will see you inside. Pull hard on that rubber band today. It will be good for you." He delivered a wink and patted my shoulder at the same time. His hand was hot hot hot. Yeah, I'll pull hard on it, Giancarlo. Innuendo much? It was lucky Chrislann was my therapist. Seemingly preoccupied now, Salt and Pepper tossed another quick glance across the street then strode purposefully inside. I turned to look again, too. The man was gone.

So I gotta admit—haven't had the best luck with guys. No trouble attracting them, but then something always seemed to go wrong, and they ended up leaving. Believe it or not, my instinct was that it wasn't me. It felt like something always "happened," something, even, that scared them. How could that be? I wish I knew. I had no idea.

Take my last boyfriend, for example. Johnny. I had met him while filming *Green Splendor I* when he was stunt doubling for one of the surfers. We lost contact for a long time, then I ran into him five years ago. We dated for six months. He proposed. Took me to Disneyland and waited until we were in the little boats for It's A Small World. The song was playing, and I couldn't quite hear him. He was what Seinfeld would have called "a low talker," except that he'd already done an episode on "close talkers."

I raised my voice. "What?"

He raised his voice. "You wanna get married?"

The automatons were doing their thing, singing about how small the world was, albeit full of tears and also fear. Now that I thought about it, that song was a little creepy, and so was that ride. What did fear and tears have to do with your happy place? It was a weird place for someone to propose. But yet that's where he chose to do it, and I accepted, under the unblinking, glazed eyes of the automatons and the disapproving ghost of Walt Disney. I figured Walt was pretty much disapproving of everyone. Then a few weeks later, he stopped calling and disappeared. I couldn't reach him anywhere. I called his brother. His brother hemmed and hawed, so I knew, at least, that Johnny was alive.

But nobody would talk, and eventually I gave up. Obviously, the guy had changed his mind. About a year later, I ran into Johnny at the Farmer's Market on La Brea. He was bent over a basket of tomatoes, picking various ones up and squeezing them while the seller watched, frowning slightly. I came up behind him and tapped him on the shoulder. He turned with a smile on his face that quickly peeled away when he saw me.

He looked absolutely terrified, as if he had been in my apartment and discovered all the newspaper clippings I had saved about the oodles of people I had been slaughtering over the years. He looked so scared that I couldn't bring myself to question him about what had happened. Anyway, it was a year later, so most of the sting had gone already, soothed by the balm of time. I had also experienced a *Twister* moment, realizing that I really wasn't that upset about it.

Johnny had turned into a vegan the last four months we were together, due to some health issues. He had no longer been a stuntman by then. He wouldn't have been able to muscle cars into flips or parkour himself up the sides of buildings fueled with some rice and a celery stick. He'd gone into business with his brother as a scuba diving guide. Hanging out with a vegan definitely shrunk the boundaries for where one could find a delicious meal to about a four-foot-by-five-foot inescapable enclosure, a situation which began to lose its patina almost before it even started.

There were other little things, too, like Johnny joking about "my skin tone" and how there could be a little "skin tone problem" when he took me home to meet his parents. I mean, what the hell was that supposed to mean? "My parents are a little conservative," he'd told me. He'd been raised in Lake Balboa, an area between Encino, Van Nuys, and Reseda. I'd been insanely jealous that he'd had the Kardashian lake, available to all, while we'd had the Greta Garbo lake, available to none. I knew Johnny had been joking, but the "skin tone" thing had always bothered me, even though his parents had been perfectly nice. The topper being that they had not just a smattering of Mexican heritage mixed in there, themselves. And then it didn't matter, because Johnny disappeared.

Which brought me to the question: Could I not love men because they were always leaving, or did not loving men make them leave? As if on cue, my cell rang. It was Rex, back from Vegas. He wanted to go out tonight, dinner and a movie. Or just dinner. Or just drinks. I knew it would end up as "just drinks." I was pretty sure Rex was an alcoholic. But he was a charming one.

"I'll pick you up," he said. "Where's your dump again?"

He was still miffed at me for moving into my cruddy apartment instead of moving in with him. He came off like *his* life had been mangled by fake Latino Ricardo and *his* dream condo in Hermosa Beach had been wrenched away, complete with undisguised contempt from the Realtor. He had a place in the hills above the Chateau Marmont in Hollywood that he had just moved into a couple of years ago, and he was between wives, so there was plenty of room. I gave him the directions, and he said he'd be there around 8:30. We disconnected, and I looked up in time to see Chrislann barreling down on me on his tiny legs across the parking lot.

"WTF, Rae?!" He screamed something in Tagalog. "What are you doing out here? Come on, come on!"

I glanced at my watch. "I still have one minute left."

"Minute, schminute. Oh, my God! Are you smoking? Oh, my God!" He stared, aghast, at my cigarette, as if it was a crack vial. "That's no good for you or your recovery! But I'm sure you already know that." Lightning fast, he plucked it out of my hand and tossed it to the cement and then stomped on it viciously. I decided not to get angry at him because I had smoked it down almost to the end, anyway. "Come on. That shoulder of yours needs all the time it can get. Come on, we're burning fucking daylight!"

I liked Chrislann's direct approach and the fact that he made it seem like we were in an action movie. I followed him inside.

CHAPTER 9

I was waiting for Rex outside my building because it was cooler out here than it was in there. The air conditioner was about 30 years old and was inside busy doing what I should have done long ago: writing a living will as it prepared to possibly die. Rex screeched over to the curb in his convertible Miata. He was a professional poker player and by now, he was a millionaire a couple times over. We didn't talk about money very much. It was considered crass.

We had met at UCLA where I was studying journalism and he was studying engineering. Just one of those things, standing in line at the student store. After he realized he'd seen me in a couple of local surfing competitions, we became best buds. We attended every surf event that time and money would allow and watched the rest on TV. I had been boning up for the Op Pro when the Tiger shark made its appearance, bringing an end to my surfing days.

Rex dropped out of UCLA the first time he won more than a million dollars at the World Poker Championships. These days, he played poker and sold a line of specially engineered surfboards that he had developed himself. Some one-of-a-kind adjustments to the fin, nose, and rails that transformed your surfboard into a hemp-inspired magic carpet. Rex *had* been smoking pot when he'd first thought up the concept. I had tested one long ago and had to admit the ride had been fast and smooth. I'd come up with the idea to brand two separate types, and the resulting logos (developed from my original doodles, by the way) featured a figure surfing a line of tumbling die for Lucky Seven while Splintered Paddle showed someone standing up in a canoe perched on top of a curling monster wave. Inspiration: King Kamehameha. Like Osiris, I'd always admired King K. because he'd united the Hawaiian Islands into one kingdom, empowering them against the clamoring Western interests. You gotta admire anyone with the balls to take on clamoring Western interests.

Soon after Rex had dropped out of UCLA, I dropped out after landing my first *Green Splendor* movie and had never looked back… until now. For some reason, although there had always been sexual tension between us, we'd never gotten together. Well, except that one time.

Rex had gotten out of the car to greet me since we hadn't seen each other in about two weeks. He was tall, about six-four, and towered over me. He yanked me to him and encased me in his arms. I uttered a muffled shriek as his grip tightened. He buried his face in my hair for a minute.

"What's wrong with you?"

"My shoulder." I moved it around, trying to loosen it up.

"Your shoulder?" He looked baffled. "Hasn't it been that way for years now?"

"Yeah. It's been years, Rex. Years."

"Here, Shark Bait, let me help you." He waited until I was in the car then pushed the door closed and jogged around to the other side. He screeched away from the curb just as Mr. Dadalian appeared on the sidewalk. Mr. Dadalian always seemed to be around when I was missing underwear and when I was speeding off in a car with some guy.

"I'm in physical therapy. I just started. But I think I'm gonna quit and let Hama train me."

One eyebrow went up. "Hama?"

"I'm not getting anywhere with this guy. He's too much of a pussy. I need Hama. I need my shoulder to be Scared Straight."

"Okay. You know what kind of fanatic Hama is. She has no feelings. If you start crying, you'll just make her mad."

"Well…" I shrugged. "We'll see." I looked at him sideways, gauging his mood. He seemed pretty up. I wondered how *he'd* take it if I told him ET hadn't been innocently levitating children's bicycles or returning World War II vets during a friendly encounter on Devil's Mountain. Rex was drumming his hands on the wheel. He was chewing gum and wearing his lucky black Fedora, which was pushed down low on his head to keep from flying out of the car. If I didn't know him, I would assume he was on methamphetamines, as I'm sure many a stranger had. But this crazy, looping energy of his went hand in hand with his mad calculating skills, making him a natural for playing cards. I gazed at him for a moment, admiring his masculine profile, the dirty, dirty blond hair kept short, almost military style, mixed with the family's Texan roots that lent him a distinctive dusky Cristiano Ronaldo-like bearing.

"I'm on a mission tonight," Rex was saying. "I'm going to get you super drunk and then talk you into something. Just letting you in on the game plan. Because I'm a gentleman." He reached up and touched the brim of his hat like a gentleman would.

I slouched down in the seat and fiddled with the radio. "You don't have to get me drunk to sleep with you," I said, before I could stop myself. *Where had that come from?* Rex stopped chewing his gum and squinted at the windshield.

"Just kidding." I was losing my mind.

"You're not kidding."

"Okay. I'm not kidding." Definitely losing it.

Rex had been married three times, and all three marriages had been very short and very annulled. I had liked two of the women and hated one. The last one had been a Vegas chorus girl about seven years ago who had been a prancing bitch. She had been insanely jealous that I had been the one to give the surfboards their logos and also hadn't understood why Rex donated so many to causes and charitable institutions all over the United States. After the marriage was annulled, I asked him why he'd married her. "I was super drunk," came the straight-faced Rex reply. By now, it would be more or less impossible to trust anyone since he was so rich. I kind of felt sorry for him. Which was absurd. Who was I to feel sorry for anyone? I was seeing things—an updated Roswellian nightmare—and I felt sorry for Rex the millionaire who couldn't find anyone to love him. *Get a life!* I thought moodily. There. I had done a complete 180. With any luck, along with everything else, I was prematurely menopausal.

"I wouldn't get you drunk first for that," Rex was saying. "And you wouldn't want or need to be drunk first." He was deadly serious.

"Oh, yeah?"

"Yeah."

I opened my mouth for more verbal sparring and decided against it. I wouldn't be able to return his rallies anyway.

"Hey, pull my Mals out." He gestured toward the glove compartment. I reached in, located the Marlboros, and handed him one. Then I dug around inside my purse and removed a Virginia Slim. Yes. Virginia Slims. We both lit up, inhaled, leaned back in our seats. I guess the beach scene had really done a number on me yesterday. I was in a worse mood than I had realized. Because I had thought I'd been Scot free, the unwilling witness to a rare event that I'd never see again in my life. But no. They were everywhere. They were all over the place, engaged in a free-for-all. And only I could see them. I blew smoke toward the windshield and Rex did a double take.

I waved my hand. "Don't ask." No. He couldn't handle it either. I couldn't tell anybody about the aliens. I couldn't tell the cops, I couldn't tell my friends, I couldn't tell my family. I was alone, alone, alone. Big surprise. I gazed out the window at the temperate L.A. evening. One good thing about this town was that during the day, you would boil to death and sweat out all your vital juices and probably wouldn't mind dying, but by nighttime, you could reanimate, refreshed, when the temperature plummeted 20 degrees or more.

"So you have anywhere in mind?" asked Rex. "Just make sure there's stiff drinks. That's all I ask." We were still in Glendale, tooling through the dark suburban side streets, going nowhere fast. I thought of the Americana over on Brand. We could pop into the Cheesecake Factory. There were a lot of little restaurants over there, but it was so crowded. I shuddered. What if they came and started plucking bodies up like choosing hors d' oeuvres off a silver serving tray? Rex took his hands off the steering wheel and cupped his mouth. "Earth to Rae…Rae…Rae. Come in, Rae…Rae…Rae."

My cell phone rang, playing a riff from *5150*. That was the ringtone for Margarite.

"Should I answer it? It's Margarite."

"What is that, Van Halen?"

"Yeah." I stared at the phone, nervous. Margarite hardly ever called me. "It's the code for a mentally disturbed person."

"I know what it is." He shook his head and stared out the windshield. "You really can't stand her."

"No, I love her. But I don't like her."

"That's apparent. Go ahead. Don't let me stop you."

I watched the phone as if it was alive. "I have a bad feeling. I have a feeling something's going on."

"How would you know that?"

I know because bad things have *been going on.*

"I don't know. I just have a feeling."

"Answer it. Answer it."

I inhaled through my teeth and pressed the button. "Hello?"

Margarite was sobbing. I held the phone up so Rex could hear.

"Hello? Rae? Hello?"

"Hello?"

"Hello? Is that you?" She was sniveling and slurring. Now *she* was drunk! "Rae? Rae? Rae! Rae!"

"Yes! I'm here! What's going on?"

"You have to come over here," she said drunkenly. "I think Diddy's dead!" She broke out into new sobbing.

"Is Diddy her husband?" Rex whispered. "I thought his name was Douglas."

"It is Douglas," I whispered back.

"Who's Diddy?"

I shrugged.

"Rae? Rae? Rae? Rae?" Her voice was inching higher and higher. I stared at Rex, holding the phone out toward his face. He winced a little as Margarite's octaves approached glass-shattering levels. We both flicked our cigarettes out of the car at the same time. It was a truly idiotic thing to do, considering me and my cop karma.

Rex said, "Come on; let's go," and headed for the freeway.

❖ ❖ ❖

Margarite and her husband lived in Brentwood, OJ's old stomping grounds. She was waiting on the sidewalk outside of her house when we pulled up. She was sitting on the curb with a bottle of wine in her hand. She got up when she saw me climbing out of Rex's car and dropped the bottle. It rolled softly onto the grass, expelling its contents. Margarite was tall, about five foot ten, had jet black hair styled in a pageboy that I wasn't fond of, and looked very pale. I guess she hardly went outside anymore. She was also quite a bit chunkier than last time I had seen her.

She started to get down on her hands and knees to either retrieve the wine bottle or perhaps suck the spilled contents out of the grass, but Rex caught her by the arm and pulled her up gently. They stood together, both of them tall. I wasn't exactly short—five foot seven— but they were much taller and complemented each other in a way that made me weirdly jealous. Rex was not Margarite's type, and Margarite had always annoyed Rex. I could tell, even now, that she was annoying him just by the way she was swaying unsteadily on her feet and peering at him as if trying to recall who he was.

"What kind of vodka are you drinking and where can I get some?" He held on to her arm.

"Unhand me!"

"What?" Rex said and then laughed. He looked at me over the top of her head and mouthed, "Unhand me"?

"You are…" Margarite had recovered and now obviously desired formal introductions. Rex smiled down at her.

"Rex."

"Rex! You're so tall!"

"Thanks."

Margarite got a weird look on her face. I realized a moment later that she was sort of lecherously smirking.

"What a specimen!" she slurred. "You're very handsome."

"Uh…"

I stifled a laugh. Margarite sagged, and Rex held her up. She put one hand up on Rex's chest and spread her fingers over his shirt and rubbed lightly. Then she started rubbing him with both hands. Like

Anderson Cooper dealing with Kathy Griffin, he grasped her wrists and gently but firmly extricated her.

"Um, Margarite, you must be really drunk to be coming on to Rex."

Margarite straightened up and whirled around in a sloppy half-circle.

"I am married!" she shrieked. "I am married!"

"Shh, shh, I know you are," I said quietly. "Come on; let's go inside." I came over and took her other arm. Suddenly docile, she complied, and we walked her back into her yard, up the driveway, and to the front door. Once inside, she broke free of us and darted away like a crazy wild animal.

"God." I sank down onto the champagne-colored living room sofa with my chin in my hand.

The room was dimly lit by one yellowish lamp on the side table. The rest of the room lay in shadow.

"Your sister's packing it on. When's the last time you saw her?"

"Three or four months ago," I said into my hand. Margarite came prancing back into the room.

"He's back here. Back here, you guys." She gestured with her head, oddly, like someone suggesting we should join them in a back alleyway.

"Who?"

"Diddy."

"Fuck," Rex whispered. "I forgot about Diddy."

I stood up. Margarite weaved her way unevenly through the furniture and out a glass side door leading to the backyard. The backyard was dark. It was hard to even make out the pool. I tripped on a chair leg, and the heavy metal screeched loudly. Rex steadied me from behind.

"Hey, M., did you guys forget to pay the electric bill?" His hands remained on my arms, warm.

"Where's Douglas?" I asked. Douglas was her entertainment lawyer husband.

"Out!" She said bitterly. "As usual." She pointed at the water. "Diddy's in the pool. I think he fell in, and he was too old to get out. He has arthritis. Had. Had arthritis…"

We approached the pool and stared down into it, almost afraid to look.

"Who's Diddy?" I asked. "A neighbor? Are you neighbors with P. Diddy? Is P. Diddy in your pool?"

Margarite flapped her hands and jogged in place. She was regressing quickly to a seven-year-old.

"No! No! Diddy. Paddy. Paddy!"

"Paddy!" I looked in the pool and could just make out a dark shape floating out in the deep end near the side. "Your dog?"

"Her dog?" said Rex, walking toward the dark shape. "He's dead? Are you sure?"

"Is his name Paddy or Diddy?"

"We just...started calling him Diddy," Margarite said between sobs, "because he'd go crazy whenever...P. Diddy was singing on the radio. He...loved P. Diddy's music."

Rex was squatting near the body, reaching over and poking it. Margarite faced me suddenly and seized me by the shoulders.

"I'm sorry I knocked you in the pool when we were kids. It was an accident. I didn't mean to do it."

"I know. It's okay." I wasn't used to Margarite touching me.

"Want me to pull him out?" Rex said. "He's definitely dead."

"But you drowned, you know," persisted Margarite.

"Well, I fell in and was paddling around a little until Mom got me out. I don't think I drowned."

"They never told you, Rae." She breathed heavily into my face, and I pulled back. "You drowned. You had to be...re-re-revived."

"Honey, no, I didn't."

"They never told you. They didn't want to upset you."

Rex was busy at the pool with the leaf skimmer, floating Paddy-Diddy toward the shallow end where the steps were.

"Rex, are you hearing this? Margarite says I drowned. In the pool. That time when I was a kid."

Rex stopped his gruesome chore for a moment and stood there looking at me. Even though it was almost pitch dark back here, I could see his face clearly, and Rex did not look like someone who was amazed at the news. Rex looked like someone who already knew.

"Oh, my *God*!" I said and threw my hands up.

Margarite grabbed me in a sloppy bear hug. "I'm sorry! I'm sorry!"

"How long? How long?" I yelled at Rex over Margarite's shoulder.

"Um…" He tapped Paddy-D's dead body with the leaf skimmer absently. "Couple of years ago. Your parents were out here throwing their anniversary party. Margarite was drunk…"

"Drunk?" I turned to her. "You got drunk and told *my* friend a family secret? And you got on my case for being drunk the other day?"

Even when she was intoxicated, Margarite remembered things. It was infuriating. "You called in the middle of the afternoon, Rae-Rae." She held up her finger. "Whenever I drink, it's at night."

Rex stood next to the drowned dog and nodded as if he agreed with her, and this was the correct and acceptable behavior for universal alcoholism.

"Yeah, so she told me." He tried to look sheepish, but he started smirking and then he stifled a laugh. My eyes were adjusting to the dark now. I could see his teeth flashing in his laughing face. He bent over and guided the corpse onto the steps then started to wrestle it out of the water.

"Your dog is gigantic. What kind of dog is this?"

"It's a Bernese Mountain Dog," I answered, because Margarite was clinging to me and quietly whispering into my hair, "I love you. I love you," and didn't appear to have heard him. Rex finally maneuvered Paddy-D onto dry land.

"Sorry," he said. "I was gonna tell you. Then I forgot. It's not that big a deal, is it?" He was smiling again and trying not to. Evidently, he found the whole thing very funny.

"Why would they lie about that? That's like waiting until I'm 20 to tell me I'm adopted!"

"I don't know." He shrugged. "You should ask them."

Margarite was staring at Paddy-D now. Her maudlin-meter swung from me back to the dead dog.

"Oh, Diddy, Diddy, Diddy!" She started to walk over there, and I pulled her back.

"Don't move, Margarite! You're going to fall in there next, and when Rex is trying to save you, you're going to try to climb on top of him to keep from drowning. Then I'll have to jump in and bash you over the head, and you'll have a terrible headache the next day. You don't want that, do you?"

"No. No more drowning," Margarite whispered. "No more drowning."

"Do you have some trash bags?" asked Rex.

We were all back at the curb helping Rex get the trashcan positioned. I didn't think it was trash day tomorrow, but the trashcan was going out here anyway. Paddy-D's tail was hanging out of the plastic bag and down the side of the can. Rex was trying to stuff it back in.

"Okay, I think that does it. We're gonna take off," I said to my sister. She rested her hand on the garbage can tenderly, lost in her thoughts, then two beats later, she was grabbing at me again.

She put her face up close to mine like we were about to get busy and spoke into my mouth. "I hate them."

Rex, busy typing something into his phone, glanced up and froze. "What? Who?"

"I hate them. Those girls. Those skeletons. The ones that are starving themselves. I hate them. I don't care if they die, those selfish little bitches. I don't care! I'm tired of giving them permission to live!" She said all this in my face, her mouth millimeters from mine. "So I've been eating," she whispered. "In direct opposition to their... their...death wishes." Rex was watching, fascinated. And, I'm sure, as all men did, hoping...

I hated to disappoint him, but I wedged my hand up between her face and mine and then slowly pushed her head back. Hama, maybe. This was Margarite. *Come on, Rex. Be serious.*

"You are invading. My personal space. Back, please."

"Come on," said Rex. "We'll walk you back inside."

Back at the house, she wouldn't let us leave. "One last thing, though." She clutched at Rex's forearm. "You should know. I need to tell you something."

I dropped my head forward and closed my eyes. Rex reached past Margarite and squeezed my upper arm to give me strength. What? What was it going to be? More whining about the anorexic girls? More bitching about her absentee husband? I wanted to say, "Margarite, I have huge problems." I felt like Rutger Hauer's character in Bladerunner: "I've seen things you people wouldn't believe…"

But Margarite surprised us both by saying, "You were dead for a long time, Rae." She started whispering, placing her hand theatrically beside her mouth. "You were under water for fifteen minutes before Mama got you out."

I looked over at Rex. "Did you know about that part?"

Rex's mouth was hanging open. "Didn't know about that part."

CHAPTER 10

I thought people tended to remember and hold on to things that should have been dust in their memories eons ago, and I was no exception. A lot of it might be things you wouldn't mind unhearing and unremembering, but it was too late. The school Margarite and I had attended in North Hollywood had been a private school, and several child actors and lots of actors' kids had gone there. The grades ran from first all the way through twelfth. Once I'd overheard two of my classmates talking about Helen Hunt. She had attended the high school a few years ago with the older kids for six months. The boy said, "Helen who?" and the girl said, "Helen Cunt." I was scandalized. But very careful not to show it. You could never show any emotion around these kids. They were like piranhas, poised to tear you apart the moment you showed a shred of vulnerability. These kids were smart asses, indifferent to being surrounded by semi-famous actors because their parents were lawyers and athletes and actors themselves.

In retrospect, I wouldn't unhear the Helen Cunt thing. I had to give that girl credit for thinking on her feet, for uttering the taboo word in order to garner a reaction from the boy, which she received in spades: his face burning bright red, followed by raucous laughter. But Red Harris was a different story. When Red Harris came to the school for a few months and one day decided, mysteriously, to tell me to "turn around and shut up," I wouldn't have minded unhearing that. I wouldn't mind, now, unremembering that.

It was so long ago, but somewhere along the line, it had become part of my permanent history. Red Harris had been a super-popular, obnoxious little blond pop star, Leif Garrett's nemesis. Leif had already been older by this time and losing his luster. Think Honey

Boo Boo. Think Justin Beiber. Think of them entering the machine in The Fly and melding together into one monstrous being. That would be Red Harris. Having Red Harris tell me to turn around and shut up for no apparent reason was like Lincoln stepping down from a poster on the wall and launching into a series of "your mama" jokes.

Of course, there was no comparison between Lincoln and Red Harris. But for a while, at least during my childhood, Red's name was probably almost as recognizable. At least in the United States. Okay. At least in Los Angeles. So the event emblazoned itself into my tender young mind and remained today one of the things I would gladly let slip, forget about, discount as so much fodder from the past. But it was too late. It seemed to be stuck there forever. And now, ranking number one above Red Harris, was Margarite's revelation about my death. Couldn't unhear it. Couldn't unknow it. Would definitely never forget it. Did it make my life any easier? No. It just compounded all the weirdness going on these days. And why had she chosen to reveal this to me now, this burning secret? It was like she'd thought to herself, "I can't be close to my sister. It's too late for that. But maybe I can insinuate myself into her life by bringing up a bizarre event that essentially makes her look like an inexplicable freak. Maybe we can get closer through those special shared memories of her impossible fifteen-minute death."

I was in Whole Foods in Glendale searching for Hama's favorite gluten-free Honey Oat Bread and moping a little bit over this latest revelation. I was going over to Hama's place for shoulder therapy. I had given up on Chrislann, even though I loved him like a son. I was skulking around in the baked goods aisle when Cola called. As usual, right to business.

"*Sand in Your Face* is wrapping up shooting in a month. The producers want you to be on the reunion show."

"Is Ricardo going to be there?"

Silence.

"Yeah, so I'd rather dive out of a plane without a parachute. Pass."

I realized that I was behaving like a prima donna—undeserved at that—and wondered for the millionth time why Cola didn't dump me. For the millionth time, I thought: Cola has a crush on me. *Cola is in love with me.*

"If you dove out of a plane without a parachute, the minute you left the plane, you'd regret it."

His dry and emotionally flat response reminded me that this theory, like always, would be dismantled immediately by a heartless team of Dr. Phils and Dr. Ruths ping-ponging their observations back and forth:

"Note zee lack of feeling in dis man's vocal chords."

"Oh, yeah, there's nothing there. If he's in love with her, he's a master play-actor, an award-winning thespian."

"Or a repressed sociopath. Otherwise, how could anyone be dis dry but hide dese feelings of wanting to trow her down and rip off her panties?"

"It would show somehow. No one human would be able to suppress feelings that strong. He, at the very least, has a distant affection for her borne of their professional relationship."

"Yes. No panties ripping off here. Ever. Dis girl lives in a fantasy world. How old is she again?"

"Well, she's no *girl*, Dr. Ruth," said Dr. Phil with an exaggerated wink. "If she's a girl, then I'm Cher."

"If you are Cher, den I am having a terrible nightmare, because you are the ugliest Cher I have ever seen!"

I heard Cola say once, from far away, "Rae."

I pulled the cell phone closer to my ear.

"My sister Margarite told me the weirdest thing the other night," I said, changing the subject. "You wouldn't believe it."

Usually silence from Cola symbolized encouragement. So I continued.

"Not only did I drown when I was a kid. I was underwater, according to her, for fifteen minutes."

Cola's silence continued for several beats. Then, "I'm not sure if that's possible."

"No shit, Sherlock!"

A thin woman walking past with a baby nestled in her cart shot me a dirty look. I guess, along with no smoking and no red meat, we weren't allowed to swear anymore, either.

"Okay," Cola was saying. He sighed deeply. I found my bread in the meantime and went to pay for it.

"Let me ask you this," he said, putting aside my fifteen minute death for now. "Has Dante contacted you?"

"Dante? I think we texted a week ago that we were going to have lunch."

"Did you have lunch?"

"No…"

"Okay. If Dante contacts you—"

"Has anything weird been happening to you?" I interrupted.

"In what way do you mean?"

"I can't say. You would know if it was happening."

Pause.

"No, Rae. Nothing weird's been happening to me."

I scanned the front of the store for the shortest line at the cash register.

"But if Dante contacts you—"

"What?"

He sighed again. It was a little weird. Cola sounded frustrated, and that was unusual. Since Dr. Ruth and Dr. Phil had made it very clear that he wasn't in love with me, I decided maybe he hadn't gotten enough sleep last night. There. Nice and normal and boring. Nothing out of the ordinary. Then Cola had to ruin it by saying, "Just watch your back. He's not what he seems."

"What?" I laughed. "What are you talking about?"

"All right, Rae, I'll talk to you soon. Read the trades. Everyone wants you back."

There was no use in pursuing this new Dante thing. Cola would say nothing more.

"That's good. I guess. Thanks."

We disconnected. I dropped Hama's gluten-free bread as I was turning off my phone. I bent over for it, and when I straightened up, Giancarlo was standing right in front of me. I almost dropped the bread again. He smiled, his eyes crinkling up in an attractive Clint

Eastwoodian way, his dusky cheeks craggy and lined.

"Rae, how are you? I saw you across the store."

"Hi. What are you doing here?"

What are you doing here? Did I actually say that?

Giancarlo gazed at me in amusement. "I," he gestured at the bread I was holding, "enjoy gluten-free products as well."

"Oh, this isn't for me. It's for my friend."

"Hmm," said Giancarlo, looking at my afflicted shoulder. "How do the sessions go?"

"Well…"

He stepped forward and put his hand out. "May I?"

"Um…"

He took the bread from my right hand and passed it over to my stumpy hand. My stumpy hand accepted the bread mutely from Giancarlo while the rest of me waited to see what he was going to do. He picked my arm up and gently began to raise it toward the ceiling. The thin lady with the baby walked by behind him as he manipulated my stiff limb in different directions. She gave me another dirty look. She was not happy with swearing. She was not happy with people doing physical therapy in the middle of Whole Foods.

"I have arthritis. But it's premature," I told her. "It's from a tetanus shot," I informed her receding back. "Be careful. If the doctor suggests that you get one this year, just tell him or her to get fucked."

The woman hissed through her teeth and hurried the cart away. I had said the word "fucked" very softly, so the baby couldn't hear. The baby was leaning around his mother so he could stare at me as he was wheeled away. He smiled a toothless grin. He loved me. I waved with the bread in my hand and he laughed.

Giancarlo chuckled softly.

"Do you know her?" He guided my arm back down to my side.

"Yeah. We're frenemies."

"Your shoulder is very stiff. Has the condition improved at all? Of course, it will take time…"

"You know, Giancarlo…" I exhaled. "Chrislann's great, but—"

"I would like to go out with you."

I hugged Hama's bread to my chest. I opened my mouth.

Giancarlo placed his hand on my arm. "I am sorry. You were not expecting that." He didn't look very sorry.

"No, no, it's fine. I just—I'm a little preoccupied. I've been having a very strange week."

"I remember this from the other day. You were hung-over." He looked down for a moment, then back up. "I find you very attractive. I find no reason to deny it."

This is what it must be like to have a conversation with Bela Lugosi, I thought dreamily. *Who says, "I find no reason to deny it"? Who?* And then I thought, *I don't care!*

"I'd love to go out." I hadn't been out on a date in *years.* There was no way I was going to tell Giancarlo that. Giancarlo was a foreigner, obviously Spanish or Italian. He was comfortable with expressing his true thoughts. I was American. I would not express my true thoughts right away. I would hold them close to my chest. No one could see my cards. On top of which, it was L.A. So triple what I just said. Take the cards and slowly push them through your skin, into your chest, and leave them inside, nestled between your ribs. I had been moping around in Whole Foods, musing about returning to school, scared to look up at the sky for fear of what I'd see, and feeling sorry for myself because a teen heartthrob had been extremely rude to me many years ago. And Giancarlo wouldn't find any of that out for weeks, months. He would be on the verge of falling in love with me and happen to mosey by a closet he had never seen before in my apartment. "What is this?" he would say innocently and open the door. Out would tumble all my skeletons. Giancarlo would crash to the floor, covered by skeletons, unable to move, unable to dig himself out.

"This Friday?"

"Okay. Wow. You don't beat around the bush, do you?" I suddenly felt guilty and, a second later, realized I was thinking about Rex. After we'd left Margarite's the other night, we'd gone to The Standard and something weird had happened. Involving me and Rex. And a kiss.

"Pick you up?" Giancarlo said, smiling.

I blinked. Rex disappeared.

"Yeah. I'll give you my number." I recited it to him while he tapped it into his phone.

When he was done, he patted my arm again.

"All right, Rae, I will call you on Friday. Take care of that shoulder."

He stared into my eyes and I stared back with a stupid grin on my face. We exchanged more eyeball electricity, then Giancarlo gave my arm a quick squeeze and strode down another aisle and disappeared into the interior of Whole Foods. If he had been wearing a cape, nobody would have noticed. It would have just seamlessly blended in with his persona and not seemed weird at all.

CHAPTER 11

I was not enjoying my rehabilitation with Hama any more than I had with Chrislann. However, with Hama, it was a different kind of torture. It was much, much worse. Hama owned a little 1940s-style house in Van Nuys where she had installed a small gym in the garage in back. This was where we were now, with me lying on the bench trying to muscle 15-pound dumbbells into the air.

"Oh my God. OH MY GOD. You're kidding me. Please tell me you're kidding." She stared at me as I struggled, her beautiful Japanese eyes bugging out of her head.

"I will kill you if you don't stop doing that," I gasped.

"Look! You can't even talk! When did you get so weak? How out of shape *are* you?"

"I will kill you."

"Come on, up, up, up, up, up!" A sharp clap accompanied each "up." "Don't stop. Don't stop. Don't stop. DON'T YOU DARE STOP."

She lunged forward and grabbed my wrists and manhandled the dumbbells into the air.

"Eight. Nine. Ten. Okay, stop."

My arms collapsed on either side of me. I exhaled in misery.

Getting set up had almost been as bad as the actual workout. Hama had started screaming immediately. We used to work out together quite a while ago, and she was very angry that I had forgotten to put all my gear on. People thought you could just walk into a gym and start hefting weight, but you had to don an extensive array of accessories, similar to all the gear you needed for rollerblading. There was the belt to support your back. You needed gloves to help minimize sweat and maximize grip. There was elbow support, there was knee support, there were lifting straps that you attached to your wrists so that later, when you told Hama you couldn't get the hundred pounds off the ground in the dead lift, she could scream at you to put on your lifting straps. The only thing you *didn't* have to wear was a helmet. And this was all amateur stuff, lightweight. Apparently, when Arnold Schwarzenegger and his crew had been working out, they lifted so heavy that their bodies would go into revolt and they needed a bucket nearby to hurl into. Not only that, when they were doing squats, which are known as the king of all weight lifting exercises, they would often wear a diaper. Such was the intensity of the workout. Such was the price of glory.

"PUSSY!" screamed Hama. "PULL THAT DOWN. PULL THAT DOWN. OH MY GOD. PUSSY!"

Now I was struggling with pull-downs, which my shoulder did not like at all. Hama had a Caribou III integrated weight machine similar to the style used during the Inquisition and very popular before, during, and after the witch-hunts. I would have been better off burned at the stake. At least I would have been dead already and resting in peace.

"This…is…hard…on my shoulder," I puffed, yanking down on the bar. "My shoulder is injured, you know."

"Don't yank it down, Rae! Pull in one fluid motion." She stood behind me and put her hands on the bar and demonstrated one fluid motion, her biceps flexing imperiously. "See? See?"

"Yeah, I—"

"Now do it. Do it!"

If Hama had been my gymnastics coach and I was a 10-year-old girl, I would have despised her. But for some reason, all the girls loved her. Now I started to wonder if maybe I *was* a pussy. I pulled harder on the bar. My shoulder shrieked in silent agony. I didn't think Chrislann would approve of Hama's treatment. It wouldn't have mattered, though, his approaching her and expressing discontent. Hama could have crushed Chrislann with one arm.

"One more. One more."

"I can't—"

"ONE MORE."

"Hama, I—"

"ONE MORE."

"Hama—"

"ONE MORE."

We would have gone on until the sun imploded and the galaxy collapsed, so I gripped the bar (using my lifting straps, mind you; and, yes, they were also obviously used for the inverse) and in slow motion, muscled the bar toward my chest while my arms quaked mightily.

I released the bar, and Hama snatched it from me and reattached it at its place on top of the machine.

Right now, I think I hated her more than anyone in the world. If she wasn't trying to help me, I would have punched her in the throat. *What a bitch.*

"Okay, you're done."

I panted, my hands on my hips. I thought I was hearing things.

"Thank God!" I turned and walked out of the garage.

"Here, don't forget to drink this!" Hama tossed a water container toward me that was full of an endurance drink packed with electrolytes and other goodies. It tasted like cherry-flavored-watered-down vinegar. Too tired to protest how disgusting it was, I upended the bottle and squeezed some into my mouth as we re-entered the house through the backyard door.

"How do you feel?"

"Like crap. That hurt like hell. You're like Mussolini."

"And who are you? Do I know you? I'd rather be Mussolini than you."

"Jesus Christ," said a voice from another room, "Are you guys about to throw down?"

Hama's boyfriend Billy was standing in the living room, having somehow slipped in silently, regardless of his mass and girth. Picture Hama with a buzz cut and about 80 more pounds of muscle packed on her.

Billy was gripping a plastic bag in one hand and a bottle of water in the other. He held the bag aloft and said, "Steaks."

"Rae was working out. She has the upper body strength of a five-year-old."

"I have an injured shoulder, Hama."

"A five-year-old who tiptoed into her parents' rec room and sneaked a few sips of her father's brandy. A tipsy five-year-old."

"Who has brandy in a rec room?"

"My parents did. My parents had brandy and lots of other booze in a bar in the rec room." And then she added, "You have the upper body strength of a fetus."

Billy sauntered into the kitchen with the bag of steaks. There had to be about 20 or 30 of them in there. He held the bag as if it was filled with feathers.

"How'd you do that?"

"A pap smear gone wrong."

Pause.

"How much did she bench?"

Billy had decided not to go there, into the world of the Pap smear. Especially one that had somehow injured a part of my body in the opposite direction.

"Two fifteen-pound dumbbells. Six reps, max. Ten when I was helping."

Pause. Billy snorted then cut it off quickly.

"When was the last time you worked out?" he called.

"It's been a while." I got up off the floor. "I'd better go."

"A few more weeks, we'll have you right as rain," said Hama.

I shuddered. "Uh…we'll see."

"Month at the most. How long were you supposed to go to physical therapy?"

"I don't know. Two or three months."

"See? Forget it. They're pussies. Don't go back there."

In Hama's world, everybody was a pussy.

Billy sauntered back into the room, his arms floating out from his body because his traps were so big.

"You wanna stay for dinner? It's steaks!"

"No. I have to go home and take a bottle of aspirin. And then drink several cocktails." I headed for the door. "Thanks, Hama."

"Rae, at least do a little more stretching. You're *really* stiff. You don't have to be that stiff."

"Hey, Rae, everybody at Gold's on your side. Just give the word. There's a couple guys over there who'd love to beat the shit out of Ricardo."

I smiled. "Why not just kill him?" I shrugged innocently like *what's the big fricking deal?*

Advocating murder was no big fricking deal. You could put a positive spin on anything with a big smile and the right attitude. I really thought if Ricardo ended up dead, I wouldn't have any trouble just looking the other way. And I would care very little. This was who I was. This was who I had become.

I had left Hama's and was finally at the border of Burbank and Glendale in the Z, puffing on a Virginia Slim, when a green Chevy pulled up next to me, and the driver, a handsome black man, looked over at me and smiled. Although I'd never seen him before, he seemed vaguely familiar. I didn't smile back. He creeped me out. The light turned green, and he pulled forward and took off. I drove about a block and a half before the light turned red again. I was behind the stagger. Somehow, the Chevy had escaped it.

Feeling eyes on me, I glanced over to my left to see who was staring at me now. I was delighted and charmed to see a police cruiser stopped at the light beside me. The passenger window rolled down. It was the same ruddy, handsome officer from a few weeks ago. What were the odds? This time there was no Soviet Bloc perp in the backseat. One good thing about Glendale was that smoking was still alive and well. Rob Reiner hadn't been able to sail his Spanish galleon into the bay here, yet, and unload his pox and typhus and ruin everything. There were just too many Armenian men to fight against, for one thing.

I smiled and raised my hand in greeting.

The cop grinned. Rather saucily, I thought. Then he pointed at me. "Guess what."

"What?"

"You're not wearing your seatbelt."

I looked down at myself. I was, indeed, not wearing it. I had been so pissed off at Hama, I had just gotten in and burned rubber out of there.

"Oh, crap," I said, reaching around for it.

"You should probably pull over and adjust your seatbelt, Ms. Miller."

He must have gone home and googled my name. Wow.

"We have to stop meeting like this," continued the ruddy cop, hanging one arm out of the window and down the side of the car.

"Sorry, officer. It won't happen again." The light turned green, and the cop car and I both started pulling forward. "Although this doesn't really count as a second time. The first time we were just talking about 280Zs."

"Seatbelt tickets are expensive," he continued conversationally. "Do you know how much they are?"

"No."

"A hundred and forty two dollars, minimum."

"That's a lot."

"It triples for not restraining a child properly in the car."

I shrugged. "Well, I don't have a child, so…"

He grinned. "And who knows if you have that hundred and forty two dollars either. It's touch and go right now, for you. You gotta get back on the show. Or get another show."

"No, officer. Not with Ricardo's skeezy, scummy ass still there, sir." I chose less inflammatory words to describe Richard, trying to be respectful and not incite Contempt of Cop. If he started using foul language, though, I might join in.

"I gotcha." He grinned at me and pushed his hat up on his head a little. Like Officer O'Hara just jawing with the neighborhood kids, reminding them to stay in school. "Well, be safe, Ms. Miller. Please pull over when it is clear to do so and secure your seatbelt."

"Thank you, Officer."

There was a pause. He seemed to be on the verge of saying something else. He left his arm hanging out the window and eye fucked me for a few seconds (in a nice way), and I was pretty sure he was going to ask me out, even though he was probably married. Then the radio squawked in the car, and he snatched up the receiver. The cruiser took off, almost causing a five-car pile-up.

I considered pulling over and putting on my seatbelt but settled for looping it over my chest and arm. I was just too tired. I turned off the main road and was nearing my neighborhood when I realized the green Chevy was in front of me at a stop sign. I could see the guy sitting there and staring at me in his rearview mirror. He sat there for so long just staring that finally I blasted the horn. And then his eyes crinkled. I could see them! He was smiling! Who were these strange men lurking around and leering at me recently? I wasn't going to take it anymore! The man took off through the intersection. I took off through the intersection. At the next stop sign, it was the same thing. Then he accelerated away and spun around the next corner, and by the time I got there, he was gone. I turned down that street and trolled along at a good clip, searching for the green color. I tossed my cigarette butt out the window, turned another corner, and came to a dead halt, tires screeching.

Ironically, the looped-over seatbelt did nothing to protect me, so I smashed forward into the steering wheel. Gasping, I straightened back up, staring out of the windshield. In the middle of the street, several people were being floated up through the sky toward a waiting saucer-shaped machine. The woman closest to me was just being lifted off the ground, so close that I could see the bottoms of her sandals. They looked like a pair of Payless leather thongs that had been worn maybe two or three times, judging by the scratch marks. Clung to her bosom was a tiny white dog. Both had their eyes open and were immobile. Down the street a little further, I could see a young girl being floated out of a fifth story window. Beyond that was a third victim, a man wearing a bright bicycling outfit, his bicycle abandoned below in the street. *The front wheel was still spinning.* It was a kidnapping smorgasbord, a felonious brouhaha.

I tossed the looped-over seatbelt off, pulled the gearshift to park, and threw open my door. *Not again. Not again. Not again.* This was fast becoming my daily motto. The lady's legs were dangling just above me. I climbed onto the hood of the Z then onto the roof. I looked up, seeing her sandals again. This woman had pictured herself walking through Glendale in these sandals, strolling along the beach in Santa Monica. Not floating into the air, disappearing into the sky. Suddenly something happened. I was airborne. I'd leaped into the air, flinging my arms around the woman's calves. Super-duper mistake. My shoulder cracked, and pain whipped through my arm and directly up into my brain. I saw stars.

I felt the woman bobble a little bit, but the slow ascension did not falter. Now, due to some mysterious element of the light, I was paralyzed, unable to let go. The stubs of my missing fingers throbbed, and my shoulder was screaming. It was doing all the screaming for me, because I couldn't move or speak. Where was the help? Where was a cop when you needed him? I didn't need a cop to nag me about my seatbelt. I needed a cop to unload his gun into this paralyzing light. Suddenly the terror came pouring in. What was I doing? This time there was no big-headed creature to startle. No bras to pelt it with. For the millionth time, I asked myself: why, exactly, had I put off getting a gun for so long? God knows I'd been with Rex to the gun range enough times. I knew how to shoot. Okay, I knew how to watch someone shoot. Here was a perfect example of it coming in handy. Get pulled onto this ship. Stand up. Unload both barrels.

Something new happened. I don't know what, but I felt it and heard it. A vibrational change in the light, a sort of adjustment. They were pulling the woman up faster! It was like they were up there looking down, seeing me, sensing my violence. "She's packing heat," one said to the other, and pushed the button that said "haul ass." The vibration seemed to click and shift again. The light released me. I dropped down onto the roof of the Z with a thud. Behind me, a car came around the corner fast. I could tell from the sound of the engine it was one of those little rice rockets. I turned my head, and in the millisecond before it slammed into the back of the Z, I was surprised to see its driver, a teenaged boy, staring slack-jawed not at me laying on the roof of my car but up and beyond me, directly at the woman in the light. He saw her!

There was a terrific sound of crunching metal and shattering glass, and I flew off the roof. I landed hard in the street. On my bad shoulder. And then on my stomach, crunching the fibroids. I spasmed with pain. My head bounced once. Everything went white. White, not black. And then the weirdest thing of all happened: I heard the sound of somebody sucking their tongue and then a thick Armenian accent saying, "You are drunk. Your car is in de middle of the road. Here. Let me help you up."

Nothing I could say would convince Mr. Dadalian that I wasn't drunk. I guess there was no other explanation for my car to be sitting in the middle of the street, engine running, door open, and me lying on the road in front of it, writhing and moaning. I guess the only thing the mind moved to was a dark saloon, an empty bottle of Jack, the sound of a shot glass slamming onto the bar. A raspy voice saying, "Gimme another one, and make it snappy."

Maybe Mr. Dadalian figured I was just a woman, getting drunk in the middle of the day because I couldn't find my pink bra, I'd lost my source of income, and I was single and had no children—at my age! He had no idea about the monsters up above him. I used to have no idea about the monsters. I had been experiencing an unreasoning anger toward Whitley Strieber lately, as he transformed before my eyes from fiction writer into autobiographer. Well, fiction for me, anyhow. How dare he be telling the truth!

The UFO was gone. The teenaged boy who had seen them was gone.

Mr. Dadalian insisted that I was too drunk to drive. He was coming back from the Korean market down the street that was operated by Mexicans and owned by a mysterious third party who made sure that among the many varied products, the "deli" was stocked with jerk chicken and curried goat. He handed me a plastic bag filled with choreg and basturma and several containers of yogurt. He went around behind the Z to survey the damage, saying tsk, tsk, tsk several times and shaking his head.

A couple of people had ventured out of their homes at the sound of the accident and now stood staring. I went back to take a look myself. The bumper was bent in and the right taillight was broken. I closed my eyes and dropped my head forward. This is what I got? For being a Good Samaritan? It was like Bigfoot appearing one day out of the Verdugo Foothills, and I was the only one there to jump on his back and keep him from making off with a toddler he'd found in someone's backyard. Then he staggered into the street with me on his back, and *I* got a ticket for jaywalking.

"I have a friend who owns garage. He can fix that for you. Good price." Mr. Dadalian patted my arm. He looked around at the street and spotted the bicycle that the monsters had chosen to leave behind this time. He wandered over and hefted it up, then walked it out of the street onto the sidewalk. He left it leaning against a tree and came back toward me frowning slightly.

"Middle of street," he commented. "Same as you. What happens here?"

He took my arm without waiting for an answer and guided me around to the passenger side and lowered me into the seat.

"I will drive de car back to building. Please attach seatbelt."

I snorted laughter. They needed to make seatbelts for the roof of your car. Standing on the roof of your car was dangerous. Mr. D. got into the driver's side, closed the door, strapped himself in, and drove us home at about twenty-five miles per hour the entire way. Once at the building, he continued to help me to my apartment, as if I was falling-down drunk and couldn't see straight.

"Mr. Dadalian," I said, "it was just a dumb traffic thing. I'm not drunk. Look…" I leaned forward and breathed in his face. He recoiled slightly then looked confused. Because there had been no drinking at Hama's place. You weren't allowed to drink when you were being tortured. You might succeed in undermining the agony somehow. I handed Mr. D his grocery bag. We were outside my door.

"Well, I do not know why you were in de street. You did not pass through windshield…" He held his chin, his mind traveling back to the scene of the accident.

"It was a hit and run. He was gone by the time you got there."

"But how you end up in de street," Mr. D. persisted, "rolling around, going, 'Ahh…ahh…ahh…?'" and here he pantomimed me holding onto my shoulder and making a hideous face.

"I got out of the car and—" I stopped and sighed. "Look, thank you, Mr. Dadalian. I appreciate it." I turned and shoved my key into the door.

"I think is best you are not on TV any longer. I do not think that show good for you."

I opened the door. Mr. Dadalian looked sincere. I guess he didn't despise me as much as I'd thought he had.

"Thanks. Maybe you're right."

He really might be right, actually.

"Okay, you go in now. Drink some coffee."

Oh, God.

"Take care. Perhaps my wife brings over some tahini roll later."

"Okay. Thank you."

I happened to love tahini rolls. I hoped Mrs. D. *would* bring some over.

"Good night."

"Good night."

I closed the door, walked over to the sofa, and slumped down into the soft pale yellow cushions.

CHAPTER 12

While I was still at UCLA and just before I scored *Green Splendor I*, I went through a period of existential angst. During this time, I was taking Philosophy 101. That wasn't the real name of the class, but that was the essence of it, although it hadn't proven to be that easy. I hadn't realized philosophy would be riddled with theorems and equations and logic conundrums. The teacher had been Bob Smith, someone we'd jokingly referred to as "Mr. Motel," because it was the kind of anonymous name you wrote down at the motel where you were cooking up speedballs or hosting prostitutes in your room.

Mr. Motel had been of average height, average looks, average hair color. One day in his office while discussing a paper I had written (Mr. Motel had pulled it out from his stack, thumbed through it, then asked, "What the hell were you talking about?"), we'd deviated into an unexpected sidebar concerning reality, existence, and the meaning of life. After this office visit, Mr. Motel had become a mentor of sorts, advising me that I, along with the rest of most of the world, was miserable because of an inability to "be in the moment." Everyone was either in the past or the future and hardly ever in the present. His list of suggested reading included Antoine Faivre, Rene Guenon, Madame Blavatsky, Gurdjieff and Ouspensky, and Julius Evola. I devoured the books with the intention of transcending the earth and taking my regrets along for the ride.

Over time, I discovered Blavatsky was fairly racist, Evola sympathized with the National Fascist Party, and my mentor saw nothing wrong with kissing me on the neck one day while we were hugging good-bye for the Christmas holidays. It wasn't the fact that he was 20 years older as much as the fact that he was married, and a picture of Mrs. Motel was sitting right on his desk, staring at us as Bob's lips pressed gently against my carotid artery.

We remained friends over the years. Bob joined an esoteric school called Now, and I dropped out of UCLA to do the first *Green Splendor* movie. It wasn't like I'd forgotten all about his advice and teachings and the books I'd read; it was just hard to live that way. I guess that was why people became monks and Zen masters. It was like locking yourself into a bio dome or getting on a space ship aimed for the next star system; you had no choice but to focus because all the distractions were gone.

Bob and I had fallen out of contact except for a few stray letters back and forth, and now the twice a year random email. As my newly re-injured shoulder throbbed, and the image of the bottom of the woman's sandals flooded my mind, I realized that my isolated childhood in Sherman Oaks wasn't going to get me all the way through this. My brain felt jittery, and my nerves hurt. None of my long-ago fallen heroes could help. If Madame Blavatsky were here visiting, lounging comfortably on my yellow couch, she would have spewed out some comment concerning my mixed heritage. But really, who could take anything she said seriously considering she had dubbed herself the Priestess of Isis? My brain would still be jittery, and my nerves would still hurt. And even though Bob had kissed me inappropriately years ago, and I assumed the organization he now attended was a cult, I figured it was better than nothing. I needed support. I needed a sympathetic ear. The only reason I didn't think that I was going irrevocably insane, complete with hallucinations, was the boy. I'd seen the boy, and I'd seen that he'd seen what I'd seen.

If Now was a cult, it wasn't hiding. I found it without incident online and dialed the number quickly before I lost my nerve. Bob and I hadn't contacted each other for a few years, so I wasn't sure what my standing was anymore. A woman answered.

"This is Now. How can I help you be present?"

That threw me for a second. My inner voice, my denial voice, was chanting *Hang up, hang up, hang up*. But what would I do after I hung up? Who did I have to talk to? Rex would laugh. Hama would call me delusional. Margarite would try her crappy head-shrinking on me, even though she'd admitted, to my face, that she hated her clients! Once I'd regrouped, the woman set me up for an introductory meeting.

She told me there would be coffee and Danish.

Next door, Annie's boyfriend suddenly began yelling. It sounded like he was in my living room with me.

"I…" I began, distracted. What had she said?

"If you have any questions before you arrive, please don't hesitate to call back. I will be here until six this evening. My name is Riot."

At least that's what I thought she said.

We disconnected just as the noise meter began to go red again next door. I sat on the sofa listening for a few minutes then got up and pounded on the wall. There was a pause next door in the yelling, and then moments later somebody's giant fist pounded back, *boom, boom, boom.* Guess who. I flung my cell phone onto the sofa and crossed the room in three strides, yanking open my front door with the intention to do God knows what, when the phone chirped timidly behind me. I strode back to the sofa and snatched it up. "What?" I barked.

Pause.

"Rae?"

There was a lot of background noise. I could barely hear whoever it was.

"Yeah? Yeah? Who is this?"

"It's Ganymede!"

My anger instantly evaporated.

"Ganymede! Hey, baby."

I heard what sounded like a jet engine roaring in the background.

"Where the hell are you?" I asked. "The Kennedy Space Center?"

"I'm across the street from the Bob Hope Airport."

Next door, Annie's door slammed. My alarms perked up, getting ready to go off.

"With your mom?"

"No."

"With the nanny?"

"No."

I tried one more time. "With your dad?"

"No."

I lowered myself to the sofa in a controlled descent.

"Did you get a ride again?"

"No, I drove here!" He said proudly.

I lost some vision in my right eye.

"You don't have a car," I said stated reasonably, picking up my purse and my keys.

"I borrowed the nanny's car," Ganymede yelled over the noise.

"You're eight years old," I said, desperately trying to make this not true.

"Ten!" he shouted. His sense of outrage came through the phone loud and clear.

"Where are you? Tell me. Exactly. Where you are."

I retrieved Ganymede on Hollywood Way and Burton, across the street from the airport as he'd said. He was standing in front of a building holding Ralph by a leash in one hand and a backpack in the other. Ralph wasn't wearing the Elizabethan collar today but was sporting a small muzzle. The Shepherd winced as I got out of the car and slammed the door closed. He was a dog, and he could smell my emotions.

I approached Ganymede. At first, I thought he was covered with blood. *Oh, my God,* was my first thought. *He ran someone over.* I almost started to turn and search for the body, wondering where we would hide it, before I realized his T-shirt was designed to look that way. I stood staring at it for many moments in a kind of fugue state.

"Hi, Rae," Ganymede said quietly.

"Where's the nanny's car?"

He pointed. Up the street a little ways, a black mini Cooper was parked crazily near the curb. It looked like Helen Keller had parked it. After a few martinis. I held out my hand. Ganymede handed me the keys wordlessly. I got into the mini Cooper. There were several pillows stacked on the passenger side. I reparked it, got out, and gestured for everybody to get in the Z. I used to love the Bob Hope Airport. It was a tiny, adorable little airport that could fit neatly on

LAX's lap, snuggling like a small child. Now it would forever be associated with Ganymede dangling a carrot in front of Death and baiting it halfway across the Valley. I had come to like this kid so much, I realized I in no way, shape, or form wanted him to die. Or even get slightly hurt.

Once he was buckled in, Ganymede said, "Are you mad at me?"

I pulled away from the curb gingerly, completely paranoid, my nerves jigging under my skin. I kept seeing a 20-car pileup happening on the 101, metal sheared off, windshields buckling, rims spinning through the air, glinting in the L.A. sun.

"Um…" I said eloquently.

"I'm a good driver," he informed me. I saw the nanny's car flipping over ten times, sailing off the freeway, and smashing into the parking lot of a Home Depot. I would be watching with Bill Murray from a rooftop. He would turn to me and say, "He could have survived that." Then the nanny's car would explode with a horrific sound, shooting fireballs straight toward the sun. Bill would turn to me and say, "Maybe not that."

"Uh…" I said again, banishing the images. "It's against the law. For you to drive. You're too young." Why was I so surprised? This was Ganymede we were talking about. It was more surprising that he hadn't constructed a transporter and teleported straight into my living room. "How did you see? You were sitting on those pillows, weren't you?"

"Yeah."

"Jesus, Jesus, Jesus, Jesus, Jesus."

"I'm sorry."

"Jesus, Jesus, Jesus, Jesus, Jesus." I could actually think of nothing else to say.

Ganymede was silent for a while, looking out the window.

"I don't know where you live," he said quietly. "I was going to call you, and then I was driving by the airport, so I pulled over."

Pulled over! *A ten-year-old was saying he'd pulled over.*

"Dad and I come here sometimes to watch the planes. I was watching them for a while."

"That's nice, baby." I paused. "Listen, unless you're over there mixing me an appletini and you forgot how to do it…let's not talk right now."

Ralph snuffled in the back area beneath his muzzle. Ganymede got the message and was silent the rest of the way home. Once there, we bumped into Mr. and Mrs. Dadalian in the hallway.

"Hey, there," I said weakly and kept going.

"Feeling better?" Mr. Dadalian asked. He eyed Ganymede up and down, glanced at Ralph, then looked back at me with an unreadable expression. Now Mrs. Dadalian was staring at me. She touched her husband's arm.

"Dis is the one?" she asked in a stage whisper. She was a smaller, rounder version of Mr. Dadalian. She was dressed in a strange getup that resembled a dirndl.

"Yes," Mr. D, said. "She is better now. You are feeling better?" he asked loudly, as if I had lost my hearing.

"Yes, thank you, much better."

Ganymede and I made to go, but the Dadalians just stood there.

"Is this your son?" Mrs. Dadalian asked. "I make extra tahini rolls for him and bring them over."

"What are tahini rolls?" Ganymede asked.

"No, no, she has no children. You will insult her. American TV women do not believe in this."

"I am so sorry," said Mrs. Dadalian. "I will still bring you tahini rolls."

"Oh, no, please don't bother."

"It is no bother. It is my pleasure."

"They sound good," Ganymede commented. "I'd like some."

"You do not live in this neighborhood." Mr. Dadalian, looking down at Ganymede. "This is your nephew?"

It was like this was a women-only YMCA, and I was out after curfew.

"This is my godson," I blurted out. I grabbed him by the hand. "Thank you, Mrs. Dadalian. See you guys later."

"All right…"

I practically sprinted down the hall, dragging Ganymede after me, and we made it safely back inside. Ganymede made a beeline for the *Green Splendor I* and *II* posters I had stacked against the wall.

"Wow!" he said, gently prying them apart to see them better. I sank down into my sofa again. Ralph surveyed his surroundings briefly, seemed satisfied, then slunk over and lay down on the floor with his head near my foot. I rooted around in my purse for my cell phone.

"What is your phone number?"

Ganymede straightened up slowly from the posters and looked at me.

I closed my eyes. "Do you know how far it is from Topanga Canyon to Burbank?"

He shrugged. "I'm a good driver."

"Just say it once. Tell me you know how far it is. Tell me you know."

"I know how far it is, Rae."

"One more time. Say it again."

"I know how far it is." He smiled.

"Stop smiling. What's your number?"

He stopped smiling, sort of, and recited it to me as I dialed. The supernanny answered the phone. There was something that sounded like wolves attacking a deer or a slew of demons rising out of hell in the background. The sound was piercing and continuous. I held the phone away from my ear.

"That's my sisters," Ganymede calmly informed me. He had sunk down onto the floor beside Ralph and removed his muzzle and was stroking him absently. Ralph's eyes were closed and he didn't move. He appeared to have passed out. With the supernanny and I yelling into the phone in order to be heard over the slaughter of crows at Ganymede's place (murder just wasn't strong enough), I painted the picture of what was going on. The supernanny began to hyperventilate and said she'd make all appropriate calls (something she was used to doing, obviously) and would pick up her car later today. She had an extra set of keys. Abruptly there was a click and a dial tone.

I looked over at Ganymede.

"What the—" I said, holding the phone out, referring to the terrifying noises I had heard.

He smiled, still stroking the unconscious Ralph. "Why do you think I came over here?"

I didn't bring up the fact that his bitch of a nanny never even mentioned picking him up.

Cue naïve young girl skipping through a field, followed by her loyal goat.

Girl: If the supernanny couldn't take Ganymede home, I'm sure Andrygen would have happily swung by to retrieve her beloved adopted black son!

The goat bleats once and looks straight at the camera, eyebrow cocked.

[laughter]
[applause]

Evidently, while I was napping, exhausted (it wasn't Hama's workout, per se, or a three-fer alien abduction, or even Ganymede jacking his nanny's car—it was all three combined on top of the fact that I actually *couldn't* get blasted now because a child was here), Mrs. Dadalian made good on her promise and brought over the tahini rolls. When I got up an hour later, Ganymede was in the living room munching on one and drinking a coke. The TV was on, and he was watching soccer. He had put some water in a bowl, which Ralph had obviously been slobbering at, because there was water everywhere on the wooden floor. Ganymede had no idea he was eating pity rolls, borne of Mr. Dadalian's unshakable belief that I was deep in the sauce. I made a mental note to bake them brownies or something.

"Is that all you've eaten?" I was a terrible caretaker. And I also had a raging headache. I felt no better now than I had before the nap. Plus which, every muscle Hama had even remotely been involved with was burning and sore. I could barely move. I felt like one of Ganymede's robots. "Let's go out to lunch."

"Okay! Where?"

"I don't know. Let me get an aspirin first." *And wash it down with a pint of beer.*

"Aspirin?" He chortled. "Aspirin doesn't do anything! Aspirin is for babies."

"I call everything aspirin. It's actually Ibuprofen. It's all the same to me." I stumbled back toward the bathroom.

Ganymede yelled from the living room, "Are you going to put those posters up?"

"Um…" My hand shook a little as I fiddled with the bottle. My shoulder was killing me. Chrislann would be so angry if he knew what had happened. Not just from a physical therapy point of view, but from a driving in L.A. point of view, considering how excitable he got over certain traffic situations. Finally, I managed to swallow a few pills with the sink water and went back out. I looked around at all the unpacked boxes and the empty ones that I had to now repack since I had agreed to move in with Rex.

"You know, I don't think so. I'm not staying here. I'm moving somewhere else."

I hadn't made effort one, though, to get ready for Rex's. I guess it was the last thing on my mind. Rex's mission, as it had turned out the other night, had been to convince me to move in with him. He said he was lonely in that big house by himself, and I had picked the worst building in the L.A. area in general to live in (little did he know!), and I was ridiculous if I insisted on staying here. We'd driven to downtown L.A. to the Rooftop Bar at the Standard. Leave it to Rex to find a place that basically only served drinks, although it offered a "lunch" menu, which was served "until midnight." And, of course, you could smoke there. So we drank like fish and smoked like bandits.

I'd given in after the second drink and would have agreed on the first but had to make it look good. Had to make it look like I wasn't desperate to get out of Glendale, get back on my show, and forget everything freaky that had been happening to me lately. If I lived at Rex's place, he'd more or less leave me alone. It wasn't a romantic thing with us. Even though sometimes we seemed to be sending each other mixed signals, and it was very confusing. Like he had paid for everything at The Standard (over $250 worth of booze, including a bottle of champagne and then the crab cakes). And then a poker nemesis, John, had shown up, and he and Rex had spent a half-hour Alpha-maleing their way through a conversation the way they did at the tables during a tournament. Poker had a subtle way of trash talking compared to, say, basketball, where they were much more up front with it.

Basketball: "Just call me the janitor 'cause I clean shit up!"

Poker: "Did you guys see that movie *Memento* where the guy couldn't remember anything except from reading notes he'd left himself, and the whole movie went backwards instead of forwards while he was trying to piece together what had already happened? All-in."

And if you had paused to consider even one syllable of what he was saying, suddenly all your chips were gone, and you were sitting outside in the street on your ass.

Anyway, when I had agreed to move in, long after John had started dancing with a sixtyish woman in a green glittery dress who might or might not have been Angelyene, Rex had seized my face and planted a huge one, sans tongue, but aggressively all-consuming. Before the kiss, he had been smiling. After the kiss, he had stopped smiling. He had pulled away, a strange, dawning expression on his face that I felt reflected in mine, and we had stared at each other for a solid eight seconds. Try it. Eight seconds of unbroken, unsmiling eye contact was like a thousand years. I think we were both stunned, wondering what had just happened, and more importantly, why did we want it to happen again? We had both turned our heads at that moment and discovered that John had finished dancing and was seated back at our table, arms crossed, smirking at us. "Are you guys that drunk, or are you going out now?" John asked.

I gazed off into space, preoccupied.

"What's wrong?"

Ralph was awake and staring at me too.

"What?"

"You have a weird look on your face."

I *bet* I had a weird look on my face.

I mentally picked up The Standard and Rex's lips, pivoted, and placed them onto a dark shelf in the back of my mind. I brushed my mental hands together. Let it go. Deal with it later.

"Okay, come on. I'll take you to Johnny Rockets. Or Fuddruckers."

"Okay!" He jumped up. What an easy kid to please.

"Will Ralph be okay here by himself? He's not going throw himself out the window or anything, is he?"

Ganymede looked down at Ralph, who was resting comfortably, head on paws. He didn't seem anywhere near as twitchy now, a few hours later. A light bulb went on over my head as I recalled the phone call with the nanny. With the sound of Armageddon, of the world tearing in half, in the background. I glanced at Ganymede.

"You know…maybe your mother didn't do anything to Ralph, kiddo. Maybe Ralph has a stress disorder because your sisters are always screaming and slamming doors and blowing things up over there."

Ganymede grinned. "They're not blowing things up."

"You know what I mean."

We both gazed down at the calm, snoozing Ralph, considering.

CHAPTER 13

I made sure the Mini Cooper's keys were somewhere safe, then we packed it up and headed for the Z.

Coming from a different angle this time, Ganymede noticed the rear end damage. He opened his mouth to say something, and I put my finger to my lips and closed my eyes. He gawked in silence. I decided to take Ganymede over to the Americana because there was a robot store there that I was going to surprise him with. I made sure we were both buckled up and drove slowly all the way there, expecting the worst every time I turned a corner. It was almost dusk now, so I guessed lunch would actually be dinner. As we walked from the parking lot through the courtyard, he garnered many sidelong glances at his seemingly blood-smeared, gore-splattered attire. Ganymede wanted to eat at the Potato Corner.

"What? No!"

"Why not?"

"You can't just eat a potato for dinner. Are you on crack?"

"No, there's other stuff there. They have chicken."

"Oh…" We walked into the Potato Corner, and I saw that they did, indeed, have chicken fingers along with their potatoes, French fries, and tater tots. Chicken wasn't exactly "other stuff," but it was something, even if it was only one thing. "Okay. Pick out the most balanced meal and order it. I have to make a phone call."

"Okay. I'll pay you back, Rae."

I looked back over my shoulder at him.

"Don't worry about it," I said. "You crazy kid."

Andrygen had really raised a sweetheart. I dug my cell phone out and went to stand over by the glass door. I hadn't checked in with

Cola in several days and figured I should at least say hello so he didn't think I didn't care. I stood by the door while the line rang. Cola answered, "Hello, Rae."

"Hi there!" I said with false gaiety. "What up?"

There was a lot of ambient noise on Cola's end.

"I'm glad you called," said Cola, all business as usual. "I have a proposition for you."

I swiveled one eye Ganymede's way. He was still at the counter.

"Stop. You're making me blush," I quipped.

Cola paused. He spoke again, lightly. "Well, maybe I shouldn't even bring this up and should just send you straight into standup."

Hah. See? He hadn't gotten miffed, and I could *hear* him smiling. Maybe there *was* something there.

Ganymede finished ordering and joined me at the door, holding up his number. I gave him a thumbs-up.

"No, go ahead. But I won't do it, whatever it is. I'm going back to school."

Ganymede heard me say this and made a face. He went on to pantomime barfing and then finished by swirling his finger around his temple.

"Why don't I just tell you in person?"

"Oh, well, I'm out on a date tonight. You wouldn't want to ruin that for me, would you?"

"I didn't know you liked them that young," said Cola.

I looked up. I looked out of the Potato Corner's glass door.

"The other way," said Cola.

He was standing outside, to the left, dressed in a dark suit, cell phone to his ear. I hardly ever saw him outside his office or when it wasn't night, so it was a little weird seeing him in the light of the dying day. It struck me, as it had at other moments, how pale he was. He really worked too much and needed to get out more. We smiled at one another just as Ganymede's number was called.

"Go ahead," I told him. "Stay up front. I'll be right back."

I went outside, walking through the dusk toward Cola. Hama was right. He *did* resemble the lead singer for Bush: lean, not as tall as Rex, but maybe six feet, thick black hair. And like I said, although he appeared to be at least a decade older than I, he seemed like a much, much older man, and I didn't know why. Living life hard and fast, I guess. The life of a Hollywood agent.

Cola came forward smiling slightly, Sphinx-like, and embraced me. His eyes were so dark they looked black. I could smell the Billy Jealousy shampoo and black pepper body wash. No CVS Dove Men + Care for Cola. We pulled apart, and I glanced over my shoulder to make sure nobody had kidnapped Andrygen's kid and made off with him to the bathroom right under my nose. He came out the door holding a to-go bag.

"Hi," he said to Cola, looking him up and down. "I've seen you before."

"Hi," said Cola. He held out his hand. Ganymede shook it delicately. "I've seen you before, too. Andrygen's son, right?"

"Yeah."

"That's an attractive shirt you have on," said Cola, gesturing to Ganymede's slaughterhouse tunic.

"Yeah, we're hanging out. Ganymede and his dog Ralph need a little peace and quiet."

"I drove here!" Ganymede blurted out.

"Uh...not cool, man. I wouldn't boast if I were you."

Cola smirked at both of us like we were a carnival act. He didn't ask for details.

"I need an evening out," I said, "to take my mind off things."

Cola said, "Things?" and cocked an eyebrow curiously.

"Like the show?" asked Ganymede. "I don't like that guy Ricardo."

"Awww...thanks. I appreciate anyone who doesn't like Ricardo."

"Well, listen, Rae, we'll get into it more later, but there's going to be a show about ex-athletes, and your name came up. That's why I was glad you called." Cola waited for my response, one hand idly trailing down his tie. It was like having Bobby Fisher as an agent, and it didn't matter what you thought or what you ultimately said, he was already a thousand moves ahead of you.

"Well..."

Ganymede grew excited. "You could go back to surfing!" he said. "You were really good. I saw both *Green Splendor* movies, but I have to see them again. I watched them on my iPhone, and it was really, really small. I'd like to see them on a regular TV next time."

"Oh, thank you, baby," I said, and ruffled his hair. He beamed.

"Well, give me a call," said Cola. He put his hand on my shoulder. "Think about it."

"Okay." I glanced around. "What are you doing here anyway?"

"Having dinner with a client at Trattoria Amici."

"Ooh la la!" I pursed my lips. "You never take *me* to places like that."

"Who was it, George Clooney? Shia Labeouf? Beyonce!" Ganymede's eyes just about popped out of his head. If they had and then landed in his afro, we would never have found them again.

Cola smiled. "No one you know," he said. He leaned over and touched his cheek to mine briefly. "We will eat there if you like. It would be my pleasure."

Cola patted Ganymede on the shoulder and left.

Later, after Ganymede and I had finished eating, I stood up from the bench where we were sitting and said, "Come on." I steered him toward what I hoped would be the highlight of his day. "How's the robot coming?"

"Pretty good. I've been studying vibrations and sound waves. I've been reading up on bats and dogs and whales."

I peered into my purse, searching for my cigarettes. "Bats and dogs and whales?" I echoed, preoccupied.

"Yeah. Oh! I'll show you when we get back. I've been testing it on Ralph."

"Pardon?"

"Well...I can't equip the robot with real weapons. So I came up with a sound wave idea."

"I'll bet." I stood up. "When I can't use real weapons, I always turn to sound waves, too." Ganymede grinned at me. "Come on, I have something to show you."

We tossed our trash and began to stroll through the lamp-lit darkness toward the robot store.

"I have to figure out how to protect everybody."

"What are you talking about? Do you guys have a gang of drug dealers after you? Why do you keep talking about 'protecting' people?"

Ganymede walked along slowly and didn't answer for a while.

"I don't know." He shrugged. "There's all the stories about the ZRs, you know. They just take people whenever they want. I think the government has a deal with them or something."

My skin went cold in the balmy air.

"Um…" I glanced around, suddenly imagining Men in Black standing at every corner. Nobody was paying any attention to us. As far as I could tell. "What are ZRs? Are you talking about what I think you're talking about? The Grays?"

"Yeah." He scuffed his foot on the pavement. "Zeta Reticuli. They're named after a binary star system. You know they eat our souls, don't you?" He raised his head and looked up at me. "I'm guessing at a lot of stuff, but I'm starting with whales and bats and… mutating them…into what I think the ZRs are. Part biological and part mechanical." He held a finger up in the air and said, "Frequencies are my forte!" in a silly voice, then laughed.

"What?"

"Huh?"

We rounded the corner. The robot store was up ahead. I had completely forgotten it even existed.

"What are you talking about?"

Ganymede glanced at me then screwed his mouth up, thinking.

"Well, did you know that people who are, like, around an ultrasonic sound field all the time have a lot of headaches or nausea?"

"Of course." What was this kid talking about? *Did* I know that? It sounded familiar somehow.

"Yeah, and then there's the fact that kids have a range of hearing extending up to 30 kHz, and guess what!"

"What?" I said faintly. My fingers had begun scrabbling inside my purse again and finally closed around the elusive cigarettes.

"It's even higher for asthmatic kids!" he finished triumphantly. Then, in a wistful manner, like a brooding Dr. Frankenstein: "If only I had a real Zeta I could look at…"

Yeah, sounds good, I thought, picturing the Gray or ZR from the laundry room sucking some of Annie's soul out through her mouth and then smacking his lips and licking his fingers just before I brained him from behind and Ganymede locked him in a cage. I'd help him do that. No problem.

Suddenly, Ganymede saw the robot store sign up ahead. He stopped walking for a second then bolted. I followed slowly behind him, my mind whirling, lighting up a Slim. The timing was amazing. A few weeks ago, if he had said this, I would have dismissed it out of hand as the ravings of an adorable sci-fi geek. But now, now… something about what he said made my hair stand on end, and not only could I not just dismiss it, I felt scared. I watched myself stampeding back into my Denial 101 classroom. I threw open the door and ran inside. Everyone in the class startled. I ran straight to the first row and crouched down behind Kara, the pregnant teenager, trying to hide.

I was busy taking more deep breaths and filling my lungs with smoke when my cell phone rang. It was the supernanny calling back, saying she had spoken to Andrygen and would it be a terrible inconvenience to keep him at my place for three days? I immediately switched from anxiety mode over to amazed mode and then slid right into incredibly annoyed mode: not at Ganymede or him staying with me, but at his horrible PETA-ass-kissing, animal interpreting mother, Madonna II. I said sure, no problem, before I remembered that Now was tomorrow (what?) and that I had a date on Friday. I dropped the phone into my purse and headed for the store.

Inside, I located Ganymede in one corner, holding a box and gaping at its contents with the expression of one who had unraveled the secret of the Higgs Boson. The look on his face made being stuck with him for three more days completely worth it. And I meant "stuck" with only the most utmost of affection. We stayed in the store for an hour and a half. I started to forget about aliens and souls that were finger-licking good. I bought him a very complicated-looking robot kit. He swore he'd pay me back, and I rolled my eyes. And even then, I basically had to drag him away by his afro.

CHAPTER 14

Ganymede must have suspected he'd be staying overnight at least one night, because he came prepared. Along with essentials like his iPod, iPhone, and several video games on DVD (he must have crossed his fingers on that one), he had stuffed his pajamas and toothbrush in his backpack, too, a change of clothes, some paperbacks, including *Dune* and *Robopocalpyse*, and several *Road & Track* magazines.

So, all we had to do was go home, have some tahini rolls and hot chocolate nightcaps, toss Ralph some turkey for dinner, watch a movie, and hit the sack. At one point, true to his word, he dug a small metal box out of his backpack, fiddled with it for a minute, then told me to watch Ralph. He pressed a button, and Ralph's head immediately went sideways and his ears stood straight up. Ganymede grinned and said, "Frequencies," and that was all.

Once he let go of the button, Ralph stopped cocking his head, licked his lips once or twice, and gave a half wag with his tail. I smiled back, strangely heartened by his mysterious passions. Hours later, I offered him my bed, but like the true little gentleman he was, he said the sofa was fine.

In the morning, I could barely move. Every muscle in my body felt like someone with a sledgehammer and a grudge had not held back. So having to get out of bed and drive over the hill to the Now meeting was about enticing as having my fingers chewed off again. After a brief breakfast of Shredded Wheat and toast, we all piled into the Z (Ralph sans the muzzle; he seemed okay; he seemed like a different dog), and I navigated poorly across town, squinting behind a large pair of sunglasses Hama had gotten for me several birthdays ago.

Now was located all the way at the end of Sunset near the beach. There was a sharp right turn onto some street I'd never heard of before. I couldn't read the sign until I was right up on it, due to my diminished eyesight.

"What does that say? What does that sign say? Quick, quick. I can't see it. It's blurry!"

After Ganymede had read it off, and I had squealed around the corner at an unsafe speed, he looked at me in a matter of fact way. "Maybe you should get some glasses," he suggested.

"No shit, Sherlock."

"Well, why don't you get some?"

Why don't I get some? Ha. Like it was that simple.

"Uh…" I navigated down the street past a few houses, scanning, searching. Up ahead, I saw a large parking lot and headed that way. "It's complicated. I can't get into it right now." Ganymede was too young to understand denial and all its subversive complexities. He had plenty of time to become acquainted with it, and I wasn't going to be the one to make the introduction. I drove up the street and pulled into the lot, and Now stood before us in all its humble glory. It was a Spanish-style red brick and tile building, set back a ways from the road and surrounded by swaying palm trees. I parked (the lot was about half full) and Ganymede waited for me patiently, grinning at all my grunts and groans while I pried my stiff, aching body out of the car. Together, we entered through the front door. I pulled my sunglasses off and shoved them into my purse. A middle-aged woman with yellow, shoulder-length hair sat at a front desk made out of what looked like a felled Sequoia tree trunk. She smiled widely as we entered. She was tiny behind the giant round desk.

"Welcome! Good morning! How are you?"

"Uh…hi."

"Rae? Miller?"

"Yes."

"Oh, good. I'm so glad you could make it." The phone rang. She held up a finger. "You have reached Now. How can I help you be present?"

Ganymede looked up at me. I shrugged. Ralph sprawled out on the cool tiles and heaved a sigh.

"Yes," the woman said very softly once into the phone, and placed the receiver back down as if she was handling nitroglycerin. "I am *so* sorry about that. Please, Ms. Miller, sign in, and I'll take you back to see Bob."

I was surprised. "I get to see Bob already?"

"Get to see Bob, already?" someone said behind me. "You get to more than see Bob. You get to give him a big hug!"

I turned around. It was Mr. Motel. He had appeared from some side hallway. He was dressed in what looked like a white karate outfit, and he was wearing flip-flops. He beamed at me, fifteen years older than the last time I'd seen him, his belly straining at the karate belt, his hair snowy white but still full. He held out his arms. I walked into them and felt his squid-like embrace encompass me. My aching body reacted badly. I felt like vomiting. I patted him softly on the back a few times. We parted.

"Rae! Rae, Rae, Rae, Rae, Rae, Rae, Rae, Rae, Rae, Rae!" He actually said my name many more times, but I lost count as they blurred together. "How long? How long has it been?"

"Um…"

Bob looked down at Ganymede. "Oh, my God! Is this your son?"

My heart constricted. I smiled.

"No, this is my—"

"Godson!" Ganymede interjected. We exchanged a look and a secret smile. Ralph continued to sprawl on the tile floor, ignoring all of us.

"Well, well, well, you look *wonderful*, Rae. What brings you to Now? Hopefully a spiritual crisis has brought you to us. And we will do our damnedest to keep you here."

"Where?" said Ganymede, curious as ever.

"Come, come, come," said Bob, ushering us down the hallway where he'd come from. "Thank you, Riot," he threw over his shoulder at the woman. Riot. I had heard right. I smiled at her as we walked away.

"Ms. Miller hasn't signed in, Bob—"

"Come this way," he said, cutting off Riot. "Come to my office." He ushered us through a doorway.

Riot called, "Perhaps before she leaves she can si—"

Bob slammed his door closed. He rolled his eyes. "That's why we call her Riot," he addressed the ceiling. "Because she tends to get hysterical."

"How do you spell that?" asked Ganymede. "It sounds like you said Riot."

Bob motioned for us to sit down.

"I did say Riot, young man." He went around a big black desk with a dark glass top and sat behind it. "That is that woman's Now name. Your moth—uh, godmother will get one too, as soon as she joins."

"What's a Now name?" asked Ganymede. Ralph was standing by the door and wouldn't come any further into the room, as if he smelled evil in here. He whimpered and turned around and crammed his nose into the hinges.

"I will go into all that soon, young man."

"You don't mind if Ganymede is here?"

Bob threw his hands up. "Why not? He might as well start waking up now. Get a head start!" He launched his head backwards and guffawed.

"I am awake," countered Ganymede.

Bob straightened his head up. "Oh, I can see that, young man. You *are* awake. Just not completely. Just not in the way that we strive for here."

"Um…I don't know. I think I'd rather send Ganymede out while we talk. I don't want to…upset him."

"Mmm." Bob leaned forward in his chair and steepled his fingers together. "That serious, huh?"

"Yeah…"

"Okay. Who am I to argue? Off you go, my boy. It was a pleasure to meet you, Ganymede. Your parents were wise people to name you after one of the moons of Jupiter. Jupiter and its moons is a very powerful symbol."

I was pretty sure Bob was dishing out a load of bullshit, but it sounded good.

Ganymede stood up and opened the door. He threw a backward glance at Bob that was rife with suspicion. Ralph's toenails clattered and slid on the floor. He couldn't get out of the room fast enough.

"Oh, there's supposed to be some delicious Danish here," I told Ganymede. "Go ask the front desk lady where they are."

"Okay." He closed the door behind him.

Mr. Motel and I were alone. I searched his desk for a picture of Mrs. Motel. There was a frame to the left, but its back was to me. For all I knew, Shakira was in that frame. There was something going on with Mr. Motel. I couldn't put my finger on it, but I was beginning to side with Ralph. I began to deeply regret coming here.

"Rae, it's so good to see you. I don't know if you know this, but I'm the director here."

"Oh, wow."

"Yes. I rose up in the ranks, as they say." He chuckled merrily. "It's grown into quite a place. Lots of members." He leaned forward. "Lots of *big* names," he whispered. He seemed a little bit like a casting agent who was new to town and the extra he had managed to hook from *Sister Wives* morphed into Idris Elba by the time the conversation was over.

"What is going on with you? How are you doing? Did you get things straightened out with your TV show, or are you still ousted? Kicked out. Banished? Is that why you're here?"

I rolled my eyes and slumped down in the chair. "Oh, God, I wish!"

"Tell me, tell me. What's been going on?"

I couldn't just blurt it out. How was I going to approach this topic without looking completely loony?

"Now, Rae...we've been friends for a long time. You know you can tell me anything. I'm not here to judge." He gestured around the room with his white-sleeved arms. "You're safe here."

"Okay." I crossed my legs and absently applied some Chapstick I had been fiddling with. I dropped the Chapstick back into my purse. "You know, I'm responsible for that kid," I said. "I really shouldn't leave him alone."

"I'll bet he's at the front desk with Riot. Here." He clicked a button. "Riot, my dear?"

"Yes, Bob."

"Is one of the moons of Jupiter hovering about your desk, by any chance?"

There was a pause, then Riot giggled. "Yes, he's here, Bob. Locked in orbit!"

"Could you leave your comm on while you two converse so Rae knows he's safe?"

Instead of being insulted and defensive, as I would have been if somebody had just accused me of being a potential kidnapper, Riot said cheerfully, "Will do, Bob!"

There was a click, and then we could hear them talking.

"I'm building a robot," said Ganymede.

"Oh, how wonderful!" Riot enthused.

Bob looked back at me. "Rae. Rae. Whatever's in your head right now…let it out. Don't hold on to the past. You can't know the future. Be in the now. Your fears are unfounded. Why did you bring them in with you?" He gestured toward the door. "Go, get up. Take your fears and put them outside the door. Then come back in and tell me what's going on."

"Oh, well, I don't need to—"

"Put them outside, Rae."

"I get it. The symbolism—"

"Outside, Rae."

"You want me to actually—"

"Sweetheart…"

"Okay. " I stood up stiffly and shambled to the door and opened it. I bent over and pantomimed placing my fears down on the floor in the hallway. I grunted with effort as I stood up. Then I closed the door.

Mr. Motel sighed. "Ah…good. What's going on with you? You seem extremely stiff. You know, we have yoga here twice a week."

"Oh…" I waved my hand. "I was working out with a friend of mine to rehab my shoulder. I'm super sore."

"What's wrong with your shoulder?"

"Nothing."

Bob's eyebrows shot up. "Nothing?" He grinned. "Mm. Okay. Next topic! Now…let's hear it. About the other things." He lowered his voice. "What's going on?"

I sat down slowly, my thighs revolting like twentieth century Russian peasants.

"Okay." Just tell him. "I've been seeing things lately. Frightening things. I'm not sure if I'm hallucinating or not."

"You're on drugs?" Bob was nodding as if I had already said yes.

"No. I'm not on drugs."

"A little drinking then?"

I paused. "Um…no more than usual. But yes. Some drinking."

"What are you seeing?"

"Aliens."

Bob's expression remained the same. He nodded and tapped his chin with one finger. He looked as if I had just said clowns or dentists or something else as reasonable but potentially terrifying and, in the end, harmless.

"What kind of aliens?"

"The famous kind. The kind we all know about. The big heads, the little mouths. They're kidnapping people. I've seen them. But nobody else seems to be able to see them. Well, except for this one kid. But he disappeared, so I don't know who he is."

"Hmm…" Bob's fingers were steepled again. "Hmm…"

"It's crazy, right? I mean…I never used to be this way. It's a recent thing. It just started happening out of the blue!"

"And you see them…doing what, exactly?"

"Floating people up to their ships. In a bright light."

"Hmm…"

In the background, I heard Ganymede laughing, and Ralph barked.

My eyes went to his desk. "They can't hear us, right?"

Bob smiled. "Oh, no, no. It's just one way. Like a baby monitor."

I put my hand over my chest. "Whew. I don't want to scare him."

"Well, Rae, I can understand that." He leaned back in his chair and surveyed me for a moment. "Because that *is* scary."

"I know. I know. Why can *I* see them? Why can't anyone else?"

"Well, first things first. What are you doing here? Do you want to stop them?"

I frowned slightly. "Stop them? I came here because I'm going nuts. I came here so you would tell me I'm not nuts." I leaned forward and lowered my voice. "And I have it on good authority that they're doing something with our souls!"

Mr. Motel stood up and came around the desk toward me. He sat down in the chair Ganymede had vacated and folded his hands in his lap.

"Rae," He gazed intently at me. "Let's say this was true and this was happening. Because I've heard of this phenomena before, of course. Everybody has. Whatever they're doing, they couldn't do it without permission."

"Permission?" What the hell was he talking about? "If that were happening to me, I wouldn't give permission! The people who are being taken—they don't look like they gave permission. And what about Whitley Strieber? He basically said he was raped. People are terrified. I've seen their faces."

Mr. Motel gave me a ghost of a smile accompanied by a wise and knowing expression. He reached over and patted my hand, then left it sitting there, on top of mine.

"And yet…they have given permission. Maybe not consciously. But something inside them, deep inside them, acquiesces."

Bob stared intently into my face, and, not breaking eye contact with him, I very subtly wormed my hand out from beneath his, leaned back in my chair, and crossed my arms. How could Bob have joined this school, become the director, and still be exactly the same as he'd been at UCLA? Oh, well. It still felt sort of good unloading the situation on him. And he was taking it very well. I supposed that he had more or less "heard it all" from the confused and searching throngs that trampled through this place at any given time.

"Well," he said, crossing his own arms now, "you are definitely in need of some guidance. I'm *so* glad that you came here." He appeared to be in deep thought.

"Because robots will take over the world one day," Ganymede was saying in the background.

"Oh, honey, I wouldn't worry about that."

"Ralphie, no! No! I'm sorry. He only does that to someone when he likes them."

"Sweetheart, I don't judge affection. I take it from whence it comes."

"You should return on Saturday," Bob told me. "It'll be an introductory meeting."

"I thought I was coming for the introductory meeting today."

"Well, it's more of a meet and greet today." He smiled. "We'll give you your Now name at the next meeting. If you decide to join, that's the name we'll be calling you by."

"What the hell is a Now name?"

He waved his hand. His cell phone rang. "It will all be explained. You came to the right place! I *knew* you would return to the flock one day, Rae!" He was busy reading his cell phone display now.

"So you don't think this is crazy—I'm crazy?"

"Crazy?" He barked a laugh. "Sorry. I have to take this. It's Clint." He looked at me like *told you so*.

He stood up and went back behind his gigantic black Darth Vader desk. "Hey, there," he said conversationally. "Are you staying in the Now?" He winked at me.

"There's other things, Bob. I just found out I was dead when I was a kid. I just found out I was under water for fifteen minutes. Isn't that impossible without brain damage?"

Bob covered the mouthpiece with his hand. "Well, you seem fine now. It was obviously meant to be." Holy shit. He was blowing me off! He cocked an ear to the phone. "Yes. That makes total sense to me, Clint. But let me give you a little advice." Bob stopped talking and looked at me pointedly. He mouthed, "Riot will help you," and waited until I'd stood up and shambled toward the door. "Try stretching a little," Bob said in a stage whisper. Then: "See you Saturday!" he half-mouthed, half-hissed before resuming his conversation with Clint. I doubt it was Clint Eastwood. It was probably just Clint Howard.

Out in reception again, I approached the front desk as Ganymede was saying, "But they are going to destroy the world."

"Not before people will," Riot answered, very calmly. As creepy as Ganymede's obsession with robots was, Riot was much, much creepier. "People will beat robots there. That's why we're here. That's what this place is for."

"For what?" Ganymede was sitting in a chair beside Riot behind her desk where they had obviously already become good friends. Ralph relaxed between them on the floor. "To hide from the robots?"

"No, honey. To change our behavior. To change ourselves."

As I reached the desk, a Led Zeppelin song suddenly blasted out over the loudspeakers, startling all three of us. Robert Plant shrilled about being confused and horny. Then it cut off. Riot looked at us expectantly, a big smile on her face.

"Woke you up, didn't it?"

Ralph whimpered. I knew how he felt. I had left my fears outside Bob's door and hadn't picked them up again when I'd exited, but somehow they'd grown legs and followed me anyway.

CHAPTER 15

Andrygen left an endless message on my cell, thanking me profusely for having Ganymede over until Saturday. The supernanny was going to be dropped off at her car sometime tomorrow (Ganymede had already called home and given directions), and Andrygen would take me out to dinner soon to thank me. Ricardo had alienated everyone on the show, and the tide of feeling had turned against him, and I should definitely think about doing the reunion.

The fact that I had missed the call and didn't have to speak to Andrygen reinforced the feeling that the universe wasn't completely cold and heartless. There was good luck and providence. There was a little wiggle room.

Ganymede and I spent Friday watching movies, baking brownies for the Dadalians, eating pizza, and generally having one continuous pajama party. Ralph didn't like pizza, so I fed him more cold cuts from the deli, which he gobbled down. Then it was late afternoon and time for me to drop them off at Hama's while I went on my date. The provision for the date, as I had explained it to Giancarlo over the phone, was to do it early, because I had to get Ganymede from Hama's afterward. She had offered to keep him overnight, but I had turned her down. I felt weirdly territorial over him. And an overnight at Hama's meant I probably should let Andrygen know, which wasn't gonna happen, so why go there in the first place?

Hama threw open the door at her place. "Hello, hello! Hi! Come in, come in!"

"Hi," said Ganymede, pulling Ralph by the leash after him into the house, grinning widely. It was already obvious they were going to get along great. I started to go in. Hama put her forearm across my throat and yanked the cigarette out of my mouth with her other hand.

"Are you shitting me? When? Why?"

"Ooh!" said Ganymede from the interior of the house. "You're in trouble."

I rolled my eyes. "Long story. I can't stay anyway."

I turned around to go, tweaking my back, but didn't let Hama see me wince. I felt slightly better than yesterday but was miffed that I had to go on my date with any muscle discomfort at all. I'd forgotten how long it took to recover from working out when you hadn't worked out in a long time.

"Wait a minute. Wait wait wait wait wait wait." Hama now blocked me with her arm. She was practically as strong as a man, so there was no getting past her.

"Hama, I have to go."

"You haven't even told me about this guy. You haven't told me anything. How well do you know him?"

I shrugged. "Very little."

"What if he's a serial killer?"

"He's not a serial killer! He's a physical therapist."

"How did you get your arms to look like that?" Ganymede reappeared and pushed between us, staring up at Hama. She bent her arm into the classic muscle pose so her biceps popped up.

"You mean like this?" she said.

"You don't want to know," I told him.

"Yes, I do."

"You're building a robot. What do you care about muscles?"

"They're so big," he said, staring.

"We can work out. You wanna work out? I'll work you out," said Hama.

"Okay, guys, have fun." I wanted to warn him, but it wouldn't kill him.

"Okay, well, take some pepper spray with you and keep your car keys between your knuckles."

I rolled my eyes and headed for the car. "See you later, G."

"See you, Rae!" he called gaily.

Mmm. Maybe she'd go easy on him.

As was the usual with L.A., the temperature began to drop as the day drew closer to dusk, reminding all concerned that yes, this was a desert and, yes, we were living in it. We shouldn't even be here, shamelessly stealing water from the Colorado. It was a nice break from the endless heat wave we'd been having, though. Back home, I changed into a pair of jeans and a white blouse that plunged somewhat in the front before deigning to present its first button, rubbed some Mixed Chicks leave-in conditioner in my hair (of all people, Margarite had turned me on to this brand; it really did keep the frizzies down), and deemed myself good to go.

When Giancarlo showed up promptly at six and rang my buzzer, I went downstairs. The swarthy physical therapist was standing on the grass with his hands in his pockets. He was wearing dark gray slacks and a thin black sweater that clung to his chest and shoulders. I felt one of my knees wanting to buckle and gave it a mental tongue-lashing. *What the fuck are you doing?* I yelled at it. *Don't embarrass me, asshole! We're not 18 years old anymore, or did you forget?*

I don't give a crap if we're 108, bitch, said my knee. *Look at him!*

I regained control and walked forward. Giancarlo finally saw me. He had been studying the late afternoon sky like some scholar of yore, engrossed by the mystery of the universe.

"Rae, how good to see you," he murmured, coming forward to hug me with one arm. "It is so beautiful out tonight. Are you ready?"

"Yeah. Thanks for picking me up. I could have met you somewhere."

"Don't be ridiculous. Of course not! Here…" He saw me starting to wiggle into my jacket and attempted to help me. I winced as I wormed my right arm into the sleeve.

"What is this?" Giancarlo said, staring. "It is worse?"

"Yeah. I sort of fell on it. Yesterday." *From the roof of my car.*

"Oh, what a shame. Do you think you re-injured it?" He stepped to my side and took my arm into his hands, a procedure that now seemed to be a tradition with us. "Let me see. Does this hurt? And this?"

He stepped in front of me, bending my arm slowly upward. Our faces were about a foot away, and I got a whiff of his aftershave. Our eyes met as he continued bending, bending, bending my arm. Neither of us broke eye contact, and I didn't even feel what he was doing with my arm. I had completely forgotten that I had one.

But then: "Ooh," I hissed between my teeth. I had felt *that*.

He immediately stopped. "Uch," he said, lowering my arm. He clicked his tongue several times. "That is a pity. How did this happen?" He let go but didn't move away. Before I could answer, he lifted his hand and cupped my chin lightly. "You must be careful, *dolcezza*. You must not re-injure yourself."

"Yeah, well…" *Don't do it!* I was screaming at my knee, which was showing signs of weakening. *I will fuck you up!*

No, my knee came back at me in a pheromone-induced rage, *I will fuck YOU up. I will fuck YOU up. I think that's how this works, sweetheart. You won't be able to walk. I will FUCK you. Keep your panties on, baby. Everything's under control!*

"It couldn't be helped." I finished weakly.

Giancarlo smiled and released my chin. "Yes, such is life. Some things cannot be helped," he murmured quietly, gazing unblinkingly into the center of my pupils. The gray streaks at his temples glowed in the waning afternoon light.

I smiled at him bravely. "Ready?"

Giancarlo stepped back, his gaze dropping briefly to my plunging neckline before it casually rose again.

"You look very beautiful."

"Thank you. So do you."

He grinned and inclined his head. We walked together, in our beauty, toward his cherry GTO.

Giancarlo had paid ahead of time for tickets to a special presentation of *2001: A Space Odyssey* at the Arclight in Hollywood. No amount of cajoling or threats of "no second date" would convince him to let me reimburse him for half, nor would he let me buy the exorbitant drinks at the lounge once we arrived. "You cannot threaten me," he was saying quietly. "I believe there will be a second date. And a third. And a fourth." His eyes bored into mine. It was impossible to maintain eye contact but simultaneously impossible to look away.

"You know, you have a lot of confidence." I studied him closely. "Where are you from in Italy? South, I would imagine."

Giancarlo sat back in his chair. "My family is descended from a great line of Moors. In the past, we had been in Spain but immigrated to Italy, where we have remained for several centuries. As you know, the Moors aided greatly in bringing parts of Europe out of the Dark Ages."

"That's so much more interesting than my family history."

"Why do you say this? Your family history already fascinates me. You are a mixture of many races also, as I am, are you not? We are very similar."

"Well, I may be a mixture, but we aren't descended from people who brought Europe out of the Dark Ages. My mother's black—Creole—from Louisiana. My father's Irish. I think both of their families were alcoholics. Dr. Drew could have a rehab show about them alone."

Giancarlo laughed. "Liquor is the great balm, is it not? Who among us does not partake?" He gestured to the glasses in front of us. "But that is fascinating also. Can you imagine your mother's rich history? Louisiana?" He looked thoughtful for a moment. "I have been there many times. To New Orleans. And the Irish…ah. Have you not heard of the Black Irish? There are many theories as to what that means, but who does not realize that the Moors were in ancient Britain? It would be silly to assume they'd never reached Scotland or Ireland." He raised an eyebrow.

"Very silly." I'd heard this before.

"Yes. Your father's people have their secrets and their history also."

I grinned. "You guys really got around, didn't you?"

He lifted his glass up and took a big sip. "We did, at that. You most likely have Moorish blood running through your veins."

I took a big sip of my drink. "That doesn't sound too bad. Having Moorish something running through me."

Giancarlo leveled a smoldering look my way. We held eye contact for several blazing hot seconds. He smiled slowly. He said, "How is your shoulder feeling?"

I paused at the abrupt subject change. Then I rotated my shoulder around gingerly. "Not bad," I said, surprised. "I'm glad I met you at therapy, but I hope Chrislann isn't too mad at me for bailing."

He rubbed his chin roughly then pushed his hand through his hair. "Ah, Chrislann, he has mentioned this. He only hopes you are taking care of yourself. He does not hold grudges. Despite the foul language he's so fond of, he is a very popular therapist there." He gazed at me fixedly.

"Oh, good. Don't tell him I fell on my shoulder. Tell him I'm working out with a professional fitness trainer."

"I would very much like to kiss you."

"Oh, my God. You're incredible!"

"Incredible in what way? I have not kissed you yet."

"You're so straightforward. I'm not used to it." Even Johnny, my ex, a stuntman who had been fairly macho, hadn't been *this* macho.

Giancarlo ignored me, got up, and leaned over my chair, caging me in with his arms on each side.

He stood there looking down at me as I looked up, my hand frozen on my margarita.

"Do you want to kiss me," he asked, "or is this too soon?"

"Oh, it's not too soo—"

Suddenly I was saying the last word into his mouth as he pressed his lips against mine. They opened slightly, and then his teeth were nipping at my upper lip, and then his tongue joined in a little, and then there was more nipping, and then he stopped and pulled back. At least I didn't have to curse my knee out this time, since I was sitting down.

"Mm…that was nice," murmured Giancarlo, straightening up.

"That *was* nice," I echoed, in a daze.

"Now let me allow you to enjoy your drink. I will return to my side."

"Or you could sit on my lap."

Giancarlo grinned, the craggy lines showing his age in a sexy way.

"If I knew I would not break every bone in your body, I would do so." He sat back down, still smiling. "You, however, would *not* break my bones," he dared.

I didn't think I could stand up, much less sit on his lap. What was wrong with me? It had *really* been a long time since I'd been involved with anyone. I couldn't believe it had been so long, though, that I was reacting this way. Like when Rex had kissed me at The Standard, and all the stars had disappeared from the sky, and time had stopped. *Oh, my God*, I thought, *I was hard up!* When had that happened?

Giancarlo took a sip of his drink, still staring at me invitingly. I liked that he was aggressive but not pushy. There was a big difference. He was cool and calm, patiently waiting for nature to take its course. It was a turn-on. I decided to be as forthright as he had been. I decided to dig my playing cards out of my chest where they were buried, deep inside where no one would ever see them, except maybe a radiologist at a hospital, and lay them on the table the way Giancarlo, who was evidently terrible at poker, always did.

"You know, I don't think that's such a good idea right now. You wouldn't be able to walk in public, and I wouldn't be able to focus on the movie."

Giancarlo dove right in, grinning. "You would just walk in front of me as my shield. That is not a problem. You would be doing me a huge favor, and you would know how huge it was as we progressed. And you have already seen this movie, no? Have we not all seen this movie?" He raised an eyebrow questioningly.

"We have all seen this movie," I said, nodding. I was starting to not use contractions now, like him. I looked around at the patio. I decided to change the subject. I was out of practice, and if Giancarlo continued rallying with me it'd basically be Stanley Kubrick who? And we'd end up in bed in about ten minutes. I had to draw it out for at least a few hours more. I meant dates. A few dates more. "Hey, I'll be right back. Ladies room." I winked. Giancarlo stood as I got up. It was like he was from the year 1800. Except for the innuendoes, which would have been unconscionable in the 1800s. But here, now, it was much more than unconscionable. It was refreshing.

I wandered to the front of the lounge area where the bathrooms were. A couple who probably recognized me from the show stared as I walked by, smiling lightly. It was verboten to stare at celebrities in L.A. You had to sort of pretend that you didn't see them or you'd come off like a gibbering hillbilly. I didn't make up these rules. This was just the way it was. Even with minor, minor, minor celebrities like me. I figured the couple was from out of town.

In the past, it would have felt kind of nice being recognized, but things had changed. The least of my worries was getting older and finding work and caring what others thought of me. My new worries involved the alteration of reality, the introduction of real terror and danger. Being on this date was just a diversion from the fact—a temporary stay from the insanity—and it was working, too. I didn't actually have to go to the bathroom. I just needed a breather from the smoldering volcano that was Giancarlo. In the midst of diverting my attention from Them, I had to further divert my attention from the sexiest Moorish-Italian physical therapist I had ever met in my life.

I was about to enter the bathroom when someone grabbed me from behind. *Oh, my God*, I thought, *what now?* The strange hands grabbed my shoulders (ouch!) and whirled me around. Dante stood in front of me, inches away. His white teeth flashed in his face, and before I could even register what was happening, he was bending toward me. At the last second, I turned my head, and his approaching lips brushed my cheek. I was stunned. He was the last person I had expected to see. My mouth dropped open, and I threw my arms around him. He returned the embrace, hard, then pulled away and signed something, his dark eyes alight with mischief.

I shook my head.

"You're going too fast. You're—"

Moeyner appeared out of nowhere, smiling smugly.

"Oh, hey—" I was thrown for a loop again.

"Hey." Moeyner popped her gum and cut her eyes at me.

"Moeyner! Oh, you guys are—"

"Yeah, we hitting the town tonight. How you doing?" She air-kissed my cheeks, and I air-kissed hers back.

"Not bad."

"You hitting the bar? Alone?" Moeyner asked pointedly.

Dante signed something beside her. Moeyner watched, then said, "I'm just kidding, Rae. Who you with?"

"No one you know."

Dante signed again, looking at me. I picked up, "you," and that's it. I shrugged.

"I'm sorry. I—"

"A'ight. I'll trans'ate," said Moeyner, tossing her weave over her shoulder. She was greatly exaggerating her "ghetto" persona. Even more than usual. "I know you ain't take the time to learn, so—"

"Well, *nobody* took the time to learn. Except you."

"Yeah, 'cept me." Her eyes were light brown tonight. I was pretty sure they'd been dark brown the last time I'd seen them.

"Well, don't single me out. Call everybody else out then, too. Where's this hostility coming from?" I was caught off guard by Moeyner's antagonism. We had gotten along okay on the show, except when we were talking about race. Whenever I would mention that I was ethnic too, she would roll her eyes so far back into her head it looked like she was having a seizure. Then she'd fling her hand up and it would essentially be "end of discussion." We got along better when she was trying to teach me the finer points of Krumping. Moeyner, of all people, considered twerking too crass.

Dante grabbed Moeyner by the shoulders and turned her toward him. He signed in her face rapidly. Then he signed something at me, his eyes lit up and dancing.

"You…don't…pretend…the moon?"

Dante threw his head back and laughed uproariously. For someone who was completely deaf, he had a very deep voice, lacking the familiar nasal quality that often occurred with the hard of hearing. I think maybe he had lost his hearing later in life, and that was why. He was wearing a colorful scarf from under which his dreadlocks flowed. Suddenly, Cola's warning resurfaced from below, shoving its way up through my consciousness. It broke through the surface, gasping, and had a coughing fit. "He's not what he seems," repeated the warning. What in the hell had *that* meant? It must be a backstabbing thing. Maybe Dante wasn't as honorable as he appeared.

Now, more people were looking over at us and whispering among themselves. The three of us were attracting attention.

"He wants to have lunch," said Moeyner. She crossed her arms belligerently.

I leveled my gaze at her. "Let me ask you something, Moe."

"Don't call me Moe."

"It's your name. What's wrong with it?"

Moeyner dropped her purse on the floor and began to casually remove her earrings.

"I'll kick yo' ass," she said loudly. "Bitch!"

In response, I dropped my purse to the floor and started to kick off my heels. I wasn't wearing earrings. Many summers during our childhood, Margarite and I had been sent to San Diego to stay with our cousins on Dad's side of the family. Between incidents in our hometown and America's finest city, we'd gotten into enough trouble with neighborhood kids that, over the years, we'd elevated our street brawling to a passable level of self-defense. I glanced around quickly to see if any loose objects were available for throwing or smashing into skulls.

"Why you so snobby?" screeched Moeyner, her fists up. Dante stepped between us, smiling, and pantomimed a catfight, as a small crowd began to gather. "You one snobby, high yella b-yotch."

"I've never been snobby to you, you dyke! You're delusional!" It was almost as if Moeyner was making things up on purpose to start a scene. I glanced around again. Was the camera crew here?

"OOOHHHHH!" Moeyner yelled, and lunged. Dante held her back with one arm. He signed something quickly with one hand.

"Hmph!" said Moeyner, and started putting her earrings back on. "Okay. *What*ever."

I waited a moment, then began to slip my heels back on. Thank God. My breasts would probably have flown out of this low-cut blouse. I tried not to groan as I bent my stiff body over.

"Okay, nice to see you guys," I said sarcastically.

"Yeah, catch ya latah, b-yotch," Moeyner called, digging around in her purse for more cunt pills. I wanted to warn her not to take any more; she was going to overdose.

I turned to go into the bathroom, and Dante caught my arm. I looked over my shoulder, and he held his hand up in the Vulcan salute while six or seven people milled about in a loose semi-circle, staring and whispering. I held three fingers up in the "west coast" sign and then pushed my way into the ladies' room.

CHAPTER 16

Someone I knew had once said, "Watch. When you're up about anything or just generally in a good mood, someone will come along and tear that feeling away from you." And how true that had turned out to be. Not just tonight, but other times—many times. Evidently, people didn't really do it on purpose. They just "sensed" your upness, and it was instinctual to reach up and yank you back down to earth to wallow in the misery with everybody else. So therefore, when the dramatic opening of *2001* began and *Thus Spoke Zarathustra* was pounding through the theater later, I couldn't get my mind off of Moeyner and her attitude. After about ten minutes, I reached across the armrest and felt for Giancarlo's hand in the darkness. I located it lying across his thigh, which he had crossed over his other leg. I laced my fingers between his, and he immediately gripped my hand, folding it beneath his other hand and placing the whole bundle on his thigh. I tried to focus on his hand, warm and strong, tried to focus on the Monolith, tried to focus on polite and emotionally dead HAL.

About an hour into the movie, Giancarlo's phone vibrated. I knew because I could feel it through his leg, which he had pressed up against mine. He pulled it out and read the ID. Then he leaned over and whispered, "Rae, please forgive me. I must take this."

"Okay, sure."

He got up and began to inch his way out of the row as things continued to go terribly wrong on Discovery One. I leaned back in my seat, which was somewhat uncomfortable because we were in the Cinerama Dome, the original theater that had never been renovated, to my knowledge. I watched Keir Duella dealing with HAL the computer. About twenty minutes later, I started swiveling my head around, looking for Giancarlo. Maybe he had forgotten where we were sitting. Maybe he couldn't see me.

"Open the pod bay doors, HAL," Kier playing Dave was saying.

"Dave, I'm afraid I can't do that," replied HAL, very calmly.

The only thing I could think of that was worse than being stuck in outer space with a psychotic computer was the fact that Giancarlo had vanished in the middle of our date. Ten minutes before the end of the movie, I finally got up and inched my way painfully out. My body had petrified in the uncomfortable seats. Kier was in the white room, experiencing the different stages of time. I felt empathetic toward him, as I was going through the same thing myself in the Cinerama Dome where I had seen such gems as *Scrooged*, *The Untouchables*, and *Hook* with Robin Williams—some in the '80s, some in the '90s. So long ago, but also like yesterday. Such fond memories. And not one of them had concluded the way this night had. This was a new one. Giancarlo had answered a phone call and disappeared to complete an undercover drug deal or whack somebody in an alleyway. What else could it be? He had left the theater to answer his phone and gotten hit by a car? What had he been doing, jaywalking across Vine to slap his ho for cutting her night, and therefore his cash, short? If she didn't get back out there and finish the job, he wouldn't have enough greenbacks to pay for our dinner later.

Hooker: My last john beat me up! He broke my nose and stole my shoes.

Giancarlo immediately backhands her on her already-bruised cheek. She sobs and stumbles sideways in her bare feet along the filthy sidewalk.

Giancarlo: (sans charming Italian accent) Call someone who cares, bitch. Put a Band-Aid on it and get back out there, or I'll cut you!

The angrier I got, the lower and sleazier Giancarlo's reasons for disappearing became. As I was exiting the building, I saw Dante and Moeyner heading toward me from a walkway around the side. I stopped and waited for them to approach, just as Giancarlo came rushing up out of the darkness. I turned back to Moeyner and Dante to find Moeyner walking forward, but Dante was nowhere to be seen. Moeyner neared from one side as Giancarlo neared from the other. I buzzed internally with frustration, unable to make a scene now because Moeyner would witness it.

"Rae…Rae," Giancarlo said, slightly out of breath. "My God, I am so sorry."

Moeyner smiled at us. "He sorry already? It be pretty damn early for dat!"

"Hey, bitch," I said sweetly. "This is Giancarlo. Giancarlo, my ex-roommate Moe. Moe the Bitch."

Moeyner had a nerve, approaching me after we'd almost thrown down in the lounge area. I was almost shaking with rage.

Giancarlo had been moving forward to shake Moeyner's hand. Now he hesitated.

"Have I missed something?"

"Naw, you ain't miss nothing, brothah." Moeyner held her hand out. "Dat's how we roll."

"Hello." Giancarlo took her fingers in his and pumped them once.

"Hel-lo, brothah!" Moeyner leered at him lecherously. Giancarlo smiled.

I searched over Moeyner's shoulder. "Where'd Dante go? Wasn't he just there?"

She turned and looked behind her.

"Yeah. Someone probably wants an autograph or a picture. That been happening all night," she said smugly. "Same for you?" She cocked an eyebrow.

"What?" I said, as if I hadn't heard her because I'd been thinking of something else. Dante *was* the most popular on the show, so it made sense. I doubted they'd wanted her autograph all that much. Shrew.

"Well, we was finnin' to invite y'all for drinks, but I think I better just go find out where he go," she declared in her best ebonics voice. *Drinks? She was fucking bat-shit crazy.*

"It was very nice meeting you," Giancarlo said politely. He had caught his breath by now and was standing calmly beside me.

"Yeah, same here." She gave him the once-over, looked at me, and cut her eyes away. "See ya, Raine!" She hefted her giant purse up higher onto her shoulder and went back the way she'd come. I waited until she had disappeared before I turned slowly toward Giancarlo and stared at him.

"I thought you had jaywalked out here and got run over by a drunk driver." I gestured toward the street. I didn't mention his being a pimp and backhanding a whore, but I was still thinking it. I was ready to go home.

"There is nothing I can say to redeem my actions. It was an emergency, and I cannot explain. But I am so sorry that it occurred during our outing."

I shook my head. "Don't worry about it. Maybe we should just call it a night, though."

There was something odd about him. It seemed like he had a different shirt on. I thought he'd been wearing a black sweater, but now it looked navy blue. I could see the blue tints clearly under the bright lights outside the theater. I guess I hadn't been looking that closely earlier, busy as I had been trying to keep my knees from buckling. He sighed and dropped his head forward.

"You are angry." He looked up. "I do not blame you." He took me lightly by the elbow. "Come, let us go."

"It's just so weird, Giancarlo." I disengaged my elbow from him. "If you were a doctor, I'd understand. Brains don't wait to get operated on. Are you a doctor? What are you? Are you not telling me something?"

We began to walk toward the parking lot.

He smiled wistfully. "I am not telling you a great many things, Rae. I am sorry I cannot explain. Not right now."

"Not right now? Does that mean that one day you will?"

He hesitated. "One day…the truth may be revealed, yes. It is possible."

"But let me just get this straight." I gave him a thin smile. "You left the movie and never came back, and you can't tell me why?"

"I cannot tell you why. "

"Are you a CIA guy or something? Are you just undercover as a physical therapist?"

Giancarlo reached out and put his hand gently on my shoulder.

"I am a physical therapist. And you *could* say I am an agent. But not with the CIA or FBI or NSA."

"I *could say* you're an agent."

"You *could* say I am an agent."

I was standing outside the Arclight doing Meisner's repetition exercises with a man who was a secret agent and maybe a pimp and possibly a serial killer. I hated it when Hama was right. I also sent a mental telepathy message to Cola and informed him that he'd warned me about the wrong person. Obviously, he should have warned me about Giancarlo.

"Okay," I said. "Let's leave it." What else was there to say? He was either lying or he wasn't. But I did sense that something unusual had happened and he hadn't just run out to play cards with some buddies on the spur of the moment.

"Thank you, *dolcezza*. Come, now. Let us go."

Giancarlo began to take surface streets, heading in the opposite direction from Glendale. The GTO wound its way up Highland and then cruised up Little Cahuenga with few traffic hindrances. Luckily, nothing was going on at the Hollywood Bowl tonight, or it would have taken twice as long to get through. We said very little along the way. The vibe was tense. I think Giancarlo was trying to stretch our time out, delay our parting, my inevitable cool gaze and refusal to let his tongue anywhere near me. We were cruising east along Riverside when he said, "I am reluctant for the night to end so badly. I will take you straight home if you wish. But since we are near my home, I thought you might come in for salami and wine."

Salami and wine? My stomach growled like a trained seal at the mention of the food. After all, we were supposed to be eating dinner now.

"Um…where do you live?" I had no intention of going to his place.

"Have you ever seen the Toluca Lake? I have a house on the lake."

"You have a *house* on the *lake*?" I looked agog at him. "I've never seen the lake, and I've lived in L.A. all my life."

"Oh, no, one cannot get to the lake anymore. No, no, no." He clicked his tongue. "I find it appalling. I believe all should be able to enjoy the lake, not just a few."

"Hmm," I huffed. I felt annoyance verging on anger. "Really. And how about Americans enjoying it, since it's America?" I was being a bitch, but it was a lot more benign than the things I *could* have said. Giancarlo *could* have been some kind of secret agent, and I *could* have been an astounding harridan. He didn't seem to take my comment personally, though, and just chuckled. Probably because he knew it was true. I was silent, reluctantly curious now about his home. Giancarlo must have sensed an implicit acquiescence, because he turned right off Riverside onto Forman and drove quite a ways down to Toluca Lake Avenue, where he turned again. This street was long and continuous, passing house after house, then curving gently this way and that until Giancarlo finally pulled into a short driveway surrounded by trees.

We exited the GTO and entered a smallish white house with a gray slate roof. Giancarlo snapped on lights and strode straight through a living room very staid and strangely similar to Margarite's toward a back wall that was made entirely of glass, including a sliding glass door. We stepped outside onto the patio. It had been cool tonight already, but it actually felt chilly out here. A light breeze blew up from across the water. I crossed my arms and gazed out over the dark lake, speechless that while I, one of the serfs, had been fruitlessly belly crawling through the mud, searching for the entrance to heaven, it had been right here in Giancarlo's backyard. Giancarlo the Moor. Giancarlo the secret agent.

He had disappeared back inside his house and now he returned, bearing a tray with two glasses of wine, cheese, salami, and what looked like olive oil sesame seed crackers—one of my favorites. He set them down on a table and handed me one of the glasses.

"Let us toast." He held his glass toward mine. "To your open-mindedness." We clinked glasses. "Thank you for not running away, even though by all accounts, I would not blame you."

"Oh, I might still run away," I said, swigging the wine, which immediately went to my head, because my stomach was completely empty. "At the very least I'm never, ever going to see another movie with you again."

"Touché."

Hadn't I just said myself, earlier, that re-injuring my shoulder "couldn't be helped"? Giancarlo had agreed and commented that, yes, some things in life couldn't be helped. So who was I to say he didn't have some equally bizarre and fascinating reason for doing what he had done? It was possible.

Giancarlo faced forward and gazed out over the water.

"Your house is beautiful. It's really beautiful here," I said, turning toward him. The moon was high and bright, illuminating the crags in his face. He seemed melancholy, and I felt a rush of affection toward him. One of my weaknesses was a melancholy man. But not the Morgan Freeman kind who understood your emotions and listened intently to everything you were saying—even though that was nice. More like the Daniel Craig kind where he looked somber because he knew he had to break your arm in four places in order to extricate you from the villain's diabolical trap. The angry, brooding Wesley Snipes kind who would skewer your nemesis with a sword and then, annoyed and impatient, sling you onto his motorcycle because, although he didn't necessarily want you around, it would be too dangerous to leave you there.

I slid my good hand onto the back of Giancarlo's neck and massaged it for a moment. He dropped his head forward and closed his eyes. After a while, he reached up and pulled my hand from his neck and used my arm like a fishing reel to hoist me toward him. He gripped one shoulder (the bad one—not too hard, but not softly either) and cupped my head with the other hand and pulled me close. But I've got to hand it to him—and myself, for that matter—even though he was pressed so hard against me that his flat belly and upper thigh were crushing my fibroids, we kept it under control. We did not attempt to steal past second base. Then, true secret Moorish Italian prince double agent assassin that he was, he drove me home in plenty of time for me to pick up my crazy, robot-loving adopted godson from Van Nuys.

CHAPTER 17

The next morning, I was awakened by several sounds at once. Sinatra's *Anything Goes* was blasting right into my ear. I sat bolt upright, staring around in confusion. My cell phone was lying beside my pillow where I did not remember putting it. *Anything Goes* was Rex's ringtone. I answered the phone just as a horrific screaming erupted outside my bedroom door. It continued in short, piercing bursts. For a minute, I thought it was the television.

"Hey." I stood up.

"Rae?"

"Rex—hold on a minute."

"What the hell is that noise? It sounds like the Zombie Apocalypse."

"I don't know. Wait a second." Half awake but shaking with adrenaline, I pulled on some sweat pants with trembling hands then counted to three and cracked open the bedroom door. My eyeballs rolled wildly, scanning the room. It appeared empty. Ganymede was lying on the sofa, half-on and half-off. It looked like he had tried to get up but had been stopped in his tracks. Ralph sat next to him on the wooden floor, looking worried.

"OH MY GOD." I shoved the door all the way open and came into the room, stumbling over his backpack. "WHAT IS WRONG WITH YOU?" I pressed my hand over my pounding heart.

Ganymede unscrewed his eyes and looked at me in terror.

"I can't move," he whispered, as if he were afraid whoever had done this to him would hear and return to finish the job. I was beginning to have an inkling of who had done this to him. Not some invisible bogeyman. Not even visible ones, like little gray alien invaders. It was much, much worse. "My whole body hurts. It feels like it's full of...of...of...of *acid!*"

Ah, poor kid. Right when my aches and pains had largely diminished, his were just starting. I stared down at him for a minute. I leaned over and poked him on the arm.

"AAAAAAAAAAAAAAHHHHHHHHHHHHHHH!"

Ralph threw his head back. "AWWWWWOOOOOOOOOOOO!"

"Jesus Christ!" I heard Rex's tinny voice and put the phone back to my ear.

"It's okay."

"It's okay? It's okay? Who's screaming like that?"

"A little boy."

"A little what?"

"Rae...Rae...it hurts...it hurts..."

Ralph stared at me accusingly. He licked his lips a few times but ceased howling. Since Ganymede wasn't screaming, there was no need to join in.

"Hold on," I told him. "What does it feel like?"

"Acid!" he moaned, writhing on the sofa like the accused in the midst of the Papal Inquisition.

"Well, that's because that's what it is," I told him, and poked him on the arm again. "See?"

"AAAAAAAAAAAAHHHHHHHHHHHHHH!"

"AWWWWWOOOOOOOOOOOOOOOO!"

Someone pounded on the living room wall.

"Rae...Rae..." Rex was laughing. "What is going on over there? I thought you gave up torturing little boys."

"Try again. Try Hama." I headed back for my bedroom and the bathroom. "Okay, Ganymede, sweetie, I'm going to get you some aspirin. But you have to stop screaming."

Ganymede was panting. "Aspirin's for babies!" he managed to gasp. "Aspirin won't work!"

"No—I mean—no, Ibuprofen."

"I have acid inside me?" he doubled back to the original comment, curious despite himself.

"It's called lactic acid, honey. It's just destroyed muscle fibers. Hama destroyed them."

"Whose kid is that?" asked Rex. "Did you kidnap him?"

"No. He ran away. It's one of Andrygen's kids."

I could hear Rex smoking on his end of the phone. Man, that sounded like a good idea. First things first, though. I delivered the meds and some water to the poor boy, then sat down on the other end of the sofa. My weight jostled the cushions, and Ganymede's body bounced a little.

"AAAAAAAAAAAAAHHHHHHHHHHHHHHH!"

"AWWWWWWWWWWWWWOOOOOOOOO!"

More pounding on the wall.

"Hey, when you're done with your kidnapping, come over here tonight. We're playing poker."

"Um…" I looked at Ganymede, who was tenderly touching his stomach and arms. Ralph lay down with his head on his paws and heaved a huge sigh. "I have to take the kid home later."

"Where does he live?"

"Topanga."

"Great. Drop him off and swing by."

"I'm taking him home in a few hours!"

"Good. We can hang."

It warmed my heart that Rex didn't mind my hanging out with him all day long until the poker game started. But I guess he also might as well get used to it if I really was going to move in there. As if he'd read my mind he asked, "Are you almost packed up?"

I looked around at my boxes.

"I never really *unpacked*, so…"

Beat.

"If you could turn procrastination into a job, you'd be *so rich*," Rex stated.

Ganymede was struggling to sit on up on the sofa. He frowned and hissed between his teeth and gasped. He didn't scream, but Ralph watched him anxiously.

"I'll have to let you know," I finally told him.

"Well, try to make it. Call me later. Oh, by the way, you're on YouTube."

"Say what?"

"YouTube. Check it out."

"Um…"

Rex laughed. "You should have kicked Moeyner's ass. Bye."

He hung up, and my heart sank.

I decided not to bother with it right now. I had to deal with the tortured boy on my sofa first. I looked over at Ganymede, who'd managed to drag himself into an almost-sitting up position. He had to stop three-quarters of the way there to recover. His mouth was open and he was still panting.

"Honey. Baby. You've got to get up and move. It's the only way you'll feel better."

"Do you have any Percodan?"

"Percodan?"

"Mom gives us half a Percodan—well, maybe a quarter of one—after the dentist or anytime someone has to get their cast put on or taken off."

"Anytime? How often do you guys have casts put on?"

"A lot." He shrugged. "Europa on the skateboard. Io in the backyard tree. I sliced my hand open last year on some scrap metal." He held his hand up, and I could make out a faint scar running between his forefinger and his thumb. Those kinds of things used to happen to me as a kid too, following me into adulthood, which was why I'd gone for the now-infamous tetanus shot. I almost felt like I should go jam my finger down on a rusty nail just to justify all the trouble I'd gone through.

"Mmm…no Percodan. But we can stop at Denny's or IHOP on the way over to your place and get some pancakes, if you want. Would that make you feel better?"

Ganymede nodded. He began the struggle of getting off the couch entirely, squeezing his eyes shut and clamping his lips together hard. But there was no more screaming. He bravely, heroically, amazingly made not a whimper.

CHAPTER 18

It was Saturday morning, the ungodly hour of ten a.m. I'd had to get up at eight in order to make it to Now by meeting time. I only half-remembered driving here.

Yesterday, after dropping Ganymede off, I'd abruptly decided not to take Rex up on his offer and left him a message. I went home and burrowed into my hole, tired and not up for chitchat. For some reason, I couldn't get to sleep later that night and stayed up until five in the morning watching a Hitchcock marathon. So now, I was sitting in the Z in the parking lot, dry swallowing some Ibuprofen and furtively smoking my last cigarette as I delayed entrance into the center. It wasn't that I didn't want to go in, exactly, but I was starting to remember what a fanatic Bob had been about waking up and being in the moment and all that was essentially opposite from the life I had led thus far. "There's no time to wait," he would say. "The human existence is over in the blink of an eye." Here, he would snap his fingers—one sharp, terrifying snap—indicating the end of a lifespan and the arrival of death.

But when you were young, that was more of a romantic notion than anything else, and Bob might as well have been speaking Latin for all that I'd actually absorbed. Even after the shark, I was never in "the now" as far as I could remember. In fact, the shark incident had catapulted denial to the front of the line, despite loud complaints from everybody else: responsibility, reasoning, acceptance. Once denial set in, all those other things became fair game to whimsy. As I would have taught in Denial 101, when one is engaging in denial, one is doing the opposite of being in the now.

And then I couldn't forget regret, either, denial's make-out partner. Lately, shock and denial had been engaging in extreme PDA in my life, locking together in a contortionist's embrace. Usually regret and denial were the ones that were eternally engaged, never marrying, but so alike in their uselessness that it was just easier to stay together. But now that big-headed monsters were kidnapping folk in broad daylight and doing God knows what with them...I was ready to listen again, or have someone listen to me. I guess being here made me feel guilty, because I wasn't really here to "be in the now." I just wanted somebody else—anybody else—to share in the terror with me so I didn't feel so alone. An aloneness surpassing Sherman Oaks.

I tossed my butt out the window and went inside. I was hoping Riot would be at the front desk, because I wanted to see a familiar friendly face, but the giant sequoia tree trunk was deserted. I stood there for a moment, looking around, and was about to wander off up one of the hallways when a man came rushing out of a doorway to my left.

"Rae? Rae Miller?"

"Yes?"

"Hi there. I'm Boom. You're late! We're all in here."

"Boom?"

"Yes," he smiled tensely. "Boom." He stared at me, as if awaiting another comment. After several beats he said, "The meeting's almost over, but you can at least get your Now name." Pause. "If you decide to become a member." Pause. "If waking up and being in the present moment is at all important to you."

Oh, that was a low blow. He was phrasing that exactly the way those activists did when they stood outside of Vons with their clipboards and asked, as you were rushing into the store, "Do you have time for the environment?" So obviously, you couldn't say no, because then you looked like an asshole who didn't have time for the environment. You only had time to buy donuts and a fifth of Jack, and the environment could go fuck itself. Obviously, that's what you meant.

I looked at my watch. "Why is the meeting over? It started at ten, didn't it?"

Boom looked down at his own watch. "It's eleven. Your watch must be slow." Pause. "Or maybe it stopped."

I looked at my watch again. I put it up to my ear. It had, indeed, stopped ticking.

"You're right! Crap. I'm sorry. I set my alarm for eight. I have no idea what happened. How could all my clocks be wrong?"

Boom shrugged. "I think this is perfect," he informed me. "It definitely shows you that you're not in tune with the moment, doesn't it?"

I thought about that for a minute. I had to admit he was right, but I wasn't going to tell him that. He was already getting on my nerves, vibrating with cultish energy. Boom stood aside with his arm out, waiting for me to go in. What was the point of going in now, if I'd missed the meeting? Boom didn't look like he put up with much nonsense, so there was no way I could stall. "Do you know your leader kissed my neck once," I wanted to tell him, "very inappropriately, many years ago?" I was thinking someone who had done that maybe didn't have all the answers and couldn't give me very good advice about what step to take next in this alien situation. But for some reason, regardless of my doubts, I always ended up back here.

We entered the room, and instead of the crowd of twenty or thirty I had expected, there were only four other people. And one of them was Riot. I brightened when I saw her and raised my hand. Riot smiled back and waved gaily. The room was a medium-sized conference room, but instead of a table with office chairs around it, there were only big, fluffy-looking chairs arranged in a circle in the middle of the room. The walls were painted a cheerful bright yellow. The chairs were also yellow. Four of the chairs were empty. The other three were occupied by the people I had pictured in Denial 101 weeks ago. There was an older man dressed conservatively in a very nice suit who had probably taken a wrong turn somewhere and was actually supposed to be at the Hyatt Dental Convention. He was beside a tough-looking hipster girl with darkly outlined eyes and elaborate jewelry on every part of her body. Last was a frumpy, middle-aged woman who was either a librarian or a stripper. It was always either-or with those types.

"Okay," said Boom. "Now we're all here."

"We're all here now," Riot echoed.

I sat on the fluffy yellow chair. Immediately, its sponge-like interior absorbed me like a starving amoeba.

"Better late than never!" Riot added. "Rae, please meet Henry, Laura, and Isobel." She pointed to the frumpy woman last. Isobel. Yep. Definitely a stripper. "I had a very wonderful conversation with your godson the other day about robots. Robots were the theme of our meeting today."

"Why?"

Riot threw her head back and laughed, while Boom chuckled deep in his throat. I glanced at the other three to see if they were laughing. Henry looked wary, Laura looked angry, and Isobel looked uneasy.

"Well, perhaps one of our new seekers can summarize why robots were our theme."

"Wait a minute. Wait. You really used robots for a theme because of Ganymede? I can't wait to tell him. He'll be thrilled."

"I know, I know!" Riot enthused. She *was* aptly named. "Laura… go."

Laura looked startled and tried to pull herself up higher in the soft chair but failed. "Um…because robots are automatic, and we don't want to be automatic anymore."

"Very good!" Boom boomed, and everyone jumped. "Automatic. You know that song, *Automatic For the People?* No, no, we don't want people to be automatic. *We* don't want to be automatic."

"That was the album name, not the name of a song," Laura informed Boom.

"And robots are programmed. We want to get rid of programming," Riot continued.

"And I don't think that's what the song meant either," Laura advised her.

Riot smiled benignly at Laura then turned to me. "We hold on to the past. We anticipate the future. We are never in the Now." Riot gazed at me for several seconds past what was considered comfortable anywhere in the world. Someone cleared their throat. "What are you holding on to that keeps you from being in the Now, Rae?" She waited. Everyone looked at me.

"Am I supposed to say it out loud or just think it?"

"Well, out loud, of course! There are no secrets here!"

A laundry list of reasons why I wasn't in the Now crowded my head, all clamoring to be heard. There was no way I was going to tell these people about Red Harris, and the pap smear-induced tetanus shot was TMI. The shark was too personal. Any mention of aliens and/or my new suspicion that there may be other beings like, say, vampires and fairies, would just get me exasperated looks. Ah. I had the perfect story.

"Well, when I was a child, my sister pushed me into the pool, and I drowned. I just found this out recently. Nobody ever told me that I had actually died. They just said I fell into the pool. They kept it secret for years. Then I found out not only was I dead, but for fifteen minutes, which is, I think, more or less impossible. I definitely can't stop thinking about that."

"They must have gotten their facts confused," Henry said, fiddling with his tie. "That *is* impossible."

"I know, right?" I shrugged.

"Why did your sister push you into the pool?" asked Laura.

"I don't know. She says it was an accident."

"Yeah, right," Laura scoffed.

"Did you have any learning disabilities when you were growing up?" Henry asked.

I wondered if he was a doctor.

"Not especially."

"I thought you looked familiar," Isobel interjected. "You're Rae Miller from *Sand in Your Face!*" It made sense that she was the one who'd noticed. She was the target audience, after all. Peripherally, I saw her and Laura now stealing glances at my left hand.

"Yeah, but seriously, no problems reading, writing? Trouble with backward and forward, right and left, opposite things?" Henry persisted, studying me. I didn't blame him. I didn't see how it was possible either.

"People, people," Boom said, clapping his hands. "We have all sorts of celebrities here, big and small, who realize that fame and fortune are insignificant compared to being in the moment."

"It's impossible to be in the moment all the time," Laura said angrily to no one in particular. "Your attention is always pulled away by something."

"That is correct, young woman," said Boom. "And that is why your Now name is Attention!"

"Come again?" said Laura.

"Attention! That is your Now name."

"Attention? Attention? That's stupid!"

"Your Now name is a dramatic word that," Riot slapped her hands together like cymbals, "is aimed at getting your attention and the attention of those around you. It states a key element of your personality. It *wakes* you up."

Suddenly music assaulted our ears. *Why Can't We Be Friends* blasted into the room over speakers mounted in the ceiling. Everyone jumped and froze, gripping their armrests. We listened as the chorus asked four times why we couldn't be friends. Then it abruptly stopped.

Riot and Boom beamed at us, mentally assigning special gold stars to those whose pupils had dilated to dime size or whose hair had just turned completely white.

"A little wake-up juice! Drink it down, everybody!" Riot sang out.

I winced internally and saw Henry's eyes narrow slightly. Poor choice of words. Henry wasn't going for the Kool-Aid. Henry wasn't going to get caught on a runway in the middle of nowhere and get mowed down while he was trying to get back on a plane out of crazy town.

"I work for a microbrewery," Isobel announced, totally surprising me. I had been completely wrong! Unless she was lying. "Maybe my name could be Beer."

"You expressed issues concerning men earlier," Riot said. "Your Now name underlines a key factor in the development of your relationships. Your name is Jilted."

"Ha ha! That's worse than mine," said Attention.

"And you, Henry," stated Boom, "will be Impotent, because of your personal issues."

"No, it won't." Henry stood up. "What personal issues? I'm not impotent."

"But you are. You said you feel powerless in the board room to change anything," said Riot.

"A faceless cog in the corporate wheel," Boom joined in.

Henry thrust his hands into his pockets. "Yeah. Come up with something else."

"You really should accept the name once it's given. They come to us instinctively and organically out of previous conversations."

"Instinctively and organically come up with something else."

"Impotent, listen—"

Henry turned and headed for the door.

"Excuse me—excuse me—Impotent. Don't go. You are in the past already. You have slipped out of the Now."

Henry put his hand on the doorknob and opened the door. He smoothed his tie down. "I only came here because my wife asked me to. She wanted me to do some meditation to deal with my stress. You people tripled my stress. You people have your heads up your asses."

"The self-realization center up the street focuses on meditation more than we do," Riot offered cheerfully.

Henry left and slammed the door.

Boom and Riot immediately turned back to us and smiled.

"That's what this meeting is all about," Riot told us, "finding out if you belong here."

"Rae, we will call you Tsunami. The unexpected power of the sea is your Now name."

"Thank you."

"Is that because she drowned?" asked Attention, smirking.

"I guess everyone can call me Sue for short," I said. Two beats. Then Riot, Attention, and Jilted burst into laughter. Boom remained stern, an island of male reason surrounded by the swirling eddies of female whimsicality.

"Bob would like to see you after the meeting, which has now concluded," said Boom, looking at me.

"Bob? Bob who, the director?" asked Jilted. She looked impressed. Everyone fought their way out of the big yellow chairs and eventually managed to stand up.

"I'll take you," Riot said cheerfully.

"Were there donuts and coffee here today?" I glanced around. "I didn't have breakfast."

"Yes, but they were all consumed." Riot half-turned and indicated a tiny table against the wall that I hadn't noticed before. It was empty except for a few scattered napkins and donut crumbs. "I'm so sorry. I have an energy bar in my purse that I'd be delighted to give you."

"That's okay."

"It's no problem. It's my pleasure."

"Is there any coffee left?"

"I would be honored to make some for you."

"Oh, don't bother."

"It's no bother."

"You don't—okay."

We all filed out of the room. Boom began ushering Attention and Jilted toward the front door like their insurance had just run out, and they weren't welcome there a second longer.

"Thank you for coming. The next beginner's meeting is a week from now, same time. We hope to see you then." Boom whipped around and pointed at the deserted Sequoia tree desk. "Where's Infidel? Isn't she supposed to be manning the front today?"

"Good luck with the show," Jilted murmured, voce sotto. "We're all pulling for you."

"Thank you. I appreciate that."

"Could you sign this for my mom?" Attention asked, holding out what looked like one of the napkins from the empty donut table. It was crumpled and dotted with crumbs. I fumbled around in my purse for a pen.

"To Carolyn," said Attention.

"Sorry, I can't find a pen."

"What?" She sighed and frowned. "Jesus Christ, your purse is big enough. I can't believe you don't have a pen in there."

"I know. I could fit a severed head in here."

Attention snorted. I couldn't stop thinking of them as their Now names. I had already forgotten their real names.

"Hey, you should have kicked Moeyner's ass at the Arclight."

"Yeah, so I've been told." I'd finally gotten around to viewing the YouTube clip of Moeyner and I about to throw down in the upstairs lounge. The sequence had been titled: Former Housemate to Krumping Champion: "Who're you calling high yella, bitch?"

At least it had been accurate.

Behind us, Boom was pawing through what looked like a schedule roster as Riot got on the intercom and said, "Infidel, report to the front desk. Infidel to the front desk."

She clicked off the intercom and turned to me. "Come this way, Tsunami. Bob's in his office."

But Bob was not in his office. He was walking down the hallway toward us wearing his white karate outfit. He flashed a big smile when he saw me and held out his arms. Oh, Jesus. Was it going to be like this every time? Riot delivered me into his embrace.

"Rae, Rae, you came, you came."

"Yes. Yes." I found myself matching his cadence.

"By the way, Mr. Smith, Rae is now Tsunami," Riot informed him. "Let me go get that coffee going," she added cheerfully.

"How *are* you?" He pulled back and held me at arm's length as if we hadn't seen each other a few days ago. He was acting as if a hundred years had somehow passed.

"I don't know. Okay. Confused."

"Confused? No, no! We can't have that. Come, Tsunami, come with me." He turned me around and hooked an arm over my shoulder.

"Let's walk and talk. Tell me what's going on. What's on your mind." We pushed through a side door and entered the yard. The grass was nicely manicured, and stone benches randomly dotted the area. "You were talking about hallucinations the last time you were here."

A black cat appeared out of nowhere and wound its way through Bob's shins. Bob stumbled and almost fell. I grabbed him by the arm to steady him.

"GET OUT!" he yelled and kicked at the cat. The cat jumped straight up and then galloped away. "That's Blackie. He's a pain in the ass. You're A PAIN IN THE ASS!" he yelled after the cat. Blackie didn't respond, nor did he return.

"Um…Bob, I don't think they're hallucinations." This was good. This was what I had come for. Someone was actually listening to me, hearing my crazy story. "I think it was real. It was really happening." I would leave it at the ZRs, as Ganymede called them. No need to bring up anything else, of which I had no evidence, just a paranoid suspicion. No need to compound Bob's misgivings. I knew he must have some.

Bob strolled quietly beside me, his arm still around my shoulders. He gently removed it and pushed his hands into some invisible pockets in his karate pants.

"Hmm…" he said.

"I can't tell anyone about it. That's why I'm here. I'm going crazy, you know? I mean…it's happened three times now. What the hell's going on? I'm to the point where I think I need to tell someone else. Not just you. But someone who could…help somehow. The government? The military?"

It was beautiful in the yard. Up ahead, I could see the land had been cleared out for many acres, and they were actually growing something out there. Bob saw me staring and followed my gaze.

"Ah, yes, the corn. We harvest corn here. For ethanol. Alternate fuel source."

"Wow. No way."

"Yes way." He rubbed his beard thoughtfully. "It helps to subsidize costs here. And everyone joins in. It's a group effort."

I looked down at my feet. Blackie had reappeared and was gazing up at me wistfully from behind a rock. He definitely had the look of a child that wanted to be picked up, but Bob's presence was destroying that dream before it could happen. Blackie opened his mouth and made a silent meow. Then he turned around and disappeared into the foliage.

We stood side by side and surveyed the rows and rows of corn.

"Is this good soil for corn? It doesn't seem like—"

"It wasn't great at first. We made it good soil." Bob seemed pensive. He waved his hand. "And we had to dig away at the hill. This isn't a naturally flat area, you know."

"I know. Not somewhere one would think of growing corn."

We stopped talking for a moment and just listened to the wind.

"One more thing, Bob," I said after a while.

"Hmm? Yes?"

"I think I brought it up last time. This thing about the souls. Something they're doing with our souls. I don't know what. But… it isn't good."

"Where did you hear that?"

I certainly wasn't going to tell him that a ten-year-old was my source.

I shrugged evasively, the way Woodward and Bernstein must have often done in their heyday, and said, "Around." The rows and rows of corn were making me dizzy. Their leaves rustled softly in the breeze. I imagined Riot and Boom, Attention, Jilted and even Impotent, returned, desperate for some peace, swallowing his pride and accepting his name, all out in the rows, harvesting tons of corn to make about a half-gallon of ethanol.

"Rae—Tsunami, I believe you. You were right to come here. We will help you figure this out. We will give you peace of mind. It's going to be all right. Trust me."

Bob moved toward me and pulled me into another embrace. He pressed his hand onto the back of my neck. Something pinched and burned there briefly. His big clumsy hand must have pulled a hair out. "Trust me," he repeated softly at my ear. And then: "I understand more than you know."

All the short hairs on my arms shot upward. I made to pull away so I could see his face but his arms tightened slightly. *What? What the hell had he just said?* Then my attention was effectively shunted aside as I felt his head shifting, moving down, as if he was going to kiss my neck—again! I pulled away, and he snapped his head up guiltily, like a kid caught at the cookie jar. He smiled lazily and rubbed my arm. I took two steps back from him. The wind continued to rustle the dry corn leaves. Sometimes, it really was okay not being 20 years old anymore, 'cause it got tiring being a dumbass. I'd let things slip back then, but not now. If I'd been vacillating at all, Bob had just sealed the no-trust deal with the double whammy of cryptic messages and adulterous intentions. It had helped to unburden myself a little, but not much. I shouldn't be here.

"Are you in the Now," Bob asked quietly, searching my face, "or somewhere else?"

At that moment, Blackie came racing from out of the cornfield, his fur standing straight up, his tail a fuzzy rigid banner. He blew past us without saying hello and headed for the building where he rounded a corner and vanished. Bob and I looked at each other then stared in the direction Blackie had come from. The rows and rows of corn leaves moved in the breeze, rustling, scraping. It was all very green and shadowy and endless out there. Not so great as an alternate fuel source. At least not here, in the—what were they—the Palisades Mountains, the Temescal Mountains? But it was really great as the perfect hiding place.

CHAPTER 19

It took a couple of days to get the taste of Now out of my mouth. In honor of Jilted, I primarily accomplished this by consuming vast amounts of beer. I laid off the hard stuff and just went for light doses of inebriation. Minor yet continuous intoxication also aided in making the baking sessions more entertaining. Mrs. Dadalian and I had, in the past week or so, wordlessly entered into an ongoing baking competition wherein she would concoct something delicious, deliver it to my door, and then I would try to one-up her with something of my own. I couldn't tell if Mrs. D. kept baking in order to keep up with each delicious food item I created or to, without saying it out loud, encourage me to keep trying. I could picture them at home after I'd delivered one of my desserts:

Mr. Dadalian: Do we even taste this time?

Mrs. Dadalian: We have run out of Pepto-Bismol.

Mr. Dadalian: I will put in trash.

Mrs. Dadalian: It is shame, but emergency room is always so crowded this time of night. Dis time, we cannot take de chance.

Like liquor, baking was a temporary analgesic that made everything seem better. Smell better. Now had become like so many other things in my life that I'd as soon forget, a decision that had seemed like a good idea at the time but had turned out to be not only not a good idea but one of the worst ever in the history of the world. And the more I thought about Bob's enigmatic statement about understanding more than I knew, the angrier I got. But baking made the bad part smell like butter and sugar and slightly burnt flour, which was bearable. Ganymede, emailing me every now and then with photo attachments updating his robot's progress, made me feel even worse, reminding me that I had exposed him to that cultish environment. I hadn't really believed, until we'd walked in there, that it was that bad. Impotent had had the right idea. I just hope that Attention and Jilted would be able to cleanly extricate themselves.

After a few days of staying holed up at my place, I convinced myself everything was okay. Giancarlo had called, wanting to go out again. He was out of town for several days and would firm it up once he got back. Conversely, Rex had called, casually inquiring about my packing progress. I told him I had made some headway but had been hampered by Ganymede's visit. He said he'd be by in a few days to pick me up and we should go surfing. He had checked the wave height forecast for the rest of the week on Surfline.com, and it was supposed to be a mouth-watering feast of dizzying, backbreaking sets. I wanly agreed, even though I hadn't been surfing in about six years. I hoped something would distract him before then. Fibroids really had no place in a wet suit.

A few days went by, and I got my wish. But not in the way I would have hoped or imagined. It was one of those rare rainy days, not only drizzling and cold but blustery. Wuthering Heights blustery. I didn't have to go anywhere, and I was glad. People would be freaked out, driving either 25-miles-per-hour or 100-miles-per-hour, unable to identify the flying wet stuff that was dropping out of the sky. The fact that the sun was gone and the view through their windshields was inexplicably obscured was on level with Orson Welles's 1938 *War of the Worlds* radio broadcast: the stuff of terror. I was multitasking—cooling some muffins, scanning an email from Ganymede, and in the middle of almost solving the mystery of how my past credits could be applied at UCLA when my cell phone rang.

Ganymede's email read: Nutmeg is dangerously poisonous when injected into your veins.

Affectionately, I made note of this.

I answered the phone.

"You will not believe what I just saw," said Rex.

"What?"

"What are you doing?"

"Um…baking and reading emails." I didn't add *from my ten-year-old boyfriend.*

"I'll pick you up," he said, ignoring me. Screw my baking. Screw my emails. "I'll be there in ten minutes."

"Are you in a Lear Jet?"

"I'm on your side. I had to drop off some boards in Granada Hills."

I wasn't going anywhere in this horrible weather unless he was in his Ram. "You're in the Ram, right?" If he'd had to drop off surfboards somewhere himself, he'd probably driven his giant Ram 3500.

"Yes. Very perceptive. Maybe because surfboards wouldn't fit in a Miata."

"They'd fit. If you really shoved."

"I couldn't get half a surfboard in my Miata."

I threw up my mental hands. "Call me when you're downstairs." Driving in the Ram was like driving in a tank. If one of the disoriented motorists out there smashed into us, we'd probably think we'd driven over a pothole or maimed a squirrel.

When Rex called fifteen minutes later, I left my apartment, pausing to place a Tupperware container of the hot muffins with pecans outside the Dadalians' door, and headed downstairs. Outside, I battled my way across the yard against the wind and started to pull myself arduously up into the passenger seat of Rex's giant black 3500. He leaned across from his side and grabbed me by my shoulder and hoisted me steadily inside, like a winch.

"Thanks."

"You got it." Rex was sporting a pair of mirrored wraparound sunglasses. As usual, he was sucking on a cigarette. He had tried to quit several times but had given up in the past couple of years. I would imagine that gambling for millions and millions of dollars for a living would make smoking something of a prerequisite, and it was amazing that anyone could muscle through those games without being able to partake. Rex had informed me that nicotine gum was a big buy item during tournaments. I bet the sellers probably charged $300 a pack the way 7-Eleven had spiked water prices during the

1994 Northridge earthquake. Yes, I still remembered that and, yes, I still held a grudge.

"So what's the big mystery? What did you see?"

Whatever it was, it couldn't be *that* amazing. Unless he'd spotted the Loch Ness Monster in Santa Monica Bay, I wasn't going to be impressed.

"Let me ask you something. What rock have you been living under?"

"What? Rock?"

Rex glanced sideways at me. "Exactly. I can't explain. Let's just go there."

"Okay, fine. Sheesh."

"Hey, what was it your sister said the other night?" Rex asked out of left field. "'Unhand me'?"

"Well, yeah, but what do you expect? Look at her name."

"Are you guys time travelers? Is that why you're so strange?" He beat lightly on the steering wheel in time with the radio.

"Why am *I* strange now? I didn't say 'unhand me.'"

"I want to see the time machine when I drop you off later."

"Okay, sure. Why don't we put you in it and send you back to the Black Plague?"

"Awwww."

"Is that a bubo in your groin, or are you just happy to see me?" I pulled Virginia out of my purse and lit up. Rex was making me crazy already.

"Just happy to see you, baby." He paused. Then, "How's the packing going? And if you don't say you're ready to go, I'm rescinding the offer."

"That wasn't a question."

"Part of it was a question."

He stared straight ahead, his forearm laying over the steering wheel. He craned his head around and changed lanes and didn't bother putting his signal on. I didn't want to get into the "moving in" conversation right now. I was extremely grateful to Rex, but part of me still mourned the loss of my Hermosa Beach dream home. And I felt like somehow I deserved to live in my present circumstances because I hadn't fought back hard enough against the Machiavellian yoga "master" and his spineless cronies.

"We have to have a talk, you and me, one day," Rex cryptically. "I think we have to get some things straight."

"Oh, my God, *what*?" I gaped at him. Traffic slowed to an abrupt halt, and we were buried in a sea of brake lights. Rex slammed his hand on the wheel, powered his window down two inches, and flicked his cigarette out onto the street.

"What the fuck?" he said angrily.

"That is a huge fine if a cop saw you, you know." Since I was in the car with him, I didn't want to jinx him.

After all, Osiris was *my* secret father, not Rex's.

Osiris: I do not know why she is so attached to that gaming hooligan.

Attendant: What would you have me do, sir?

Osiris: Summon the officers. Have him executed.

The traffic lightened up, and we were moving again. Rex fiddled with the radio. Suddenly, weirdly, "Why Can't We Be Friends" was booming into the car, and he cranked it up. I listened intently to the lyrics.

"What does that mean?" I raised my voice over the music. "He called her, but she couldn't look around? Is she wearing a neck brace? Is she being held hostage? Why can't she look around?" I was trying to lighten the mood. Rex drove at least half a mile without saying anything.

Finally: "Maybe he fucked her over."

I chortled and stubbed my Virginia Slim out in the ashtray. *Fucked her over?* I stared at Rex's profile but could discern nothing from it, especially with those wraparound glasses on that vaguely resembled the eyes of my new nemeses: the Zetas. They looked like big-headed praying mantises. They looked like bugs that walked on two feet. I shuddered slightly and looked away. Rex continued to be silent. If I didn't know any better, I'd think he was brooding. I could never tell—poker face and all that. I thought of topics I could bring up, one after the other: Margarite hating her clients. Hama destroying Gamymede's muscle fibers. Mr. Motel and my Now name. My date with Giancarlo.

I could hear his responses now: Margarite's having a midlife crisis. Hama's on steroids. Now is a cult, and Bob is Jim Jones. I'm surprised you're dating at all, after Johnny dumped you.

Instead, I said, "I'm not procrastinating about moving in." Lie. "Well, I am procrastinating, but not because I don't want to move in."

Rex silently turned his sunglasses toward me. I shuddered.

Bugs.

"It's just that a lot of weird shit's been going on lately." That seemed so lame. I looked down at my hands. "I'm just trying to deal."

"Really?" He looked forward again. "What kind of weird shit?" Then, abruptly, "Oh, we're here."

We pulled up outside of a Barnes & Noble in the West Hills. The rain pummeled us as we hurried into the store. We jostled by a line of a people that was snaking around the aisles and disappeared into the distance.

"Oh. Must be a book signing," I observed brightly. I looked at Rex who was shoving his sunglasses to the top of his head. He smirked.

"You didn't see the gigantic banner outside, did you?"

I sighed. "I didn't see anything. I'm not attuned to whatever has your attention."

He grabbed me by the hand and pulled me along the line of waiting people.

"I want to go to Outback and get a huge cheeseburger after this," he stated.

"Um…"

"Trust me. You're going to need the protein."

"God. Fine. What is it? What's going on? *Show me!*"

It had better be Jesus Christ standing there, or even Jimmy Hoffa, otherwise I was going to be pissed.

"Look," he said.

And there it was. Just like I'd been saying.

More weird shit.

Ahead of me, the line ended, and sitting at a table signing books was someone who looked a lot like Johnny. There was a huge poster set up beside him featuring a blown-up shot of his serious face gazing out with thoughtful determination. It was Johnny. A mixed bag of memories came flooding back as I stared at Johnny's black hair and sun-baked, watered-down Latino complexion. He had never been clear which side of his family the Mexican roots had come from. He never wanted to talk about it. Beneath the photo was the blurb, "The tale of a bewitched love gone wrong." Beneath that was the title of the book he'd written: *Supernatural Bullies: A Stuntman's Freefall into the World of Magic*. Below that, in the corner, was an image of something that looked like a cross between a gremlin and a chupacabra in a circle with a line going through it.

I looked at Rex.

Rex looked back and shrugged.

"Just thought you should know," he said. He turned to go. "Ready for that cheeseburger?"

"I'm going up there."

Rex stopped. "Say what now?"

"I'm going up there."

"Um…"

I started walking toward the table. A representative of the bookstore intercepted me while a few people called out, "Hey!" and "The line's here, lady!"

"I'm sorry, ma'am," said the store clerk. She was tiny and dressed in a smart pantsuit. "You can't approach the author."

"I know the author. We were engaged."

"Okay. But are you still engaged?"

"No. But he was a stunt double in *Green Splendor I*."

The clerk paused. "No kidding? Wow. *Green Splendor I*?"

"Yeah."

"What is that, a movie?"

Behind me, Rex snorted laughter.

"Who's talking about *Green Splendor*?" Johnny called out from the table, his pen hovering above an open book. He glanced toward us quickly, then did a comical double take. His eyes widened. He shoved the book, unsigned, toward the woman standing there and stood up. "Holy crap! Rae!" He spotted Rex behind me. "Oh, my God, Rex!" His mouth dropped open. "Da foe Defoe! I saw that clip, man!" I figured Johnny was referring to the now-famous clip of Rex coolly calling someone's bluff while a fistfight broke out around him.

Johnny waved us over. "Come here, you guys!"

The store clerk, who had been blocking my path, grudgingly stepped aside and let us pass. People in line gazed after us jealously and murmured amongst themselves. Up at the table, Johnny leaned forward awkwardly and gripped me by my shoulders. "I can't believe it!" He shook me a little. Still holding on, he lifted his head and addressed his fans. "This is my muse, everyone! This is the muse that started everything!" He was talking loudly. No more the soft talker was he, evidently.

The crowd murmured louder, excitement gathering. Outside, a loud clap of thunder rent the air.

"Started what?" I asked. I was stunned.

Johnny released me and waved me around. "Come back here. Come back while I sign." He thrust his hand out absently for the next person's copy. I threw Rex a glance before I sidled around to the back of the table. Rex narrowed his eyes in disbelief. I shrugged, just as confused as he was.

"Oh, Mr. Soto," said a young woman wearing a tight sweater and granny glasses, "I wanted to—"

"Holy shit! This is amazing!" said Johnny, ignoring the woman completely while he signed her book with a flourish. He snapped it shut and held his hand out for the next person.

"What's this about?" I gestured to the poster. "Supernatural bullies? Is this a fantasy novel?"

"No, Rae, it's not a fantasy. It's about us."

I stood still. I think I stopped breathing. I glanced over at Rex again where he leaned against a wooden pillar, his arms crossed.

"It's the reason why we broke up. Or I broke up with you. Because of this. This situation that happened. Nobody believed me. But my brother…" he said, signing another book, "convinced me to write my story. And it took off."

There was something even more amazing than the fact that Johnny had written a book. I was right. *I was right. It hadn't been my fault!*

"Could you make this out to—" began a man wearing a suit and tie.

"I had no idea," said Johnny, cutting him off and scribbling his name, "how big it was gonna be."

The man took his copy back, frowning slightly, and left.

"They're gonna make a movie of it." He grinned. "It's already green lit. Cameron's attached. So is Brad Pitt."

"Brad Pitt?" I guess there was no point in addressing the fact that Brad Pitt wasn't Mexican.

The next person in line, a middle-aged woman, looked at me appraisingly. "You're on that show, *Midlife Crisis,* aren't you?"

Johnny chortled. He apparently was well aware of *Sand in Your Face..*

"No."

If she couldn't get the title right, I wasn't going to say I was on it.

"Would you sign my copy, too? Since you're his muse?"

"Um…"

Johnny laughed again. "Go ahead, Rae! Why not?" He was in the middle of laughing gaily, enjoying his moment in the spotlight, enjoying his generosity, when something caught his eye. The change in his face was instantaneous. He shot to his feet, his pupils dilating. Rex and the store clerk and everyone in line turned to see what he was looking at. There was a man standing across the store, leaning against a pillar like Rex, arms crossed, staring at us. There was nothing special about him. He was average looking, dirty blond, scruffy. Everyone turned back toward Johnny just as he grabbed me by my upper arm and yanked me against him.

"Who is it? Brad Pitt?" someone asked in confusion.

Whatever remnants of washed-out South American pigment remained in Johnny's skin drained silently away as he turned bone-white and started shaking. He clenched my arms and began to back up slowly, taking me with him. I watched as Rex approached.

"Johnny," he said, "let go of Rae."

He came around to the back of the table.

The store clerk joined us. "Sir, I have to ask you to step back."

"Johnny, let go of Rae," said Rex, oblivious to the clerk.

"It's *him!*" Johnny trembled. He was standing half behind me, his fingers digging into both my arms, claw-like. The fans in line shuffled around, a commotion growing as the thunder boomed outside.

Rex grabbed Johnny's wrists.

"Mr. Soto!" The store clerk said, switching her attention to Johnny, "Let go—" Briefly, she gripped one of Johnny's wrists along with Rex, but pulling yielded no results. "SECURITY!" she screamed.

"BULLY!" someone in the crowd yelled, and the line surged forward, unchecked.

"NO!" yelled the clerk, "EVERYONE REMAIN CALM!"

The crowd plunged toward the table. Rex ripped Johnny's hands off me, and I stumbled away sideways. The tiny clerk clung to Rex as the fans surged around them. Their sheer boiling numbers dislodged her, and she disappeared beneath the surface. Johnny, his face twisted with terror, hurled a book toward where the blond man had been standing. It sailed past Rex and slammed into a woman's chest. The woman grabbed her breasts with both hands and shrieked. The blond man, in the meantime, was gone. Rex seized me by my shark hand and yanked me with him back around the table.

"BULLY!" someone yelled, while someone else screamed, "TERRORIST!"

"Oh, my God!" a woman said. We both glanced backwards to find Johnny scrambling onto the signing table. Next, he launched himself off it straight at Rex.

"Oh, fuck me," Rex breathed, incredulous.

Johnny plummeted down, spread-eagle. They crashed to the carpet. An errant leg knocked me sideways. Rex's sunglasses somersaulted through the air. Every woman in the room screamed. Johnny and Rex rolled around on the carpeted floor, grunting and grappling.

"NOT AGAIN," Johnny bellowed, "NOT AGAIN! I WILL KILL YOUR SUPERNATURAL ASS!" As I stared in horror, something bizarre happened. Something *more* bizarre. Clearly superimposed over Rex's face was the face of the blond man from earlier, and from the adrenaline-fueled terror in Johnny's expression, I knew that that was what he was reacting to. I quickly glanced around. No one else seemed to see it. Rex, displaying great restraint, managed to shove Johnny off him just before security arrived. Both quickly gained their feet.

"COME GET IT, MOTHERFUCKER. GET SOME MAGIC, COCKSUCKER!" Johnny roared. Women gasped and covered their children's ears. Johnny swung. Rex leaned back. Johnny's momentum spun him around, straight into a pyramid display of books. He pitched face forward. The books torpedoed off the table amid gasps and shouts from the crowd. A tangle of fans grasped at Rex, clawing blindly. I lunged sideways, shoving at random bodies. Two security guards sprinted forward, elbowed the throngs aside, and helped Johnny up off the floor. The store clerk had resurfaced, unharmed. She gazed stonily up at Rex, as if this was all his fault.

"Sir," she said panting, "I'm going to have to ask you to leave." She turned to me next. "And you, ma'am."

"You don't have to ask," said Rex, breathing hard. He half-turned and grabbed my shark hand again. We started fast-walking toward the exit. The crowd, gaping, parted reluctantly to let us through. Cell phones thrust into the air, busily snapping pictures and taking video.

I heard Johnny saying behind us, "IT WAS HIM. IT WAS HIM. MOTHERFUCKER. FUCKING CHEATING ASSHOLE GOBLIN!"

"Who?" said one of the men. "The tall guy?"

"IT WAS HIM. OH, MY GOD. HE WAS HERE."

"The tall guy? Who?" In a panic, the guard spoke into his walkie-talkie. "Stop the tall guy at the door. Do not let the tall guy out."

"No," the store clerk said. "There was somebody else. Let the tall guy go. Let him go."

"Cancel that. Let the tall guy go. Do not detain the tall guy."

"Find a blond guy. He's in the store somewhere."

"New orders. Blond guy. Look for a blond guy."

Radio static. Then a voice, annoyed, "What blond guy? More *specific*, please?"

Rex and I reached the front door. Nobody was there. Nobody tried to stop us. We stepped outside into the pouring rain. Rex half-shoved me ahead of him, and we made a break for his truck. The thunder rumbled, and lightning flashed. We sat in the Ram, panting a little, not saying a word, for at least five minutes. I knew what was on his mind before he said it because of the grin on his face.

"Don't say it."

Rex stared ahead. He held it in for quite a few minutes.

Then: "You were gonna *marry* that guy?"

"Shut it. I will kill you."

"Kill *me*?" He looked out the windshield in amazement. "What just happened?" He looked back at me.

"I don't—"

"Wait. Wait, wait, wait."

"I—"

"Hold on—wait, wait." Rex held a hand up and then squinted, thinking. "He didn't see me, Rae. His eyes were glazed. He was *out* of it."

Something was slowly starting to occur to me.

That guy staring from across the store had looked like those guys that were always following me around, those random men gazing at me everywhere in town. For some reason, one of them was, or had been, stalking Johnny too. And it was magic. So, that meant only one thing. It was Them again—the ZRs. Oh, my God, they'd been in my life much longer than I'd even imagined. And they terrorized Johnny. They had it in for Johnny. So much so, *Johnny had turned into a writer.* Johnny, who was not only *not* a reader or writer but an anti-reader and writer. Similar to antimatter. He had the same mass as particles of ordinary readers and writers but with an opposite charge and quantum spin.

Reflexively, Rex patted the top of his head and realized his glasses were gone. "Shit," he said.

"Want me to go back in and get them?"

I felt guilty because I could have just turned around instead of approaching the table. Had I turned around and just left? No. I had not. But I'd found out important information. *Those beings had been stalking me for a long time. They had been intervening in my life. They had screwed up parts of my life. Why?*

"Uh…I wouldn't suggest that. No, sweetheart."

"I'll get you some new ones."

"They weren't from CVS; they were Oakleys."

"I can afford Oakleys."

"No, you can't. You're unemployed."

"I'm not broke."

"You will be. Soon."

"Sorry. I had no idea Johnny was gonna jump off a table in Barnes & Noble and try to kick your ass."

Rex started the Ram and put it into gear. "Yeah, *try* being the operative word. Guy's certifiable," he said, pulling out into traffic. "You're lucky he dumped you."

I said nothing and stared out into the rain.

"You ready for that cheeseburger? I'm ready for that cheeseburger."

Oddly, I was ready for it. Especially if it was made out of vodka, gin, tequila, and rum.

Hold the buns.

CHAPTER 20

There were bruises on my upper arms a few days later, reminding me that all was not well. Rex was behaving strangely, Johnny was an author. I was slowly making a dent in my pile of money. Rex was right. I *would* be broke if I kept going this way. Aliens were everywhere, doing whatever they wanted, appearing as humans. I believe the widely known term was known as "screen memories." The Zetas disguised themselves as all sorts of things—owls, wolves, authority figures, clowns. No wonder some people had an inexplicable terror of clowns. Despite—and because of—all this, I was online again, actually getting ready to sign up for the fall semester at UCLA when Cola called. I had to at least *act* like I was moving forward in my life. I stared for two more beats at the computer then turned it off. It really was beginning to seem like someone was trying to stop me from going back to school. Was my secret father, Osiris, not pleased?

Osiris: I do not want her attending that institution at her age. She will be a laughingstock.

Attendant: (delicately) How…old exactly is she, Lord?

Osiris (shrugging): I do not know. We are not certain. None amongst us are certain.

Osiris (shrugs again): Fifty? Sixty?

Pause.

Attendant: Surely not so old, sir?

Osiris: What know I? She has ceased to utter the number aloud. I have long since forgotten.

Attendant: Then what does it matter, if nobody knows her age?

Osiris (angrily): They will know! The humans sense these things about one another. Especially the *Los Angeles humans*.

Attendant: Yes, sir. I will have her banned from all institutions of higher learning immediately. Truly, you are a great and caring father.

Cola wasted no time, as usual.

"Rae, you're on YouTube again. How did you get banned from Barnes & Noble?"

I opened my mouth and nothing came out.

"Don't worry about it. It's good PR. But you and Rex are going to have to buy books somewhere else for a while."

I minimized the UCLA website and started searching for the YouTube video.

"Okay, listen up. I got an audition for you. "

Online, I watched a shaky cell phone video documenting Johnny's terrified expression as Rex pried his hands off my arms. Next came the mosh pit leap and the ensuing havoc. The title of the video read: "Ex-*Sand in Your Face* actress & poker star "Da Foe" Defoe instigate bookstore riot."

 Slowly, I closed YouTube and said, "Sorry…what?"

"You're looking at YouTube, aren't you?"

"Not anymore."

"Don't look at it, Rae."

"Well, I can't unsee it. It's too late."

"Okay, forget about that for now. I got you an audition. Announcing at surf competitions a few times a year. It might lead to other things."

I listened to Cola for once and pushed Barnes & Noble aside and instantly perked up. Sports announcing? Could lead to other things? That was the reason I had gone into journalism in the first place, to end up announcing for either surfing or gymnastics or both. That would segue into reporting, surf writing, editing a surf magazine, getting in Gymnastics Magazine. Although I had never risen to the level of a Lakey Peterson in surfing or a Gabrielle Douglas in gymnastics, I had competed and won many times, albeit small competitions. But I knew my stuff, although people would probably remember me more for the modeling and movies. I couldn't believe that Cola was calling with an opportunity like this. Frankly, I was speechless.

"Rae?"

"Wow, that's—you caught me off guard." I looked out the window. "What—there's an audition?"

"Just a quickie thing, just to see how your sportscasting chops hold up. How rusty are you? You up for this?"

"Yeah!" I said, enthused. "Are you kidding? Yeah! When is it? When does this happen?"

I could hear the smile in Cola's voice. He was happy, which was rare for Cola.

"Thursday. Two days from now. You even have a little prep time. I'll text you the details later today."

"Okay. I was applying to UCLA when you called. I guess I'll just put that on hold for a moment…"

"You can put it on hold but don't forget it. It would behoove you to finish that degree."

"Behoove me, huh?" I had a big, stupid grin on my face. An announcing gig! "I don't deserve you," I said. "I'm sorry I've been such a deadbeat lately."

"I'm sorry, too." This, delivered dryly, but he definitely was pleased. "Okay, talk to you soon."

"Tally-ho."

I put my phone down on the table and stared at it for a moment, hardly able to believe the turn of events. Was it possible that things were looking up? Was something good about to happen instead of something weird and inexplicable? It felt like a page had turned, the tide had turned. As if to prove me right, seconds later the phone rang again.

It was Giancarlo, back in town, hoping we could go out next week.

"I would like to take you to a showing of *Lawrence of Arabia*," he said.

"Ha ha."

"I have missed you. I have thought of you often."

"Same here," I said. I may have still held a slight grudge for the whole disappearing act, but I had thought of him often, too.

"Chrislann sends his warmest regards. He hopes you are doing well."

"Aw! Thank you. How was your business out of town?" I asked him. "Was it physical therapy related?"

Two beats.

"You could say it was…physical. At the very least. Yes."

Mmm. Mysterious Giancarlo. I let it lay. We penciled ourselves in for next weekend. Giancarlo ended the conversation by saying, "I cannot wait," and then hung up without waiting for a response. Now, that was confidence. But then again, what did one expect from someone who had a house on mythical Toluca Lake? Someone who, for all intents and purposes, may not even be an American citizen?

My eyes settled on the living room and the still-half-packed boxes. If I was going to be a sports announcer, that meant I actually could pack everything up now and move over to Rex's. Not that Rex needed or wanted any money from me, but it was a simple matter of not being 18 anymore. Living with people for free didn't feel the same way it had back then when everybody understood that you were young and still had to get your life together. I was in such a good mood, I started shoving things back into boxes and taping them up with my industrial-sized, giant packing tape. I would call Rex later tonight with the good news. In the meantime, though, after clearing away half the stuff from the living room, I decided on the spur of the moment to go get a couple of cigars for Cola up at Planet Tobacco. I knew he liked Punch Double Coronas and something called a Cabaiguan Guapo, so I'd have to get a couple of each if they were there.

It was getting dark outside as I hopped in the Z and headed over to Glenoaks Boulevard. I rolled the window down, enjoying the almost-balmy 78-degree weather. Whenever I ran into people from the East Coast who had moved out to California, specifically L.A., and who were bitching endlessly about traffic and shallow people and how crowded it was but how separated everyone was at the same time, I always asked them, "If you hate it so much, why do you stay here?"

They always looked at me as if I'd just said, *Do you wear your skin out of convenience or is it just there already every day when you get up?* before they answered, "Because of the weather."

❊ ❊ ❊

I was bent over at Planet Tobacco, surveying the cigars that were way down low in the glass cabinet, when someone came in the shop door behind me.

"Like, God, I know, Mom! But he wasn't even, like, in the top demographic. What do you effing expect?"

The Valley Girl voice, low and throaty, was a stranger's voice but oddly familiar.

"Darling, please don't use the eff word in public," a woman replied, whispering the last part of the sentence. "What did I tell you?"

"God! I didn't, Mom, I said effing! I said effing on purpose. *Purposely*. So we wouldn't be having this conversation. *This* conversation—right now! Pfft! What's the point? Where are the Cohibas?"

"No, no, sweetie, Daddy doesn't smoke Cohibas anymore."

"Not for Daddy. Not for Daddy. For *me*. *Me*. I'm smoking Cohibas now. You get Daddy's stuff. I'm going over there."

I straightened up and turned around and stared at the woman who was now walking away to the other side of the shop. She was wearing sunglasses (at night) and one of those bright dreadlock hats with the pretend dreads hanging out of it. She had on a pair of flowered culottes, flat sandals, and a prim white blouse. I crossed the room and stood behind her. She turned around, suddenly, sensing someone there, and gasped when she saw me. It was Moeyner. How *dare* she gasp? *I* should be the one gasping. We stood staring at one another, aghast.

"Oh…my…Go—" I started.

Moeyner grabbed my hand. "Rae, be quiet! Shh! Oh, my God," she whispered in her throaty Valley Girl voice. "I knew it wasn't a good idea to come in here. I told my mother to go to Compton. I know somebody there. But she refused."

I twisted around and looked at Moeyner's mother, a woman wearing a beautiful black and white sundress with pearls around her neck. I turned back. Moeyner pushed her sunglasses down her nose and regarded me appraisingly. I could practically see her operating an invisible scale in her mind, weighing the odds of getting out of this unscathed.

"How did you win the Krumping Championship?" I said accusingly. "Are you even *from* North Long Beach?"

Moeyner shuddered and rolled her eyes, horrified. "God, no! Are you kidding?" She grabbed me and pulled me over to the corner for more privacy. I didn't know why. There was nobody in the store but us.

"Anybody can join a dance competition, you know. You don't have to be from the 'hood." She continued to grip my arm painfully. "Rae...Rae, you can't say anything. Please."

"I'm not going to say anything. I'm not part of the show anymore."

"Are you saying if you were on the show you would throw me under the bus?"

"Is that the same bus you were rolling backwards and forwards over me at the Arclight?"

Moeyner paused. Her eyes went up to the left, thinking. Had she actually already forgotten?

"Oh, that!" She waved her hand. "I was just acting. I have to play the tough chick."

"For who? To get that stupid little blip on YouTube?"

"Yes!" she hissed. "Yes! Those little blips did a *lot* for our PR, you know!"

"*Our* PR?"

"I saw your little thing in the bookstore. That was crazy, girl! People are talking." Moeyner pushed her sunglasses back up her nose and tossed a fake dreadlock off her shoulder.

"But why put on an act?" I persisted. "Can't you just be yourself?"

Moeyner huffed. "They already had *you*, Rae. I had to be blacker, or they wouldn't have taken me."

"Had to be—wait. What?"

"Oh, come on; don't be naïve! You're not that naïve, are you? Oh, my God! You're a wannabe. Don't you realize that?"

It was so disconcerting hearing words like "naïve" coming out of Moeyner's mouth that I forgot for second or two to be insulted. Then I said, "Wait a minute! I'm not a wannabe. I'm half black! My mother is black!"

"Shh," Moeyner hissed, crouching down a little as if the NBC news van was right outside. "It doesn't matter! You don't really *look* it, and you definitely don't *sound* it. So, in the eyes of everyone concerned, you are *not* it! Get it?"

"But your friends and family know…how do they…how does the truth not get out?"

Moeyner smiled. "Really? Seriously? I mean, my God, everyone in Hollywood knew Rock Hudson was gay except his fans." She peered over my shoulder for a moment. Reassured that the cigar man wasn't tweeting our entire conversation, she said, "Remember when we all found out Spike Lee wasn't from the ghetto but was upper middle class? Does anyone remember that today?" She shrugged. "Everybody's acting," she concluded. She flashed a tense smile over my shoulder as somebody approached us. I turned around and faced Moeyner's mother.

"Mom, remember Rae? From the show?" she said shrilly. "Well, guess who's here buying stogies, too!"

Moeyner sounded like she was about to pop a blood vessel. Her mother already knew what was going on, obviously. Why was she so stressed?

"Oh…hello there," said Moeyner's mother. "I'm Mrs. Clifton." She cocked her head to one side. "I think it's simply terrible what they did to you, honey. I—"

"Come on, Mom, we have to go!"

"Moeyner, I was speaking—"

"I got my period, Mom. We have to go. It's an emergency!" Moeyner stamped her foot and then headed for the door.

"Your per—" Mrs. Clifton placed a hand over her heart. "Good lord!"

"I have a tampon in my purse," I called after Moeyner sweetly. I didn't actually have one. I knew Moeyner wasn't coming back.

"Moe! Moe! Did you hear her? She has a tampon! Rae has a TAMPON!"

"No bathroom," called the cigar man from behind the counter. Even though he didn't speak English very well (I'd been in here several times before), it had only taken him seconds to discern what was going on. He chopped his hands in the air. "No bathroom."

"Oh, dear—all right." Moeyner's mother followed her daughter to the door. "So nice meeting you, Rae. Good luck!"

"Thank you, Mrs. Clifton."

"Moeyner, Moeyner," she called as she exited, "do you have cramps? There's some Midol in the glove compartment."

The cigar guy and I were left alone as the door swung shut. We stared at each other for a beat or two, then he broke out into a wide grin and waved his hand.

"What?" I said.

"What she gonna do, put a tampon in here in middle of floor?" He looked around at all the cigars as if they would answer him or suddenly break out into song. "I have five daughter. Five. This never happen to them. Never."

"What? Using a tampon in public or in a cigar shop?"

He laughed and waved his hand. "Both! Psshhh!" He kept waving his hand. I went ahead and picked out Cola's cigars, my buoyant mood rapidly draining away. Oh, my God! Moeyner was the cause again! I had been happy at the Arclight until she had shown up. I had been happy tonight until she had shown up. And she had shown up tonight as a white girl, practically! She was, in reality, a dyed-in-the-wool Valley Girl, probably born and bred in Woodland Hills or in some sprawling mansion on Laurel Canyon. She had transformed from Malcolm X into Taylor Swift in 5.3 seconds.

The cigar guy didn't have the Cubans I wanted (surprise) but he had the Guapos, so I bought four and got the hell out of there. I walked cautiously to the Z, expecting Moeyner and her mother to come revving out of an alleyway in a BMW with their lights off and mow me down because now I knew their secret. But it was quiet outside, and nobody was around. As I drove back down the boulevard, I saw an old man waiting at the corner to cross Glenoaks. I did a double take; it was Mr. Dadalian. I pulled over, got out, and walked toward him.

"Fancy meeting you here," I said as a greeting. The night was turning stranger with each moment, so I decided to just go with it. Maybe if I didn't fight it, it would go away.

Mr. Dadalian turned. "Ah, Miss Rae. Where you come from?" He peered around as if trying to locate the Stargate I had stepped through.

I pointed to my car down the street.

"I just came from Planet Tobacco."

"Ah, so do I. I just come from there!" Triumphantly, he held up a bag in his right hand. "A couple of cigars, dey last me the whole week. I did not know you smoke cigars."

"Would you like a ride home? I'm going back to the building." It *was* within walking distance from our place to Planet Tobacco, but nothing I had the patience for tonight.

"Ah, yes, that would be fine," he said and began to follow me toward my car.

"Mrs. D. won't be jealous, will she?" I ribbed him.

"Da Missus will be angry dat I not walk," Mr. D. answered sternly, patting his belly. "I'm on diet and exercise."

"Oh…then I guess we'd better just leave you here," I said gaily.

We both laughed and continued down the sidewalk.

"And these aren't for me," I said, holding up my bag. "They're for my agent. He got me an audition."

Mr. Dadalian smiled in the darkness. "I am so happy. I am so happy. He get you something better dan rotten beach show?"

"Yes," I said, smiling back, feeling the satisfaction from earlier returning. Thank *God,* I had bumped into Mr. Dadalian. He loved me now, and his wife and I were BBBs—best baking buds. As we neared the car, Mr. Dadalian clucked his tongue and said, "Oh, I see you did not get rear taillight fixed." Jesus, he had good eyesight! I never would have been able to make out something like that in this low light.

"I tell you I have friend who can fix, gives you good price. Remember?"

I did, in fact, remember that, and made a mental note to take Mr. D. up on his offer. Why not? I didn't know any mechanics personally. As we took a few steps closer, something strange happened. The hair on my arms stood up, and my stomach squeezed tight. Mr. Dadalian was in mid-sentence, still commenting on the car, when the cone of light shot down, encompassing us both. The light felt like nothing, but the paralysis was immediate, as was our ascension toward the sky. I didn't feel my feet as they lost touch with the earth. What a bizarre sensation—almost like flying, what flying would be like—and I couldn't enjoy it. I couldn't move, but I was still thinking, I was conscious. I could see the Z getting further and further away. *Oh God, oh God, oh God.* I hoped Mr. Dadalian wasn't conscious. I hoped it was only me. His heart was aged. What if it just stopped?

The familiar terror from the first time, the time with Annie, came rushing back. It clawed its way inside me, bored down through my pores. I wanted to vomit and felt a scream trapped in my lungs. Cars drove obliviously by beneath us. I heard snatches of radio and laughing voices. As our heads reached the height of the street lamp, two things happened simultaneously: I heard a voice in my head saying *We have the one spoken of. One who sees*—except it wasn't in English, I only heard it in English—and then two distinct blurs, fast-moving figures, swirled around me as if battling for my body. And then abruptly, I was released from the light and plummeting down. I think I screamed. Someone/something grabbed me and slowed my descent. I felt hands on my upper arm, my lower back. I touched down softly, and sat with a soft bump onto my ass. I sensed the other above, wreaking some kind of havoc up there. I heard growling, a shrill shrieking, almost like a whistle, a cacophony of noise.

Then silence. The light was gone. I looked all around. Mr. Dadalian was gone. I looked straight up. The ship, which I hadn't seen, was gone. I craned my head in every direction. The two blurry, impossibly fast moving figures were gone. There was nothing there. I was alone, sitting on the sidewalk on my butt beside my Z. My brain was split between thinking, *poor Mr. Dadalian. Poor, poor, poor Mr. Dadalian* and then the more realistic right-to-the-point question, *God, do those gray motherfuckers have a hard-on for the people in our building or what?*

PART 2

"The optimist proclaims that we live in the best of all possible worlds, and the pessimist fears this is true."

— James Branch Cabell

"How come if alcohol kills millions of brain cells, it never killed the ones that made me want to drink?"

— Author Unknown

CHAPTER 21

I woke up lying on the floor at the foot of my bed. There was an empty bottle of Jack beside my elbow. I didn't know what time it was. I couldn't remember coming into my bedroom at all. My head throbbed, and my neck was kinked up. I heard a distant banging and realized someone was knocking at the front door. *Wait a minute, wait a minute, wait a minute…*

We have the one spoken of. One who sees.

I sat bolt upright, banging my elbow against the bottom of the bed.

"AAAAHHHH!" I screamed and cradled it drunkenly. My head swam, buried under tons of invisible ocean, the pressure overwhelming. Oh, my God, I had the mother of all hangovers. I picked up the empty bottle of Jack, tilted it up onto my tongue, capturing the last few drops. *Hair of the dog…*

At the front door, the knocking continued.

"I'm coming," I called weakly. I struggled to gain my feet. "Coming." A little louder. "HOLD ON," I bellowed, rubbing my elbow and shambling across the floor. I entered the living room, bright with afternoon light. I shrank away from it like a vampire, shielding my sensitive pupils. My stiff neck shrieked from the unexpected movement.

"ARRRGHHH!"

We have the one spoken of. One who sees.

Holy shit times a billion imploding red giants. What the fuck?

I stood, lost in my thoughts, until the banging started again. I ripped open my door just as I realized the knocking was not for me. Yep. Nobody there. Except Mr. Dadalian, about to enter his apartment. He turned around, his eyes widened slightly, and he faced his door again.

"Mr. Dadalian, how—" I stopped myself with a show of woozy self-control. I had to act like I knew nothing. What could I say? Yes, I abandoned you. But it wasn't my fault. Somebody or something saw fit to intervene on my behalf and didn't give a crap about your cigar-smoking ass.

"Hi there…" I fumbled for words. "Did you guys…get my muffins?" I couldn't actually remember the last thing I had delivered over there. It could have been a pile of rocks with whipped cream sprayed on top, for all I knew. Mr. Dadalian continued to keep his head averted. He addressed the opposite wall.

"Hello, Rae." He paused. "You are not decent."

I was immediately hurt and about to object when I stopped and looked down at myself. All I was wearing was a bra and panties. I closed my eyes and opened them again. Unfortunately, Mr. Dadalian was still there, and so was I. I wasn't dreaming.

"Um…sorry about that. Guess I'll talk to you later."

"Did I not see you last night on Glenoaks? I thought I did, then…" Mr. D. continued to address the opposite wall. "I find myself later way far down street. My wife have to come get me."

I was holding it together pretty well while random images shot through my brain of me and Mr. D. rising into the balmy Burbank night sky, the Z getting smaller, *the sound of their voices, like bees, bugs, something itchy and repellent: We have the one spoken of…*

Mr. Dadalian looked down at the carpet and shook his head. "Is very, very strange…" he muttered.

"Well…I'd better get going," I slurred slightly. I'd almost said, "I'm glad to see you" but wasn't sure if that was appropriate. Since his body hadn't been discovered, sans internal organs, in a deserted Metrolink station, I just said, "Glad you made it back okay. I'll, uh, bring some dessert over…later…" I trailed off, wishing I hadn't said that last part.

"Okay, Miss Rae." He stuck his key into his door, and I pushed my door quietly closed.

* * *

When we had been around eleven years old, Patric had taught me and Hama and a couple other girls how to do backflips on the balance beam. Basically, you started out on the floor doing hundreds of backflips on a painted line then progressed to the low beam, four-foot beam, then finally the high beam. The high beam, though, was a different world entirely. Suddenly you were up in the air, expected to hurl yourself backward into empty space. Yes, you had just performed the feat zillions of times on the low beam, but down there had been much less distance to fall. Who could say if you would land on your feet, your groin, or your neck? Feet would be good, groin would be humiliating (and painful), and neck would be bad.

Who could say if you'd land on one foot, slightly off, slip, and slam your temple into the four-inch wide beam on your way down? And then wake up later in a hospital, terribly thirsty, unable to raise your limbs, and when your mother, teary-eyed and looking *a lot* older, wept with her head bowed, you found out that no, you hadn't been in a coma for several weeks or a month or several months. You had been sleeping for fifteen years! And, yes, while you were thankful that your family had been able to keep you here and that you hadn't needed machinery to stay alive and you'd finally woken up, now you were a thirty-year-old virgin who hadn't finished the tenth grade, had no idea how complicated Windows 27.5 was, and all for what? Doing a trick in a gym? Trying to impress Patric?

Thankfully, none of that had ever happened to me, obviously, but the thought had gone through my mind many a time. That was why I hadn't been that great at the balance beam. I still remembered the feeling I'd get just before I hurled myself upward, and no amount of creative visualization could completely dispel the sense of utter vulnerability and blooming alarm.

Right now, after the attempted abduction, and the weird voices scratching in my head, I was camped out on that high beam but way too drunk to get down, much less attempt a backflip. I was on my belly on the high beam, clinging to it with my arms and legs like a baby orangutan to its mother. I was drowning in vulnerability and choking on blooming alarm. If the commander from my gymnastics childhood had returned and found me here, paralyzed by abject panic and shock, he would have snorted in disgust, blown snot out one nostril for the sole purpose of grossing me out, and given me a dishonorable discharge on the spot.

The hours rolled by indiscriminately the way hours tended to do while one drifted through an ongoing inebriated dream. Immediately following Mr. Dadalian's exit, I had felt okay. But then, little by little as the day had gone on, paranoia had begun to spout little arms and legs and a little pug-like scrunched up face lined with worry, and had started following me everywhere in the apartment. It was like a needy, worried, scrunched up mutant pet that clung to my calf as I tried to read emails, galloped after me as I went to the bathroom, threw its paws around me in terror when someone knocked on the door. Of course, I didn't answer, and when I tiptoed over there later and cracked it open, I found a Tupperware container of some kind of meat wrapped up in soft flatbread, roasted eggplant, and feta cheese strudel. Attached was a note that I had to rear back near-sightedly to read: "I knock." That was all.

I scooped up the container and retreated back into my burrow with my prize. Mrs. Dadalian was upping the ante and moving on to real food, I saw. I would have to respond in kind. But unless I could somehow transport myself interdimensionally to the store, it wasn't gonna be today, 'cause I wasn't leaving my apartment. And that must mean it was time for another drink.

True terror came several hours past dinnertime with the realization that I was almost out of booze. Even this news wasn't enough, however, to get me dressed and out the door. I actually wasn't sure I'd ever be able to walk out of this building again. While I paced the floor with my hands pressed to my head, seriously considering going next door to see if Annie had any liquor lying around, my cell phone rang.

I waited until the caller had left a message then scrambled to the sofa and pressed the phone to my ear to hear it. It was Cola, calling about the audition for the sportscasting position—which had come and gone. My jaw swung open. The audition! I'd missed it! I stared down at the phone in a hazy stupor and tears swam in my eyes. Oh, my God, those big-headed ZR assholes had fucked up my opportunity, fucked up my life. No. No. I had *let them* fuck up my life. No, no. My life had *already been fucked up*. I could hear Bob Smith now. He materialized, unbidden, into my apartment through the nearest wall and stood in the living room smiling patronizingly at me. "If you had stayed in the Now, you would have gone to the audition. You're in the past now, Rae. You're a prisoner of time."

"No, I'm a prisoner of the balance beam. Don't you see me here on top of it?"

A smug smile. "Same thing, Rae. The past. Let it go. Let it go..." his ghostly voice echoed, and I threw my cell phone at his dematerializing body. It bounced against the throw rug and smacked into the wall with an unhealthy sound. "Next you'll be telling me to forgive Leif Garrett's nemesis! Quack!" I shouted after him. I crawled along the floor toward my last bottle of rum. It was three-quarters empty. Which meant one-quarter of an opportunity to keep my buzz alive and well.

At some point, I had two brilliant ideas. One—order groceries over the phone! Two—push my bedroom dresser against the front door. That was what everybody always did in the movies to keep the zombies and psychotic pecking birds out. I knew deep down it was fruitless, but on the surface, it felt good. As I struggled with a pen and paper, happily jotting down the kinds of alcohol I wanted, I decided on the spur of the moment to cook something fantastic for Mr. and Mrs. Dadalian. For God's sake, they deserved something special, considering what they'd just gone through. Mr. Dadalian thought he was going crazy. Mrs. Dadalian probably figured Mr. Dadalian had simply sidetracked to a bar on the way home.

I got on the Internet, my mutant pug paranoia pet temporarily forgotten in the excitement, surfing for recipes. Happening across several colorful and wet-looking pictures, I decided on flan. Flan! It was the answer to everything, wasn't it? Even its name inspired international joy and happiness. The way you pronounced it— Flahn—plucked you out of everyday life, shoved castanets into your hands, and demanded that you dance. Yes, Mrs. D. had provided an entire meal this time, but I wasn't up for anything beyond dessert at the moment. I'd have to rise to her latest challenge at an as-yet-undisclosed date.

I scribbled down all the ingredients I would need and called Vons. Then I went to my bedroom and began the arduous task of pushing my heavy dresser through the living room and into position across my front door. The commander had returned and now observed my activities from the sanctity of my pale yellow sofa with his arms crossed, nodding somberly.

"Won't stop Charlie," he said angrily and spat. "But at least it's something."

Later when the groceries arrived, I had an embarrassing moment of tugging the bags through the allotted space, glaring while the delivery boy smirked. I still tipped him generously, showing that I was the bigger person. He had no idea, after all, what was going on. *I could be saving his ass in the next five minutes.* He wouldn't remember later, but that was beside the point. I was on the balance beam, no spotter, alone, expected to perform incredible feats. How much was I supposed to take, exactly? Was this torture going to go on for the rest of my godforsaken life? I had a question, though, better than all the rest. How had they known me? *How had they known me?*

CHAPTER 22

The hours dragged by as I hunkered down in my living room, wavering between nostalgia and sentimentality and then prolonged drunken terror. I cried and slumped over and fell asleep and woke up with a headache and cried again and shivered with fear. This was me, going partially bat-shit crazy. But not completely. Not completely.

There were several attempts at making flan that went astray each time I got to the whisking part, and one time in the oven where I burned it beyond repair. Something about whisking the milk and egg and almond extract together without "incorporating any air into the mixture." Was that even possible? Wasn't that like asking someone to try not to breathe? Apparently, I also wasn't tapping on the counter correctly to get rid of the extra bubbles, because when the flan emerged from the oven, the texture was horrible.

I decided to devour some more of Mrs. D.'s delicious meat and eggplant, thinking it would give me the brain power to concentrate better, never taking into consideration that not drinking would help too. Not drinking would allow the mutant pug pet back in, letting it gaze up at me with its worried, scrunched-up face. Not drinking would make me remember the voice. Not drinking would remind me that two unidentified fast-moving beings had unlocked me from the alien light, kicked some Zeta ass, and lowered me back to earth—not necessarily in that order—and I had no idea why. Who would I be beholden to now? It was like someone trying to rape you in an alleyway, and John Gotti just happened to be moseying by on his way to the corner deli, and he pulled his gun out and blew the would-be rapist away. So, yes, you'd gotten out of the rape, *but now what would John Gotti want from you?*

I dove into my third attempt at making almond leche flan. The poor, overburdened air conditioner chugged and wheezed as it struggled to provide tepid air for the apartment. My TV glowed against the wall, muted. I focused on the picture, realizing a moment later that the credits for *Sand in Your Face* were flashing across the screen. Wait a minute. *Sand* only came on once a week—on Mondays. How many days had gone by? I'd completely lost track.

I walked over from my kitchen nook and sank down onto the sofa. The minute Ricardo's face appeared on my TV, my gorge rose. Then Dante's face popped on screen, his hands dancing and dreadlocks flying as he made some dramatic point in sign language. My gorge dropped back down. You had to give it to the guy: sweet, sexy, deaf, Jamaican Dante. The first hearing-impaired "actor" to be on a reality TV series in a sustained "role."

When someone knocked on the door, I bounced to my feet and stood still for twenty full seconds without moving. I don't know what I was doing. Listening for something? The sound of hovering engines? Another knock. I came back to my senses. Obviously, it had to be one of the Dadalians. I lurched forward and staggered across the room, clipping an empty box of sugar that went somersaulting across the wooden floor. I climbed on top of the dresser and peered through the peephole, suddenly hoping it was Rex. A surprise visit from Rex would be wholly welcome, even if he chided me about being the worst procrastinator alive. He could help me finish packing. We could move out of here tonight!

But no, it was Dante. Weird. I pulled back from the door, swaying and thinking. What were the odds? I vaguely remembered passing him my information, but couldn't remember if it was before or after the Arclight. I unlatched the door and yanked it open. It slammed into the dresser and stopped, and we stared at one another through the half-foot gap. Dante didn't lose a beat and flashed his sexy grin at me. "Trouble with the ex?" he signed as I tugged the dresser away from the door. Except that he hadn't signed, he'd spoken. Or someone had spoken. Someone with a deep male voice and a deep male laugh that followed. I straightened up from the dresser and looked past Dante into the hallway to see who was there. Mr. Dadalian, obviously. Or

Annie's boyfriend. But no one else was there. I stared and stared, searching for the other man in the hallway, my brain trying to make sense of the fact that it was empty. Dante gestured to the tiny space I had created.

"Can I come in?" he asked in a deep male voice.

He waited the many, many, many seconds that slowly ticked by until I said, "Sure…" then he shoved the dresser back (like it was made of feathers) and immediately slipped inside, sideways, like a shadow.

Dante strode straight to the sofa, tossed aside the newspaper and frozen pizza boxes and printouts from the computer, and dropped down onto the cushions. I closed the door slowly and turned around. I hoisted myself up onto the dresser and sat there swinging my legs, staring across the living room at Dante, a slow grin peeling back my lips. I was wearing a thin, white tank top and shorts because the apartment was like a sauna, what with all the baking and the malfunctioning air conditioner. Dante sat on my sofa and stared at my legs for a while. Nothing new. He hadn't changed.

"Did you miss me?" he said. *He said.* He smiled slightly and glanced at the TV and saw that *Sand in Your Face* was playing, made a moue, and cocked his head. I waved my hand dismissively.

"I'm not watching. Believe me. It just came on, by accident. I didn't even know it was Monday. I've been in here for three days straight. Maybe more. I lost track of time." I was still slurring slightly. A normal person would have been surprised by what I'd just said, possibly expressed concern. Dante just sat there regarding me with what seemed like amusement.

"Keep talking," I said, grinning. "Keep talking, you son of a bitch." It was like being in *Cuckoo's Nest*, the hallway scene with Nicholson and giant Chief and the chewing gum. Or even more shocking, that scene from *The Crying Game*. "Oh, my God, you son of a bitch." I couldn't stop grinning. Dante grinned back and shrugged.

"Wanna call me a son of a bitch one more time?"

"Yeah, you son of a bitch." I jumped off the dresser. "You lying, cheating son of a bitch."

"Yeah, no shit." He glanced down at his wrist at his very expensive watch. "Tip of the iceberg, darlin'. Just the tip."

I stepped toward Dante, swaying slightly.

He settled back into the sofa, entirely relaxed. The pale yellow cushions were surprisingly complementary to his skin tone. He patted the empty space beside him.

"Rae, come here. Sit."

Something in his voice compelled me to do so, so I did.

"I can't believe you can talk. I can't believe you're not deaf," I murmured in drunken wonder.

"You have no idea," he murmured back. He raised his hand and studied his nails. "Andrygen spoke kindly of you the other day," he said in an odd, exacting way. "And Moeyner misses you."

If I had been drinking something, I would have sprayed the coffee table with it. Say what?

"No, no, no," I shook my head, almost falling over with the movement. Dante started to put his hand out to steady me. I straightened up. "I just saw her. A few nights ago. She's not who she says she is, you know." I paused. "She's not from the ghetto. She's from—I don't know where—Beverly Hills? Manhattan Beach?" I stared at him accusingly.

Dante smiled sympathetically, acknowledging the loop-de-loops of mendacity. He tilted his head a little. "Well…" he shrugged. "It's show biz. You're a little too old to be this naïve, Rae, don't you think?"

"Naïve?" I seethed. *She* had said the same thing. God, was it true?

"Come on. They needed variety. You're a sister…but just barely. So, Moeyner had to fill that space. They couldn't have two bougies on there, right? It would have been redundant."

"Re…dundant?" I quoted him, hardly able to get the words out. I watched as he absently picked up some of my mail, scanned it, smirked, and tossed it aside.

"I know what happened to you, Rae," said Dante.

I started, still trying to sort out the race labeling that had just occurred. I should be used to it by now, shouldn't I? How many people, after all, had stared at me, uncomprehending, when I'd told them that I was black? How many people had out-and-out laughed and said, "No, you aren't!" right to my face? It had happened my entire life. Dante was right. Too black for Sherman Oaks but not black enough for Hollywood. Go figure.

"Um...what was that?" I struggled to rein in my thoughts.

He reached out and patted my thigh. My skin tingled beneath his touch. "Let's cut to the chase."

"What chase?" Hadn't we already cut to the chase? What else could there possibly be to talk about? I wondered.

"They're interdimensional beings known more popularly as the Grays. They can appear in public, in daylight, unseen, wherever and whenever they like, to continue the experimentation that has been going on for eons. But of course, some can still see them."

He leveled his gaze at me.

"Oh, my God," I whispered. *This* I had not been expecting. "You've seen them?" I closed my eyes. "I'm not crazy." *This* was something to talk about. *This* was amazing news. I could not believe it. Another witness!

His face was grim. "I've seen them for hundreds of years, sweetheart. They're getting stronger. Humans are a means to an end in their search for eternal life. Their search for the soul."

Hundreds of years? I frowned, distracted. Humans? Then, as he continued, I thought: *maybe I really should have been more like Margarite, complete with conked-out pageboy and blasé living room color scheme.* Because if I had been more like Margarite, gone down the path more traveled—trampled, stampeded—I probably wouldn't be here, now, with Dante saying, "I know this because I'm a vampire. Our kind was here long before theirs, and we need soldiers to join us in the war against the beings that would destroy you all."

I smiled slightly. One corner of my lips. Slowly, I held my hands up, two rigid stop signs. I battled to think clearly, but my depraved days-long drinking bender wasn't helping. Wait a minute. Wait a minute. What if all of this was part of a giant prank, all abductions, Annie and the surfer and the little white dog? No. No. That little dog had been frozen. You couldn't train a dog to do something like that. Hope, momentarily strong, stumbled without warning. It rolled backward, downhill, and disappeared out of sight behind fear and loathing.

"I know what you're thinking," Dante suggested. "But, we only borrow your blood for sustenance. We don't destroy. We preserve."

That hadn't been what I was thinking. But it was good to know.

I stood up stiffly, my head abruptly clearer.

"Stop shitting me."

"I'm not shitting, you, Rae. I would never shit you."

I spelled "Really?" as sarcastically as I could in sign language.

Dante stood up now, too, smiling benignly. Or so it seemed.

"I've been alive for 500 years, Raine. The show, the act…" he signed the rest quickly, and I picked up a few stray words: either something about boredom and hobbies or boogie boards and hobos.

"A few drops of blood you can live without. Your soul, you cannot live without. Not many can see them, as you can, but you can still be controlled. If you become like me, they will not be able to control you, because it's the soul, the spark, that is your weakness. Without that, they have nothing."

A few weeks ago, loony bin time. Dialing 911 as innocuously as possible, then visiting Dante every other Wednesday at "the center." But now, weeks later, that wasn't even a realistic concern. Because if Dante was crazy, then I was crazier. On top of which, I had sort of forecasted this, hadn't I? If there were aliens, why not vampires, werewolves, fairies, trolls? *Called it!* Mentally, I pumped my fist.

"Wait a minute." I smiled and sat back down on the sofa at the furthest point from Dante. I continued to smile, taking my time. He was not going to pressure me into whatever the hell he was talking about. Becoming like him? I wasn't liking where this conversation was going. I didn't like this talk of souls. What was Dante getting at?

"You're saying the one thing that makes me human, makes me alive, is my soul, but you want me to give it up. That's not very convincing, Dante." Even as I argued with him, another part of me, the twelve-year-old part, was warming to the idea of screwing with Ricardo in ways never before imagined. I couldn't shake an image of me holding Richard aloft by the throat and observing the un-yoga-like look on his face as I whispered tenderly, *"Namaste, motherfucker."*

Dante stood up and approached me in one sinewy movement. "I meant the royal you. Not you, specifically."

"Wait a minute, wait a minute," I said in a panic, scrunching myself back into the sofa. "I haven't agreed to anything. What are you doing? I need my soul!"

Dante shook his head slowly, back and forth, back and forth. He crossed his arms and gazed down at me the way a cat calmly watches a tiny mammal, charmed and amused that it would even consider trying to escape.

"When you are human, you need your soul. The undead do not need such things. I can give you great power to replace it." He glanced toward the kitchen and sniffed. "Are you making flan? I love flan."

He turned and started to walk toward the front door.

I stood up.

"Where are you going?"

"I'm leaving. I'm not going to pressure you, Rae. It's your decision."

"Okay, well, thanks."

At least he was being reasonable. Wasn't he? If he was really a vampire (and I had no reason to believe otherwise) he could pop my head off if he wanted to, pour my bodily liquids into my Cuisinart, toss in some Sauza tequila, and make a margarita. But he wasn't doing that. He was just leaving.

Dante side stepped around the pulled-away dresser and reached for the doorknob.

"You know where to find me," he said and winked. Then he walked out.

It took about twelve hours for a series of repeating events to change my mind. Twelve hours wasn't very long to contemplate whether or not it was a good idea to give up your soul, but at least I wasn't planning to do it for selfish reasons like John Cassavetes' character in *Rosemary's Baby*. At least I hadn't driven over to the audition Cola had set up for me and drawn a pentacle in chalk on the passenger seat of the Z and chanted a conjuring spell to Beelzebub, promising him my life's essence if he gave me a career in sportscasting.

No, the series of repeating events came and went in cycles, all attended to by my ongoing inebriation. All I had to do was try to leave the apartment and fail several times, careening backwards into the room quaking and hyperventilating. Although the safety of the apartment was an illusion, I clung to it desperately. All I had to do was hear the phone ring and spasm as if someone had just run me through with Excalibur. All I had to do was listen to the escalating messages of concern from the usual suspects and weep uncontrollably, unable to bring myself to call them back and tell them I was okay, though I was *not*, obviously, okay. All I had to do was recall the vicious look that thing had given me as it stole Annie up into the sky during the first encounter. All I had to do was sit with my arms around my knees, rocking back and forth on my living room floor and asking myself why I was suddenly able to see invisible alien space ships. Had I hit my head? Had Richard slipped me a roofie under the guise of some calming pretentious yoga tea while we were filming, wiping my memory, and rewiring my circuitry?

At least this way I could ease my regret a fraction, be proactive in the fight against evil, feel like I had an ounce of control. And because of all those things and no small amount of liquor, I called Dante the next night. Actually, I texted him out of habit, forgetting momentarily about the lie. He showed up so fast, it was like he'd been sleeping in the hallway outside my door. Except he hadn't. Because I'd been peering through the peephole randomly all night long, spying on people as they walked past.

Dante arrived, and when I opened the door, he walked inside like it was all right. He chucked me under the chin and grinned. He appeared to be in a good mood.

"Didn't want to meet me, eh, woman?"

It was still so weird hearing him talk out loud.

I sat down on my sofa carefully and whispered, "I can't leave."

He approached me and sat beside me and put his arm around me and was actually quite tender.

"I know, baby. I know," he said, pressing his forehead against mine. "You won't be afraid anymore. You will get your mind back. You will get your life back."

"But I'm also super-drunk," I pointed out.

"But you are super-hot and soon will be super-powerful," he countered. He must have known this would catch me off guard and shut me up, because I said nothing, having no comeback. I was still on the balance beam, clinging with all my limbs, and Dante was diligently prying them off, one by one.

"Why is all this happening? Why now?" I whispered, addressing no one in particular. It was really just rhetorical.

But Dante said, "You've always had magic in your life. You're just realizing it now."

Softly, he pressed a finger under my jaw and gently turned my head toward him. He lowered his mouth toward mine. Oh. We were going that way first? His lips brushed lightly over mine, moved across my cheek, then abruptly dipped down directly onto my carotid artery. Right before he bit, he whispered in my ear, as if he could read my mind, "And Rae...don't bother fucking with Ricardo. He's not worth it."

The last thing I uttered as a human being was, "You know, he's not even really Hispanic." I hated the reproach I heard in my own voice. I hoped dying would make me a less catty person.

CHAPTER 23

I thought L.A. was one of the best places, besides Transylvania, probably, to undertake the life-changing experience of becoming undead. I figured that in Transylvania, a person's cultural heritage would be a plus: you were already in the know about what was going to happen. Same with L.A., our heritage coming from the movies and TV. There was an old joke: what's the difference between L.A. and yogurt? Yogurt has culture. But in this case, the media environment worked to my advantage. I was expecting to pass out. And I did. I was expecting to wake up later feeling like there was molasses in my veins. And I did. Dante had laid me out on the sofa. I sat up, mouth dry and head pounding, momentarily bewildered. Then I remembered everything, and so far, I wasn't impressed. All this felt like was the mother of all hangovers.

I noticed the sun poking through the slats of my blinds. It was morning! I raised my arms and looked at myself. Nothing looked different. Shouldn't I be somewhere more protective than on my living room sofa? Why hadn't Dante wedged me under my bed or stuffed me into my closet? Cautiously I gained my feet and shuffled toward the window. Everything seemed so normal, so lacking in drama, that it took a few moments of experimenting with my blinds to discover that while the sun didn't cause me to burst into flames, it was undeniably...uncomfortable.

Suddenly, with the worst timing in the world, I remembered Cola's warning about Dante. He's not what he seems? Is that how he had put it? Surely, he had been talking about the deaf act. Surely, Cola didn't know Dante was a vampire. *Oh, my God,* I thought, *Dante is a vampire.*

Oh, my God. I am a vampire.

I rushed into the bathroom to see myself in the mirror. No fangs yet. Relieved that I also hadn't turned bone white or grown spherical ears, I realized that having no reflection must be one of the vampire myths. Idly I wondered how many more were myths. Garlic? The cross? I wandered around the apartment for a while, preoccupied, alternating between the window and the bathroom mirror. When my phone shrilled (Cola again), I noticed that my nerves had calmed to the point of nonexistence. Nonexistence.

What did it mean to be undead, exactly? It was my usual M.O. to research it now, after the fact. Googling this on the computer had brought me no closer to any concise explanation, although I was disturbed to discover a painting from the 1400s entitled "The Undead Lovers" presenting two desiccated corpses standing side by side, grinning, modestly half-draped with white sheets. I do believe a frog or toad was either entering or exiting the female corpse's privates, its intentions unclear. Wow. The undead concept had been around for quite a while. I felt like I had the flu and wondered how long it was going to last. Dante, of course, had left no instructions, written or otherwise.

One thing was for sure: I was off the balance beam. I picked up my cell phone, keys, and wallet and headed for the front door. I was out of liquor again and figured I should get more—why stop now—and wanted to test my sea legs. I listened to Cola's message asking where I was. He didn't sound angry or annoyed that I had up and disappeared and completely flaked on a super-duper dream opportunity. In fact, he sounded worried and tense. He sounded like a father calling his daughter's cell phone, wondering why she hadn't come in from her date last night.

The steadily building agoraphobia and accompanying paranoia had disappeared. I successfully exited the building without vomiting and/or passing out (I had nearly done both a couple times over the past several days whenever I tried to leave) and headed for the Mexican/Korean/Jamaican market. It was late morning and weirdly humid. As I walked along the sidewalk under the trees, I tried to categorize whatever physical sensations were going on. The sunlight continued to make me feel uncomfortable —not in pain exactly, but it was definitely nicer under the trees.

I lit up a cigarette even though I wasn't really craving a smoke, just lighting up out of habit because I felt a little nervous. I'd done such a big thing, after all. It was kind of like going out and having a penis attached without telling anybody. Like traveling to Bavaria and purchasing a castle on the spur of the moment. I realized I had been a lot drunker than I'd previously thought and worried briefly about that. I walked along smoking and thinking.

At the market, the usual tiny "welcome" sign was hanging on the door. I tossed my cigarette, went inside. I was standing in the spirits aisle reading bottle labels with no problem when I realized that I could see everything super-clearly. Oh, thank God. I could cross "get eye exam" off my to-do list where it sat four or five spaces beneath "fix shoulder" which sat four or five spaces beneath "go back to school" which was number one on the list. Nothing on the list had included becoming undead, but in this new world I lived in, populated by aliens and vampires and now, undoubtedly others I didn't even know about, the list was old school, last year. Passé.

One thing was for sure: *Interview with the Vampire* had certainly used poetic license whenever somebody had been turned. Aside from my improved eyesight, nothing had been overtly fixed on my body. The fibroids were still in my abdomen, and my fingers were still gone. The only difference was, I noticed, that none of it hurt anymore. My stubs weren't throbbing and sore, my abdomen didn't feel tender and vulnerable, and my shoulder, although still limited in movement, did not hurt. Chrislann would be so happy for me if he were here. I was sure of it.

"Fucking physical therapy or a fucking vampire!" he would have shouted exuberantly. "Whatever works!"

I glanced up from studying a bottle of 1800 Coconut Tequila as someone else entered the liquor aisle. It was Annie. At first, she didn't see me. She spent about five minutes perusing the whiskey shelves, selected a bottle, then straightened up, cradling the booze like something precious to her chest. Again I thought, as I had so many times before, *Annie's so tiny*. It was like watching a child buying booze. Here we were, full circle. She had been the start of everything. I had been powerless then, helpless. Everything was different now. Well, for me, at least. Annie in the liquor aisle didn't bode well. As I was standing there thinking all this, she suddenly caught sight of me, gave an unfriendly half-wave, turned on her heel, and left.

Back home, I put the booze in the kitchen and headed straight back out for the Z. At Tobacco Planet, I purchased the same Guapos I had lost during the abduction then as an afterthought, bought several for Mr. Dadalian, which I hung from their doorknob in a plastic bag. Then I hopped back in the car and started driving to Century City and Cola's office. I'd decided, on the spur of the moment, that it was time to pay Cola a visit. I could explain in person what had happened to me, why I had missed the audition. I'd come up with some tale. Obviously, I couldn't tell him the truth.

It actually felt really, really great to be off the high beam. Patric wouldn't have been happy with my dismount. You weren't supposed to dismount off the high beam by letting a vampire sink his fangs into your neck, but I considered it being proactive. Because the alternative—cowering in my apartment, the agoraphobia flooding past the containment barriers and consequently necessitating psychotherapy and handfuls of anti-anxiety medicine—was unthinkable.

No one seemed to know anything except me and Dante (and the rice rocket boy). No one seemed to be doing anything about it except me (and that was very little). I had never expected to find myself being transported through the air toward a nightmarish destination, and yet I had been and had been powerless to stop it. It didn't matter how many legs I grabbed on to—the creatures would continue to perform their kidnappings and experiments—whatever the hell they were doing. Rex was at risk. Giancarlo was at risk. Margarite might be better off after an experience with the Zetas. Who was I to say? Maybe she'd loosen up a little. But now, according to Dante, they had no dominion over me. Us. And together, the vampire army would handle The Uninvited.

How, exactly, I had no idea. Would we slaughter them? I looked down at my hands, imagining them slaughtering a Zeta. At the moment, I couldn't really see that happening, considering that I was loath to kill a spider when I found one scampering across the back of my sofa. I tried to catch them in a glass and then deposit them back outside in their natural environment.

Somewhere in the middle of my drive over to Culver City, I started to feel nauseated and realized I was overheated. The sunlight, uncomfortable before, was now making me sick, and my limbs felt like overcooked sausages stuffed inside my skin, which was hot to the point of turning a bizarre purple. I pulled off the freeway without even seeing where I was and drove until I saw some shade and floored the gas until I was parked under it. Here I sat for many moments, panting slightly and trying to keep from vomiting.

It was about twenty minutes before I felt in control enough to even start to think again. I raised my arm. The purple color had started to fade, and the sausage feeling began to diminish. I glanced up at the sky, recoiling slightly from the light, then closed my eyes and put my head back against the seat. Fleeting thoughts zoomed through my head, in and out like buzzing flies, but I heard them anyway: *What if this was a mistake? Did you think this through? Was this a good idea, making the sun, the giver of life, your deadly enemy?*

Shut up, I told the thoughts. I treated them as if they had come from somewhere else, a planet light-years away, not from my own brain. *Shut up and get a life.* (Not sure how thoughts were supposed to get a life) *Everything isn't perfect. It'll work out.*

After I'd finished panting and gagging and lowering my core body temperature again, I was able to focus enough to make out a blurry CVS sign a ways down the sidewalk. I got out of the Z and started walking toward the store. This turned into power walking and then into an all-out sprint. I almost knocked an elderly woman over who was trying to exit with her walker as I blasted through the doors. She pivoted on her walker as I held the door open from the inside, waiting for her last wheel to disengage from the arc radius of the door. Slowly, slowly, slowly, it rolled away.

"Thank you," she called in a shaky voice.

Inside, I bought a baseball cap, light jacket with hoodie, and some sunscreen. After purchasing them, I donned and applied them before I even left the store. Then I trudged back to the car slowly, testing it out. It helped somewhat. At least I didn't feel like I was tied to the post anymore with the fire licking at my feet and the crowd screaming, "Burn the witch!" Now I just felt like I was waiting for a pizza inside a Papa John's where the air conditioning had gone out.

Back inside the car, slathered by the sunscreen, jacket on, hoodie up under the cap, was even better. But I still found myself pushing the Z up to 80, 85 several times. After a harrowing twenty minutes or so, I tore off the 10 freeway and started making my way down Westwood Boulevard toward Cola's office. Once I'd jammed my car into a spot in the street, I stood outside the glass doors, listing on the sidewalk, disoriented from the drive and the sun until Nora the security guard stuck her head out the door and called, "You okay, Ms. Miller?"

I gazed at her, dazed.

"Um…"

Nora came out and peered up into my face.

"Have you been drinking?"

"Yes."

She clicked her tongue and took me by the arm.

"But it was a long time ago," I amended. "I'm just hungry—hung—hung-over."

My nostrils flared. Something smelled like a bouquet of fresh-cut flowers.

"Yeah, you're still hung-over, all right. Come in here."

She led me inside saying, "Let me get you some water."

I hadn't even thought of the whole inviting in thing until after I was in the building. I waited complacently while Nora disappeared in the back and then returned with a plastic cup of water. It was very cold. She handed it to me and watched as I gulped some of it down. It was tasteless and unsatisfying. Why was it always so hot outside? It was probably much easier to be undead in the Antarctic.

"Thanks, Nora."

"No problem. Going up to see Mr. Georgiou?"

It always sounded weird when people used Cola's last name, so used was I to his nickname.

"Yeah. He got a great audition for me, but I missed it."

Nora clicked her tongue.

"I hope you got a good reason, girl. Well, get going."

"Thanks, Nora."

I was still gripping the cup of water as I rode the elevator up. Muzak was tinkling subtly in the front office as the elevator doors opened into Cola's foyer. His thousand-year-old secretary, Irene, was seated behind her desk, typing in slow motion on a laptop. A young woman resembling Olivia Wilde was sitting on the sofa to the right. For once, I could see everyone and everything beyond my limited scope crystal clear. I could tell right away it wasn't really Olivia Wilde. I approached Irene. She sat at her desk, typing and typing, either ignoring me or completely unaware that I was there. I cleared my throat. Irene glanced up. Her eyes widened behind her gigantic eyeglasses.

"Raine Miller. How nice to see you."

"Hi, Irene."

I didn't really have a plan. I sort of half-intended to walk into Cola's office and glamour him, *True Blood* style, into creating my overnight superstardom. If I was going to fight the good fight and battle to save mankind, I might as well be rich while I did it. It wasn't like Cola wasn't always trying on my behalf, but maybe now I could really get him going by planting the idea in his head that I was the next Stacey Dash—sans Republican leanings—or a Halle Berry wannabe.

"Mm. So nice to see you again. You're looking…" Irene began, and trailed off, at a loss for words. She fastened curiously bright and piercing eyes on me. Something changed in her face.

"I've been under the weather." I raised my plastic cup and sipped some water. I glanced over at the Olivia Wilde lookalike. She was staring at me. She looked away. I wasn't sure if she was staring because of my new "energy" or because I was still wearing the hoodie and baseball cap and sunglasses. I probably looked like I was in methamphetamine withdrawal. I *felt* like I was in methamphetamine withdrawal.

"Mr. Georgiou was expecting you?"

"Uh…not really. He called me."

"Well, please have a seat while I tell him—"

Irene stared wide-eyed as I turned and headed for Cola's office.

"Ms. Miller!" Her creaky voice raised in alarm.

I opened Cola's door and walked in. Moments later, Irene tottered in behind me saying, "Mr. Georgiou—" but Cola, across the room at his desk, only raised his hand quietly, like he was making a bid at a silent auction. The door clicked shut behind me. I stood in the darkened office, still dissipating heat and panting. Cola watched me from his desk. There was an air of anticipation, almost as if he had been expecting me.

"You missed the audition."

His voice was quiet.

"Cola, I know. I know. I'm sorry about that."

"Have you seen Twitter and read the blogs? Have you been to your website?" He said quietly. There he was. The jet-black hair. The ridiculously form-fitting muted Caraceni suit. "The fans are rabid. They all want you back. I have a conference call with the network in twenty."

His voice sounded strange.

"Cola," I started, "Sorry I missed the audition. And I appreciate everything you've done for me…" He had, after all, saved me. During the long dry spell following *Green Splendor I* and *II* and my modeling days, the lingering death knoll that usually precedes either a nine-to-five or prostitution (or a coaching spell at Patric's gym), Cola had swept me out of the clutches of ruin. And I was thankful. But I had to exert some control; I could not always be the one the shark went after.

"But something happened—" I continued.

"I know." Cola stood up, his face unreadable. I stopped, my mouth still open.

"Y-you know? Know what?"

And then something really weird happened. I noticed that Cola had fangs.

He stood there looking at me with his fangs hanging out for several seconds. Hours. Centuries. Don Cheadle could have suddenly appeared, stepping through an interdimensional doorway saying, "Hey, Cola, I think I left my invisibility cloak here," and I wouldn't have noticed. It seemed like Cola stood and stood there like he had always been standing there, and I had always been staring at him. Nothing outside of us. Me. Him. The pointy teeth he had that he shouldn't have had retracted back into his mouth. He slowly slid his hands into his pockets.

I decided to test my neck. I could move my head. I gazed around the office because I could think of nothing else to do at the moment, noticing for the first time how dark it was in here. The windows were covered by steel shutters. I stumbled forward a few more steps, my knees weak, and braced myself against the front of Cola's desk with one hand. I was still gripping my cup in the other. Some water sloshed out onto the pale salmon Savonnerie carpet. Cola materialized by my side. He gripped me by the elbow the way men used to do when ladies were about to swoon or start a scene in a public place.

"Rae," he murmured. "Rae."

I figured out what was wrong with Cola's voice. He sounded sad.

I cleared my throat nervously. "I wasn't—"

He cut me off bluntly. "No harm done."

I stared at him. He stared back, unwavering. His hand was cold.

I asked shakily, "How long have you—"

"Hundreds of years." He tried to move me. I still had one hand on his desk and had trouble letting go of it. He pried my fingers off gently, one by one.

I swallowed. "Did you know—"

Cola's jaw flexed. "Dante." He closed his eyes for a moment, and it seemed like a slew of emotions fought for control. His usual calm won the battle. "What's done is done," he said in clipped tones. Then, softer, "Now everything changes. You actually don't even need the show anymore. You can have your own show. You can have your own movies. You'll be a star."

I laughed suddenly, then choked it off.

"What?" said Cola attentively.

"Dante," I breathed, about to pass out. I laughed again. "He's not what he seems.'" I raised my cup and took another sip of water. I coughed and laughed. For some reason, the water tasted terrible. "I thought you were talking about him not being deaf. Because how could you know the truth? But you *do* know. Because…" I trailed off, declining to state the obvious.

Cola was busy inching me around in a tiny U-turn, but he still smiled lightly.

"Well, yeah, he *isn't* deaf. That's a fact."

My knees were shaking, and I was hyperventilating slightly. I had come here prepared to use force, and Cola was already five steps ahead of me. My agent was a vampire. Dante was a vampire. What was that song? *The World is a Vampire.* "Dante's a good actor," I whispered grudgingly, my mind awhirl.

"Mm-hm," Cola murmured, intent on somehow getting my unresponsive corpse across the room.

"How did you know—"

He looked amused. "Rae." He chuckled but said nothing further. He guided me to the vegetable-tanned calfskin leather sofa. I swayed. He lowered me down to the soft surface then plucked the cup out of my hand. "It's going to be okay, Rae. Don't worry."

It occurred to me that I couldn't recall ever having seen Cola in the light of day except for maybe a handful of times. But this had never struck me as unusual, because at least half the people I knew didn't go outside until the day was mostly over.

Suddenly, I recalled the cigars I had bought for him. They were crammed into the pocket of the cheap jacket I was still wearing. I fumbled for them and yanked them out.

"I-I got these for you. They're your favorite."

He smiled at me as I handed him the sealed plastic bag.

"How thoughtful, Rae." The plastic rustled slightly as he peered inside. "I love these. Thank you."

"I was almost abducted a few days ago," I said. "In case you were wondering." I gazed down at my nails. "That's mostly why I folded and let Dante…"

"Shh, shh, shh," said Cola. He put his cold hand on my head and actually rubbed my hair like I was a child. "I know, I know, I know."

How did he know? He frigging knew everything!

"You know about the aliens?" I asked, confused.

"Shh, shh. Of course I do. Don't worry. We'll talk about it later."

I sighed and decided to let it go for now. When Cola wasn't budging, there was nothing you could do. "Can I…sleep on your sofa till sunset?" I asked timidly, thrilled that he wasn't going to dump me as a client. Or slaughter me—I don't know—in some kind of vampiric territorial frenzy. "It's really hot outside."

He brushed a strand of hair off my face in a very un-Cola-like fashion that freaked me out a little. At the same time, I turned to Dr. Ruth and Dr. Phil and stood with my hands on my hips, glaring accusingly.

Cola didn't answer me about sleeping on his sofa. Again. But I guess not saying no sort of maybe meant yes.

CHAPTER 24

My cell was ringing. I woke on Cola's sofa. He had placed a thin cotton covering over me. The familiar gigantic painting of Denzel Washington in some action movie spread over most of one wall while the beautiful mural of the Mediterranean Sea and surrounding hills that I had always loved covered the other. That was probably where Cola was from. I had never asked him, and he never spoke about himself. He was very private. I glanced around. He was nowhere in sight. The steel shutters had been lifted from the windows, and I could see the gray-black sky outside.

I stretched, refreshed. I felt great.

Giancarlo was on the phone, wanting to push our date up to tonight.

"I hope you are free. I know it is short notice."

"Your date with J.Lo got cancelled, huh?"

Giancarlo laughed softly. "I am not dating anyone at this time." Loaded pause. "Except you."

Whatever effect he had intended by saying that, he succeeded, and I stammered, "I didn't—what—?"

He laughed again. "I am always catching you off guard. I enjoy doing so."

"I enjoy you doing so, too."

What, me, undead? Here I was, flirting as if nothing had changed!

"Very good, very good. You are available for more enjoyment? What time then, *dolcezza*?"

"Mm…" I glanced at my watch. It was seven thirty. The sun was just setting. "Eight thirty, nine?" I heard myself saying, even as some part of me hesitated. *Was this a good idea?*

"That is perfect for me also. I will pick you up, *dolcezza.*"

We disconnected. I paused. I guessed it would be all right to go out with Giancarlo tonight. Annie hadn't screamed when she'd seen me, and no one, including Olivia Wilde's double in the waiting room, had reacted badly. Reassured, I stood up and opened Cola's door. After being so rude to Irene earlier, I was sure she would be holding a grudge, and I didn't blame her. Happily, though, the waiting room was empty, so I scooted out of there fast, always thrilled when an awkward apology could be delayed for another time.

On the way home, my phone chimed. I was rocketing down the 101, almost back to Burbank. I pulled off at the Laurel Canyon exit and answered the phone. Though it was illegal in California and many states to talk on a cell phone while driving, I don't think anybody actually cared. However, with my cop karma, it was always a crapshoot.

It was Cola. "Rae," he said, "try wheatgrass. It'll help." Almost on cue, I felt my insides cramp as a terrible sensation of undefined need flooded my belly.

"Oh." I gritted my teeth. "Ugh," I groaned. "Really?" I glanced into my rearview mirror and did a double take. There was a cop car right behind me.

"Crap. I have to go. There's a cop behind me." Inexplicably, I was whispering.

"Okay. You shouldn't have answered while you were driving."

"Yeah, thanks, Dad." I was still whispering. "Sorry I barged in on you like that. And Irene," I added.

"We'll speak soon."

Cola disconnected. I hung up the cell and tossed it onto the seat beside me. Too late. A shrill *whoop whoop* pierced the air, and the cop car flashed its lights at me. *Jesus Christ.* I pulled over to the curb and watched in my rearview as the officer started to get out of his patrol car. Suddenly, the air was rent by the sound of screaming sirens as several police cars appeared out of nowhere and raced past us at top speed. The cop leaped back in his vehicle and pulled up beside the Z. He mimed talking on a cell phone then losing control of the car, threw his arms up and screamed as the imaginary crash occurred, then turned and shook his head sternly at me. I nodded and so did the cop. Satisfied, he stomped on his accelerator and disappeared down the street after his brothers in blue. I leaned back in my seat and sighed. It was my curse to bear.

In the Whole Foods on Coldwater Canyon, I hobbled around, gripping my middle with one hand while I searched for wheatgrass juice. The only thing I could find that wasn't powdered was a two-ounce container that included an eyedropper thingy to dole out the drops. And it was fairly expensive—almost fifteen dollars for such a small amount! I bought it anyway, of course, trusting Cola implicitly. Back in Glendale, there was a large plate of cookies covered with plastic wrap in front of my door. I picked them up, immediately guilty that I had failed so badly at my flan. I would just have to try again later, I guess, either before or after I helped the vampiric army march on the alien interlopers. Inside, after squeezing past the dresser, I was confronted with the chaos of the last several days. It was truly terrifying. A band of escaped Howler monkeys couldn't have been more destructive than I had been. But I didn't have time to clean up now.

Gripping my spasming stomach again, I popped open the dropper and dumped half a teaspoon of the liquid into some orange juice. After gulping it down, it seemed like almost immediately I felt better. I looked at my phone. Rex had left three or four messages. I would call him later tonight. Strangely, I felt guilty that I was going out with Giancarlo. It was like Rex and I were married, and I didn't want him to know that I was "having coffee" with a coworker. When Giancarlo called to say he was here, I shoved the phone in my purse. As an afterthought, I grabbed the tiny bottle of wheatgrass juice and shoved that in my purse too. Downstairs, I pulled open the front door of the building. Giancarlo was standing on the front steps this time, half-turned away, studying something across the street. He was dressed in his usual impeccable manner, topped by a dark brown leather jacket for the almost-chilly night.

"Hi," I said. The air outside smelled wonderful.

He turned around to face me, smiling. And then the smile trembled. And froze. Then he wasn't smiling at all. Then he backed up a step and seemed to lose two shades of color. "No..." he said softly, his face twisting, tortured. Then louder, "No!" His eyes widened. I gasped. Something was wrong. Something was terribly wrong. Giancarlo was having a heart attack! He was going to grab his chest and drop to his knees. As it was, he had stumbled backward, off the porch. He was going to die, here, on my doorstep! Panicked, I reached into my purse for my phone. Giancarlo said quietly, "This is not so." He moved forward a step and seemed to sniff the air around me. He staggered slightly. Louder: "Tell me this is not so!"

"I'm calling 911! Giancarlo, hold on!" I fumbled for my phone.

"Fuck!" he yelled.

I startled and almost dropped the phone. Giancarlo reached into his leather jacket—*it must be his aspirin, his heart pills*! I thought. *Oh, my God, I had no idea! He seemed so healthy!* He removed a short object, snapped it downward with his wrist. Six inches of wood turned into a foot of wood with a lethally pointed tip. While I was still trying to absorb what was happening, he leapt toward me, aiming the wood at my chest—a stake, it was a stake—and shouted, "*Fuck me!* You're a fucking bloodsucker!"

The swearing stunned me almost as much as the sudden violence. I had never heard him swear before, and my mind balked, wondering if it was even English. He swiped the weapon at me, and the tip brushed across the top of my breasts beneath my light summer sweater as I instinctively dipped backward out of range. I whirled around and ran back into the building, slamming the door in Giancarlo's face. He stopped it with his foot and kicked it back open.

"Jesus!" I heard him shout in a throaty, masculine voice full of tears as he tore after me down the first floor hallway. Giancarlo had morphed into a murderous hitman before my eyes, and *he* was the one who was sad?

"GOD!" I heard him shout gruffly, "Rae, stop! Wait—"

"Yeah, right!" I screamed over my shoulder and peeled down the carpeted hallway at full speed. Soon, I had out-distanced him, even though I had barely been trying, and I realized this must be part of my new self, my new strength and speed. I was so fast! I was probably strong, too. Maybe I could wait for him and straight arm him to the ground as he ran past. I didn't want to try it, though. I was too scared.

Someone started to come out of their apartment, and I screamed, "Stay inside! Stay inside!" as I bolted past. Whoever it was pulled back immediately and obediently slammed their door shut. I rounded the corner and saw a side exit and made for it at top speed. Far behind me, I heard Giancarlo call, "Raaaaaeeeee!"

I kept going. I ran outside into the cool evening air, straight across the neighbor's driveway, hopped a fence, (slamming my phone as I did so, because I was still mindlessly gripping it), and then leaped into a tree situated behind a garage. I sat cradled within the branches, waiting and watching, yanking my purse back up onto my shoulder. I was breathing somewhat hard, which I found odd. Giancarlo burst out of the same side exit and stopped running immediately. He held the wooden stake down by his leg and stood listening. He swiveled his head slowly right, left, back again, listening, waiting. I sat in the tree and watched him, a poisonous melancholy settling over me like a fog. *My date had tried to kill me.* I watched as Giancarlo slowly folded up his portable stake, shoved it back into his leather jacket, and strode purposefully around the side of the building. *My date was a vampire hunter.*

"Rae," he called out in a conversational tone. He returned from the side of the building. He appeared to have calmed down somewhat. He stood and ran his hands through his hair distractedly. "Rae, come out. I know you are there."

I sat in the tree and didn't say anything.

Giancarlo turned and went to sit down on the steps. He held his head in his hands for a moment. Then he looked up and called out again, "Rae, please…I am sorry. I reacted…automatically."

He said the last word so softly, I almost didn't hear. He muttered something under his breath to himself, and then he laughed and stood up and pushed both hands into his hair. Slowly. One. Two. Three times. He shouted something in Italian.

Then he sat back down, pressing his palms together before him.

I decided to take my life into my hands only because he had pulled himself together enough to apologize, and I figured that was a pretty hard thing for a vampire killer to say to a vampire.

"You didn't even hear my side of the story!" I called out from the tree.

Giancarlo's head snapped up. He looked blindly in my direction. He stood up, and I could see his fingers twitching, itching to grab the stake out of his clothes again. He didn't, however. Instead, he shoved his hands into his pockets. He looked at the ground then, back where he'd heard my voice come from.

"Rae…" he shook his head. Even from this distance, I could see he was having trouble speaking. After a while he said quietly, huskily, "What happened?" He stood shaking his head. "Who did this to you?"

I decided to get down from the tree. He really, really seemed sorry. I could have been wrong, but I didn't think so. Gingerly, I dropped down. Now I couldn't see anything, because I was behind the wooden fence I had jumped earlier. I heard Giancarlo saying something else, sort of half-talking to himself and half-talking to the wind. I took the time to drop my cell phone back into my purse, leapt up, grabbed the top of the fence, and flipped over it in one movement. Patric would have been pleased.

I walked slowly toward Giancarlo back across the driveway. He saw me and stopped talking, stopped moving. I couldn't even imagine the long, involved conversation we were going to have. We would have to find a cozy table in the corner of a restaurant or huddle on two barstools at the end of a bar while my tale unspooled before him, starting with Annie in the laundry room that fateful afternoon. I could tell him everything, because if he knew about vampires, there was no reason why he couldn't know about the Zetas, unless he already did. Finally, *finally*, I had someone to talk to. Well, someone human, someone not supernatural. I don't know why that seemed to make a difference, but it did.

Giancarlo stood under the cold moonlight and watched me as I approached him.

He said, "Rae, please forgive me," and lunged in my direction. His hand swiped the air, and I ducked beneath it and stumbled into a run. *Shit!* He caught a fistful of my hair and yanked viciously backward. It tore loose from my scalp as I jerked away.

"AAAAAAAAAAAAAAAAHHHHHHHHHHHHHHH!" I screamed and stumbled. Giancarlo was on me like white on rice. He threw his arms around me from behind, heaved me into the air, and then sharply downward, trying to get me on the ground. Where was Mr. Dadalian *now?*

"What—you—why are—you apologized!" I grunted between the grappling.

"I do…apologize," he grunted between wrestling moves. "I am… so sorry…Rae. But I cannot…let you…go free!"

Where was my vampiric strength now? He was so strong! Suddenly, we were both on the ground with Giancarlo straddling my stomach. Under any other circumstances, this would have been incredibly sexy. I could feel his muscled thighs pressing inward, trying to immobilize me. The wonderful odor that had been in the air around him on the porch had now entirely disappeared. *Sweated off all your crappy aftershave?* I thought bitterly, struggling against the legs that relentlessly tightened against me like determined anacondas. With steely rage, Giancarlo whispered, "Who did this to you? I shall kill them. I will kill them all," as he removed the stake from his jacket.

"Go for it! I'll wait here."

Then, ignoring me, very softly and politely, Giancarlo whispered, "Please remain still, *dolcezza.*" He repositioned the stake to a more lethal-friendly position. The plunging motion never came. Giancarlo half-grunted, half-shouted, "I cannot!" at the same time that I bucked my hips upward. He flew sideways, and the stake spun out of his hand and clattered across the cement. I scrabbled backward. He threw himself at me again. I automatically raised a knee. It struck him in the stomach, and he doubled over with an "Oof."

I screamed wordlessly and threw myself over onto my hands and knees, trying to gain my feet, while Giancarlo went for the stake. He was quick. I had taken a few steps when he grabbed me from behind again. Without thinking, I head-butted him backward. He grunted, and his grip loosened slightly. I wrenched myself free. His clutching fingers briefly grasped my purse but lost purchase as I sprinted across the driveway. I raced around the building with Giancarlo hot on my tail.

"You asshole!" I screamed over my shoulder. "You liar!"

"Rae," he panted, "it is nothing personal!"

"You're crazy! Not personal? It's called a dictionary! Look it up!"

"Jesus Christ! Rae! Fuck!"

Running flat out, I was able to gain a lead again and soon lost him somewhere behind me around the other side of the building. Inspiration struck, and I detoured abruptly toward the street. As I ran, I dug my car keys out of my purse. I sprinted toward the Z, unlocked the door, and jumped in. I started it up and sat there for a moment, letting it warm up. This was torture similar to movie scenes in elevators when the monster was galloping toward the characters and no amount of stabbing the "close door" button made the doors move any faster. I had to let it warm up, though, or it might stall. True to the nature of the evening, Giancarlo burst around the side of the building and headed right for me. He threw himself at the passenger door, tried the handle, then scrambled across the hood (son of a bitch—my paint!), and cranked on the driver's side handle seconds after I locked the door.

"Rae, I must speak to you!" he shouted through the glass. *Speak to me?* He pulled his arm back as if to smash through the glass, and I shrieked, "No, Giancarlo, no, it's a classic!" at the top of my voice. He paused long enough, his eyes wide, for me to punch the gas, crunch the car parked behind me, put the Z in drive, and tear out of the parking spot. I was about to burn rubber out of there when I noticed he was just standing in the street, staring at the car I had smashed into. I craned my head around to see it. It was Giancarlo's GTO, parked right behind me. I cranked the window down a crack and addressed him in a loud voice. It seemed to break through his fog. "There are aliens abducting people in broad daylight, Giancarlo! I only became this way so I could fight them—stop them! I'm one of the good guys!"

He stared at me like he had never seen me before, his chest heaving up and down. At least there was one good thing about this night, I thought, as I peeled away at top speed. I now had a new horrible memory that I'd still be holding onto 20 years from now that made Red Harris look like stupid kid stuff.

No pun intended.

CHAPTER 25

I had no destination in mind, of course, so I just drove. Whenever someone came up behind me in a car, I broke out into a cold sweat and couldn't breathe. Just ten minutes of running around and fighting with Giancarlo, and I had post-traumatic stress already. Obviously, I would be a terrible candidate for the military. But apparently, either Giancarlo had given up or he'd been so shocked that I'd damaged the GTO that he couldn't even move, because none of the cars behind me turned out to be him. Maybe I would go back home tonight, and he'd still be there, standing in the street and staring at his car. Maybe I would tell all the vampires in the world that he was mercilessly hunting down that this was his Achilles heel; just casually key the GTO as you were fleeing, and it would be a guaranteed get out of jail free card.

I found myself transitioning from the 101 to the 405 and heading south. I should drive the other way, take the 405 north to the 5, heading for San Francisco. That might be a good idea. Get on the Golden Gate Bridge and at some point in the middle, just drive off the side of it. Was I moping? Yes, I was moping. I was in a fairly bad mood. I'd really, really liked Giancarlo. But here was more of my bizarre history with guys in action; not only my usual bad luck but, even worse, now I'd gained a mortal enemy.

I guided the Z without really seeing. My head was pounding, and now I was feeling that stomach-clenching thing again. When was the last time I'd eaten? I didn't know. Abruptly, I recalled the wheatgrass juice and leaned over sideways, fumbling to get it out of my purse. I shoved the tip of the bottle into my mouth, squeezed, and sucked down the juice greedily. Immediately, I felt much better.

I made a mental note to thank Cola later for his advice. Of course, when someone *loved* someone, like Cola obviously did me, they gave you good advice. Unlike Dante, whom I was beginning to see more and more was, indeed, not who he seemed to be. Not just because he wasn't deaf and not just because he was a vampire. Because he was a gigantic asshole.

Quite a while later, I was driving through Hermosa Beach, making my way toward my forsaken condo from what seemed like a million years ago. I parked in the street in front of the building and gazed with melancholy at my lost dream. Maybe it had been a small dream and very ordinary, but it had been mine. This would have been mine. There were palm trees outside of the building swaying gently in the evening breeze. I could hear the big fronds rustling like someone shuffling through dry leaves in a forest.

I thought about what Cola had said, that I didn't even need the show anymore. I could have my own show, my own movies. It sounded like it should be a good thing, but it was different, wasn't it? The condo would have been hard-won, a personal, private accomplishment. I know I had consciously traveled to Cola's office bent on worse: hypnotizing him into making me an overnight success. But now that I thought about it a little, a movie franchise acquired as a vampire would be nothing, like entering a party and having someone automatically pass you a glass of champagne. No thought, no effort on your part of any kind except showing up.

My eyes drooped shut as I wavered between self-pity and grandiose fantasies. Slipping into a stress doze, I opened my eyes again an hour later, feeling none the better. I slowly drove away from the condo and headed toward the beach. I slipped my car into a spot at the curb, got out, and headed down to the sand. Over to my left, the pier was lit up, and people were strolling around and leaning against the railing staring out at sea. Nobody was on the beach. I walked down to the water's edge and gazed into the churning dark waters. For some reason, I found myself thinking of my old nemesis, the Tiger shark. I walked forward, wading into the frigid water. It was much colder than I thought it would be or thought I would feel. Maybe it was just phantom nerve endings that were "remembering" how the ocean felt at night. I didn't know.

I continued to wade forward, the water up to my hips now, pushing through deeper and deeper. Suddenly, I reached a shelf and plummeted beneath the waves into the cold darkness. I lingered under the water, swaying with the tide, and a series of belated bubbles escaped from my mouth and traveled upward. I inhaled deeply and waited for the killing pain, the panic, the struggle for the surface. It never came. I could breathe! Or whatever it was. Not breathe? I was standing under the water, not drowning, not dying. I opened my eyes wide, straining to see into the distant gloom.

Tiger sharks lived for a long time. The one that had chomped me, if it had lived a safe, relatively risk-free life, could still be alive. Wouldn't it be surprised to be swimming along and see me swooping down from above? And before it could react, wouldn't it crap its pants to feel me unceremoniously taking a huge bite out of its dorsal fin? Then let *it* go through the rest of its life with everybody in the ocean staring at its mauled dorsal fin, feeling sorry for it or disgusted by it. Let *it* try to get modeling jobs and watch the photographers get increasingly frustrated trying to find creative ways to camouflage the damage. Let *it* start drinking and drugging, despite warnings and concern from the few sharks that still cared, and then, years later, wonder what had happened to its life. The perfect revenge story. Full circle.

Done daydreaming, I shot to the surface, swam to shore, and trudged back toward my car. In a deep melancholy, I drove to the Valley, heading for Margarite's neighborhood. I drove by Margarite and Douglas's place, stalker-style. The gate was open and the lights were on. For some reason, this warmed my heart, and I felt a little better. Maybe they were having a dinner party in there. People would be laughing, clinking glasses, flirting with each other. Maybe Margarite was hosting a special dinner for all of her anorexic clients. Every single plate would be returned to the kitchen, untouched. Later, after everyone had left, Margarite would walk into the kitchen as if she was going to do dishes and scarf down each uneaten portion. Douglas would have to rush her to the ER later to get her stomach pumped. I hoped she was getting help and that the next time I saw her, she could still fit through her front door.

I decided to stalk Ganymede's place next. I pulled up half a block from the house facing the wrong way and stared at it in my rearview mirror.

This house also had all its lights blazing, and I could hear voices distantly on the wind. The shrill voices of three crazy little girls. Everything seemed normal here, too. The relief made my stomach unclench a little. Next, I would have to go see if Rex was all right, make sure no cones of light were shooting down into his home. Make sure he wasn't being floated, surfboards and all, up into the sky. The only place I couldn't go, which is where I actually should have been and needed to be, was Now. Something was going on there beyond the everyday kooky attempts to get people to remain in the moment. I couldn't put my finger on it, but Bob had seemed evasive. Hadn't he? Maybe he had simply become evasive because he was running a school of enlightenment. Maybe it was standard operating procedure, like with politicians, to dance around certain subjects.

As I was sitting there musing, my cell phone rang. I looked at the caller ID. It was Ganymede.

"Hello?" I looked at my side view mirror back at the house to make sure nobody was sneaking up on me.

The yard was deserted.

"Hi," said Ganymede cheerfully. "Is that you parked out there?"

"Um…"

"I'm coming out."

"Oh, sweetheart, no. You'd better not."

Pause.

"Why not?"

"How did you see me? I'm like half a block away parked in the dark."

"I was looking out the window when you drove by. I just happened to see you."

"Oh, okay." I sank down into my seat, feeling awkward. I hadn't wanted anyone in the house to see me stalking them. "I was coming from my sister's place, and I decided to swing by this way…just to… check on you guys. See if you're okay."

"She lives nearby?"

"Um…yeah. Sort of."

"On Topanga?"

"No."

"Ventura Boulevard?"

"Um…the other side of the hill."

"PCH?"

"She lives in Brentwood." God, he was persistent. "I can't really explain how I ended up here."

"I know," said Ganymede guilelessly. "I'm always checking up on people, too."

"You're protecting them, right?" I said. The creepy way this kid acted and the whole robot thing…I was beginning to think he and his family might be having similar adventures to mine. The possibility of this filled me with such rage, I thought the top of my head was going to blow off.

"Yeah. But I can't do enough," he said simply.

We were quiet for a moment.

"I'm coming out," Ganymede said again, decisively.

"Can you get past your sisters?" I hedged, trying to stall him. My clothes were still wet, and I didn't want to have to explain that and I wasn't in the mood, anyway, for Ganymede's eccentric sweetness. I needed to boil and baste in my fury for a while. I needed to feel this, absorb and accept where my life was right now: condensed down to a tiny enclosure where I was regaining consciousness, stunned and bewildered, chained to a pipe, listening to a gruff voice ask over a scratchy P.A. system, "You want to play a game?"

Ganymede was thinking, weighing the odds.

Finally, he said, "I don't think so." He sighed deeply. Then a few seconds later, he said brightly, "Could you go to the store and get some ice cream? You could bring it back and just leave it on the doorstep. I'll come out and get it."

"Ice cream, huh?" I smiled at my phone, picturing Ganymede's enormous afro. "Why haven't you just driven down to the store yourself?" I teased.

"Ha ha, very funny. I'm totally banned from driving."

"Well…" I said. "The stores up here are closed. It's pretty late, you know. I could drive down to the Valley and get some, but it might be a while. Will you still be up in forty-five minutes?"

"Of course I'll still be up. A documentary on the making of *Robopocalypse* doesn't start until eleven-thirty."

"Okay, baby, I'll be right back. What flavor?"

"Oh!" He said excitedly. "Neapolitan! Thanks, Rae."

"You got it."

"I'll pay you back," he promised.

"No, you won't. My treat. Don't worry about it."

We disconnected, and I pulled away from the house, heading down into the Valley. The spontaneous mission was just what I needed, however odd it may have been. I couldn't help myself. I loved that kid to death.

When I returned from below and was pulling up to the house again, I saw a small, dark shadow disengage itself from the front porch and come running across the lawn full tilt. Ganymede had been waiting for me outside, obviously, eager to get his robot-building mitts on what I considered one of the most liberal-minded of ice creams, melded as it was with three very different flavors. Leave it to Ganymede, resident egghead and deep thinker, to crave Neapolitan. Probably a subconscious desire for peace at the homestead.

As I opened the door and put one foot down to go meet him, the worst possible thing in the world happened. A cone of light suddenly filled the yard, surrounding Ganymede and stopping him in his tracks. I lurched all the way out of the car, dropping the bag of ice cream into the dirt. I tilted my head back and saw the machine. A confusion of sounds and voices swarmed my mind. *She who…get the boy…not now…*

As was foretold earlier in the evening, the top of my head blew off. Oh, no. This was the wrong night. Oh, no, no, no. This was the wrong, wrong, wrong night.

I walked into the light and stood beneath Ganymede who was floating up into the air. Casually I reached up, hooking one hand around his ascending ankle. After a few minutes of tug of war with the beam of light, a being appeared in the air. It focused its glaring, insectoid eyes on me, but to no avail. I did not freeze. I did not let go of the boy. Instead, I bared my teeth. Slowly. When it saw this, it tried to disappear. I didn't let it. Now I let go of the boy and moved, lightning fast. It started to screech. I didn't let it. My vampiric voice emerged, producing a sustained note of havoc. It tried to fight. I didn't let it. It tried to keep living. I didn't let it. I vibrated, superhuman, monstrous, no feeling, no thought. All I could see was Ganymede, in my mind, his soft afro, his trusting eyes. I sank my hands into the creature as if it were made of water, or sand. I unleashed pernicious violence upon it. More voices filled my head, disconnected and panicked. I understood nothing that was said. Within seconds, I had reduced the being to a purplish, brackish pulp. I had reduced it to its origins, its mysterious beginnings. I stood panting in the yard, white-knuckled and burning hot. Before me, the remains liquefied and disappeared.

I felt eyes on me. I whipped my head around. Another Zeta was standing on the dirt just outside the circle of light where Ganymede was still slowly rising. I lunged toward it. Immediately, ridiculously, it flung its hands in the air like a car-jacking victim. I stopped, thrown by this. Ganymede's heel was just reaching eye level. Distracted, I reached up again and grabbed his shoe and held on like I was flying a kite while I stared down the being. Why was it just standing there? There was something different in its flat shark-like eyes from the other ones. I felt it more than saw it. Something not quite like empathy but something leaning toward it, something striving toward it.

I gestured at Ganymede with my free hand. "Do you mind?"

The Zeta ducked its head once. Was that a nod? It kept one palm raised placatingly, shot up into the air, and disappeared. A moment later, so did the light. Ganymede plummeted down. His foot wrenched from my grasp. He thudded into the dirt. The hovering ship was gone. The voices were gone. Except one, from down below:

"Ow," said Ganymede.

I turned around. He was sitting in the dirt, looking at his elbow. It was cut and bleeding a little. Crap. I should have caught him. He looked up at me with anticipation mixed with his usual guileless adoration, but then his grin dimmed several watts. He frowned, looked back down at his elbow, then back at me. "I think I tripped," he said hesitantly. Several beats pulsed by as he gazed at me, then he seemed to shake it off. "Where's the ice cream?" he asked with a watery smile.

Mutely, I returned to the car. I was still shaking a little, somewhat stunned at events. I had murdered, killed. But one of them had been different. I had let him go. I searched around in the dark, found the bag half-rolled behind the front tire. The Neapolitan had definitely seen better days. Ganymede took the bag from me and smiled openly, his previous uncertainty apparently gone. He made no comment about why the ice cream had been lying in the dirt under my car.

"Thanks, Rae!" He pressed his elbow. "I have to get a Band-Aid and some Neosporin. I don't want to get the flesh-eating disease."

Oh, boy. "I don't want you to get the flesh-eating disease either, honey."

"You should come in and have ice cream with us."

"Yeah. That's a good idea. Maybe some other time."

"Okay…" He deflated a little.

I tried to think of something to cheer him up. I tried to think of something to take my mind off Them and my murderous rage and how easily I had pulled that thing apart *and how good it had felt. And how I would do it again, without hesitation, if given the chance. And how I would kill them all, without hesitation, if given the chance.*

Except the ones that held their hands up and seemed sorry…

"How's the robot coming? The last pictures you attached were from about a week ago."

"He's almost done. Just a few adjustments. The sound waves—"

He was cut off as the front door flew open, and a torrent of atonal shrieking and howling assailed the quiet night. Ganymede whirled around as his sisters swarmed the yard, then turned back to me, panicked. "RUN!" he yelled, gripping his elbow and his ice cream. "RUN!"

It was almost more terrifying than an alien abduction. I ran.

CHAPTER 26

I jumped in the Z, turned it on, and spun in a tight circle out of there, headed back for the Valley, my tires squealing. In my rearview, I saw one of the girls waving at me while the other two tackled their brother, trying to wrestle the ice cream out of his hands. I drove around a bend, and they were out of view.

Immediately I began thinking of odds. Ganymede conveniently getting abducted while I was here. Same with Mr. Dadalian. What were the odds of that? It seemed pretty suspicious. But it was also very confusing. Hadn't they been stalking me for a long time, and wasn't Johnny proof of that? But the dangerous stuff had only recently started. God. Crap. What was I going to do now? Where was I going to go?

Even though I was almost one-hundred percent sure that Giancarlo wouldn't be waiting for me at home, I was afraid to go back there. I could go to a hotel, spend the night on Mulholland Drive in my car, or beg for sofa rights at Rex's or Hama's. I realized I was potentially putting both of them in danger if my theory was true, but something deep down told me there would be no more abductions tonight. And call me selfish, but I just didn't want to be alone. I called Rex first but got no answer. Hama's phone rang and rang. *Please, Zeus, God, Horus, Vishnu,* I prayed, *please don't make me have to call Margarite. At least do me one solid tonight.*

I was just about to hang up when Hama cheerfully answered.

"Hey, chica," I said. "Um…I don't want to be alone tonight. Long story. But you can say no," I said quickly. "I don't want to—"

"You get over here, girl! We'll be waiting," said Hama, and slammed down the phone.

When I knocked twenty-five minutes later, both Billy and Hama threw the door open wide.

"Rae!" yelled Hama as Billy shouted, "Get in here!"

I exhaled, relieved. No weird pauses, no staring, no stakes. They yanked me inside and the next thing I knew, I was the middle component of a spontaneous group hug.

"I've been calling and calling!" Hama was saying emotionally. I tried to react, but the combined strength of their arms made even the thought of moving just a delightful daydream. I didn't even think my new power was any match for them. Bill laughed uproariously and squeezed harder. I realized they were both blasted.

"Come here! Come here!" he shouted, pulling both of us closer. After a moment, he released one arm and sort of half-shoved me aside to get to Hama. They fell on to each other as I stumbled sideways across the floor and almost plunged into the glass coffee table. When I looked again, they were tongue-deep in each other's mouths and rapidly shifting from light porn to X-rated. They were super-drunk and by all appearances super in love, and I was super happy for them.

I tiptoed out of there and into the kitchen where I found the remains of many enchiladas, eight empty beer bottles, and three half-drunk bottles of wine. I picked one up and dumped the contents down my throat before I remembered the wheatgrass again. I dumped some of that down my throat, too, just for good measure. Then I sat staring at my hands, looking for the telltale signs of murder. There was nothing on them except a little dirt. I got up and washed them in the sink then picked up one of the enchiladas and absently started gnawing on it while I turned on the TV with the remote control.

There was silence from the other room, thank God. Hopefully they had both passed out in the middle of tearing each other's clothes off.

Oddly, the first thing that came on the TV was the *High Stakes Poker* clip of the famous fight with Rex sitting in the middle. There was Rex at the table, slouched in his seat, wearing a Dodgers baseball cap pulled down low. The player ahead of Rex called all-in. The argument broke out between two other players. The melee began. Fists flew and Rex ducked, calling his bluff. I smiled, watching the familiar scene. The station was playing it in slo-mo this time, so now it looked like the Matrix with the fist arcing toward Rex's head, missing him by agonizing millimeters. In the background, the announcers commented, laughing in amazement.

"If I had someone doing a Mohel on me, I'd only want this guy to do it!"

"Well, that sounds kinda weird, Jeff, but I get what you're saying."

"Hostage negotiator, anyone? Call Rex Defoe at *High Stakes Poker*! He won't mind. It'll only help him focus better!"

"Rex 'Da Foe' Defoe! A minor disturbance in the Force, indeed, Jeff. Oh, my God, what's going on? An 8.0 is shaking Las Vegas! The Palazzo is crumbling! Dafoe's ducking the balustrade and still makes the call!"

"Holy cow! A sheet of metal just sliced his right arm off at the elbow, and he still calls!"

"Blood is everywhere! How many pints of blood are in the human body, Jeff?"

"Missiles fired from North Korea head for Vegas—"

"North Korea doesn't have that capability, Jeff."

"I heard the news that day, too, Ronny! Get your head out of your ass. They've got missiles."

"I'll remove mine if you'll remove yours. Their missiles can only reach Guam, Jeff."

"But we all know what would happen if they could reach Vegas, Ronny! Need I even say it?"

"You do not need to say it, Jeff. You do not need to say it."

Then, together, shouting: "He still makes the call!"

It went on like that. And then my cell phone rang with *Anything Goes*, and I answered happily, feeling better than I had in days and days. Could be Hama and Bill, so normal, so in love. Could be the magical wheatgrass, a seeming balm that right now was coating all my insides and soothing the terrible clenching. Could be the wine. Or maybe it was just Rex's voice. I went the first eighteen years of my life not hearing or knowing Rex's voice. I went the last…whatever… years of my life hearing it and knowing it always.

"Hey, Shark Bait," he said in a throaty undertone.

"Yeah. Ha ha." Not shark bait anymore. Now the Tiger shark and I, we weren't so unalike. "Guess what I'm watching. Your famous clip."

"The call clip?"

"The call clip."

"That was a crazy night."

"How much did you win that night?"

"Um…a lot." He paused. "I don't remember. Where are you?"

"Visiting Hama and Bill."

"Are they working out?"

"No, they're not working out."

A sudden image of Giancarlo jerking me back by my hair filled my vision, and I stifled a small sob.

"Was that a sneeze? Are you getting the flu?"

"No," I said, fingering my scalp where the hair had torn out. It wasn't sore anymore. I lifted the little bottle and gulped more wheatgrass. Whatever it was, it was doing the trick. Then I picked up the wine bottle and upended it over my open mouth.

"Anyway, woman, what were you calling me for?"

"My date tried to kill me tonight."

"What date?"

"This guy. That I was going out with."

Pause.

"Have you ever thought of doing stand-up? You're actually really funny. That would be a great opener."

"I know. It's so funny, right?"

Pause.

"He tried to stick a piece of wood through my heart."

I heard ice cubes clinking as he drank something.

Next logical question: "Where'd you meet this guy?"

"Physical therapy."

"Did you get your money back?"

"Well, he's not my therapist. He's someone else's therapist."

"You're going on and on with this. It almost sounds like it's true."

"I'm just kidding." I laughed. "Are you crazy?" I'd said enough. I don't know why I had said it to begin with. It just felt good to say it out loud to someone. Maybe also so that I had a witness in case Giancarlo succeeded sometime in the future. Rex wouldn't be able to do anything about it because Giancarlo would hide his stakes and deny everything. But still…

Pause. Pause.

"What is going on with you? You sound weird."

"I do?"

"Let's get together tomorrow night. I've been thinking about you. Remember when we saw that re-release of *Pulp Fiction?*"

Pulp Fiction? How weird that he would be thinking about that! I didn't even think he remembered. Me, Rex, and Hama had gone to see *Pulp Fiction* together in a small celebration after I'd scored *Green Splendor II.* Afterward, we'd gotten blasted somewhere in Miracle Mile, almost started a riot at the pool tables, lost a $500 bet (Hama's fault), taken a cab back to Rex's place in Marina Del Rey (very expensive, but no matter, because Rex was super-rich by then), immediately gotten into a screaming fight over something I no longer recall, and ended up rolling around on the carpet, ripping each other's clothes off while Hama passed out on the sofa. That time. The one-time sex time. Did I remember?

"I'm surprised you remember," I commented dryly.

"Why wouldn't I remember?"

"Never mind."

"I think we should talk."

"What? What do you mean?" I asked, alarmed.

"I'll pick you up."

"What kind of talk?"

More pausing. I heard him smoking over the phone.

"Nothing that can't wait. Just try not to get killed by one of these random men you pick up in the street."

I rolled my eyes. Did I detect a note of jealousy there?

"I'll swing by," he said again.

"That's okay. I'll come to your place."

"That's ridiculous. I'll pick you up."

"Ridiculous? My license wasn't revoked. What's the problem?"

"I know how much you hate to drive."

He was right. I did hate to drive. But I loved driving my Z. It was sort of a paradoxical situation. It was just typical life in L.A.

"It's okay. I'll suspend my hatred for one night." I emptied the bottle of wine down my throat. I felt a little lightheaded. It was a nice feeling. Being lightheaded was much better than your heart hemorrhaging because of piece of wood was lodged through it.

"Okay, I'll see you tomorrow. Dinner and a movie."

"Can't wait."

"Love you," Rex said, and immediately disconnected. Rex always jumped off the train before the other hobos could say they loved him back. He wasn't great with pillow talk. He was Giancarlo's complete and utter opposite.

My throat tightened, and I half-coughed, half-sobbed. Belatedly I wondered if Rex, now, would notice anything weird about me. He knew me better than anyone. Would he see? I stood up and tiptoed to the kitchen door to see where Hama and Bill were and walked right into Hama. She blinked in the bright overhead light, yawning.

"Sorry. We drank a little too much and fell asleep on the floor."

"Don't apologize. It's your place."

She put her hands on her hips and looked around imperiously.

"You're right. What was I thinking? GET OUT."

I laughed.

"You sort of look like crap," said Hama.

"Why, thank you." I batted my eyelashes.

"Are you okay? I'm glad you're here." She pulled me to her and squeezed hard. I did not even want to imagine what sex was like with Hama and Billy. Being sandwiched between the two of them had felt like being trapped in a car crusher. "I never even asked you what's going on. What's going on?" she asked.

"Nothing serious. Just feeling lonely."

"Aww…" She abruptly became serious. "How's the shoulder?"

As I displayed the dazzling arc range of my newly recuperated shoulder, she expressed guarded amazement and demanded to know what I'd done. Greatly editing the details of the last 24 hours or so, I told her about the wheatgrass.

"Wheatgrass?" She wrinkled her nose. "*Wheat*grass? Since when?"

"So you don't know everything in the world about health and diet."

"I do know everything in the world about health and diet. Wheatgrass isn't that great."

"It's pretty great."

"It shouldn't have healed your shoulder. You must have done something. You must be having sex again."

"Yeah, sex healed my shoulder." I chortled loudly. "Or did it heal *your* shoulder?" I asked pointedly.

Hama grinned. She reached out and pumped my arm up and down, angling it in awkward directions suspiciously and carefully watching my face for the impending scream. It never came. "Amazing…" she murmured. Suddenly, an unbidden image of Ganymede floating up into the night sky flooded my mind. My throat tightened and, as was my new pattern, I hiccuped back a little sob. Hama's head shot up.

"Did that hurt?"

"No. I was thinking of something."

"Wheatgrass…" she whispered, engrossed, not even interested in what I had been thinking. "Well, okay. Looking good there, lady." She let go of my arm. "I'll get the sheets for the pull-out."

"All right. Thanks for letting me crash."

"Don't thank me for that. Thank me for your shoulder."

"Why?"

"'Cause I figured out what happened. It was the workout. My workout shocked your shoulder back onto the road to wellness. That was the catalyst. My workout." She thumped her chest. *"You need pain to get rid of pain."*

"What a wonderful code you live by."

"Thank you."

I dozed on and off through the night, not really sleeping, and was already awake when Hama got up around six a.m. to make her protein shake in preparation for her first workout of the day. I thanked her again for her hospitality, and as I left the room, she swatted me on the rear so hard tears sprang to my eyes. There was no way I was going to let her see that and just continued bravely forward to the front door. I decided to bite the bullet and go home. For some reason, the daylight gave me courage. On the way there, I stopped at a Cheesecake Factory and picked up a red velvet cheesecake for the Dadalians. Maybe if I showed up at home with a red velvet cheesecake in my hand and Giancarlo was camped out in his GTO waiting for me, he'd hesitate before he pulled the stake out of his jacket. How dangerous could someone be holding an entire cheesecake? What kind of vampire even *went* into the Cheesecake Factory to begin with?

Anonymous Vampire: Hi. Give me a red velvet cheesecake and hold the cheesecake. In other words, give me a cheesecake made out of blood or I will slaughter you and your family and everyone in Van Nuys. And believe me, I would be doing Van Nuys a favor.

I didn't think that would go over well. I trolled past the building slowly, overheated from the drive. Paranoia quickly eclipsed all other sensations. I continued around the block. I didn't see the GTO anywhere, although that meant nothing. He could have moved the car and returned, now dressed all in black, sunk back into the shadows. But as I hesitantly parked, exited the car, and fast-walked into the building, nothing happened. No one rushed me. No one jumped me. I hustled inside, went upstairs, scratched a quick note that I hadn't had time to bake but wanted them to enjoy this, and left the cheesecake outside the Dadalians'. Then I pushed my apartment door open, smacking it into the dresser, fully expecting Giancarlo to come hurtling out of the kitchen. But no one was there. I scooted past the dresser and slipped inside.

I rinsed the ocean's salt off and dropped my body core temperature simultaneously in a cold shower, then fell thankfully into bed, slipping into a dreamless sleep. I awoke at dusk, putzed around, surfed the 'Net a little. Later, I got ready to go out and chose a sexy little sundress to wear. Rex wouldn't care. I figured that night at the Standard had been an anomaly. I noticed that I was low on wheatgrass and decided it could wait. I figured that I wasn't going to turn into a blood-thirsty monster within the next couple of hours. When I left, I did my paranoid spy routine in reverse, skulking cagily back outside, into the car, and not relaxing until I was accelerating away into the night.

In Hollywood, Rex threw the door open wide, smiling, and I realized I was nervous. What if *he* saw something? What if, unbeknownst to me, Rex was a poker-playing surfboard-designing Vampire Slayer? While I waited tensely, he eyed me up and down, taking in the sundress with no small amount of amusement. And then, conveniently, he uttered the magic words, "Come on in, Shark Bait," and I crossed over the threshold without incident. "Back in a sec," he called, disappearing around a corner. I exhaled deeply, feeling silly that I felt so relieved. So far, Ganymede had merely frowned, Hama had said I looked like crap, and Rex hadn't noticed anything. It looked like maybe I could get away with this after all. I gazed around the foyer and over at the living room. It was so sparsely decorated, it felt like Rex was still moving in. He just wasn't into buying stuff. He had paid off his parents' house years ago. He was an only child, so there were no siblings to provide for. But he had set up some education funds for several of his cousins.

I was nosily perusing the refrigerator when Rex appeared in the doorway with a light jacket on. "Wanna skip the movie and just get blasted? But you should eat something. You're a lightweight."

I stared at him. I sniffed the air. I gazed around the kitchen. He was baking cookies? Why hadn't he told me? Something smelled so good! Was that a pot roast? Mmm! I bent to peer into the oven, but it wasn't on.

"What's going on now?"

"Huh?" I straightened up.

"What are you doing?"

I looked around in confusion. Where was that delicious odor coming from? I locked in on Rex. "Wow, you smell great! What is that, Drakkor Noir?"

"Drakkor Noir?" he asked, amazed. "Are you high?"

I pivoted around and closed the refrigerator door and stood with my back to Rex for a minute. The light bulb went on over my head. I swallowed. My mouth felt crispy. Oh, yeah. That. I was smelling *that...*

I revolved slowly back around, looked anywhere but at Rex. For the second time in a short period, I realized how woefully unprepared I'd been to take this side step into second reality. *How drunk had I been, exactly?* Yeah, Rex had been super drunk when he'd gotten married the third time. But after that, he wasn't barred from entrance everywhere, wasn't subject to this clawing desire. So many other things were just myths, like no reflection in the mirror, bursting into flames in the sun, the whole cross thing. But this, this...

This was something else entirely. This was undeniable. That was why people had been smelling so good lately: Giancarlo and Hama and even remotely, Annie in the liquor aisle. I hadn't been prepared for this. Rex smelled like a double cheeseburger with onions and pickles, hold the special dressing, *and I wanted to eat him.* Completely stressed and freaking out, I put my hands up to my face and burst into tears.

I could only imagine Rex standing there, baffled. But I couldn't see him, because my eyes were covered. And I didn't want to see him. How could I face him? *What had I done?* I heard footsteps, clothes rustling. The cookie/pot roast/warm chocolate smell increased. Then Rex was pulling me against him, wrapping both arms around me while saliva flooded my mouth. He rubbed my back, saying, "Shh, shh, shh." My forehead pressed into his neck, nudging his Adam's apple. His arms were lean and strong.

"It must be depressing going through menopause prematurely."

"Shut up!" I said, pulling back. I pounded him on the shoulder with my fist. He grinned, and then we both laughed.

And then, out of left field, he said, "If it makes you feel any better, you're the one I should have married."

Weirdness! Despite that, even though that would have essentially made me the fourth choice to the prom, it was still sweet, and I appreciated it.

We were walking up a semi-dark side street near Nine Thirty in Westwood, coming back from Rex's quest for a pack of cigarettes. Dinner had been delicious. In the movies, vampires never ate solid food. I had squeezed out the last of the wheatgrass an hour ago into one of the many cocktails I had consumed, and I had to admit I was feeling pretty funky. I had consumed so much alcohol, Rex was flabbergasted that I was still vertical. After the first two drinks, when I'd noticed nothing happening, I'd just kept drinking and drinking, wondering when the buzz was going to kick in. My undeadocity obviously spelled a sad end to drunkenness. I'd had so many cocktails and beers, I'd insisted on paying for all the booze. Rex had shrugged like, "Sure, go ahead," and when the check came, he grabbed it.

"You're unemployed," was all he said when I started to argue.

I was happy. It felt like something was happening with me and Rex. The weird thing was, Rex and the shark were intertwined. Something had happened to us after the shark came into our lives. We had changed. No, I had changed. The shark, the monster circling below our dangling arms and legs, had seized so much more than my hand. It had seized my mind, my will, my life. The years had gone by, and I'd become like Ripley in *Alien 3*. At one point, as her endless nightmare continued, she'd told the alien, "You've been in my life for so long, I can't remember anything else." And that was how I felt. Bob, for all his faults, was right. We were never in the Now. Because the past or the future always had us by the balls.

Walking back to the truck later, Rex dropped his arm around my shoulder like he'd done a thousand times before. But tonight, it didn't feel like a thousand times before. It felt like the first time. And something weird was going on. The baking cookie smell was increasing by the moment, mixed haphazardly in with that smoldering energy particular to long-buried sexual tension.

"You're driving me crazy in that little dress," Rex said suddenly, as if reading my thoughts.

I shot him a look. "Are you coming on to me?"

He exhaled, the smoke curling away into the night. He removed his arm from my shoulder.

"I'm admiring your tiny, flimsy dress."

"It's not that tiny."

"It's really short. And flimsy." He stared down at my legs.

"It was hot today."

"It wasn't that hot. You put that dress on to drive me crazy."

"I wasn't aware it would have that effect."

What a liar!

Silence.

"I mean, you haven't cared about that...in *years*," I elaborated, fishing.

"What? What makes you say that?" He looked confused.

"Well, because I—"

"I'm not sure you're up for this conversation," he said enigmatically, cutting me off.

"What conversation?"

"The one you've been avoiding since we were kids. Youngsters. Young adults."

"Avoid—what—kids?" My mouth dropped open.

Rex walked along and smoked for a while. Walking and smoking. Smoking and walking.

"I don't—you—" I stammered, my attention drawn to a vein in his forearm. I wondered what he'd do if I affixed myself to it and started sucking. "We were—but—" I trailed off, staring dreamily at the vein.

Rex was looking at me like he was weighing something. He threw his cigarette to the ground and crushed it as he stepped toward me. He pushed his hand into my hair and pulled on it lightly so that my face tilted upward. He stared down at me for a few seconds, his eyes moving to my lips the same way mine had moved to his vein. Then he started to back me up across the sidewalk and into a tree. I felt the tree trunk press into my back like an insistent boner. Rex lifted my arms above my head and pinned them against the tree. He never could have done that just a few days ago. I would have shrieked in agony in this position. I think I even saw recognition of this fact, that I wasn't shrieking, pass through his face right before he pressed his body against me, keeping my arms above my head, and stared at me steadily. I stared back, my mind contorting like a bendy straw, and all reason fled. Taking my fugue state for consent (which it was), Rex began to lower his face toward me, pressing my hands harder into the tree, and we were thus engaged when a voice said beside us, "Sheesh. Classy."

We pulled apart. A medium-sized, ordinary looking guy with five o'clock shadow and big, spooky eyes was staring at us.

Rex let go of my arms immediately. He said, "What?"

"Classy. I said *classy,* dude. Geez. Get a room already."

Rex tensed beside me.

"Do I know you?"

Rex always assumed he was bumping into one of his betting acquaintances, usually someone he'd beaten the crap out of in a game somewhere.

"Do I know you?'" the guy said sarcastically, imitating Rex. "No, dude, you don't know me. But you know *this.*" He held his hand out. He was holding a knife. "Gimme your fucking wallet," he said. His eyes darted cagily right and left. It was completely surreal. Weren't we in Westwood? Westwood was the home of UCLA, our alma mater. Westwood was a nice neighborhood! For a moment, I was scared out of my mind, completely forgetting that I had torn a living creature apart just a few hours ago. I was more trained to respond to human danger than I was to ZR danger, which was murky at best; who even knew if, in the end, they just wanted to be friends? This guy, however, did not want to be friends. Something inside me uncoiled with a sickening need. I moved forward. To what? Tear his head off? Plunge my fist into his heart? But suddenly, there was a barrier. Rex's arm was across my chest, stopping me. Then he yanked me behind him. Abashed, I let him.

"Seriously, man?" said Rex to the guy.

"Don't call me bro," the man said angrily. "I ain't your bro."

"I didn't call you bro," Rex said.

"I just heard you, dude. You said, 'Seriously, bro?'" He swiped the air with the knife. "And I say seriously, bro. Seriously. Gimme your fucking wallet!" He jabbed at me. "And your purse. Now!"

Rex didn't say anything else. He nodded agreeably, one hand up in compliance, and reached into the big side pocket of his cargo pants. He pulled out not a wallet but a gun. He immediately aimed it at the guy's head. The mugger's eyes opened wide and got ten degrees spookier.

"Drop it." Rex spoke in an undertone. "Drop it."

The mugger dropped the knife. He held up his palms, reminding me of the alien being yesterday.

"I'm sorry. Sorry about that, bro. Sorry." He didn't sound sorry at all.

"That's all right, bro."

"That thing loaded, bro?"

"Yeah, bro, it's loaded."

Rex stepped forward. The mugger stepped back.

"I wasn't gonna hurt you. I just need—"

Rex kicked the knife away and then slammed the gun viciously across the man's face. There was an audible crack.

"AAAAAAAAAAAAAHHHHHHHHHHHHHH!" the mugger screamed and lashed out blindly, grazing Rex on the cheek and jarring his hand. The gun, dislodged, clattered to the sidewalk. The man swung at Rex, blood pouring down his face from his nose, while I darted in and scooped up the gun.

"RAE, GET BACK," Rex shouted hoarsely in a voice I recognized but couldn't place. A second later, I realized it was the voice that had shouted "shark" that day so many years ago, just before he had saved my life.

The mugger threw two roundhouse punches toward Rex's head, which he neatly dodged. Then Rex brought his fist up from below straight into the mugger's chin. He put all 6'4" of his body behind it. The man stiffened like he was receiving the mother of all wedgies then collapsed rigidly onto his back. He was like a marionette whose handler had abruptly decided to go grab a pint of beer. "Fuck this puppet stuff," said the handler and dropped the strings and walked out. The mugger's head bounced two or three times off the sidewalk. Rex was panting slightly. His cheek was cut. He turned to me. I was holding the gun with both hands, pointing it down at the sidewalk. Gently he removed it and, glancing at the prone mugger, pulled me against him.

"Fuck," he said into the top of my head. "Fuck."

"Are you okay?"

"Fuck. Motherfucker. Fuck." He whipped around and kicked the guy viciously in the ribs. "Fucking motherfucker!" He was like an enraged gorilla. If he had had a rock, he would have smashed the man's head in.

He leaned over and retrieved the knife from the ground.

"What are you gonna do with that?" I asked.

"Not leave it with him," Rex said tersely. "Come on, let's go." He took my hand and started walking. "Let's get the fuck out of here. Motherfucker!"

We started to head back for Nine Thirty and the Ram.

"Come on," said Rex. He had spotted the truck ahead and was making for it fast. Both the gun and knife had disappeared inside his pants.

"You don't have a license to carry concealed, do you?"

"Rae, let's go. I don't want to get involved with any fucking cops right now."

I took that as a no.

We reached the truck, and he came over to my side to help me. He placed both hands on my ass and pushed as I clambered in. I half-turned and said, "Thanks" sarcastically. He grinned then strode to the other side. As he climbed in, he was already lighting up. I still had very little desire to smoke anymore. No drunkenness, no smoking. The population at large would have been surprised to know that becoming a vampire simply involved converting to Mormonism. I gazed at Rex with a sudden wrench of feeling. He, too, had been in my life for so long, I couldn't remember anything else.

But in a good way.

CHAPTER 27

Rex slumped in his seat a little and closed his eyes.

"Fuck," he said, fingering the pocket where his gun and now the knife was. "And, no, I don't have a carry concealed permit," he informed me. "I didn't qualify for good cause." He sunk lower in the seat. I slumped down in my seat, too.

"Too bad you didn't have that gun at Barnes & Noble," I said.

Rex laughed slightly. We were parked on the street in front of the restaurant. My eyes ticked toward the cut on his cheek. I felt an unwelcome heat bloom in my belly. I removed a tissue from my purse and twisted in my seat to dab at the cut. Rex hissed between his teeth.

"You don't have any Neosporin, do you? So you don't get the flesh eating disease," I added absently. I stared at Rex's cut and my vision dimmed.

"What?" He looked at me.

"Neosporin," I said, dabbing gently. My almost undead heart was pounding.

"Yeah, I got some right here," he said, patting his pockets. He grinned at me around the cigarette. It was getting very hot in the Ram, and my head felt like it was full of cotton. I kept dabbing at Rex's cut like a robot whose program was jammed, *dab dab dab*, even while in some part of me alarms were blaring and warning lights were flashing. There was a big iron gate ahead that was slowly closing, and I had the feeling the only chance for both of us to be safe was for me to run and dive beneath it before it locked shut. Rex sucked his cigarette down to a nub and shoved it into the ashtray.

"Okay, let's get out of here," he said, and pulled conservatively away from the curb, not his usual style. Probably because of the gun and now the knife in his pants. I sat quietly in my seat, listening to a high-pitched ringing in my ears. I lifted my purse up and pawed around until I found the wheatgrass bottle. I removed the stopper and tried to squeeze some drops directly into my mouth. None were forthcoming. Rex observed all this without comment. We wound our way slowly through the Westwood streets in silence.

"Shit was crazy, huh?" said Rex, maneuvering onto Wilshire Boulevard.

"Hell, yeah," I said I said vaguely. It was taking all my will just to keep it together

"What did that fucker say? 'Get a room?'" He was lighting up again.

"He was disgusted by our PDA," I croaked, staring at his mouth. *I was going to suck his lips off.*

He glanced at me, looked away. Looked back.

"Are you okay?"

"Rex, I'm sorry I put off moving in with you," I blurted out. I could see him listening intently. "I actually got good news from Cola the other day…" I stopped here to swallow with effort. It was difficult to remember words. "And I was going to call you…" Here the cotton swelled as a red haze filtered in from the sides like an encroaching fog. "But then something happened…"

They took me. Mr. Dadalian and I. They took Ganymede. I shouldn't even be here with Rex. What if they came to get Rex? And then I gave up my soul. And on top of everything, I didn't even know what the hell was going on with us. One minute we were best buds, fishing Margarite's dead dog out of the swimming pool. The next minute we were in *Fifty Shades of Grey*, about to do it against the side of a tree in the middle of Westwood. It almost felt like a spell was lifting, and we were picking up right where we had left off years and years ago. We had been on the verge of something back then, but it had just mysteriously never taken root. This was beyond the shark and anything I was doing. This was beyond me. It felt like the same kind of thing that had happened to Johnny. *Had those things put some kind of spell on me, on my life?*

Suddenly I remembered something Dante had said in my living room. Something about magic always being in my life but I'd only noticed it now.

"What happened?" Rex said quietly. We had made our way over to Fountain and were winding our way steadily toward his place.

"What?"

"You said something happened."

Oh, yeah. "More weird shit." The fact was, I couldn't move in with him now. Not like this. "But also…we're friends. We've been friends forever. It'll get ruined if we change it." *It'll get ruined if I run out of wheatgrass. It'll get ruined if I drink your blood.*

Rex was silent. He kept driving until he was pulling into his driveway. He turned the engine off and stubbed his second cigarette out in the tray.

"You shouldn't be living in that shitty apartment."

"It's not that sh-shitty," I stammered. I could hear his heart thundering. At least that's what it sounded like to me. "There's a lot of n-nice people there."

"I'm sure there are," he said patronizingly. He patted my shark hand. "Just think about it. Come on," he said, and got out. "Come in and tell me about some of this weird shit that's going on." He headed for the front door, fumbling with his keys.

I stepped up beside him while he was trying to find the right key. Unceremoniously, I reached up and grabbed his head, pulling him toward me. I bit his ear, then rammed my tongue into the cut on his cheek. It was like Frenching a light socket. My whole body juddered. Rex turned toward me, lips parted in surprise. His keys clattered to the stone porch. His beautiful brown eyes darkened even more as he took in what was happening. The thin, red haze began to fill my vision while the rest of the world slowly winked out of existence. It was a familiar sensation. After a beat, I realized it was almost identical to road rage.

Rex grabbed me around the waist and helped himself to a fistful of hair. I snaked my arms around his neck, my teeth plucking at his lower lip. He grunted and ran his hands up my thighs and under my dress. *Stop. Stop. Stop.* The alarms were blasting, and the big iron gate that harbored sanctuary slammed closed. Without me. I dug my fingers into Rex's shoulders and jumped on him, wrapping my legs around his waist. He cupped my ass then hooked his fingers into my panties and almost tore them off. *Stop. Stop. Stop.* I could not stop. Rex smelled like a T-bone steak. I wanted to lick him all over. Then I wanted to suck out the marrow. Rex pivoted and my back slammed against his front door. The gun and the knife clattered in his pants. He pressed against me, pinning my shoulders. His gaze swept downward, then up. We locked eyes. Five seconds. Ten seconds. Fifteen seconds. We breathed hard into each other's mouths.

Out of nowhere, he pulled back.

My legs slid from his waist.

I gripped his shirt like a drowning victim.

He grabbed my arms and held them.

"Don't worry about condoms," I muttered. I struggled, trying to free myself. The road rage sensation continued, full throttle. The world had disappeared, and all of my vision had tunneled down to Rex. But instead of seeing Rex as the object of my fury due to some driving infraction that had occurred, cutting in front of me at a high speed without signaling, say, I saw, smelled, and sensed him with every cell—living or dead—of my body.

"Rae, hold up, hold up."

"I said *don't worry about condoms.*" My voice was guttural. I had turned into Linda Blair.

"Stop, baby. Stop."

"What?"

"Rae—"

"Nobody says stop," I panted. "Are you crazy? Nobody says stop." I think it was a documented, universally accepted fact around the world that nobody said stop in the middle of ramping up for crazy sex. I reached out and tried to unbutton his shirt before I realized there were no buttons. He grabbed me and spun me around so my back was against him.

"Be good, be good, come on," he begged me quietly, "or I'm going to fuck you right here on the front lawn."

I could definitely confirm that he was ready to do just that. I ground myself backward against him. He groaned.

"I'll fuck you right here." He almost sounded angry about it. "But you won't be happy later."

"I won't?" I found this incredibly difficult to believe. "I think we'd both be pretty happy."

"We'd be happy five minutes later. Tomorrow we wouldn't be happy."

"I think we'd be happy five minutes later *and* tomorrow we'd still be happy."

I squirmed around, trying to break his hold. Weirdly, I felt very weak, as if Rex could overpower me if he wanted. Try as I might, I couldn't break his grip. I was in an uber-horny blood frenzy, and I had lost my vampiric strength. Rex held me against him. I felt his blood pumping against my back.

"You can't drive home like this. You had way too much to drink. Come inside."

"Can we sleep in the same bed?" I pressed.

Rex tightened his arms around me. "Yes," he said, "we can sleep in the same bed." He spoke into the top of my head. "And have a long talk."

That again?

"Talk about *what*?"

There was a long pause, then Rex let me go. I turned around and faced him. I averted my eyes from the cut on his cheek. The haze lifted. The roaring in my head began to fade. I felt like I was coming out of a dream. Neither Dante nor Cola had warned me that among the side effects of becoming a vampire was raging nymphomania. Nobody had told me that I would turn into the biggest slut in L.A. As if to pound the fact home, I felt my underwear slipping down my hips.

"You ripped my panties," I said petulantly.

"Sorry. I'll get you some new ones."

I sat down on the porch. Rex remained standing, leaning against a wooden post.

"I mean, come on," he said after a long pause. Then, "We're not getting any younger, are we?"

Those were the worst words ever. Those were the words I never wanted to hear. They didn't really apply to me anymore, but I still hated them.

"What the hell does that mean?" I asked angrily. "You don't want to fuck me?"

"Have you lost your mind?"

I closed my eyes and nodded. "Yes," I whispered.

"You are acting really weird. What was in that dropper? Are you on something?"

"No…" This barely audible.

"Listen, Rae…" He paused again and the seconds ticked past, the silence continuing uncomfortably. Finally, he said, "I don't have time for this anymore. Either we're friends or we're something else. But I'm not playing games."

I opened my eyes. He gazed down at me, unsmiling, his arms crossed.

"Uh…please correct me if I'm wrong, but I recall someone backing me up against a tree tonight." I quirked my lips, as if thinking. "Oh, yeah. *You*. It was *you* backing me up against a tree."

"Yeah." Beat. "I didn't see you fighting very hard."

"I wasn't fighting very hard." I threw him a frustrated grin. "God knows what would have happened if that nice young man hadn't mugged us."

Rex decided not to address that. Then: "I've been thinking about you a lot lately." Pause. "Not that I ever stopped," he added. He pulled a cigarette out and lit up. He cleared his throat. I waited.

"Come inside," he said, "it's cold out here. Aren't you freezing in that little dress?"

I stood up. "You have a lot of will power," I said with grudging admiration. "But just remember, *you* backed *me* up. I'm not the one playing games."

"Really? Why'd you wear that dress tonight?"

Why *had* I worn this dress tonight?

"I didn't think you'd even notice. You never notice."

Rex looked thoughtful as he took a long drag. "How's that planet you're living on? Can I visit sometime?"

"*You* kissed *me* at the Standard. You stuck your tongue down my throat."

He gestured toward me. "Case in point! Who sticks their tongue down someone's throat that they don't even notice?" He paused. "And I don't think I stuck my tongue down your throat."

"You might as well have. And tonight—"

"Because you're wearing that dress."

"I wasn't wearing this dress at The Standard. So who's playing games?"

Rex tucked his hands into his armpits and slowly doubled over, cigarette clamped between his lips. After a few seconds, he straightened up. His eyes were closed.

I sighed. My head was spinning. "I have to go."

Rex squinted at me through his cigarette smoke. I guess I was lucky he had made a spontaneous secret pact with the God of Abstinence when I hadn't been looking. Who knows what might have happened otherwise? I only knew one thing for sure: I had to get out of here, and I needed more wheatgrass. Okay, that was two things, but they were made out of the same idea.

"O...kay," he said. I could tell he was not happy. "I don't think you're good to drive. You drank a shitload tonight."

"Do I seem drunk to you?"

He studied me briefly. "No," he admitted. "You don't seem *drunk...*" I knew he was searching for the word that described what I seemed and could find it nowhere in the immediate vicinity.

"Yeah. Even if I got pulled over, I wouldn't get a ticket." I waved my hand dismissively.

"What?"

"Never mind. Long story."

Rex walked me to the Z. I remembered to lead him around the front so he wouldn't see the damage to the back because there was no way I could explain any of that to him tonight. He closed the door once I was inside. I was still vibrating like I'd drunk a thousand Red Bulls. I had no idea what to say to him. He was guarded and wary now, almost like he was dealing with someone he had just realized was a mental patient.

There was a long, strained silence. Rex smiled lightly, but he looked somber. My heart was almost breaking, because it felt like Rex and I were doomed. And it almost looked like he was thinking the same thing.

I drove away and dug my phone out of my purse once I was out of sight of his house. I pulled over, not emotionally prepared for an encounter with the law, started to text out of habit again, then redialed Dante's number, angrily stabbing at the buttons, and bellowed into the phone, "Is there going to be a meeting or what? Do you guys even HAVE a plan? I've been through some shit, Dante. I can't do this alone. *I THOUGHT THAT WAS THE POINT!*" I screamed the last part and hung up. I sat panting for a while and tried to calm down. Absently, I checked my messages. Something from Margarite. A message from Rex several days ago. A text message. From Giancarlo. "We have to talk," he'd written.

We have to talk.

I had incurred the wrath of Europe's Premier Vampire Hunter. Except now he wanted "to talk." I could just imagine how that conversation would go:

Me: Hey, Giancarlo. How's it going?

Giancarlo: Hello, Rae. It is good to see you. How is your shoulder doing?

Me: Oh…better. Good. Fixed. But you knew that already.

Giancarlo: I suppose I did suspect as much, yes. I am so sorry, but could you please come forward and hold very still…

I had to go out and do something to burn this raging energy off. How dare Giancarlo try to kill me! How dare those monsters try to abduct my unofficial godson! How dare Rex say we were getting older! Okay, maybe right now I couldn't do anything about that other stuff, but there was one thing I could do. *One thing.* And I was going to do it now. I was so amped up, I felt like I would just step outside, lift up into the air, and fly to Venice Beach. Wasn't I supposed to be able to do that anyway? What kind of vampire was I? I had no fangs to speak of yet. Even if I'd *wanted* to suck Rex's neck, I wouldn't have been able to break the skin with my flat incisors. I couldn't fly. Had Dante somehow bestowed the price-cut undead package on me instead of the complete edition? With an effort, I reined myself back in. None of that mattered. Right now, I was going to do what I should have done a long time ago. Even before I'd died. I was finally going to go tear Ricardo a new one.

Right after, I went home and changed my clothes. I had torn off the failing panties and tossed them onto the passenger seat. Once home, I grabbed the ruined underwear and my purse, completely expecting Giancarlo to come leaping off the roof or out of a tree. I sprinted for the front of the building as the wind kicked up, briefly exposing my nudity before I Marilyn Monroed my dress back down. I picked up a container full of brownies that didn't seem very Armenian-like, slipped inside my place and, once there, decided to finally clean up a little. I left the brownies in the kitchen and didn't touch them, suddenly afraid that Giancarlo had made them, peppering them with wooden splinters that would tear my insides apart. Then, once I was done cleaning, I actually fell asleep for a few hours. I awoke in a panic, not knowing where I was, and missing Rex terribly. I looked at the clock. Two thirty a.m. This would be a good time to go to the beach and deal with that dick, Ricardo. Everyone asleep. Fewer witnesses.

In Venice, the idea that I could simply stroll into the house and engage in my fantasy of holding Ricardo up by his neck with one hand was quickly thwarted when it dawned on me, once again, that I couldn't just walk in wherever I wanted anymore. It was past three thirty in the morning as I lurked outside the *Sand in Your Face* abode. The house was tucked away two short blocks from the beach on a stretch with a lot of other aging hippy-like dwellings. Cayman, the Wyoming cowboy, was trying to talk Kairi and Moeyner into a threesome. I could hear their voices through the walls—not words exactly, but I knew what was going on anyway. I sensed that Kairi was into it. I could tell that secret Valley Girl Moeyner was completed repulsed by the idea but playing along. Moyener had a crush on Dante, not Cayman. The crew was set up, filming the seduction. Ricardo and Andrygen were in their respective bedrooms, sleeping alone, Ricardo snoring like Bigfoot. I didn't sense Dante at all.

I loitered outside, nimbly avoiding miscellaneous members of the crew as they wandered around smoking, checking equipment, and making phone calls. I had just worked up the nerve to approach one of them and get her to invite me in when I felt a whoosh of air. My arm was almost jerked from my socket, and suddenly I was two hundred feet away, standing in the neighbor's yard under a blossoming bougainvillea. I guess I shouldn't have been surprised to see Dante and his white teeth flashing at me in the dark.

I slapped a hand over my chest.

"SHIT."

He laughed. "You are such a drama queen."

I smiled tensely. "Yeah, I'm so used to being jerked hundreds of feet through the air at the speed of sound. I overreacted. Sorry."

Dante just smiled.

"I called you. Did you get my message? You should have. I screamed the last part."

Dante eyed me coolly, still smirking. "I haven't checked my messages." I couldn't tell if he was lying or not.

"Well, listen. I just tore a ZR apart with my bare hands." I looked at him. "I learned from my godson that's Zeta Reticuli." I paused. "I know they're interdimensional and not from Zeta Reticuli, but I'm used to this nickname now." Dante continued to watch me in silence. "When I killed that thing, it felt good, but…" I paused, searching for the right words. "But, um…when is the big meeting going to be? You know. We all get together, map out the plan."

"There is no meeting," said another voice, behind me. I whirled around. It was Cola. He materialized out of the darkness, intently fixed on Dante. "Is there, Big D?"

Dante's grin expanded. He placed a hand over his heart, as I had moments ago, but sarcastically, feigning emotion. "Georgiou. So good to see you. Where you been?"

Before either of us could blink, Cola was a blur, closing the gap between them. Then his hand was wrapped around Dante's neck.

"Oh, my God!" I stumbled backward.

"I should annihilate you," Cola said in a low voice, barely moving his lips. "I should tear you limb from limb and let the sun do the rest."

Dante choked and grabbed Cola's wrist. Unfazed, Cola held on. After several beats, he let go.

"Hey, hey, hey!" I said, trying to lighten the mood. "Whoa! I didn't know you cared…"

"What do you want?" Dante snarled, backing away, massaging his throat. "I've always liked her and wanted to taste her."

It took a few seconds to sink in. *Say what now?* It was my turn to lunge at Dante in a rage. Cola's arm shot out across my chest, stopping me. He stood beside me, not a hair out of place, and placed his fingers lightly on my arm. Our eyes locked. He didn't have to say anything. I got it. I had been suckered.

"Taste me?" I was astonished. "*Taste* me?"

"Who do you think you're dealing with?" Dante asked with contempt.

My feelings, unused to the ribald world of vampires, were wounded.

"Ever heard of restraint?" asked Cola. "Or has it eluded you, along with rationality and common sense?"

"Oh, man," Dante laughed, "Don't saddle me with that crap, just because she's your—"

Cola snarled. Dante stopped talking. He was still grinning, but he stopped talking.

"What has to be said," said Cola menacingly, "isn't necessarily what should be. You've put me in a position—"

"Speak for yourself," said the other. I had no idea what they were talking about and wasn't sure that I wanted to know.

Dante turned to me. He'd had enough of Cola admonishing him, apparently.

"Listen, sweetheart, there is no vampire army. Aliens will come, and aliens will go. And there are other beings. There always have been."

"No kidding."

He shrugged. "What are you complaining about? You'll never get old now. You'll never die. You'll become insanely rich." He addressed Cola, as if trying to prove a point. "Tell me I'm wrong. And on top of everything, you don't have to take any shit from anybody. Least of all, Them. They can't control you. Your will is your own."

"But I've lost my soul."

Cola gripped my arm. His suit tightened along his arm, over his biceps. Hmm. What kind of undead body was under that suit that I had never noticed before? Did you still have to do sit-ups when you were no longer alive, or were you frozen wherever time had left you? What had Cola been doing, maneuvers with the Roman army, hoisting a heavy sword night and day? Loading bag after bag of grain onto wagons under the hot sun? While I drooled a little, preoccupied, Cola said, "Tell her."

Dante crossed his arms and remained silent.

"There's still time for Undoing. If she's balked at her decision. There's still time." Cola looked at me with an expression approaching tenderness. "The wheatgrass has been working?" he asked me quietly.

"Oh, yeah, thank you! What is it, anyway? It seems like it…makes the blood smell less good. And my stomach doesn't hurt as much."

Cola nodded. "Also get some iron supplements. It helps."

Dante chortled and rolled his eyes far back into his skull. "She will need blood. Sooner or later."

I made a quick mental note to stop by CVS as soon as possible.

"Wheatgrass is as close to blood as you'll get," Cola informed me. "It's seventy percent chlorophyll, and the chlorophyll molecule is identical in structure to human hemoglobin…"

Dante threw his head back and guffawed.

"…Except that where human beings use iron as the oxygen-binding element of the hemoglobin molecule, plants use magnesium as the central oxygen-binding element in chlorophyll."

"Holy shit!" More raucous laughter followed.

Cola gazed steadily at Dante. "If she wants to not consume blood, there are ways around it."

"Ha!" Dante scoffed and crossed his arms. "Did *you* find a way around it?"

"Cola, Dante, listen," I changed the subject before more strangling started. "I don't know if you're aware of this, but those things—the Zetas—they know who I am. They know that I can see them." I looked at them beseechingly. "If there's no vampire army fighting them off...what am I supposed to do?" It was like being stuck at a job with sexual harassment. I couldn't leave the job, and they were just going to keep coming after me.

Cola and Dante exchanged a look. Wordlessly, Cola turned to me, placed his hand on the back of my neck, and reached under my hair. My skin tingled under his cold palm. I was half-terrified and half-turned-on. He rubbed his cold, cold hand there, slowly increasing in rhythm until it was burning my skin.

"Lean your head forward a little, Rae," he said softly.

And I did. My hair fell on either side of my face like a curtain. And then he plucked something off me.

"Okay," he said. I straightened up. Cola held his palm out. I looked down at it but saw nothing.

Dante clucked his tongue. "Goddamn energy suckers," he muttered.

I looked closer. In the center of Cola's palm was a tiny dot, barely visible. It glinted in the moonlight. It was metallic! Cola put it between two of his fingers and pressed them together. Distinctly I heard a cracking sound. He brushed his hands together.

"Okay, they won't be able to find you now," he said casually, as if he had just removed a piece of lint from my jacket.

"Someone put a tracker on me?"

"Someone put a tracker on you."

"How did you know where it was?"

Cola smiled, as if I was a child. "That's where they always put it," he answered.

"Who?" I was starting to freak out again. I felt it coming on slowly, the way the ocean would build its wave behind me, slowly, inexorably gaining mass and speed, and there was nothing I could do about it except ride it or get out of the way.

"Yeah, it's the company you keep," Dante said. "Some people who have it out for us." As I continued to stare at him blankly he rolled his eyes again and said, "Your boyfriend with the stake."

"Giancarlo?" I looked from one to the other, baffled. "No! Why—when? No. That makes no sense."

"Don't listen to him," Cola said, as close to exasperated as he could get and still remain reserved and calm. "It's that esoteric center. Now. Don't go there anymore."

"What?" I reached up absently and massaged the place on the back of my neck where the tracker had been. It felt hot and itchy. Abruptly Cola cocked his head, listening. His steely fingers released my arm and he backed away. "Please excuse me. I have to go. But Dante...tell her. It's her right."

We locked eyeballs again, and something glimmered deep down in there. I don't know what it was, but it made my heart hiccup and my brain tilt. And then Cola was gone. I appreciated the fact that he was hundreds of years old and probably had lots of other things on his mind, but he had taken the time out to face down Dante. And he was really pissed about it, too.

"Listen, sweetheart, I told you not to come here and dick around with Ricardo." Dante sounded miffed. His vampire pride had been bruised by Cola's snarling and protective instincts over me. "I told you he wasn't worth it."

"Don't change the subject. What's the Undoing?"

"Ahh…" He waved his hand and rolled his eyes. "You still have a fortnight before your soul is completely gone. If you think you've made the wrong decision, we can change you back. Well, we can try. Sometimes the process is fatal."

The bougainvillea seemed to glow in the moonlight as I absorbed the information. What was a fortnight again? Surreptitiously, I did some mental math.

"You mean I'm not really undead yet?"

"You are almost undead."

I sensed the conversation wrapping up and decided to leave the nymphomania issue for another time. I didn't have the energy to deal with Dante's guaranteed leering strip club reactions. The next thing

I knew, he was right in front of me. I hadn't even seen him move. I guess that's how the Zeta had felt. I was still amazed at how much the movies had gotten right. Dante's depthless eyes fastened on mine and he placed his forefinger beneath my chin. "I've always liked you," he whispered. "Just remember…I'm your maker."

"Meaning?" I pressed him. What did that mean exactly? That I was beholden to him? I was pressing the empty air, however. Like Cola, Dante was gone. Out of the night, echoing on the wind, came Dante's voice: "You are mine, and you are one of us. You have sacrificed day for night. The long, eternal night…"

CHAPTER 28

Being almost undead was screwing with my sleep pattern. It was exactly the same thing as when we had to fiddle with the clocks for Daylight Saving Time. Whenever we had to go forward in spring, Hama said her sleep never returned to normal until we fell back in fall. Now I commiserated with her greatly since it was very difficult to sleep at night anymore. I drove south aimlessly for a while, resupplied myself at a 24-hour CVS in Marina Del Rey and got a chocolate shake from an all-night IHOP. Then, as was becoming a personal tradition to check up on folks, since I was headed that way anyway, I made my way to Margarite's neighborhood.

I was driving along slowly, slurping the last of my shake, when I noticed a woman with an enormous ass walking a white dog in the murky darkness and realized two beats later that it was my sister. I drove past her and pulled over to the curb. When I got out, I watched as Margarite, wearing a knee-length overcoat cinched over what looked like a pink bathrobe, was yanked along the sidewalk gripping the leash in both fists, trying to hold on. It was obvious what Cesar Millan, the Dog Whisperer, would have to say about this. He would be disgusted. Margarite was busy letting the dog pull her past me when they both did a double take. She let out a tiny screech and the dog's tail windmilled crazily. He lurched at me, smiling.

"Oh my God. OH MY GOD. Where did you come from? WHAT ARE YOU DOING HERE?" Margarite's hand was over her heart. That had been a common theme for tonight, hands over hearts. The dog leaped up on me. He was almost glowing in the pre-dawn morning.

"Hey, sis," I said. For someone who despised Margarite so much, I was sure over here a lot. I felt a tender, inexplicable tug in my guts, like affection. How long did sibling rivalry go on? We should have ended ours a long time ago. The dog continued to leap up on me, and I patted him.

"Bunny, NO!" She yanked on the leash. Bunny choked and coughed and continued to smile at me. "This is too weird. What are you DOING here?"

"Aw, Bunny. That's cute. I guess this is your new dog," I said, stalling.

"How did you guess?" said Margarite. "What are you DOING here?"

My mind whirled, searching for an answer.

"You know, I go to this meditation center down the street. They had an overnight thing, but I left early."

"What meditation center?" She turned her heard this way and that, as if it the building would materialize before her. "The self-realization place?"

"No…"

"Okay, but what are you doing on my street?"

Leave it to Margarite, Ph.D., to not let it drop.

"How about a hi? Do I get that at least?"

Bunny leaped forward, pulling Margarite, who sighed, peeved.

"Yes. Hi, Rae. How are you?"

"Do you always walk your dogs in the middle of the night?"

"It's almost morning. And yes. I do. I walk them whenever I can't sleep." Suddenly she glared at me. "If you were a man, I'd think you were stalking me."

"Well, I'm not a man." There was no way around it. I *was* stalking her. But not for malevolent reasons. Still, I was in the same boat as a stalker. Neither I nor the stalker could explain what we were doing here. And beyond that, even, I couldn't imagine a man in the world who would *want* to stalk Margarite.

She glowered some more. "You look…pale."

"I feel pale."

"You look very strange."

"I feel strange."

Margarite sighed.

I squatted down to play with Bunny. He panted and leaped about.

"Well, I can't really talk about you," Margarite informed me, glancing around at her Brentwood neighborhood. "I've put on a lot of weight lately."

"Really?" I said. No way I was going there. "I didn't notice. I just thought you were pale too. We're both pale. We're losing our skin tone. Remember how the girls at school would admire our skin?"

"The white girls? They loved our mocha skin. The cup o' Joe with cream. It was almost the exact shade they tried to duplicate with that spray-on stuff."

"Except Jarna Lewis. You didn't know her. You were gone by then."

"Who was Jarna Lewis?" Margarite inquired. It was a weird time and place to be having this conversation.

"She was a sister. But darker. She always made fun of me. She'd ask, 'Why are you so light?' I think she knew Dad was white. She just wanted to…you know."

"It never ends," said Margarite. "Either you're too black or you're not black enough." She paused and gestured with her elbow. "Wanna come in, get some coffee?"

I smiled. Bunny saw my teeth and took this as a friendly invitation and hurled himself against the leash.

"Bunny, NO!"

"Okay, sure." I gestured to my car gallantly. "Hop in," I said, and as Margarite took a step forward, the unthinkable happened. A shaft of light shot down from the sky, surrounding her and Bunny. Immediately, they froze, Margarite in mid-step, Bunny in mid-wag. My jaw dropped and I looked up. As my hands clenched into fists and my almost-undead adrenaline started to flow, a small ZR appeared on the sidewalk, sort of stepping out of the light as if from behind a curtain. No! Cola destroyed the tracker! *Did I have another one on me?* He brushed by Margarite whose bathrobe shifted a little as he passed and shuffled toward me, hands in the air like the LAPD had him surrounded. If it was physically possible, my jaw dropped another two inches. Holy shit. It was the ZR from Ganymede's abduction. The one I had let go. It had to be. Who else did the perp walk? I stared down at it, speechless. Immediately a voice buzzed in my head: *One that Sees, they are not harmed, I will not harm, need to speak with you now.*

"What...*the fuck?*" I spoke out loud, the old-fashioned way. "What...*the fuck?*" I couldn't think of anything else to say.

Creature: *One that Sees, I come in peace with offering if you not believe.*

It shuffled forward a few more inches and reached inside its coveralls. For a millisecond, I imagined it removing a Glock and aiming it at my head like Rex had done to the mugger a few hours ago. That would be some karma, huh? Instead, it pulled out the opposite of a Glock. It pulled out my missing yellow bra with the little silk florettes decorating the front of it. My favorite yellow bra.

Creature: *One that Sees, I have warning.*

I reached out and snatched the bra from it. "Holy shit," I muttered. "*You* took this? Was that *you?*" I glanced at Margarite as I stuffed it into my pocket. The creature gazed at me blankly for a few seconds then began to blink rapidly as if it was about to have a grand mal seizure.

Yellow Bra: *No, no, no, no, no, no, no, no, no, no, no, no, no, no, no. Not me. Not me.*

It seemed very upset that I had insinuated it was a thief. We both waited to see who would speak next.

"You have a nerve coming down here..." I stuttered into silence. Then: "How did you find me?" I stopped myself from mentioning we had destroyed the tracker.

Yellow Bra: *I lose signal. But I follow car.*

I frowned. I pictured a helicopter during a high-speed chase on the freeway.

Yellow Bra: *You letting me live. I live to shine. Shine, not burn.*

"What?"

Y.B.: *We follow you. You shine, not burn. We want to shine, not burn.*

"JESUS!" I threw my hands up in exasperation.

The ZR looked nervous and shuffled its feet around a little.

Y.B.: *Souls. Souls. Shine, not burn.*

"Oh," I said. Then, with dawning, "Oh…"

That expression sounded vaguely familiar somehow. I think I had read it in a romance novel once.

"You guys just…burn when you die? Instead of…floating off like we do?" I was making a handful of assumptions for both of us. But suddenly I was excited. I was getting an explanation, some answers! I wished I understood him a little better, though. I wondered why, if they bothered to learn English, they only sort of half-learned it, like they'd acquired a defective Rosetta Stone from a dumpster somewhere.

The Zeta was staring at me with its big wraparound eyes.

Y.B.: *Not English. Not English. You see ships. You understand us also.*

I frowned. Evidently, I was tuned into them in more ways than one. Although I was hearing him in what sounded like broken English. Not unlike Spanglish. In this case Zenglish.

Y.B.: *Yes, burn, ashes, gone.*

Y.B. continued, gently directing me back on point.

Y.B.: *No float. No shine. Want the shine.*

"I can imagine." I felt slightly embarrassed that I might have willingly given away something they were trying so hard to achieve. But who knew? Souls and spirits were supposed to be different. As far as I knew, I still had my spirit, though my soul was in jeopardy. But this wasn't about me. I clicked my tongue and shook my head. Poor little buggers.

Y.B: *Big take coming. This is my warning. Big take of many at once. Many not to be returned.*

I narrowed my eyes at Yellow Bra.

"What? When?"

Y.B.: *Soon. Now. Tomorrow.*

"Tomorrow? *Now?!*"

Yellow Bra glanced up past the light toward his ship. He seemed antsy, like he was double-parked.

Y.B.: *Or day after. Not sure. Soon. I go now.*

Yellow Bra started to float away, up into the light.

"Hey!" I whistled sharply, as if hailing a cab. Yellow Bra stopped floating away and looked at me. He was at eye level with Margarite who gazed blankly outward at nothing. "Let me warn *you* now, since we're doing all this warning. First of all, thank you. I appreciate it. But we're going to have to kill you guys. You do realize that, right?"

Yellow Bra paused a moment, thinking. Then he did the approximation of a shrug.

Y.B.: *I warn ones on your side not to be on ships. Thank you, One who Sees.*

"Thank *you*. I'm sorry." I flapped my arms. "I wish you guys were doing things differently…" I had a what-are-ya-gonna-do? look. Yellow Bra's face moved a little in a weird way, and a moment later I realized he was trying to smile. It warmed my heart and made the hair stand up on the back of my neck simultaneously. He floated up some more into the light then disappeared altogether, and a moment later the light was gone too.

Bunny made a weird snorting sound, barked, then stopped and ran in a circle, wagging his tail, completely confused. Margarite's foot dropped heavily down to the ground from her mid-step. She looked at me blankly for a moment then blinked several times. I could smell her life force, but it was dim and oddly cloying.

"Let's go get that coffee. Come on, get in."

Shine not burn. How weird. I almost felt sorry for them. And I really felt sorry for Yellow Bra. And these mysterious others like him. It was quite the turn of events. It was the last thing I would have ever expected to hear: some of them on our side. The sky was starting to lighten up. I knew I wasn't going to catch on fire, but it would be hard to stay awake. And then Margarite would accuse me of being bored, and we'd get into a huge fight as if we were twelve years old. Because even with being almost-undead and Rex refusing to have sex with me and aliens returning my missing underwear and my whole reality standing on its head, some things never changed. 'Cause Margarite and I, we burned, burned, burned. We did not shine.

I was back at my place, playing my messages. There was one from Bob's secretary reminding me about another meeting. I thought of

Cola warning me to never, ever go there again. I withdrew my newly returned bra from my pocket and tossed it onto the coffee table. It landed beside the panties Rex had mangled. If Mr. Dadalian had seen them, he would never have imagined the unbelievable story behind both items. He would just think I was a terrible housekeeper, this stemming from my being unsuitable for marriage and childless and a lush to boot. Exhausted, I crawled into bed, eager to sleep the day away.

I woke at dusk, disoriented. My phone was ringing. I had been having a terrible nightmare involving Bob. He had been chasing me through the UCLA campus at night as he had transformed into a werewolf. While we had both had two legs, I'd been pulling ahead, obviously in superior cardiovascular condition. But once he'd acquired four legs, he gained on me with terrifying speed, and as I rounded the corner of Royce Hall, he'd leapt into the air, paws forward, claws out.

"Bob! No! Leave me alone!" I'd shouted, diving out of his way.

"I want your guts!" Bob had growled through his half-human, half-dog muzzle. "Give me your guts!"

I followed the sound of the phone. It was lying on the floor beside the bed for some reason. I answered it without looking, thinking distractedly of Rex. We hadn't spoken since last night, the night of the mugging. Or night of the blood frenzy. Or night of the crazed nymphomania. Take your pick.

"Hello?" I said.

A voice exhaled deeply. "Rae," Giancarlo rumbled. "I did not think you would answer."

I completely froze and almost dropped the phone. I really needed to get an appropriate ring tone for Giancarlo. *I am a Nightmare Walking* or *Kiss With a Fist.* Pause.

"Hello?" he said tentatively.

"I didn't know it was you. I didn't look first."

"Ah…"

Pause.

"Well, I am glad you did not screen me. I would like to speak to you. Are you free to speak now?" he asked.

"Um…yeah." Oh, so polite when he wasn't trying to murder me. Silence. Silence.

"There is very little I can say."

"There *is* very little you can say," I agreed. Was I holding a grudge? Fuck, yeah, I was holding a grudge. *Silence. Silence. Silence.* I stared across the room and out the window at the coming night.

Giancarlo exhaled deeply again.

"I am calling, Rae, because…" Exhale. "I believe I may be…" Long pause. "mistaken about you." Here he coughed. But he must have turned his face away courteously, because the cough was muffled. Nobody had manners like that anymore. I guess that's how Moorish vampire-hunting royalty rolled.

"Uh, yeah, I'd say you were mistaken."

"You do not understand, Rae."

"Obviously."

"My family…for generations this is what we do. I have been trained from a boy. This is what I do. I could not believe it when I saw you there…changed. I could not believe it."

I waited, staring at the window.

"I reacted…instantaneously. As always. As I have been trained."

"No shit. I remember."

I was simmering, hearing his voice again, having flashbacks of that night. But then I suddenly remembered something. When he had been straddling my stomach, about to plunge the stake down, he hadn't done it. He said he couldn't do it. I had completely forgotten this until just now.

"Why didn't you do it, Giancarlo? You had me. But you didn't do it."

"I could not do it, Rae."

Pause.

"It is not only that I am so attracted to you. That is not the only thing."

I smirked, despite myself.

"You are not bad." He exhaled again. "You are not bad," he repeated, not like he was trying to convince himself, but like he was amazed that it could be true.

"Yeah, I know. You're preaching to the choir."

Giancarlo and I were silent on the phone for a long time. It was very peaceful. Finally he said, "I remembered what you said before you drove away. I did some research on this subject. I have found…" He sighed. "Disturbing evidences."

"Evidences?"

"I had heard of these things before. But it was not in my reality, you understand? My reality revolves around…your kind. What you have become."

"I only did it so I could fight them. I told you. I don't kill people. I don't drink blood."

Giancarlo cleared his throat.

"How do you survive, may I ask? If you do not…"

"Wheatgrass. And iron supplements."

Silence. Silence. Silence. Silence.

"You smelled really good that night, right before you attacked me." I wasn't sure I should be telling him this. I got up and walked over to the window, searching for him below on the dark lawn where he would naturally be waiting to ambush me.

"But then when you were after me, you didn't smell good."

Giancarlo was silent. I pictured him sitting in his lake house in a darkened room, patiently sharpening about three hundred stakes, one after the other. He would nod as he sharpened the last stake, saying to me on the phone, "Tell me more about this. Perhaps here, at my abode. Can you come over now?"

Instead, he said, "I have heard of this before." He cleared his throat. "Well, this is all very interesting. I have never…had this experience before."

"What experience?"

"Of calling up…one such as you. Of…apologizing for my behavior."

"Well, generations of vampire slayers. It's in your blood. I guess it's not really your fault."

"Thank you, *dolcezza,*" he murmured.

"Do you always spot them—us—immediately? That's how good your training is?"

Giancarlo gathered his thoughts.

"No, not at all. You were obviously…just turned. It is simple when one is new and fresh. We can spot them immediately."

I wasn't sure I liked that "we" he mentioned. No, I did not like that at all.

"Older ones—ones who have been around for a long time—they have a way about them. They cast an aura that shields them from detection."

This immediately made me feel better about Cola and even Dante.

"I think you guys need to rethink your ways," I suggested. "I don't think every vampire in the world is necessarily bad. I don't think you can just indiscriminately come after us just because we're vampires. Was that what you were doing," I added, "on our date? Out slaying some unsuspecting vampire?"

Giancarlo chuckled. "I understand what you are saying." Pause. "The one I helped to dispatch that evening," he said carefully, "was far from unsuspecting or innocent."

Pause. Pause.

"The problem is, Rae…" He trailed off. "Many start out one way. They are fine in the beginning. But as time goes on, they change."

"Oh."

"In fact, the majority change, I am sad to say."

I pictured myself a hundred years from now, as white as a sheet, my fangs twisted in my mouth, slipping into an orphanage and sucking half the children dry and then jumping into the Z and racing to the nunnery across town for a nightcap.

"If I may ask…have you had much success in your present form… with the battle against the gray ones?"

"Not much, no. The guy that made me…said there was a vampire army. But he lied. There's no army. But I did kill an alien with my bare hands the other night. It was supervising the kidnapping of my godson, so…that wasn't gonna happen."

Giancarlo sucked in a sharp breath. "What a nightmare. A waking nightmare."

"But I'm going to check out some shit soon."

He was instantly alert. "Shit? What shit?"

"Well, I got a heads-up about something. A warning." I should go to Now and spy on Bob. Maybe he knew something. "I can't tell you where I'm going. What if you show up and try to kill me again?"

"Rae, I am calling as a truce. I am not going to try to kill you anymore."

"Why not?"

"Because I believe you. I believe you meant to do good by doing this. I believe you will not change..." He paused. "Anytime soon." When he spoke again, there was a smile in his voice. "And I can prove to you that I mean this."

"Let's hear it."

"You do not need to tell me where you are for me to find you. As long as your cell phone is on, I can find you. I have known where you are many times already. I have not acted on it, as you can see."

I stiffened at the window. There was no one on the lawn directly below me, but he could be anywhere.

"I know, for example, that you returned home late last evening. Briefly. To change your clothes."

Oh, my God. He had been following me. Suddenly I thought of the panties in my pocket and the wind blowing outside. As if reading my mind, Giancarlo said, "You were wearing..."

Pause. Pause.

"An *extremely* short dress."

And I heard him smiling again. God. He'd seen it. He'd seen the dress go up. He'd seen my ass.

"I am jealous," said Giancarlo deep in his throat, "of whomever you were returning from."

"Well, I—something happened to my—and so I threw them out—oh, forget it." Obviously, I wasn't going to tell him about being in the throes of an orgiastic stupor, although I'm sure he would have enjoyed that tale a great deal.

He chuckled. He definitely was his old self now, relaxed and charming.

"I will speak with you soon, Rae. I would like to stay informed on your progress with the other beings. I believe we are in the same boat, both of us fighting against a powerful foe. It is a hard battle, and it never ends."

"Wow. I feel better now. Thanks," I said sarcastically.

"I am so sorry I threw you to the ground and treated you so roughly. I would much rather have been caressing your face and..."

Pause. Pause. Pause. Silently, we both filled in the blanks with the various things Giancarlo would have rather been doing to me.

"Well, you know. I must not muse about what...may not be."

May not be? Not cannot, not will not. *He was trying to keep an open mind.* At least he was reconsidering things a little bit. You couldn't really toss a blanket over all of it and label it as one thing, could you? I mean, why would anybody want to kill Cola? And what about Dante? Yes, he was a liar and a really good actor, but wasn't he more or less harmless?

I sighed. "I'm really glad you called. I actually do feel better."

My call waiting signal beeped.

"Could you hold on one second, Giancarlo?" Oh, so polite when we weren't running pell-mell through the yard, one in pursuit, one running for her life.

Eh. It was what it was.

"Yes, *dolcezza*."

I pressed the button and the next minute heard Andrygen asking if Ganymede was with me. My internal alarms went off full blast. I didn't even need to hear anything else she was saying. My living room transformed into the opening scene of *Saving Private Ryan* when the explosion left Tom Hanks's character deaf and everything was muted. I felt like Tom Hanks's character. Temporarily deaf, muffled explosions, chaos diligently knitting a giant annihilation sweater that I just didn't want to put on. "No, thank you," I said amiably, but it just kept weaving, making the sweater bigger and bigger, until it gradually encased everything in its path. There was no need for sizes. It was one-size-fits-all.

I grappled with the phone, pressing buttons blindly. I couldn't get back to Giancarlo.

"Oh, my God, oh, my God, oh, my God," I muttered.

"Rae. Rae. What's happening? Did you receive bad news?"

I had fumbled my way back somehow.

"Giancarlo, I've got to go."

I hung up on him.

Somehow, I got back on the other line with Andrygen when I'd meant to just turn off the phone. In mid-sentence, I hung up on her. Only one thing was going through my mind: They had Ganymede. *They had Ganymede.* I don't know how I knew, but Andrygen had spoken, and I knew. I knew it in my almost-undead bones. I knew it in my almost-undead heart.

And Andrygen was absolutely the worst, the most god-awful mother in this world and the next. Okay, that was two things that I knew. But they were one in the same.

PART 3

"I am a brother to dragons and a companion to owls; my face is black upon me and my bones are burnt with heat."

~ The Watchmen, *Job 30:29*

CHAPTER 29

I remembered being fascinated by the fact once that blue whales could hear each other from thousands of miles away. It seemed almost impossible, like the kind of rumor PETA would start for whatever purpose they had in mind to up the cause of the whale. But that night, I experienced it myself. I didn't call the whales. But I called something else. I didn't remember getting into the Z. I didn't remember driving away. I didn't remember where I was going, and I wasn't sure how I was able to steer or how I kept from driving off the road. I was just suddenly aware that I was driving down Sepulveda with a foggy idea in the back of my mind to find Cola while a conflagration roared through my head and a strange mewling filled the car. I didn't even know it was I that was whimpering until I had stopped. My throat ached the way it had after Margarite and I had had a screaming argument as kids.

I blinked in bewilderment. The car was stopped, pulled over to the side of the road, and both Cola and Dante were standing there. I didn't remember any of this happening. Cola was leaning past me through the open window and removing the keys from the ignition. His shoulder brushed my chin and the smell of cigars wafted off him. Dante bared his fangs in the moonlight, whipping his head around in all directions, searching for the foe that was after me. His head blurred, he was moving so fast.

"Rae," said Cola, straightening up. He pocketed my keys. "Come on. Get out for a minute." He pulled the door open and held his hand out.

"Who is it? Who's torturing her?" Dante kept up his super-sonic blurry surveillance of our surroundings. His voice was a throaty growl.

I gripped Cola's hand and got out of the car. I stared up at the sky as if Ganymede would be right there. But the sky was just gray-black and empty.

"I—they—I don't—"

"Rae, Rae," said Cola, bending his knees to bring himself down to eye level with me. He held my hands tightly.

"They—Ganymede—"

"I'll slay them! Where are they?" bellowed Dante in the background.

"Calm yourself!" Cola barked at him. He turned his attention back to me. "And you, you have to calm down too, Rae."

"I'm calm."

"You're not calm, Rae."

"I'm pretty calm."

"No, you're not."

"I'm okay."

"Calm down, Rae."

Wasn't I calm? I looked away. The Veteran's cemetery spread out across the street, filled with identical upright headstones, except for where they abruptly disappeared. I knew that was where they had started using stones laid flat in the grass. I wondered how people were supposed to find anyone that way. I took deep breaths, considering this, while Cola rubbed my arm and murmured, "That's it. That's my girl. That's my girl."

"ARRRGHHH!" Dante growled.

I looked at Dante. Why was he so wound up? He was in a frenzy. Cars whooshed past us on Sepulveda, and he growled at every other one, enraged. *Geez, I didn't know you cared.* I glanced at Cola. He gazed steadily at me with such caring that I felt both alarmed and deeply grateful at the same time.

"Where did you come from?" I asked, confused.

"We heard you." He glanced at Dante, back at me. "We're connected."

Mmm. Vampires.

Dante whirled toward me. "Rae, what happened? Why did you cry out like that?"

I looked at him, baffled.

"I didn't cry out. What are you talking about?"

"It's as bad as crying out, Rae," explained Cola, the reasonable one. "It was as loud as a scream."

"What? The whimpering?"

Dante growled and threw his hands over his ears. "Arrrggh. Don't remind me!"

On top of everything else, we were empaths *and* had supersonic hearing? Ganymede would have been fascinated to listen in on this conversation, given his interests. I half-hiccuped, half-sobbed. Ganymede.

"They've got Ganymede," I said. I looked at them beseechingly. "I'm…ninety-nine percent sure. He's on a ship somewhere." I looked up. "They've got him. Right now." I looked back down. "We've got to get him. Can we get him? Is it possible? Can we find him?"

Cola grabbed my hands again and pressed them between his own.

"Did you hear her?" he addressed Dante, not taking his eyes off me.

"I heard."

"What do you want to do?"

"Kill them all," Dante bellowed. "KILL THEM ALL."

I stared at them in wonder. "We can do it? We can get him back?"

Cola squeezed my hands then gently let them go. He turned toward Dante, considering.

"They're smart. Let's move quickly. No lingering."

"Lingering?" Dante said in disgust. "I'LL LINGER TO TEAR THE LAST ONE TO PIECES."

"No, Dante. No revenge. There are other ways to keep them away."

"There are?" This from me. "I thought it was hopeless. There's no army. There's no way to stop them. And there's going to be more. There's a mass take coming, maybe tonight. I was warned."

The vampires turned as one to look at me.

"Warned?" asked Cola.

"By who?" said Dante.

They both sounded extremely dubious.

"A Zeta. It warned me that they're doing a big take."

Cola and Dante eyed one another uncomfortably as if one of my other personalities had surfaced and claimed to be Winston Churchill.

"I'm not crazy! They were trying to take Ganymede a few days ago. I killed one of them and let the other go. It came back to warn me."

"Why would you let an energy sucker go?" Dante asked, astonished and disgusted at the same time.

"It looked scared. It held its hands up like I was robbing it." Saying that out loud didn't sound as reasonable as when it had actually been happening. "Some of them are on our side."

"So what?" said Dante dismissively. "We know. We don't care."

"You...know? You know some are on our side?"

"Who doesn't? Don't matter, girl. We still hate them."

"You can't hate all of them equally," I said, thinking of Giancarlo. "Anyway, *I* care," I said as if Y.B. and I were BFFs. "It took balls."

Cola was scanning the night sky.

"Ah..." he said, searching. "Dante. You see?"

We all craned our heads back. Now we could see, dotted throughout the city, up very, very high, hovering ships. There were no lights shooting out of them. Not yet. But there was a shitload of them all over the place.

"Oh, crap! It's happening. It's actually happening." I started shaking. "We've got to find Ganymede."

"There's still time," said Cola. Dante grunted.

"For what?" I looked away from the ominous sky with a force of will.

"To gather the others. We may not have an army, but we can summon one."

I stared, waiting for someone to explain, but no one did. Cola and Dante were eyeballing each other again. Then they turned to me together. "Close your eyes, Rae. You can help. Think of your brothers and sisters."

"What brothers? I only have a sister."

"Woman," grumbled Dante, "you were only playing a bimbo on the show. You're not one in real life, are you?"

"Playing a bimbo on the—"

Cola put his hand up for silence.

I bit my words off, glaring at Dante who glowered back at me and then closed his eyes. What a moody Jamaican vampire he was! One minute he was going to tear the world apart on my behalf, the next he was critiquing my thought processes. How long had he been a vampire? Hundreds of years? It had barely been twenty-four hours for me. I didn't think of other vamps as "brothers and sisters" yet. I was still adjusting.

Cola had also closed his eyes. I followed suit and closed mine. Whatever we were doing, it didn't take very long. I just pictured the word help in giant red block letters and sent it whirling out into darkness over and over. It took about six minutes, give or take. I began to hear sounds all around us. Voices. Murmuring. Car engines. I opened my eyes. We were surrounded by a crowd of people, and it was growing. All ages, all colors. They were milling about, spilling into Sepulveda Boulevard whooshing out of the dark sky, gravitating toward the center where we three stood beside my Z. Several cars whipped around the corner far down by Wilshire or sped along Sepulveda from the opposite direction, tires screeching as they headed our way at top speed.

An older man who looked very familiar was skulking near the rear bumper of my car. He put his hand out to touch it, and I said sharply, "Hey, hey, paint job." The man pulled his hand back and glanced up at me. I immediately felt chagrined for worrying about my paint job while Ganymede was kidnapped somewhere on an alien ship. I looked closely at the man. When he turned his piercing gaze on me, I froze and wheezed slightly. It was him, the…the…the talk guy! What was *he* doing here?

"I wasn't gonna key it, darling," he said with a deep Brooklyn accent in his casual interview voice. "I had one of these 20 years ago." He kept staring at it admiringly. "It's cherry," he murmured. "Cherry." He liked my car! He squinted in the dark down at the bumper where the damage was. "Except for that," he added. He lifted his head slowly, his expression recriminating. I felt my cheeks turning red, if that was at all possible.

"Aren't you…" I began, and he threw me a look like, "Really? Are you really gonna go there?" I dropped it and just stared, smiling. He reminded me of a geriatric newsie, suspenders and all.

"Hey," he continued conversationally, ignoring my groupie-like stupor, "you should get a really small sticker that says 'Luceo non uro.'"

"What does that mean?"

"It's Latin for 'I shine, not burn.'"

I didn't even have the energy to respond. I ogled him speechlessly. His observant eyes raked my face from behind his glasses. Glasses I knew, now, which were for show and that he didn't really need. "You've heard it before, I see."

"Yeah…"

"It's engraved inside my ring," he said, holding up his left hand and displaying a simple band. "I love it. *Luceo non uro.* Most people know it from a Scottish motto," he continued as he stared down at the Z. "1200s or so…"

I glanced around. Some of the vampires nearest us were actually eavesdropping. I think it was programmed into all of us to automatically listen when this guy was talking. I was glad that he'd kept the dream alive and moved on to the internet.

"They yelled it when they ran into battle. The Mackenzie clan," he continued. "But they got it from the Grays, who have been saying it for a long, long time. The Mackenzies just adopted it. And then time went on…" he trailed off. He shrugged. "They thought they came up with it." He shrugged again. "Who knows where we get stuff from that we think we came up with." He grinned at me, then gazed down at the car again and murmured, "Mm. *Almost* cherry…"

I stood, slack-jawed, trying to absorb both his presence and the information he'd just given. When Cola started talking, he glanced up, distracted from his love affair with my almost-cherry Z.

"All right," said Cola. A soft hum filled the air as various conversations took place among the vamps. It felt like intermission at a Broadway play, just before the last half happened. The pre-Mackenzian Zeta Reticuli finale.

"Okay, listen up," Cola raised his voice. Cars were squeezing by through the crowd. I could see assorted random drivers, mouths hanging open, trying to make sense of this bizarre crowd in the middle of Sepulveda. Very few of them honked. Most quietly skirted past and then floored it once clear. You couldn't tell by looking around that these were supernatural creatures, but there must be a serious vibe the civilians were picking up on.

"Okay, we all know who these beings are. They've been around a long time," yelled Cola. For the most part, the vamps stopped chitchatting and turned to listen. "Tonight is different for two reasons: There's going to be a mass taking tonight," yelled Cola. "We don't know if they're taking for good or what, but let's put a kink in their plans."

"DESTROY THEM!" yelled Dante.

The vampires' voices rose in the night, excited, keening. Cola and Dante were getting them worked up like a football team.

"They're taking our food!" someone yelled from the crowd.

There was general laughter. Cola faced where the voice had come from.

"Besides relying on the humans for sustenance, we have achieved a stable coexistence with them. Let's not forget," he said. "We were all human once."

"Ha!" barked the legend behind me. "That was a *long* time ago." He was still loitering by my bumper. "What was the second reason?" he asked like a true talk show host, guiding the meeting forward.

Cola continued. "Someone close to us has already been taken by the night beings. We regard this as a personal affront as it was already made clear to leave this one alone. Great suffering has been brought to one of your sisters and we must—"

"AVEEEEEEEEENGE HERRRRRRRRRRR!" Dante shouted, and that was all she wrote. I don't think that was what Cola was going to say, but it was too late. The crowd murmur spiked to a frenzy, and the vampire crowd immediately began to break up as various vamps shot willy nilly straight up into the air. Someone zoomed past me overhead, close enough for his shoe to almost graze my hair. I whipped my head around. It was him, the subject of my veneration, taking off for parts unknown. A Tyra Banks look-alike, dressed in full ball gown regalia, including a velvet cape, texted furiously into her cell phone. Then she shoved it into a tiny beaded evening bag and rocketed into the sky like Superman, cape flapping in the wind. I decided she was *not* Tyra Banks. In moments, the huge crowd had been reduced to just a few who remained, still chatting with one another as if they had nothing better to do.

Beside me, Cola said to Dante, "Have you located the ship?"

"I have located the boy."

"Okay, me too. Rae, come here." Cola held out his hand. He was dressed similarly to fake Tyra Banks, as though he had been attending an awards ceremony or spending the night in Monte Carlo for an evening of Punto Banco.

"Come." Cola held his hand out to me, and I took it. Immediately, my feet left the ground. And then we were twenty feet in the air, thirty, fifty. The tombstones in the Veteran's cemetery became tiny dots within seconds. Westwood's buildings and lights blurred past. We curved around and headed for Bel-Air, climbing steadily upward. The air grew colder. We went into clouds and everything turned gray and wet. Out of the clouds, into the frigid night sky. Up ahead, way high, high in the darkness, I saw a tiny light. We zoomed toward it at what seemed like the speed of sound. Cola's arms were like a vise around me, holding me close to his body. He trailed close behind Dante who led the way.

The light gradually grew bigger until suddenly we were upon it. It was one of the machines, one of the ships that took people. I was wondering how we were going to gain entrance when I felt Cola's mouth at my ear. He whispered, "The boy is here. Seek him out with your mind. Tell him to invite you in. Even unconscious, he will hear."

Someone was hovering to our left. I turned my head in the freezing night air, an icy wind blowing my hair across my eyes. Another familiar face looked back at me. The white guy who had made Blaxploitation cool again. After the legendary TV and radio personality, I had no more room for surprise. Blaxploitation, or Blax, as I thought of him, was floating beside us, holding onto a man who, in turn, was busy videotaping the bottom of the ship. The moon reflected off the vast expanse of Blax's forehead. He was Blax now. I was completely stressed and couldn't remember his name. He licked his lips and lifted his chin once like: Come on. Get us in. He stared at me voraciously, barely able to contain his excitement.

I turned away from his boring eyes and did as I was instructed. Sucking winds whipped our clothing. The cloth snapped sharply, as loud as gunshots. I heard an airplane flying by, far below. I sensed that we were so high up, outer space was right there, just at our fingertips. The stars, the planets, the galaxy were just there, just there. I sent my mind out like an invisible reel, out and out. I thought, *Ganymede, we're here.* I thought, *Ganymede, let us in.* I thought, *Ganymede, baby, we've come to get you.* It didn't take long at all. I heard it, a tiny voice, loud inside my head. *Come in, come in, come in.* And my heart breaking to hear, *It's scary here. I want to go home. I want to go home.*

I turned to Cola and said, "We're in."

Beside me, Blax snarled in anticipation.

CHAPTER 30

The vampires reacted immediately.

The vampires dove straight up through the bottom of the ship. They pummeled through it, fists first. Whatever material it was made of sliced apart like butter, and we were through. We were standing in some kind of corridor with the wind howling around us. It was dimly illuminated and deserted. Blax and his cameraman were already gone. Even as I gazed down at the hole we'd come through, several more unidentified vampires came shooting through from the outside. They disbanded immediately without a second glance at us and took off in different directions.

"You find the boy," Cola said. And then he disappeared. I whirled in a circle. Dante was gone. Briefly, I thought, *wait!* A cold terror was seeping through me, and I couldn't move. *We were on the alien ship.* Distantly, I thought I heard voices rise in alarm. There was shrieking, a shrill whistling sound. I ran forward in a panic, then abruptly stopped. I closed my eyes, stood still. Someone brushed past me roughly, and I didn't even look to see who it was. I went to my Happy Place and found comfort there: a bright, windy day on a sparsely populated beach. There was a seal that was friendly, like a dog. Well, seals *had* been dogs once, hadn't they? Back in prehistory. It barked and rushed forward on its flippers to meet me, overjoyed. Slowly I turned back the terror. I sent my senses out, let my pores inform me. The seal and I ventured forward.

I turned left and ran down a slanted corridor that was so low I had to stoop over slightly. Short little bastards. There was movement in a kind of oval doorway to my right. A big gray head and large wraparound eyes appeared. It was holding something that looked like a sheath of bright papers or shimmery material. It was like I'd startled it coming out of the bathroom. It balked and then tried to turn away. I was on it like a tsunami, tearing it apart. My seal buddy barked his approval. Barely pausing in my forward motion, I kept going in the direction my senses pulled me, leaving the mangled corpse behind.

Creatures appeared several more times, always in a panic, caught off guard each time as I yanked out eyes, popped heads off, and twisted spindly necks until they cracked. I did this all in a fugue state, operating as if on autopilot. A few of the ZRs were able to dematerialize somehow before I could reach them. But most did not react quickly enough to do that. Once in a while, I passed another vampire busily involved in similar activities. Hardly any of them acknowledged me as they blew past searching for more Zetas to destroy or appeared to randomly attack the ship itself by tearing sheets of material off the walls or pounding through the floor or ceiling. They were behaving like crazed rock stars in a suite at the Four Seasons.

The last Zeta I ran into as it came jogging around a bend in the corridor. If you could call it jogging. More like a rambling, rolling kind of quick shuffle. I smelled its dread before I saw it, and when it saw me, its only thought was *The one who sees!* just before I pulverized its gigantic head. The seal rolled on his back and waved his flippers in the air.

Finally, I arrived at an antechamber with no doors, just a low arch at the entranceway. I felt something here, so I ducked inside. It was a lab-like enclosure, antiseptic and efficient-looking, brightly lit, although I couldn't tell where the light was coming from. And then I saw Ganymede. He lay on what looked like a metal slab protruding from the rounded wall. Beside him were two ZRs that were intently studying his robot. I recognized it from his emails. It stood between the two creatures, at least a foot taller than them, as they poked and prodded its metal exterior. They were gesturing to one another silently in excitement, obviously having an entire conversation telepathically.

Boy, had they dropped the ball on this one. One of the Zetas discovered the robot's remote control, which had been attached by what looked like magnets to its torso, and greedily snatched it off in its four-fingered little hand. I took three steps into the room and brought my fist straight down into the closest one's head. The head detonated under the blow, spewing purple goop in all directions. The other Zeta dropped the remote, its mouth a tiny O, as I drove both hands into its wraparound eyes and out the other side. It shimmied on the end of my arms for several seconds, then went still. I yanked my arms free. Blood poured from various cuts and slashes on my fingers. Without a second glance at them, I moved toward Ganymede. He appeared to be unconscious. My seal friend gazed up at me with liquid eyes and barked once. He seemed to be saying, "You got this." He slowly faded away.

As I was bending to retrieve Ganymede off the table, a panel in the wall slid open and Bob came rushing into the room. He was dressed in his usual karate outfit, texting in a frenzied manner on his cell phone just as fake Tyra had been doing moments ago. He glanced up and saw me and stopped typing, his finger motionless above the tiny keypad. A slew of emotions rippled across his face, shifting from incomprehension to dawning in seconds. I, however, was still frozen at incomprehension. Bob shoved his cell phone away without looking at it or evidently finishing his message. His eyes ticked from Ganymede to me to the downed Zetas.

"You went over to the other side," said Bob, nodding slowly. "Wow." Pause. "Brava."

"You know about them? Us?"

"Them? A lot. You? A little bit." He spoke casually, as if we'd just bumped into each other at the post office.

"I knew I shouldn't have given you the benefit of the doubt."

"You should never give anyone the benefit of the doubt." Pause. "Are you going to tear my head off now?"

I was too flabbergasted to form a lucid thought. I was too flabbergasted to tear his head off. The gleaming curiosity in Bob's eyes seemed to slowly intensify. "How did it happen? Did it…hurt?" We stared at one another for a while. When it became apparent that I wasn't going to enlighten him, Bob decided to change the subject. He looked down at Ganymede for a moment.

"They're drawn to him, you know. His spirit shines bright."

He shines, I thought. *He shines.*

"What are you doing, Bob? You're in with them?" I raised my arms. "Why are you helping them?"

"Rae, Rae, Rae…" said Bob. He stumbled slightly as the ship juddered and a distant booming sound filled the air. "Let me explain something to you."

"No, don't explain anything. Don't explain anything. They're fucking with our souls and our DNA and who knows what else. *What are you doing here?*"

Bob arched an eyebrow. "Which is it? Don't explain or tell you what I'm doing here?" He paused dramatically, then: "Nobody is hurt. It's harmless."

"Some people don't come back." My head swirled with overlapping panicked voices, snatches of words: *The One who Sees…Blood men are here…Release the masses…*

He shrugged. "Very few. A price has to be paid for knowledge. Knowledge isn't free. It isn't just handed to you. You have to earn it."

"Wow," I said. I sensed movement behind me, but could not tear my eyes away from Bob.

"'Things that matter most must never be at the mercy of the things that matter least,'" said Bob, using his professorial voice, the one that had put me and half the students in his class into a semi-waking coma.

"Goethe," he finished.

I stared at him, open-mouthed.

"You're quoting Goethe, and you put a tracker on my back so they could find me? And do what? Kill me? Dissect me?"

"They're fascinated with those of you that can see the ships. They might have probed your brain a little. But they would have left it intact."

"They would have killed me and eaten my brains."

"You're thinking of zombies, Rae."

I abruptly stopped talking and made a move for Ganymede.

"Wait!" said Bob. "Let me apologize, Rae. I should have been up front with you." I scooped Ganymede up into my arms. He was limp and as heavy as a sack of potatoes. I half-heard Bob talking. I was already blocking him out, as if I was back in class. He started talking faster as I began backing up.

"I've been taken since I was a child," he said so quietly I found myself straining to hear. Something painful flashed through his eyes then disappeared. *Oh,* I thought. And then, *Ohhhhh...*

"At some point, we began to...interact, let's say." He shrugged. "I'm here to learn. To observe..." He shrugged again, smaller this time. "The mysteries of the universe." The tiniest shrug yet. "It's an honor, you know."

Mmm. Hadn't seen *that* coming. But *should* have. You either wanted to transcend existence because you knew it was a tedious, eternal catch-22, or you had, at some point, been shown the Earth from the starboard portal of a space ship. I thought of Y.B. actually trying to communicate with me, warning me, in fact; the very reason I was here. I guess some of these little guys could be confused and think Bob was someone worth confiding in. Or if they'd actually known him from childhood, maybe they thought of him as a red-headed stepson, dim-witted and endlessly amusing. As I kept backing up, I saw Bob's eyes move to whatever was behind me that I had been ignoring. At the last minute, I whirled around. Two ZRs rushed forward. One was holding something blunt and dark, aimed at my heart. It shot the object off and a weird disjointed light surrounded and flowed past me. Nothing happened. I stood there holding Ganymede and put one foot forward menacingly in their direction. Both startled, and the one with the weapon turned and bolted. In mid-running step, it dematerialized. Instead of kicking the head in of the one that was left, I said out loud, "Shine, not burn. Right?" The equivalence of being struck by lightning shot through its face. "This isn't the way," I said, and shook my head. I glanced over my shoulder. Not surprisingly, Bob was gone, having disappeared back through the sliding panel. I shoved past the remaining ZR, who was now paralyzed with indecision, and headed out of the room.

Back out in the rounded corridor, I sensed more than heard or saw the encroaching panic. The atmosphere was charged with terror and confusion. Most of the corridor had been newly renovated, vampire-style. The walls displayed ragged holes and drooping, mangled materials like aluminum siding that had been wrestled away from a house. One of the marauders had spray painted a giant penis in bold black and then added the head of a ZR leaning toward it. Really? I rolled my eyes and ran blindly down the low corridor with Ganymede bouncing on my shoulder. At one point, a creature appeared in a doorway and froze when it saw me. I stopped running and stared at it, Ganymede lying over my shoulder. I stepped toward it, murder in my eyes. Then I remembered the Scottish motto and the effect it had produced a moment ago. Instead of killing it, I could just render it immobile by sending its logic circuits into a loop. Out of nowhere, Blax appeared and dropped sideways onto the ZR like a wrestler, bringing his elbow down in the vicinity where an ear would have been. The creature's head bent in sideways beneath the lethal blow. It jerked and then lay still. The cameraman stood four feet away, filming everything. Slowly, Blax rose from the floor. Finally, he noticed me staring.

"What?" he said defensively. He glanced back at his cameraman. "It makes great footage. No one'll believe it actually *happened*." He shrugged. "But come on…" He gestured around him. "I'm **not** gonna get this on film?"

From far away or in my head I heard a voice. "RAE. RAE."

I hoisted Ganymede up higher, catching Blax's eye.

"Whoa, hey," he said, taking two steps toward me. "Are you taking a snack with you? Can I get a bite?"

"What? No!" I frowned at him. "This is the one we're saving. Remember? Down on the ground? The speech?"

"Oh, right," he said, "great suffering to one of our sisters. Blah-de-blah-blah. Gotcha."

I was beginning to remember his liberal use of the N-word in his movies and outrage began to muscle past fear and panic. Before I could get sidetracked, I whirled around and continued sprinting down the corridor, leaving Blax and his cameraman behind. I didn't know where I was going; I just ran and ran until Dante and Cola appeared. They were both panting, a crazed look in their eyes. All of us had bloody hands, Cola's shirttails had come loose, and one sleeve of Dante's shirt was in ribbons.

"She has the boy. Let's go," said Cola.

"Wait!" I heaved Ganymede up again. He kept slipping down. "Can one of you go get his robot? It's back there. Down the corridor. On the left." I gestured with my head.

Cola opened his mouth, and Dante stared at me in disbelief.

"Are you *kidding*?" he said. "Are you fucking KIDDING?" He lunged at me in a feral rage. Cola was between us in an instant, his hand pressed against Dante's chest. "WE HAVE TO GO," said Cola. "GET THE ROBOT."

He released Dante, and the minute he did, Dante blurred—gone. I thought I smelled smoke, and it felt like the ship was listing. There was a persistent high-pitched droning that seemed to be coming from all directions at once. Dante returned seconds later, holding the robot lightly under one arm even though it probably weighed over a hundred pounds. As we stood there, a crowd of strange vampires jogged by. One was dragging a limp Zeta behind him, and they all were bleeding from various places on their bodies. They barely glanced at us as they went by, disappearing moments later around a corner.

"Did you get the remote?"

Dante's mouth dropped open.

And then something weird happened. Okay, *weirder*. One would have wondered, realistically, how many of those things could still be alive? We had been punching and kicking and destroying right and left, moving at the speed of sound. But yet now, seemingly from all directions, we were swarmed by a sea of Zetas. They poured in from doorways and sliding panels, they climbed up out of the floor, they cascaded in droves down the hallway. In moments, the three of us were surrounded, inundated. The Zetas began to climb up on us like mindless worker ants. I tried to fight them off with one arm while I held onto Ganymede. Cola battled his way toward me but made little progress. Dante set the robot down and launched into the mob, unfettered, but was barely able to make a dent. Something occurred to me just then, now that this new thing was happening. We may not get out of here alive. I began craning my head around, searching for Blax and his cameraman. Where were they? Maybe they could do something. Of all the people in the world, wouldn't the guy who served up violence in spicy, diet-destroying servings have arrived packing heat?

Another panel slid open and smugly, imperiously, Bob came strolling through. He was actually smirking. He watched for a moment as the three of us struggled to keep the ZRs from covering us like a mudslide. We were failing, though. There were simply too many of them. I didn't care if I died, but not Ganymede. The universe was a cold, heartless place. Not Ganymede. I locked eyes with Cola as we struggled beneath the tide of tiny bodies. All he could do was stare grimly back, arms moving so fast they were a blur.

"Ah…" said Bob. "Maybe you should have just stayed home and watched *True Blood* on Netflix."

Dante's head snapped up. Growling, tossing the aliens off him by the twos and threes, he managed to wade forward, and before Bob could react, grabbed him by the throat. Dante was going to kill Bob, and we were all going to die. I felt my gorge rise as the floor tilted at an alarming angle. I stumbled, slamming hard into the robot. My shoulder jammed into a button, depressing it. The effect was instantaneous. The clinging mass of creatures tumbled off me as one to the floor and rolled around there, little hands pressed over their midsections. Though we heard nothing ourselves, every single ZR surrounding us and crowding the corridor fell over, writhing on the ship floor in what could only be immense physical torment. Many of them were vomiting up a disgusting gelatinous material that they then proceeded to roll in, oblivious, in agony.

Cola didn't hesitate. He scooped up the robot and yelled, "Dante, let's go!" as the entire side of the ship suddenly dematerialized. The black night sky came rushing in. In an instant, ferocious winds sucked Cola and I out amongst the wispy clouds, and then there was only whirling darkness as I spun out of control. I squeezed Ganymede to my chest. After several seconds, the spinning slowed. When I opened my eyes, I saw the ship above me receding at a rapid pace. I was plummeting backward toward earth, away from the ship, away from the stars. Before my eyes, the ship grew translucent as a piece of glass. A second later, it winked out existence.

The air roared past, tearing the air from my almost-undead lungs. We were in a rollicking descent heading straight for the mountains. Possibly Brentwood. Wouldn't Margarite be surprised to wake up in the morning and find me floating in her swimming pool holding onto a small boy with a large afro? In that instant, her entire life would be validated, convinced she had made all the right choices— the ones opposite from mine. In the movies, the hero would say to the person they were protecting, "Close your eyes, baby." But luckily, I didn't have to do that now, because Ganymede was already unconscious. Below me, I sensed the earth rushing up to meet us and waited for oblivion. It would be horrible, the worst thing ever in the world, if I survived but Ganymede disintegrated into a million pieces. What if the aliens were going to give him back? What if we had only made things worse, the vampires and I?

But of course that never happened. Out of nowhere, a blurry figure swooped down, latched on to us, slowed our descent. By the time we reached the ground, we touched down like feathers, like a snowflake kissing the top of a tree. Cola released us with one arm and set the robot down with the other. I sat on the ground with Ganymede on my lap, gazing at him with an aching relief. Many, many minutes went by. We were back on Sepulveda, up the road just slightly from the car. I tipped my invisible brim to Cola. Pretty good aim. All around us, a dizzying variety of high-end sports and luxury vehicles were haphazardly parked where the over-eager vamps had left them. There were only a couple of Hondas and Civics in the mix. A few of the undead were dallying together at the side of the road. I think those were the ones who had been chatting before and had never left to begin with. As I watched, several got into their Mercedes Benz SLs, Audis, and Jags and took off at top speeds in pairs and different directions.

After several more moments of silence I said, "You weren't in Burbank a few days ago, were you, when my neighbor and I were getting abducted in the middle of Glendale Boulevard?"

Cola kept staring up at the sky. Slowly he leveled his gaze at me.

"Maybe," was all he said. He held my eyes for several seconds until I beta wolfed and broke contact.

"Um…if you *were* there," I ventured hesitantly, "did you happen to notice if someone else was there with you?"

Cola kept staring upward. "Maybe," he said again.

I was going to get nowhere with this. But maybe that was enough for now.

We went back to silence for a while and me gazing at Ganymede and Cola scrutinizing the sky.

"It looked like it disappeared. Where did it go?"

Cola sighed. "They dematerialized back to their dimension."

I craned my neck, trying to see. What, I don't know. I had witnessed it for myself, the ship disappearing.

"Shit," I whispered.

Cola looked at me.

"Yeah, I know," he said, and we were quiet.

Dante hadn't gotten off the ship. Neither had Bob. Supposedly, they were somewhere now in the dimension of the Zetas. I couldn't even imagine what that would be like. A world of fractured light? Picasso-like images, incomprehensible and terrifying? "Oh, my God," I whispered. *Dante.* I wracked my brain for any and all accumulated vampire lore: they must be alive—or Dante was unalive, at least—because I was still a vampire. I think I was supposed to revert back to human if he had ceased existing.

"Rae, it's all right. They'll be okay."

"How do you know?"

Cola didn't answer. He looked off, preoccupied. He obviously didn't know.

"Look," he said softly, "we stopped them before they finished the abductions. We never would have done that if you hadn't warned us."

I nodded once, sadly. "But it's temporary, isn't it? They're always going to be here. They're always going to do this to us—them. People."

Cola sighed. "It's been going on a long time, Rae." He shrugged. "My kind has been here a long time." He glanced at me. "Our kind."

There was a long silence. "You got the kid back," he said finally. "Isn't that all that matters?"

He was right. I was still in shock over Dante and Bob and would deal with it later. But right now, he was right. I looked down at Ganymede, his slumbering face, with a love that I maybe did not deserve to feel. If I were a villain, I'd take him. Away from Jupiter and the crazy moons. But I wasn't a villain. I was just me: college dropout, ex-actor, fallen human. I felt honored to inhale his innocence, awed to know his sweetness. I kissed him lightly on the forehead and glanced at Cola who was now contemplating me with a tenderness I found somehow familiar. I paused, staring, something buried deep inside edging toward consciousness. Cola looked away, back at the sky, and the sensation vanished.

"He's a genius, you know," I said, gesturing down with my chin. "His robot saved our lives."

"I think you're right. He's an amazing kid."

"Someone wanted to eat him. That Blaxploitation director."

Cola frowned. "What?"

"Thank you," I said, changing the subject.

"You're welcome, Rae," he said quietly, continuing his vigil of the empty night. "You're welcome."

There was a suddenly flurry in the air. Fake Tyra Banks zoomed down from the sky, satin skirts billowing, cape flapping. She landed with practiced grace in the middle of Sepulveda Boulevard, lifted a finger to swipe the sides of her mouth in a genteel manner, licked her lips once, and glanced at us. Then she supermodel-walked to a sleek black machine that looked like a Scorpion parked at a crazy angle behind a monster truck. She got in, revved the engine, and screeched off into the night.

Watching her go, I said to Cola, "How did everybody else get on the ships?"

Cola watched the high-end sports car drive away. "They got invited in, the same as you. If abducted humans were on board." He shrugged. "Or…by deceiving the aliens…to admit them."

Or what about aliens on our side? I pictured Y.B. leaving the equivalent of a side door unlocked and then tip-toeing off to hide in a cabinet.

I studied my hands. They had been cut and slashed and bleeding freely just moments before. Now they were almost completely healed. I wasn't quite vampire, wasn't quite human. I remembered reading *The Watchmen* long ago and coming across that quote from the Bible and wondering what it meant. After tonight, it was obvious. At least for me. I was a brother to dragons and a companion to owls. I was a predator. I was a creature of the night. I was the shark. But there were still bigger monsters than me out there in my opinion. I couldn't believe we'd lost Dante, or Bob, for that matter. It didn't seem possible. And what about Blax and his cameraman? I had no idea if they'd made it or not. All that potential film footage possibly lost. But we were lucky. Everyone in *Alien* had died except for Ripley. Everyone in *Private Ryan* had died except for Private Ryan. Here, I think, we'd suffered fewer casualties. We'd killed the monsters and gotten the boy. We'd even gotten the robot, and even though we'd left the remote, in Hollywood this was what we liked to call a happy ending.

CHAPTER 31

"Are you sure you want to do this?" Cola asked.

He bent over me, staring into my eyes with a veiled expression. If I wasn't completely crazy, I'd say he was hiding fear.

The minute I realized he was scared, I was scared. I closed my eyes and took deep breaths. When I opened them, Cola was still leaning over me, staring. I was lying on the sofa in his office, and Irene was buzzing busily around in the background, preparing things.

"Why? You think I'm gonna die?"

Nothing on Cola moved except his eyes. They ticked up and over, so he was focused somewhere near my left ear. "I've told you," he said, addressing my left ear, "sometimes it doesn't work. And sometimes it's fatal."

I grinned crookedly. "You wouldn't let me die." My voice shook a little. "If you did, Dante would come back and kill you."

Cola's eyes shifted back from my ear to my face. Behind him, Irene tottered around in the room, setting down objects and mixing liquids. She was humming Rhianna's *Umbrella*.

"Dante can't kill me. And he wouldn't try."

He was dressed, as usual, in an immaculate form-fitting suit. The only difference was his tie was loose at the throat and the first two buttons of his shirt were undone. That was the sloppiest I'd ever seen Cola. Except after the battle the other night. It wasn't very reassuring.

"If you guys were werewolves, you'd be the Alpha wolf."

He smiled lightly. "Or an Alpha vampire, since I'm not a werewolf."

"So you're the Alpha vampire," I said, trying to keep my mind off upcoming events. "What is it, just because you're older?"

"Basically." He sighed, then cranked his head around, tracking Irene. "We almost ready?" He sounded irritated and nervous. So then, of course, *I* became irritated and nervous.

My cell phone rang, and I nearly rolled off the sofa trying to reach it. Cola scooped it up off the coffee table and handed it to me. I scanned the ID. It was some 800 number. It wasn't Rex. My hopes plummeted. It was several days after the battle with the Zetas. Rex and I had been playing a serious game of phone tag, but it had ceased to be amusing and now was simply distressing. I wanted to at least speak to him, because it was possible I would never see him again. I had already called up my parents, Hama, and Margarite and engaged in cryptic, coded conversations which had creeped them all out. My father hadn't been home. If I died, I would not have said good-bye to him. My mother had asked me if I was all right. Margarite (as usual) said I sounded weird. Hama asked me if I was smoking a bong.

I wrote an email to Ganymede, telling him how proud I was of him. I texted Giancarlo a pleasant message saying how great it was meeting him and how I admired his passion. I even wrote and notarized a living will, sorting out my belongings and my bank accounts to various people, including Margarite. I was ready.

Everybody was accounted for, except for Rex.

But I had to do it anyway. I wanted out. I mean, the battle was over, wasn't it? More or less. I felt a fluttering excitement at the thought of returning to normal. The Undoing sounded like the "control-Z" command on the keyboard. Whoops. Undo that. Go back.

Cola was standing with his back to me, arms crossed, while he spoke quietly with Irene. I closed my eyes and then I heard him say, "Remember that you still have time. Just under a week. You don't have to decide today."

I opened my eyes.

"It's okay, Cola," I said. "Everyone has to die sooner or later."

Something constricted in his face and his jaw worked.

"I just got you back," he said and then stopped, as if he hadn't meant to say that.

"Back from where?"

There was a long pause.

"If we succeed," his jaw worked silently, "you'll be mortal again. Stay this way…you'll never die."

"I recall someone who was *really pissed* after Dante first did this to me. Now you don't want me to go back."

He waited, his jaw flexing, pulling himself together. After a moment, he managed to smile.

"I got used to it," he admitted.

Beat.

I reached my hand up and he took it immediately, squeezed it once, then set it gently down. He turned abruptly and gestured to Irene.

"Okay. Let's do it."

Suddenly he was all business.

"The first drink is a neutralizer. The second drink is a concentrated rhododendron tisane. The third drink is the cleanser."

"Wait—what? Rhodo what?"

"Rhododendron."

"Isn't that a poisonous plant?"

"Rae, don't do this to me."

"A deadly, poisonous plant?"

"Rae. Not now. You can't do this now."

"Yeah. Yeah, yeah, yeah. I know. I know." I closed my eyes and clenched my hands together.

"Yes or no. Decide. This is the way it's done. But you have to be sure."

"Yeah, I'm sure."

"You're ready to do this?"

"I'm ready. I'm sorry I asked about the poison."

"I'm sorry you asked, too. All right, let's go."

Irene set a tray down beside me with the three glasses on it. They looked like ordinary glasses. Like the kind of glasses you'd have juice in. Apple juice. She patted my arm with her papery hand.

"One after the other, Ms. Miller. Don't breathe. Don't pause. One after the other."

She sounded like she'd been through this before. Like she'd done this a thousand times.

"Have you ever personally seen the Undoing work?" I asked her, fully expecting a reassuring nod, an enthusiastic, "Why, of course, Ms. Miller. Seven out of ten attempts, we are successful."

Instead, she blinked rapidly several times, then shot a look at Cola. They said nothing and something bounced around inside me. I think my gall bladder had slipped its moorings. I thought I was going to vomit.

"Sit up, Rae."

I sat up.

"The effects are fast."

"The faster the better…" I trailed off, mesmerized by the glasses. I glanced up to see both of them staring at me. "Okay, well…"

"Just do it, Rae. If you're going to do it."

"I'm going to do it," I said, feeling like I should get up and run out as fast as I could. Instead, I picked up the first glass, tipped my head back, and downed it. No taste whatsoever. Middle glass. Poison. I squeezed my eyes shut, emptied the contents into my mouth and swallowed. I felt Cola and Irene's eyes on me, burning like hot coals. The poison had a vaguely cinnamon taste but nothing beyond that. Quickly I picked up the third glass and gulped the liquid down. Nothing happened. I waited about thirty seconds, then I stood up, flapping my arms in frustration. Disappointment flooded through me.

"I feel fine. Nothing happened," I said.

They ignored me. They were moving toward the sofa. I turned and saw myself there, flung backwards as if from an unknown force, askew against the cushions. The two of them straightened me out, lifted my legs up. I looked from them to myself and back to my body.

"HEY!" I screamed, and they ignored me and began speaking together. Cola bent forward and smoothed the hair off my face.

The walls rushed in on all sides and the room disappeared.

I was sucked into a vortex of swirling color that broke apart like a kaleidoscope, little by little, gradually revealing a vast ocean down below. It twinkled and curled beneath the yellow sun. I plummeted like a stone into the water, down, down, down. Bright, sunny day. Light filtering through. It was beautiful here. Now.

Jolt.

I was in the Now.

I lifted my head. I was sitting on a surfboard, back to the sun. Rex was beside me, bobbing on the waves. His lips were moving, but I couldn't hear what he was saying. We were eighteen years old. We sat with casual grace on our surfboards, our lives ahead of us, the world ahead of us. The sun dried the salt water into a fine layer over our skin. Our hair was bleached in streaks and curled wetly against our cheeks and foreheads. Rex whipped his head once and sent the hair flying, drops spinning in brilliant whirls. He smiled and my heart leapt. What a smile. What a smile! Our lives were ahead of us, the world was ahead of us. We sat on the skin of the ocean with carefree abandon, serene, unhurried. We peeled the skin of the ocean back with our fingers and toes, the fins of our boards. We rode it, our hips bucking in uneven rhythm.

I looked at him again. He wasn't eighteen anymore. It was Rex from today, older, hair shorter, a smile cracking his face into sun-baked creases. But my feelings were exactly the same. What a smile. What a smile! And still our lives were ahead of us. And the world was ahead of us. We sat quietly riding the sea for a long, long time.

Jolt.

Now.

I was in the Now.

I started. Dante and Bob were seated on a couple of surfboards, bobbing in between me and Rex.

"Oh, my God, what are you guys doing here?"

Dante sucked his tongue, disgusted. "You threw my gift away like trash? You tossed it into the garbage without thinking twice even?"

"I thought twice about it. Does that mean it's working?"

"Woman…" He rolled his eyes in contempt and wouldn't look at me.

"Are you guys still alive?"

Bob answered. He was wearing the same karate outfit he'd had worn on the ship, and the ocean lapped at his pant legs gently.

"We're alive. We're okay. What about you?" He cocked an eyebrow at me. *What was that supposed to mean? Was he insinuating that I was dead?*

"You're not really here. I'm just dreaming," I informed them.

"Oh?" Dante said in disgust. "Don't be too sure of that." He leaned forward and paddled furiously toward me. He reached out and grabbed my wrist, hard.

"Ow!"

"Don't be too sure!" he said again, incensed. Then he let go and lay back on the surfboard as if exhausted.

"One thing's for sure—you're here. Now," said Bob.

Jolt.

Now.

I was in the Now.

The female bicycle cop who had made me pick up my trash at the beach appeared beside Bob. She was sitting on her bike, and the bike was balanced on top of a surfboard.

"Hey, there," she said.

I spread my hands and looked around.

"Not smoking. Not littering," I told her.

"I know."

"What are you doing here? Are *you* dead?"

"I'm your subconscious, honey. I'm just here to make sure you *don't* litter," she said. "But also because I know that you admire me— the cop, not your subconscious—and I want you to know it's not too late. You can still go back to school and have a career too."

"You know, whenever I'm applying to UCLA, the phone rings—"

Suddenly Cola was there, interrupting my pathetic excuses. He popped in from thin air. He was still wearing his immaculate suit. But, as if this wasn't a dream and he was actually here, he had rolled up his pants to his knees so that only his naked calves dangled in the water. I could see them under the water, full and bronze-colored. He was also barefoot. I gazed down at his calves, entranced, as Cola cleared his throat.

"Rae, stop looking at my calves and listen. You've been in a coma for twelve hours. If you don't wake up, I'm taking you to a doctor in another hour."

With a force of will, I tore my eyes away from Cola's calves. I saw Rex watching silently from down the line of surfboards.

"Yours are great too," I called. He was getting further away, as more people were appearing. "Yours are better!"

"Did you hear me?" asked Cola. "Rae, this is important."

"I heard you. I've been in a coma for twelve hours. What is that, the vampire coma limit? Twelve isn't bad but thirteen is? Maybe you should take me now."

"Rae, I have to go. You're seizing. Wake up. Wake yourself up."

Cola popped out of the picture to be replaced by a Tiger shark. *The* Tiger shark. It lay on a surfboard too, on its belly, and turned its weirdly pointed head, regarding me.

"Oh, shit," I said. "You."

"Yeah, me," it spoke around its mouthful of teeth and sounded like it was lisping. "It's me, baby."

It tried to lower its dorsal fin into the water but couldn't quite reach. "Listen, you let me ruin your life. I let go. I let go of you. But you never let go of me."

"No shit, Sherlock." I knew this already. Didn't I? "Tell me something I don't already know." Frigging fish had a nerve.

"You've already died three times. Right? What do you have left to be afraid of?"

We all sat on our various surfboards in a line, bobbing up and down on the skin of the sea. Rex at the far end, Dante and Bob, the bicycle cop, the Tiger shark. I thought for a minute.

"Three times?" I asked, uncertain. I counted them off.

"When I was two years old. One."

"One," said the Tiger shark.

"When I became undead. Two."

"Two," said the Tiger shark.

I stopped. "Okay. Then where? What's number three?"

"Seriously?"

They were all looking at me, except Rex, who was quietly standing up on his board even though no waves were coming.

"Now?" I said.

"You heard him!" yelled the Tiger shark. "Wake up, Rae!"

Jolt.

I was in the Now.

Rex's board began to lift out of the water and float away with him still standing. He was floating toward the sun. He looked back once, straight into my eyes. Poker face. Completely unreadable. Something was happening. Something was wrong. I should have paid more attention to him. I should have packed up and just moved in with him. But I had a million excuses.

"Rex!" I yelled. He ignored me and continued floating up into the sky, rapidly becoming a small figure, then a speck, then swallowed by the clouds. In a panic, I turned to the line of surfboarders, including Tiger Shark, but only gently moving ocean was there. Somewhere in the background I heard a wispy, trembling voice singing about umbrellas, telling us where we could stand. The ocean continued to move, softly lapping. Everybody was gone. So I finally closed my eyes and made myself gone too.

I was lying half on the sofa, half off, my head in Cola's lap, my feet on the floor.

"Jesus," said Cola, cradling my head.

"I didn't know we were allowed to say that name," I quipped immediately. "Aren't we supposed to burst into flames or a least get really angry when we hear it?"

Cola's grim expression lightened two degrees and then his mouth quirked.

"You were having—"

"A seizure? I know." I struggled to sit up. Cola helped me.

I thought of Rex on his surfboard, floating off into the heavens.

"Did Rex call?"

"No, Rae, Rex hasn't called."

"How long was I here?"

"Twelve hours."

"Oh, yeah. I was in a coma for twelve hours. But thirteen was the magic number. You were gonna call 911 when that happened."

Cola sat beside me on the sofa looking frazzled and, if possible, overheated. I had never seen him out of a suit jacket before. I think one of his hairs was out of place. It was extremely disconcerting.

"I was talking to you," he said. "I knew you'd hear me."

I took in a deep breath. I let it out. No surprise there. I lifted my hands and looked at them. I didn't feel any different. I tested my shoulder. Not sore. Stumps. Not sore. Eyesight crystal clear. Uh-oh. Well, maybe there was a delay. We sat quietly on the sofa in the darkened room. Someone had opened the steel shutters over the windows a tad, and I could see that dusk was approaching fast.

"Anyway…" Cola stopped and cleared his throat. "I'm sorry." It almost sounded like his voice broke. I whipped my head around to look at him. Even though there was no clock in the room, I could hear the seconds ticking by one by one as it became apparent what had happened.

"Oh, my God," I said. "*Oh my God.*" I covered my eyes. "It didn't work."

"It didn't work."

"It actually didn't work."

"It almost killed you. You seized and were…gone."

"What does that…even mean? I'm already dead."

"You are undead. We are undead. Even the undead can become dead-dead."

"What a pain in the ass. What a waste of time!"

Without further ado, Cola reached over and pulled me to him. Something very strong emanated from him that some part of me deep inside picked up: It was love but very paternal. Definitely not romantic. After crushing me in his arms for many moments, he released me suddenly and was all business again. He stood up.

I stood up. Woozily.

"Here." Cola bent over, picked a glass up off the coffee table, and handed it to me. It looked like one of the glasses that had killed me earlier. "Drink it. Blueberry juice with wheatgrass and some iron."

"Is that the glass that had the poison in it?"

"The poison? No, Rae."

"The rhodo—are you sure?"

"I'm sure."

"It looks exactly like it."

"All three glasses looked like this."

"Okay, so is it?"

"Rae, even if it was, the residue would be so small it wouldn't affect you. But we clean things around here. Irene sterilized the glasses."

"How? Do you guys have a dishwasher somewhere in here?"

Cola made an executive decision and switched gears.

"I did get a call earlier," he told me.

"But not Rex." Hesitantly, I received the glass from him.

"No. Not Rex."

I fretted and started to bite my nails.

"I kinda thought this was going to work." I looked at Cola ruefully. "I can't...move in with Rex. Not like this. I can't really...do *anything* with him."

Cola gazed back, unblinking. Then, impassively: "You'd have to tell him. Eventually."

I tore my hand out of my mouth to stop myself from biting my nails.

"Okay, listen. We have a business offer. A movie. Sci-fi. He called specifically asking for you."

My jaw dropped. "Are you talking about who I think you're...he made it out?"

"Of course he made it. Where did you think he was?"

I threw my hands up. "With Dante and Bob? I don't know! Anywhere. All he wanted to do was bite Ganymede. I started running, and he didn't follow. I thought he got left behind." I paused. "How did he know who I was?"

Cola cocked an eyebrow at me.

Oh, yeah. I was in a different world now. For good. That kind of thinking was apparently passé.

"Want to talk about it over dinner? I'll take you out."

"He was filming up there. Did you see him? You know how kids film themselves beating the shit out of somebody and then post it on YouTube or their Facebook page and that's how they get arrested? He had someone filming him roaming around and pulling the heads off Zetas."

Cola regarded me silently. Then he shrugged. "At the risk of sounding impervious, it would make good footage."

"Oh, my God! That's what he said!"

That must be the agent in him speaking. That must be Hollywood speaking.

"Let me guess—this sci fi movie. Does it have anything to do with aliens? And vampires?" I smirked.

"Let's go. I think you could do with a nice bloody steak. Are you up for it? How are you feeling?"

"You eat solid food?"

"I can. I have." He took me by the elbow and walked me to the door of his office. He was busy pulling his sleeves down and buttoning his shirt back up. I guzzled down the wheatgrass-infused blueberry juice and immediately felt less woozy.

"I can't ever repay you for everything you've done. You always have my back."

"It's my job," he said.

I shook my head. "No." I shook it some more. "That's way beyond your job description."

He opened the door. The brightly lit office came flooding in. Irene appeared behind me and plucked the empty glass from my hand.

"I'll take that," she murmured. She turned to me. "I'd just like to say…it was a good try. You were very brave, my dear. I am so sorry your expectations were not met."

"Uh…thanks, Irene. At least I'm alive." Pause. "Unalive." Pause. "Whatever." I was extremely down.

"Good evening, dear." She patted my arm. To Cola: "You are off for the night?"

"The next several hours at least," he answered. "I'll bring an order back for you if you like."

"Oh, no, I'm fine, Mr. Georgiou. But thank you." Irene turned disappeared through a side door near her desk. I guess that's where they kept the dishwasher. And the poison.

"Okay, let's go," said Cola, taking control. "I'll take you to Trattoria Amici."

Aw, he remembered. It felt good to surrender. I was stuck being a vampire. Embrace it. If I was back in the ocean with everybody again, my human self would have appeared on a surfboard too and said, "You're undead. Let it go."

I let it go.

CHAPTER 32

Twenty-four hours later, I had achieved the impossible.

Battled monsters, survived an impossible fall, saved the world? No.

Well, yeah. But I was also completely unpacked.

The boxes had been emptied and flattened. I had stored everything on shelves and in closets. Even my *Green Splendor* posters were mounted on the walls in the living room. This was my home for now. I was accepting my fate. What else could I do? In retrospect, making a decision to let a vampire turn you while you were raging drunk probably wasn't the smartest move in the universe. Maybe for once I had to admit that denial might not be the best route to take when dealing with one's life. Maybe I had to abandon Kara and the gang and close down Denial School and reimburse half their tuition and open up a new place: Face Reality University. A-type personalities need not apply. The conflicted always welcome.

But here I was. And, really, it wasn't all for nothing. We had won. Sort of. For now. A Zeta Reticuli had communicated with me. Bob was removed from the equation. Dante was probably alive. There was a bruise on my wrist where he had grabbed me in the vision. Irene and Cola might have done that, restraining me as my body had seized, but I really didn't know for sure. Best of all, Ganymede was saved. And lastly, Blax wanted me for a movie. I had recalled his name in the meantime, but I now felt a nostalgic fondness for this moniker.

And very lastly, I had finally unpacked.

You're such a pussy, some part of my brain lashed out at me. *Why are you doing this?*

I can't move in with Rex. It's impossible.

Just tell him. He'll understand.

He'll understand? He'll **understand?**

God, I wish I was in somebody else's body. Being inside you is like being inside a coffin. You're boring. You know that song, "Your Body is a Wonderland"? Your body is a wasteland. Your body and mind are a scrabbly, sun-ravaged wasteland.

Scrabbly?

Scrabbly, sister. Scrabbly.

Keep talking. All I have to do is hang out in the sun for a while. Without sunblock. Without a hat. Or a quick call to Giancarlo. Remember him?

Silence.

Nothing more issued forth from that part of my brain.

Smugly, I returned to the computer and continued to plumb the depths of online registration at UCLA. As I searched the pages, I idly wondered what would happen if I called Giancarlo up out of the blue and asked for a favor. I'd drive out to the beach. It would be magic hour. I'd be super-depressed and I'd have given up, but I might as well make my last scene a romantic one. The world would be painted yellow and gold as the sun slowly lowered to the horizon. It would be a very flattering light to die in. I pictured myself dialing and saying, "Hey. What up? Just wondering…could you come over here and kill me? I'm at lifeguard tower number thirteen in Zuma Beach near PCH."

I sat back in my chair and stared down at the UCLA website, unseeing. On top of the fact that now I couldn't get *Your Body is a Wonderland* to stop playing in my head, I couldn't believe I had just imagined asking Giancarlo to kill me. And yet there was something strangely, vaguely reassuring about the fact that I had that as an option, no matter how remote an option it might be. Something poetic. I was sure he would be very gentle. He might not even be able to do it. I might have to talk him into it. As I sat musing and wallowing in self-pity, the last thing on earth that I expected to happen finally happened. I felt an incredibly sharp pain near my canines, like a madman with razor blades was sawing through my gums. Abandoning the computer, I sprinted for the bathroom and lifted my lips back before the mirror.

Fangs. The fangs. It was the fangs. They had shoved down in front of my canines, crowding the normal teeth behind. They sparkled in my mouth, super-white and pointy. Making my other teeth, which I was careful to regularly whiten at the dentist's, look grungy and off-color. Slowly I let my lips lower back down. It was difficult to close my mouth over the fangs, but I managed. I looked like I had a mouthful of food I hadn't chewed yet. I squeezed my eyes shut and mentally willed them back up. Belligerently, they remained.

Opening my eyes again, I regarded the new fangs with a sense of helplessness bordering on despair. It was like being twelve again and realizing menstruation was here to stay. It was a cause for celebration in other cultures, but in America, certainly in Sherman Oaks, California, I had only felt blindsided, burdened, resigned at its arrival. At twelve, I secretly had been hoping it would never come. Same with the fangs. I realized I had been yearning for their continued absence. Maybe they would never appear. That would make me only part vampire. That would make me only partly committed.

I wandered back into the living room and quietly closed my laptop, shutting UCLA out of my life once again. *This is it*, I thought. *This is your life.* I probed the fangs gently with my tongue, jerking at their sharpness. What next? Was flying not far behind? Leaping into the air, surging through the clouds? I looked around at my apartment distractedly. If only I hadn't walked in on Annie in the laundry room. Why did my procrastination have to end on *that* day specifically? Why couldn't I have done my laundry two days later? I guess it didn't matter. They had turned out to be everywhere. I would have run into them sooner or later.

The Undoing hadn't worked, and I had died/almost died. I pictured myself lying unmoving on Cola's sofa while Irene hovered in the background making him tea and lighting his cigars. Then the two of them, later, in the thirteenth hour, rushing me to the emergency room. Except they could only shove me out of the car and burn rubber out of there, leaving me rolling along the driveway, because nobody, of course, could find out what Cola was. And possibly Irene.

I wasn't sure about her. As for me...could doctors save a vampire's life? Maybe Cola had been referring to a "special" doctor, like the ones criminals always went to in the movies to get bullets removed and have their faces rebuilt.

This is it. This is your life, the obnoxious part of my brain piped up, daring to taunt me after I had threatened it with death.

Suddenly I thought, it doesn't have to be.

What the eff is that supposed to mean, b-yotch?

Figure it out, genius.

Magic hour, also known as the golden hour, was universally accepted as the first and last hour of sunlight during the day when a specific photographic effect was achieved due to the quality of the light. The world was magical, sexier, more romantic. Like the beginning or end of a movie.

I was sitting on a surfboard wearing only my underwear. Behind me, the sun was setting and a wave was coming. The water felt warm. It was magic hour.

I leaned forward, starting to paddle.

"You got it. Go for it!" Rex yelled.

I glanced over as I rode the rising swell. He was sitting on a surfboard several feet away. He grinned, then put his head back, eyes closed, his long, taut throat exposed to the world. To me.

Just Rex.

No one else.

It was magic hour.

We moved with casual grace on our surfboards. Some of our life was behind us, but a lot of our life was ahead of us. The lowering sun had dried the salt water into a fine layer over our skin. Our hair curled wetly against our cheeks and foreheads. Rex brought his head up and shook his hair, drops spinning in reddish jumbled whirls in the dying sun. He was wearing a pair of swim trunks because he kept several pairs lying around in his truck at all times. He kept boards stacked up in the back. He kept towels. He kept goggles. He kept surfwax, he kept skimboards, he kept wetsuits.

I had been calling him all afternoon.

I had gone Glenn Close in *Fatal Attraction* on him.

On the sixteenth try, I began to feel nuts and decided to throw in the towel.

Then my phone had rung, filling the air with *Anything Goes*. Because anything did go. And it already had.

We had been out here for hours. Riding the skin of the ocean with carefree abandon, serene, unhurried. Rex had desperately needed to relax. We weren't eighteen anymore, and we were somewhat stressed out. But when we peeled the skin of the sea back with our fingers and toes, the stress was gone, no more than myth and memory. Rex was on a Lucky 7. I was on a Splintered Paddle. I was going to tell him. Now or never, now or never, now or never. *I was going to tell him.*

"Take it!" he yelled, watching the wave grow.

It was magic hour.

I had died three times. What was harder than that? But I was still afraid. The waning light, the churning wave. The beautiful dusk, the dying day. At the last minute, I stopped paddling and sloped sideways into the water, letting the wave drive by. I pumped my fists into the ocean and pulled myself toward to Rex. He watched me coming with an amused expression. He had offered me one of his swim trunks to wear, but I had elected to keep on my virginally white boy shorts.

"You missed it," he said. "What happened?"

I pushed hard, and our boards bumped. Then I was climbing onto Lucky 7 even as Rex was reaching to pull me over simultaneously. I sat facing him, straddling the board. We bumped up and down, our hips bucking in uneven rhythm. We were so close, I could see granules of sand on his skin. The cut on his cheek had had a few days to start healing. It was safely closed off by a protective scab, and I was happy to realize that I felt nothing as I looked at it. Maybe the crapload of wheatgrass and iron supplements I'd scarfed in the parking lot was helping; I don't know. I was just glad I didn't want to lick his bones anymore. Rex plucked some ocean fluff off my shoulder.

"You know your underwear is see-through now, don't you?"

He politely kept his eyes on my face as he announced this.

"How's that cut doing? Does it hurt?" I was at least an inch long. I wondered how hard it would be for me to find that knife mugger and what I would do to him.

Rex delivered a ghostly smile. "It's fine." He offered nothing beyond this.

Next question.

"If I told you I was a vampire, would you still love me?" I blurted out.

Rex waited as if more was forthcoming, like a punchline maybe. Then, realizing there wasn't, he said, "Yeah. I'd still love you if you were a vampire."

Pause.

"Are you…a vampire?"

Pause. Pause.

"Would you believe me if I said yeah?"

The water lapped at our legs. The sun dipped down.

"I don't know." He studied me. "Your teeth do look a little weird."

I saw his finger coming closer, pointing, and closed my lips. "Those two in front. They're, like…pushed back."

"Pushed back?"

"They weren't like that before. Were they?"

"Thanks for noticing. How long have we known each other?"

"I can see through your underwear. You heard me before, right?"

"I heard you. I don't care."

I was also wearing my favorite yellow bra, returned to me from the alien dimension.

"It's like you're naked," he continued. "You might as well be naked." Then he smiled. What a smile! His face cracked into sun-baked creases. We sat facing each other on the skin of the sea, grinning like idiots. Guys were always so happy when there was nakedness involved.

It was magic hour.

It was very flattering light to be happy in.

I was going to tell him, but not now. Not today. I was just glad he had answered. And anyway, I had just sort of, kind of told him. Later when he said, "I thought you were kidding," I would say, "Well, I wasn't kidding," and at least it would be on the record. I had said it. Out loud. The seagulls were my witnesses.

We sat facing each other, our hips bucking softly. The Splintered Paddle board, attached to me by a leash, floated quietly nearby. Rex closed his eyes and whispered, "You…are…" He opened his eyes and stared at me. "*so crazy.*"

Dante had said my life was full of magic but I just hadn't noticed. I wasn't sure about the past, but I felt it now. It spun around us like a glittering web, encasing us both. I was aware only of a few things, nothing else: The lapping water. The crying seagulls. But especially the thing I felt when I saw him, when I saw that smile, and even if I died, or died completely, it would still go with me, whatever was left of me: I would shine, not burn. Shine, shine, shine.

Not burn.

ACKNOWLEDGEMENTS

Special thanks to Scott for all his help,
to James Mason for permission to use lines from "Love Poem,"
and to Marsha for being there.

ABOUT THE AUTHOR

Stacey E. Bryan was raised in the San Fernando Valley but born in San Francisco, where she left part of her heart. She received a BA in English from UCLA, studying under world-renowned Irish journalist and novelist, Brian Moore. Her work has appeared in several literary magazines in New York and L.A., including *Ginosko* and *The Rag*. She is currently working on various short stories and the sequel to her novel *Day for Night*. She lives in "beautiful downtown Burbank," as Johnny Carson used to say, with her husband who is also a writer.

312306